SWORD AND VERSE

KATHY MacMILLAN

HARPER TEEN

An Imprint of HarperCollinsPublishers

HarperTeen is an imprint of HarperCollins Publishers.

Sword and Verse
Copyright © 2016 by Kathy MacMillan
All rights reserved. Printed in the United States of America.
No part of this book may be used or reproduced in any manner whatsoever without written permis-
sion except in the case of brief quotations embodied in critical articles and reviews. For information
address HarperCollins Children's Books, a division of HarperCollins Publishers, 195 Broadway,
New York, NY 10007.
www.epicreads.com

Library of Congress Control Number: 2015943570
ISBN 978-0-06-232461-0

Typography by Ellice M. Lee
15 16 17 18 19   PC/RRDH   10 9 8 7 6 5 4 3 2 1
❖
First Edition

IN MEMORY OF ANNETTE BLEDSOE

"Find ecstasy in life;
the mere sense of living is joy enough."

—EMILY DICKINSON

THE GODS

Gyotia, king of the gods

Sotia, his sister, goddess of wisdom

Suna, his sister, goddess of memory

Lanea, his first wife, goddess of the hearth

Lila, his second wife, goddess of war

Qora, son of Gyotia and Lanea, god of the fields

Aqil, son of Gyotia and Sotia, god of sacred learning

First came Gyotia, many-limbed and all-seeing, born from the mountains of hidden fire into the darkness. Keeping only two arms and two legs, he molded the land from his other limbs and guarded it jealously as his own flesh.

"All is mine," he said into the wide silence.

ONE

I NEVER KNEW Tyasha ke Demit, but her execution started everything.

On the day the king sentenced her to die, I was with the other palace slave children, cleaning the high friezes in the Library of the Gods. Naka and Linti wouldn't stop talking about the execution—in low voices, of course, so the guards far below would not hear and shake our precarious platforms. The Qilarite guards never liked being assigned to the Library on cleaning days, and strictly enforced the rule of silence.

"How long before she dies?" whispered Linti anxiously, brushing her white-blond hair out of her face.

Naka shrugged and looked over at me. "How many times will they burn her, Raisa?"

My stomach turned. "Hush," I told them, too loudly, earning myself a shake from the guards below. I was lying on my back cleaning the ceiling, and so only had to grab the platform's side to maintain my balance. Arnath child slaves did not stay alive as long as I had unless they learned how to stay atop the platforms. Many children had fallen to their deaths on the stone Library floor—the thick rugs were always removed before the cleaning. No one wanted to sully the carpets trod by the gods with the blood of Arnath slaves.

I couldn't fault the younger children for their grim fascination; Naka was eight and Linti only six, and it wasn't every day that a prince's Tutor was executed for treason. I'd heard the rumblings about it all day in the palace. The king had ordered that the whole city attend, even—or perhaps especially—the slaves. For, though the Tutors held a privileged place in Qilara, they were still Arnath, like us. They wore the green clothing of slaves too, even if they also wore white. Tyasha would die, and another Arnath girl would be chosen to take her place as Tutor-in-training.

I slid along the platform, leveraging my weight against the edge so that I could push my rag into the molding above the statue of Gyotia, king of the gods. Though I was still small, my body had finally seemed to realize that I was almost fifteen, and had begun to soften and develop that year. No doubt the guards would soon complain about my weight on the platforms, and I would be sent to serve in one of the temples; the only Arnathim permitted to live in the palace were the Tutors and the children who cleaned the high places.

When I dropped my rag to signal to the guards, they turned the crank and lowered the platform. I dangled my legs over the side as it descended, watching the white friezes give way to the honeycomb of openings full of letters to the gods written by all the kings of Qilara. The letters, I had been told, were written in the higher order script known only to the king and his heir—and, I thought with a jealous pang, their Tutors. Tyasha ke Demit, Arnath though she was, would have been able to read the letters—if she had ever been allowed in the Library.

The higher order symbols were forbidden even to the nobles, who proudly called themselves the Scholar class because they alone could read and write. But the Scholars were only permitted to know the lower order writing. Qilarites of the merchant and peasant classes, like the guards, couldn't even learn that.

For a common slave like me, writing even one symbol would mean death.

Still, the Library of the Gods fascinated me. The walls were rounded, save for the straight one at the northern end. There stood an enormous statue of Gyotia, built into the wall itself, one face staring out over the Library, the other looking out to sea on the outside wall of the palace. Statues of the other gods ringed the Library.

My eyes were drawn against my will to the statue by the door: Gyotia's son Aqil, god of sacred learning, triumphantly holding a branding rod to the cheek of his mother, bound and gagged at his feet. Sotia, goddess of wisdom, whose crime had been wanting to give the gift of writing to all people. Statues all over the city repeated the image; some were even painted to contrast Sotia's pale skin with the olive skin of the other gods. And Sotia always had a small nose and close-set eyes, with hair that waved like mine. The Qilarites always showed her as Arnath.

No matter that it was forbidden—I recognized the symbol

Aqil was branding onto Sotia's cheek. *Rai.* The first part of my name, as my father had taught me to write it so long ago.

Kiti, his brown curls gray with dust, was already cleaning Aqil's statue, so I plied my rag to the statue of Suna, goddess of memory. At eleven, Kiti was next oldest of the children. He and I were the only ones left from the long-ago raid on our island. He'd been a toddler when the raiders came, so he didn't remember the Nath Tarin, the northern islands where the Learned Ones secretly passed on ancient teachings between Qilarite raids.

Being in the Library, however, only brought more back for me. My strongest memories were of papermaking days, when the whole village would abandon crops and help lay and press reeds. We'd share a feast while the paper lay drying in the sun, spread across tables, rocks, and branches, like thousands of clouds fallen to earth. When the paper had dried, the children would gather it up. I'd loved the soft heft of it under my fingers, like mist turned solid.

As I polished the statue, my eyes strayed over the letters to the gods in the slots covering the walls from the bottoms of the friezes down to the floor. The edges of the letters were yellowed, crinkled in places. I wondered if they were as soft as the paper we'd made on the islands. As soft as the page that held my heart-verse, given to me by my father on my sixth birthday as a symbol of who I was, who I was born to be. It was to have been the first thing I would learn to write.

The raiders had come two days later.

My fingers tingling with the memory of the soft island paper, I glanced at the guards; most were busy watching the children on the platforms. Keeping my eyes on the nearest guard, I reached out my left hand, angling my body to hide my arm. My fingers connected with the edge of a scroll. I looked down at it. It felt brittle, like paper that had been left out too long in the sun and had begun to shrivel. Useless for writing, my father would have said.

"What are you doing?"

I froze.

"What are you doing?" the guard's voice barked again. Before I could move, he grabbed my shoulder and threw me to the ground. The scroll I'd been touching slid from its slot and fell to the floor, unrolling and revealing lines of symbols.

The guard stared at the letter. Two others, who'd run over at his shouts, skidded to a halt beside him and gaped at me.

My heart thudded. I swallowed hard and tried to explain that it had been an accident, but all that came out was a squeak that resounded in the silent Library. The other children watched with round eyes, their cleaning forgotten.

The guards exploded into shouts that rang from the bare floors and stone walls. I only made out a few words, but I understood immediately that, edgy as they were in the wake of Tyasha ke Demit's treason, frightened as they were of being accused of breaking the law themselves, they would never believe that what I'd done was accidental.

Two guards hauled me to my feet. Another, who seemed to be in charge, barked orders and led the two gripping my arms out of the Library. I caught a glimpse of Linti on her stomach, gripping the edges of her platform as the guard below gave it a sharp shake.

Out in the hallway, the only sound was the strike of the guards' boots against the tiles as they dragged me to the left—toward the dungeons, I realized with a wave of dizziness. Of course we were going that way—Tyasha ke Demit and her accomplices were there, awaiting their execution the following day. Would they condemn me too, burn me beside her?

I swayed on my feet at the thought, but the guards just pulled me along as though I were a very light, very dangerous sack of grain. Black spots clouded my vision.

Someone was walking toward us from the direction of the dungeons; it wasn't until the guards knelt, pushing me to my knees, that the blurry shape resolved into a handsome young man with straight black hair and olive skin. Prince Mati. Fear swallowed me whole.

"What's this?" said the prince. I peeked up at him. Though he was not much older than I was, he seemed impossibly tall. Whenever I had seen Prince Mati before, he'd been smiling as though amused by some private joke. But he wasn't smiling now.

The lead guard cleared his throat. "This slave has committed an act of treason, Your Highness. We are taking her to Captain Dimmin." I cringed.

Prince Mati's brow furrowed. "What has she done?"

"She removed a letter from its place in the Library of the Gods, Your Highness."

"How do you know this?" said the prince sharply.

The guard to my left spoke up. "I saw it, Your Highness. She took the letter as she was cleaning the statue of Suna."

A small noise of indignation escaped my throat. The prince

turned to me at once, cold interest in his eyes. My face flooded with heat. "Is this true?" he asked.

I shook my head. My voice was barely a whisper. "It . . . it was an accident. I brushed against the letter and it fell out." Of course, this was not exactly true, but I couldn't very well tell them that I'd been distracted thinking of papermaking on the Nath Tarin.

Prince Mati's eyes narrowed. I forced myself to meet his gaze now, so he might believe me.

At last the prince turned to the ranking guard. "It seems to me," he said evenly, "that troubling my father with such a trivial matter would only annoy him, given the current situation. Let her go."

"Your Highness?"

"Unless you'd prefer to irritate the king," said the prince in an offhand manner, studying his fingernails. I realized, with a jolt of surprise, that he was not nearly as sure of himself as he wanted to appear.

Nevertheless, the three guards shifted uncomfortably, and I knew why—the king had banished the guards assigned to Tyasha after they'd failed to keep her from treasonous activities. He might punish these men for not watching me more closely.

The ranking guard cleared his throat. "No, Your Highness."

"Good," said Prince Mati with a smile. "I will apprise Captain Dimmin of the situation personally, so you needn't worry about that. Let her go."

"Er . . . Your Highness," said the ranking guard, almost timidly. "The letter that she . . . that is, the letter is still on the floor of the Library."

Prince Mati nodded and led the way back to the Library. The guards held my arms loosely now, as though the sack of grain had ceased to be dangerous because the prince said it was so.

As Prince Mati stepped into the Library, the children's whispers stopped, and a row of fearful faces peered over the platforms. Kiti hovered behind the great wooden case at the center of the Library, a guard monitoring him so closely that he could hardly move his arm to clean.

The letter lay half unrolled beside Suna's statue, my abandoned rag a few feet away. The guards and children had all moved as far away from the letter as possible, a barrier of fear around it like the ones around victims of the coughing sickness on the city streets.

The prince picked up the letter. Both guards' grips on my arms tightened painfully.

Prince Mati held the paper out to me. "Do you see what it says?" he asked.

I averted my eyes. I could see the symbols, of course, but they meant nothing to me.

The prince turned the letter around and read it silently. The corners of his mouth turned up. Suddenly I wanted to smack him. It was, perhaps, fortunate that the guards still gripped my arms.

Prince Mati let out a low laugh as he rerolled the letter and tucked it back into its slot. He looked around at the children, then at me. "How old are you?"

My voice did not work properly; it was still barely above a whisper. "Fourteen, Your Highness."

"A little old for Library duty, isn't she?" he said to the ranking guard.

"Mistress Kret is responsible for the children, Your Highness. I would be happy to tell her you said so," said the guard. He seemed relieved to have someone else to blame.

"I rather think," said Prince Mati coldly, "that it's Laiyonea ke Tirit you ought to be informing. Or have you forgotten that a new Tutor-in-training is to be selected?"

The guard spluttered apologies, but I watched the prince. Something in his tone had made me suspect that he was as appalled by Tyasha's planned execution as I was. He caught me staring and straightened his tunic.

"Take care of it," he said, cutting off the guard's babbling with an imperial gesture.

"Yes, Your Highness," said the guard, but the prince had already left.

Only when the guards let go of me did I realize that it was over, and I wasn't going to the dungeons.

Still, the Qilarite head servant, Emilana Kret, denied me supper and threatened to give me five nights in the Stander, the tiny, cramped closet in the corner of the farthest bathhouse, where even the smallest child could not sit down, only lean against the damp stone walls and kick at the creatures scuttling around in the black darkness. As it turned out, Linti smuggled me some cheese, and I only had to endure one night in the Stander. The next day, after Tyasha's execution, I was summoned to join the girls being tested to take Tyasha's place.

Linti clung to me before I left, but I whispered comforting words and begged her to stop crying so that Emilana would not hit her. Then I kept my head down as the guards led me away to join the other girls. I couldn't let anyone see how much I wanted to learn to write. I'd long ago learned that wanting things too much was a sure way to have them taken from you.

The foul-smelling potion they made us drink turned everything into a haze, and I fumbled through the testing, scribbling symbols that meant nothing to me, while the faces of the watching council members blurred together.

I must have done something right, though, because at the end of it, Laiyonea ke Tirit, the prince's Tutor, tied a green sash around my waist and announced that the oracle of the gods had chosen me to be the new Tutor-in-training.

From earth and stone Gyotia made Lanea, goddess of the home, to be his wife. He lay with her, and Qora was born. Gyotia, pleased, named his son god of the fields.

But the fire of the mountains had not died after Gyotia's emergence. His keen eyes spied a figure springing from it: Sotia, goddess of wisdom.

TWO

BRIGHT SUN REFLECTED off the paving stones in the Adytum, the sacred courtyard where we worked, but the canopies kept the glare off our pages. I inked my quill and carefully set it to the paper.

It had been exactly one year since I had become Tutor-in-training, and had entered this place in my Tutor's dress of white and green, terrified and exhilarated at the idea of learning to write. I'd spent each day with hundreds of symbols swimming before my eyes, but whenever Laiyonea had made me go through my work and name the word that went with each symbol, Prince Mati had always mouthed the ones I forgot across the table.

I had learned much, mastering the four thousand and eighty-seven lower order symbols. A more effusive teacher might even say that I had done extraordinarily well in such a short time.

"Sloppy," snapped Laiyonea, leaning across the table to

examine my tenth attempt at the symbol *gift*. "Do it again."

It had also been exactly one year since Tyasha ke Demit and her accomplices lay dying on a stage outside the Temple of Aqil, their hands removed and harsh symbols branded all over their bodies. No one spoke of it, but the knowledge of this sober anniversary hung over the Adytum like the heat of the midday sun. Laiyonea had been harder to please than usual, and Prince Mati, normally full of jokes and good humor, had kept his head bent quietly over his paper for the better part of an hour.

I held in a sigh and dipped my quill again. *Gift* was my least favorite of all the many symbols I had learned so far, not just because it took me a Shining and a Veiling—a full cycle of the night sky—to get it right even once. The last line always wanted to curve up instead of down.

Os, came my father's voice in my memory. That was what he had called a similar symbol, on the island. At first I fought the sound in my mind; I did not understand why the symbols each stood for a word here, instead of a sound as my father's writing had. Why would the writing mean different things? The Arnathim and Qilarites spoke the same tongue—our ancestors, as the Qilarites liked to remind us, had been banished from Qilara long ago for the crime of believing that the writing of the gods should be available to everyone.

But then, the Qilarite lower order and higher order scripts also represented the same spoken language; it was just the writing systems, the gods' gifts, that were different, with the more powerful higher order writing serving the king in his role as High Priest of Gyotia. The higher order symbols were used only to communicate with the gods.

So where did my father's writing system fit in?

I pushed those thoughts away; they wouldn't help me get this symbol right. Carefully I placed the first line, then exhaled as I wrote the next, and the next. The last line curved down just as it should. I lifted my quill, unable to hide my smile.

Laiyonea nodded her approval. "Now fifty times more to make it stick."

Beside me, Prince Mati snickered sympathetically. *He'd* never had to write anything fifty times to make it stick—his writing always flowed off the quill, quick and polished and lovely. But then, he'd been studying here in the Adytum since the age of four.

Prince Mati also didn't have the rather unfair disadvantage of having to study next to himself. Realizing how close we sat on the bench, I scooted away from him and swung my hair forward to hide my blush. He'd always been kind to me, I told myself, that was all it was. It wouldn't do to forget my place. I was a Tutor now, but no less a slave.

Laiyonea tapped the prince's hand with her quill. "A little more effort from you wouldn't hurt, Mati," she said. "Raisa's showing you up."

I peeked through my curtain of hair at the prince. He only bent back over his paper. No one outside the Adytum would believe that an Arnath slave spoke to the prince like that, but Laiyonea was the prince's Tutor, so he had to listen to her.

Would I speak that way, when I became Tutor to the next prince? *You'll never find out if you don't master all the symbols*, I admonished myself. I tapped my quill nervously against the inkpot.

I worked carefully, starting over each time I botched a symbol, grateful for the breeze off the ocean that stirred my hair. At the far end of the courtyard, asotis cooed on their perch. Above us, the enormous stone face of Gyotia, king of the gods, stared out over the Olsunal, the sea-without-memory.

When Laiyonea looked over the prince's finished writing, she pointed out two errors, then said sternly, "I expect that you will not let the pantomime distract you from your work." The Festival of Aqil was coming up, and the highest born sixteen-year-old boy of the Scholar class traditionally played Aqil in the dramatization of the story of the gods. This year it was Prince Mati's turn. I was looking forward to the festival; I hadn't been out of the palace since becoming Tutor-in-training, but surely everyone in the City of Kings would attend the pantomime if the prince was in it.

The prince mumbled something that I didn't catch.

Laiyonea lowered her voice, though no one could have heard us from the beach far below. "Your father told you?"

The edge in her voice made me look up—and the fierce gaze she sent me made me look right back down.

"Yes," said the prince, subdued. "I have to find someone else to play Sotia."

So one of the Qilarite girls had dropped out—not exactly surprising. No Qilarite girl from a noble Scholar family would want to play the displaced goddess of wisdom, the goddess worshipped by the Arnathim. Whichever unlucky girl played Sotia would spend most of the pantomime on the ground, bound and gagged, with Prince Mati as Aqil standing with one foot on her back. Just like the statues found all over the city.

"Hmm," said Laiyonea. "The War Minister's granddaughter could do it . . ."

I began a new row of symbols and let her voice fade into the background. Maybe today I would get up the courage to ask Laiyonea when I could start the higher order symbols, the ones known only to the king and prince and Tutors. Then I would be that much closer to knowing—

"Actually," said Prince Mati, breaking into my thoughts, "I thought Raisa could do it."

My quill slipped, ruining a whole line. I stared at him, but surely my expression of disbelief was mild compared to Laiyonea's. The prince's face fell. "S'just an idea," he mumbled, playing with his quill.

Laiyonea cleared her throat. "Raisa is too young."

"She's almost sixteen!" the prince protested. "The Gamo twins are only thirteen, and they're doing it."

Laiyonea's nostrils flared. "Your father would never agree, today of all days—"

The prince tensed, but he looked up at Laiyonea from under long black lashes. "He would if you suggested it," he said. Even I knew he was right—whatever typical anti-Arnath prejudice King Tyno felt, he relied on Laiyonea more than any of his advisers on the Scholars Council. He often called her to attend council meetings; even Tyasha's treason had not changed that. But then, Laiyonea and the king had grown up together, studied side by side in the Adytum themselves. By all accounts, Prince Mati and Tyasha had once been just as close.

Had Tyasha been as protective of Prince Mati as Laiyonea seemed to be of the king? Tyasha had been seven years older than the prince, after all. She'd been selected as a young child, and Laiyonea had presented her as a wedding gift to the king and queen before Mati's birth. The fact that I was younger than the prince whose son I would teach was but one of the peculiarities of my situation.

Laiyonea pursed her lips. "You haven't asked if Raisa *wants* to do the pantomime."

The prince turned to me quickly. I couldn't avoid the impact of his dark eyes. "Do you?" he asked, so enthusiastically that it was hard to remember why I *didn't* want to. "Come on, it'll be fun. Time away from studying . . ."

I frowned. Time away from studying meant it would be that much longer before Laiyonea felt I was ready for the higher order symbols. I opened my mouth, but, as if sensing my refusal, the prince swiftly said, "Just think about it, all right?" He gave me a pleading look.

I nodded and looked down, willing my pulse to slow. I'd accepted long ago that the impossible feelings he stirred in me were nothing but a distraction, but that didn't stop them rearing up when I least expected them.

Abruptly, Laiyonea gathered our papers and crossed the courtyard to slip them into the firepit. I started to protest—I hadn't finished writing *gift* fifty times, and she hadn't checked my work yet!—but she spoke over me as she returned to the table.

"I need to step away," she said. "Raisa, write out the last fifty tensets, twenty times each. Mati, you continue the story of Aqil's quill."

I sighed and flexed my hand as the gate closed behind her.

"You're not even considering saying yes, are you?" said Prince Mati. I steeled myself before I looked into his eyes this time, but I wasn't prepared for the hurt I saw there.

"I never said that." I couldn't understand why he didn't just order me to do it. Both Laiyonea and the prince acted as if it were my choice. Was that what it meant to be a Tutor, that I could say no?

"I just thought that *you* would understand," said the prince, turning back to his paper.

"Understand what?"

His quill stabbed the page as he spoke. "You know how my father is. If I can't find someone to take Hailena's place . . ."

My hand actually rose as if to touch his shoulder. I forced it back to my lap. It wasn't fair that Mati worked so hard, and his father never saw it. The king viewed his son's kindness and humor as frivolity, and rarely missed a chance to tell him so. I wondered if things might have been different, had the queen survived the illness that took her when Mati was a toddler.

I cleared my throat. "None of the Scholar girls want to play Sotia?"

"Oh, Hailena wanted to do it. The Trade Minister learned that Hailena's father had been selling weapons to the Resistance. Someone inside the ministry tipped off the family and they escaped yesterday."

My mouth dropped open. I'd heard whispers about the Arnath

Resistance ever since I had come to the palace as a frightened six-year-old, but the executions of Tyasha and her accomplices last year had supposedly shut it down. So it was shocking enough that there even was a Resistance for the man to sell weapons to, but to find that a Qilarite Scholar was supporting the Arnath rebellion right under the king's nose! That was inconceivable.

"So," continued the prince, "I thought I'd better have someone I can trust up there with me, someone I like. And . . . you were the first person I thought of. I know you won't say anything stupid to the High Priest of Aqil or irritate the eastern vizier's son. You always think so hard about everything." He laughed. "See, you're doing it now." He touched my forehead, which was furrowed as I processed his unexpected compliment. His fingers sent jolts of lightning across my skin. I leaned away in surprise, and he snatched his hand back, his cheeks reddening.

As I stared, too shocked to speak, he picked up his quill and dashed off a few symbols. He forced a laugh and bumped my elbow with his. "And you're not whiney like Soraya Gamo and her sisters. You should have seen them at the first practice. Soraya kept complaining that the air was too wet and her hair was going to curl like a—" He broke off abruptly.

I grabbed my quill and started writing again, pretending not to understand what he'd been about to say. Soraya Gamo had a sheet of straight, black Qilarite hair. Of course she wouldn't want her hair to curl like an Arnath's—like a slave's.

Prince Mati cleared his throat. "I'd really like it if you'd do it," he said quietly.

My quill slowed. There was no part of me that wanted to

participate in the pantomime—the thought of acting out Sotia's punishment while the whole city looked on made my stomach churn. But a larger part than I cared to admit wanted to please the prince.

"I know you don't want to," the prince went on, "but what if I did something for you in return? I could get Father to let you go to the First Shining Festival, or sharpen quills for you, or . . . I don't know, what do you want, Raisa?"

No one had ever asked me that before, especially not with that serious expression, like he was actually interested in the answer. Did *I* even know what I wanted?

Freedom. Not the answer he was expecting, and anyway, not exactly true—if I weren't a slave, I wouldn't be Tutor-in-training, and I wouldn't learn the higher order symbols. . . .

So there it was. But I was afraid to say it—would he mock me? I couldn't stand that, not from Prince Mati.

I realized I was mangling my quill, and my left hand was covered in ink. I grabbed a blotting cloth and spoke down to it as I wiped my fingers. "I want to learn the higher order writing."

I peeked up at his face; his brows drew together and his head tilted to the side. I cursed myself. If he guessed why I wanted it . . .

"Laiyonea thinks you're not ready," he said slowly. "Why are you so eager to start on the higher order?"

"Oh," I said, "I'll just feel . . . safer . . . once I know them all." It was true enough. The more I knew, the less likely it was that I would be removed, as long as I didn't do anything stupid.

Tyasha ke Demit's name practically blew on the air around us.

Prince Mati grimaced and nodded. "Makes sense," he mumbled. His quill scratched over his paper. "All right," he said at last. "If you do the pantomime, I'll . . . teach you myself."

I looked up at him in shock.

"So you'll do it?" he said, his eyes locked on mine.

"Yes," I whispered.

Gyotia, mightiest of the gods, flew to the mountains in an
instant and overpowered Sotia.

Gentle Lanea nursed Sotia through her childbirth, and Aqil
was born. Lanea refused to lie with Gyotia again, so the king of
the gods reached deep into the earth and gathered stone and fire to
make Lila, goddess of war, his second wife. Together, Gyotia and
Lila overcame Lanea and subdued her to Gyotia's will.

THREE

LAIYONEA RETURNED AT fourth bell with a tray
of tea and honeycakes that meant she intended to keep us working
in the Adytum for hours yet. She frowned when she heard that I'd
agreed to do the pantomime, but not nearly as much as she did an
hour later, when she finally gave up trying to teach me anything;
I was simply too preoccupied.

She and the prince left, but my work wasn't done. I swept
hastily—as only the three of us ever used the Adytum, it was
rarely dirty—and refilled the asotis' seedbowls, then carried dip-
pers from the rain barrels to fill the basin at the center of their
cage. We called it a cage, though it had no bars, only a raised
lip around the edge of the waist-high platform to keep the sand
from spilling over. That had puzzled me when I'd first watched
Laiyonea plucking the asotis' feathers for quills; even uncaged and

complaining, the birds did not fly away.

"They *are* caged, when they're first born," the prince had explained, when I'd timidly asked about it. "Soon they're so used to the bars that they won't fly away even without them. They fight less without the bars, though. Makes for fewer damaged quills."

I scooped droppings from the sand and threw them over the wall, then turned to my least favorite task: gathering feathers. The birds protested but didn't struggle as I whispered apologies to them. Many Scholar homes kept the small gray birds for their quills, but I remembered seeing them flying free on the islands when I was a child.

My work finished, I made a circuit of the courtyard, peering over the wall to make sure the beach below was empty. My eyes flicked nervously to the guard towers atop the rocky outcroppings on either side of the inlet. Those were always manned, but the guards would surely be watching the sea for enemy ships or storm waves that might warrant raising the floodwalls to protect the palace.

At last I went to the clump of red poppies and chamomile at the far end of the Adytum. I pushed aside the flowers and removed the loose stone in the wall, then pulled out a roll of paper. Sitting back on my heels, I unrolled it so that the tattered scrap inside remained in its cover.

The symbols on the thin paper were faded, some blurred beyond recognition, others running into their neighbors. Some greeted me like old friends, my father's voice whispering sounds in my memory even as Laiyonea's voice intoned words. Other symbols meant nothing to me.

This scrap had come with me all the way from the Nath Tarin, and I was no closer to understanding it than I had been on my sixth birthday, when my father had presented it to me.

"This is your heart-verse," he'd said. "Soon you will learn to read it, and to write the language of the gods yourself. When you are grown, I will train you to take my place among the Learned Ones." I had been thrilled at the idea of one day serving among the council of four who arbitrated disputes and passed on the teachings of our people.

My mother had made a special pouch to hold my heart-verse. I'd pinned it to the inside of my skirt, and kept it with me always, even when the raiders attacked our village.

When my mother turned to me and my fifteen-year-old brother and said, "Go to Margara's house," I obeyed without question, though my brother darted away to help Father. I watched through the window, my mother's best friend sobbing behind me, as the raiders plunged their swords into my brother and set fire to my house. I didn't see what they did to my parents; Margara made me look away. But I knew even then how the Qilarites exterminated the Learned Ones and their families every chance they got. I didn't need Margara's whispered instructions to know that I had to pretend to be her daughter when the Qilarites lined us up outside. Amazing, really, that they believed I was Margara's daughter; she and her children were fair-haired, and I had my mother's auburn hair and my father's features. But all Arnathim looked the same to the Qilarites—like slaves.

My heart-verse had traveled with me on the sweaty, dark ship and on airless carts where we sat packed together in chains. Over the years I had hidden it in bundles of clothes, in my straw pallet in the palace slave quarters, and finally here, behind a stone in the Adytum.

And still I had no idea what it said, this message from the past. Even the few symbols I recognized didn't make sense, not the way they'd been strung together. I had learned all four thousand and eighty-seven of the lower order symbols, but a mere handful of them appeared in my heart-verse. Surely the mystery symbols would be found among the higher order sets. Whatever I had to do in the pantomime would be worth it, if the prince kept his promise to teach them to me.

Somewhere beyond the green ocean, on the chain of islands where I was born, lived people who could read my heart-verse easily. "Nath Tarin" was what the Qilarites called our home— the name literally meant "northern islands," and we were called "Arnathim" here, which meant "of the islands." But I had never heard those words before I'd come to Qilara. Each island had had its own name, though I no longer remembered them. And we'd called ourselves the people of Sotia, because our Learned Ones, my father among them, passed down the goddess's gift of writing to all, no matter how many raiders came from the south.

The survivors of the raid would have hidden in the caves for days before daring to emerge. But I had no doubt that there had been survivors. For generations, the Qilarites had been raiding the Nath Tarin every ten years or so, punishing the descendants of the ancient, banished chieftain who had dared to spread Sotia's gift of writing among all his people. Though the exact timing of the raids was unexpected, the fact of their coming never was.

Every ten years or so. It had been nine years since I had come to Qilara. Since the last raid.

The gate creaked below. Heart pounding, I rolled up the paper and shoved it into the hole, leaping clear of the flowers just as Prince Mati appeared on the top step. I grabbed the comb to smooth the sand below the asotis' perch.

"You're still here," said the prince. I tried not to notice how happy he seemed about it.

"Just cleaning up." My voice was unnaturally high.

Mati reached up and touched my hair, making my breath catch.

"Leaf," he said, awkwardly taking his hand away and dropping the leaf onto the freshly swept paving stones.

I flushed, but he didn't question how the leaf had gotten there. Instead, his eyes fell on the tea tray. He made a sound of discovery and reached for my untouched honeycake.

"Oh!" I said. "I was saving that for . . ."

Prince Mati paused with his hand halfway to the cake and smirked. "Lamp Night isn't for days, Raisa."

I flushed. If a girl ate a honeycake and slept with a crumb of it under her pillow when Gyotia's Lamp shone full in the night sky, she would supposedly dream of her true love. The prince would never have dared to make that joke if Laiyonea were here; as Tutors, we were supposed to remain utterly chaste and dedicated to Aqil. "No," I stammered. "It's for . . . the children."

Prince Mati's brow furrowed. "The children?"

My fingers tangled in my skirt. "The palace . . . children." It was a delicate moment. He of all people knew that I had been one of those children before becoming Tutor-in-training, but we'd never spoken of it.

The prince's face registered understanding. He frowned at the cake, surely thinking that it was too fine for their grubby fingers.

"This little bit?" he said at last.

That startled me into answering truthfully. "It's really just for Linti. She's the youngest . . . sometimes the others take all the food. So before I . . . left, I promised I'd hide food for her when I could."

"How do you get it to her?"

"There's a place under the stairs in the front hallway . . . you won't tell anyone, will you?" Why had I said anything to him in the first place? No matter that Prince Mati acted like my friend—he was still a Qilarite.

"I won't," he said softly. He cocked his head. "You're just full of secrets, aren't you?"

My eyes darted to the poppies. "Not at all. Just that one."

"That, and a burning desire to learn the higher order writing." I didn't know how to respond to that. Prince Mati's dark eyes studied me, and something softened in his face. "I'll . . . show you the first tenset now, if you want."

"Now?" I squeaked.

"Why not?" He went to the writing chest and snatched up paper, ink, and quills, then plunked them down on the table and swung onto the bench. "Come on," he said, patting the place beside him.

He's just making sure I won't back out of the pantomime, I told myself. But it didn't feel that way. It didn't even feel like his usual offhand kindness. There was something different in the way Mati looked at me now. My heart thumped painfully. Had he guessed about my hidden page or about who my family had been? Or had he simply realized how much his nearness affected me?

And, gods, which was worse?

But he held out a quill to me, and I shook myself out of my stupor. He was offering to teach me the higher order symbols, right now, and why didn't matter.

I took the quill and sat beside him, and he started writing. I copied the symbols—*honor, star, power, council*—as quickly as he showed them to me, soon forgetting my embarrassment as I leaned closer to see the order of the lines. These symbols seemed lovelier than their lower order counterparts, more fluid.

More surprising was how often my father's voice came back to me. It had only happened sporadically before, but today I remembered sounds for three of the first five symbols the prince showed me.

He sketched something and pushed it toward me. "That means *spit*. Not exactly the excitement you expected, is it?"

I blinked. "I thought the higher order symbols were . . . more dignified than the lower order."

The prince laughed. "You'd think so, wouldn't you? But you can write anything in the higher order writing, and a lot more easily than in the lower order writing too."

The symbol he'd written had two spouting curves that might represent water arcing from a man's mouth. It was hard to imagine *that* helping me read my heart-verse.

"It doesn't matter," I told myself out loud as I traced my dry quill over the page, imitating the prince's strokes.

"No, the vertical line is first," he said. I tried it again, then dipped my quill in the ink. The result was incomprehensible.

Mati laughed. "Don't press so hard on the second line." He hesitated, then put his hand over mine and guided my quill. "Just let it flow . . . like that."

My hand shook so badly that I had to try five times before I got the symbol right.

The prince cleared his throat. "Now, ten times to make it stick. See, I'm not as bad as Laiyonea."

I smiled and wrote the symbol again.

"In the higher order sets," said the prince, "there are a lot more precise symbols to choose from. Especially when it comes to things like bodily functions." He snickered.

I'd never had to write about spitting before, but now that he said it, I realized that I wouldn't have known how. Though there were lower order symbols that represented *star* and *council* and the other higher order symbols he had shown me, there was no lower order symbol for *spit*. "If the higher order symbols are only for the king and prince—"

"And Tutors."

Now, it was true that the Tutors learned higher order script to teach the next generation of rulers. But only the king, as High Priest of Gyotia, actually used the higher order writing for its true purpose: communicating with the gods. By law, Tutors' writings could only exist here in the Adytum, and had to burn in the fire-pit each day. Failing to burn even one page could mean death.

But Prince Mati did not seem to appreciate the difference,

so I only said, "If the Scholars aren't allowed to know the higher order symbols, how do they write about . . . bodily functions, if they need to?"

He grinned. "They use the lower order symbols creatively. They actually pride themselves on that. They have competitions to see who can come up with the best euphemisms. Laiyonea showed me a report once on a priest found 'mouse against rooster' with a temple slave."

I frowned, trying to untangle the meaning, and blushed when I did.

Prince Mati laughed. "Remember that day in the Library? That letter was King Makal asking Suna for relief from his bowel troubles. Even the Scholars wouldn't have known what to make of that one."

"I remember that you laughed," I said. "Actually . . ." I paused, but something about the intensity of his attention made me feel at once safe and precarious, like balancing on the cleaning platforms after years of experience. So I went on. "Actually, I remember wanting to slap you, for showing off."

"A fine bit of gratitude," he said in mock indignation.

I gave a little shrug. "I didn't slap you, did I? I was grateful. I . . . still am." The humor drained from his face, replaced by something tentative that made the day seem suddenly warmer. For some reason, I couldn't stop talking. "I wouldn't even have been in the Selection if not for you. If you hadn't come along just then—"

"I'd been down in the dungeons." His voice was so low that I had to lean forward to catch his next words. "Visiting Tyasha."

I started—speaking her name out loud was forbidden, but of

course that didn't apply to the prince. Abruptly he straightened. "I wanted to ask her why she did it. She was always opinionated, and Laiyonea let her get away with a great deal. It was no surprise she got herself into trouble. She forced my father to punish her." He glanced at my face, as if trying to determine whether I believed him.

I didn't say anything, and he turned away. He scribbled another symbol, then pushed it toward me almost defiantly. "Here, this one means *traitor*."

I registered his words, but did not grasp their meaning. Instead I stared at the symbol, a symbol I knew—the only symbol, in fact, that I'd really known before I had come to the Adytum. The symbol that began my name in the Arnath writing, the one I'd seen branded on Sotia's cheek on the statue on the Library. The symbol that stood for the first sound in my name: *rai*.

At last I found my voice. "What . . . what did you say it means?"

"Traitor," said the prince. "What's the matter?"

To him it stood for a concept, not a sound. The idea of a symbol representing the sound *rai* would be preposterous to him. I curled my fingers around my quill in sudden dread—what if this writing was too different from my father's, and I never learned to read my heart-verse?

"Raisa?" said the prince. "What is it?"

I shook my head. "Nothing." I bent over my paper, and for the first time since I'd begun my training, I got it exactly right on the first try.

Gyotia, well-pleased with his own handling of his wives, nearly missed seeing Suna emerge from the mountains of fire, and Sotia got there first. Sotia diluted the poison of the lantana plant with her own tears and fed the mixture to her new sister. By the time Gyotia arrived, the lantana had scarred Suna's face so that Gyotia, repelled, would not touch her, and she remains the virgin goddess. So it shall be until the gods read out the scrolls.

That was the first time Sotia defied the king of the gods, but it was not to be the last.

FOUR

ON THE DAY of the pantomime, we performed on a stage outside the Temple of Aqil, with a raised portion at one end where all the scenes featuring the gods took place. Whenever the gods visited the earth, we rode across the stage to the lower end on a wheeled platform pushed by temple slaves—among them, my old friend Kiti, who had recently come to serve at the temple, having grown too heavy for palace cleaning work. I'd been delighted to see Kiti, but hadn't dared to speak to him. Laiyonea had warned me to be quiet and careful, especially around Penta Rale, the High Priest of Aqil and chief of all the priests. After the things Tyasha had done, every move I made outside the palace would be scrutinized, and Rale especially disliked the Tutors.

In rehearsals, I had surprised everyone with my ease on the rolling contraption; having spent most of my childhood atop cleaning platforms, I barely had to lift my arms to keep my balance. Still, when I stepped onto it at the performance and saw the crowd for the first time, I almost fell over. Everyone in the City of Kings must have turned out to see the prince play Aqil.

I had only one line, in the scene where Sotia questioned the two ancient chieftains, and then presented the tablet of language to the one who vowed to share it with all people. Then I escaped behind the partition to wait, nervous and sweaty; I knew that my true humiliation was yet to come. I began to wonder if my bargain with the prince had been worth it.

I traced my favorite of the symbols Prince Mati had shown me the day before—*dream*—into my left palm. It had been worth it.

The prince was on stage now with Annis Rale, the high priest's son, who was playing Gyotia. Annis seemed to think that good acting meant shouting as loudly as possible, but Mati's approach was subtler. He even managed to infuse sadness into the speech where Aqil vowed to capture his mother and give the language of the gods its rightful place of nobility.

Mati came behind the partition to await his next scene. We were alone in the cramped, dark space.

"Well done," I breathed. I realized he couldn't hear me, so I slid closer and repeated myself.

"You too," he whispered hoarsely.

I had nothing else to say, but I didn't step away, even as I flushed at his nearness. Annis Rale was delivering a long speech as Gyotia on the other side of the partition, but my ears weren't working right—instead of his strident voice, all I could hear was the prince's uneven breathing.

And then Prince Mati touched my arm. My skin went hot all over as his warm fingers moved hesitantly up to my neck and then to my cheek, and I was paralyzed, horrified only at how much I hoped he wouldn't move away. He shifted closer in the darkness.

"Raisa," he whispered.

This couldn't be happening. This couldn't happen.

"My costume," I whispered frantically.

The prince went still, then his hand left my cheek. Disappointment lanced through me, but I handed him the bindings and he wrapped them around my upraised hands—more loosely than he had in rehearsal, I noted distantly.

If only I could see his expression.

Did I imagine his hands lingering at my face as he tied the gag over my mouth? I was hyperaware of where he stood, a point of heat close by. I was so dazed he practically had to push me through the curtain when our cue came. I kept my head down so I wouldn't have to see the crowd.

He pushed me to the ground, where I lay, more or less helpless, and he rested his foot lightly on my back. This was the part I hated most, but there was no getting around it. The image was central to the festival and the pantomime. I tried to push the roil of emotions out of my mind and focus on the scene.

The others stood grouped around Annis Rale's makeshift throne. Every one of them was tall, even the girls, with olive skin and glossy black hair. And there I lay, small and pale and Arnath and humiliated, on the ground.

Annis Rale looked fierce in a golden cape as Gyotia. "This treachery, sister, is unacceptable," he said, his voice ringing out across the crowd.

I glared back at him in what I hoped was a credible imitation of Sotia in the statues. Somehow it was easy to channel my confusion into anger.

"Goddess of wisdom though you may be," Annis went on, "your store of it has run out. Did you think that you could spread the language of the gods to all mortals without our knowledge? The ones you have corrupted will trouble us no longer. I have banished them from this land." He lifted a hand, and the temple slaves behind the stage turned the cranks to make the wooden cutouts of ships at the lower end of the stage heave up and down, imitating the perilous journey across the sea toward the Nath Tarin.

Annis turned to Mati. "Well done, Aqil. Where are her tablet and quill?"

The prince slung the pack from his shoulder and held it out. "I took them at once, mighty father," he said. Did his tone seem more flat than it had in rehearsal?

Annis-as-Gyotia nodded gravely. He pulled a quill from the pack and broke it into pieces, launching into a long diatribe. Halfway through, he turned and lifted the round stone tablet that had been hidden behind him; to the audience it seemed to appear magically, and they gasped in appreciation. "Aqil," he bellowed. "I name you god of sacred learning, in place of Sotia the traitorous."

Prince Mati stepped forward. The instant he removed his

foot from my back, I scrambled up and lunged at Annis, knocking the tablet from his hands.

It hit the stage with a crash—out of the corner of my eye I saw many in the crowd jump. I hobbled after it, until Prince Mati touched my arm and I fell again. To the audience it would seem he had thrown me to the ground, but we had practiced so that he wouldn't hurt me.

I rolled onto my side, panting. Aliana Gamo, perfectly cast as Gyotia's timid wife Lanea, lifted the tablet from the ground. Aliana had to turn the tablet as she lifted it, so that the side with the missing piece, previously hidden, faced out. She heaved it into Annis's arms, and he let out a convincing howl of rage.

I looked out over the crowd as he and Mati exchanged several lines about the missing piece. King Tyno sat in the middle of the front row with his arms crossed, showing no hint of pride in his son's performance. The other Scholars on the benches wore expressions ranging from polite indifference to outright boredom, as did the rows of city dwellers and servants standing on the slope behind them. Emilana Kret and the palace slave children stood near the back. The white-blond puff of Linti's hair was intermittently visible as she craned her neck to see over the people in front of her, but her blocked view seemed a blessing. I hated the idea of her witnessing me like this.

A clump of green-clad Arnathim stood at the back corner of the crowd, where a stand of palms obscured the view; a few even perched in the trees. Lying on the raised stage, I was level with them, and a familiar face caught my eye—a young man with sand-colored curls whom I'd seen often at the market, back in my days of running errands for Emilana Kret. My cheeks flushed at his disgusted scowl.

"What have you done with it?" Annis bellowed, grabbing my hair and turning me to face him. I stared back at him defiantly, conscious of the Arnath gazes in the crowd. He pushed me away. "No matter," he said, but his voice seemed to have lost some of its certainty—probably because I wasn't behaving as meekly as I had in rehearsals. "One symbol will not save you."

Annis produced a branding rod, which he handed to Prince Mati. "Mark this traitor, and we shall have done with her."

Mati pressed the cold rod to my cheek, but my face burned as if it had been red-hot. The fact that it was the prince holding the rod seemed far worse now than it had in rehearsal.

The curly-haired slave jumped down from the tree and I lost sight of him as he pushed his way through the crowd.

It was time for my grand exit. Penta Rale had developed a new trick this year; the crowd seemed suitably impressed when I was lowered through a hole in the floor of the stage, while the others chanted, "Imprisoned in walls of stone forever. Behold the cost of betraying Gyotia."

As soon as my head was below the stage, I jumped down from the moving platform so that the high priest himself could take my place. I landed sideways on my ankle, but scrambled back up in time to see Rale slipping onto the platform. He held a long metal tube up to the level of the stage; when he did something to one end of it, flames shot out of the other. Heat rushed down into the close space under the stage, and I heard screams and gasps from the audience.

I pulled the gag down so it hung around my neck, but decided to wait until I got back into the light to deal with my bindings. I slipped into the cool, quiet temple, which was empty but for a few slaves preparing for the offerings. I forced myself to walk a measured pace to the steps, not allowing myself to think, or to wonder.

Or to wish.

I hurried to the basement to change, glad of a few minutes alone to process what had happened with Prince Mati. But when I opened the door to the dressing room, someone was already there.

Lanea saw her husband's fury that Sotia had gotten to Suna first, and she offered herself to distract him. She could not bear to see proud Sotia suffer at Gyotia's hands again. The others, she knew, would assume that she acted out of weakness, for they did not understand her kind of strength.

FIVE

THE CURLY-HAIRED SLAVE sat at the dressing table, tapping his fingers as if I were late for an appointment. I considered shouting for help, but before I could even open my mouth, he had lunged at me and clapped one hand over it.

I wasn't really frightened until he did that. I struggled, but he tightened his hand and grabbed my wrist.

"I only want to talk to you," he said. "But I can't have you calling the guards. If I let go, will you listen to me?" He smelled of sweat and wine, and something else, a bitter scent that I vaguely recognized.

He wasn't much older than I was. He didn't *seem* dangerous, but still . . .

Curiosity won over prudence. I nodded, though my heart thumped.

He released me and took a step backward. "You know what Tyasha ke Demit did?"

My mouth went dry.

"Well, do you?" he asked.

I nodded slowly.

"Then you realize you have an opportunity to serve your people as she did."

I gaped at him. "Serve . . . my people?"

He glowered as though he thought I was being stupid on purpose. "Of course. You can give back the knowledge that the Qilarites have taken from us. Do you really think those idiots were the first group that Tyasha taught? She went years without being caught."

Abruptly I realized what the bitter scent was: ink. I swallowed hard. "And you want me to . . ." He couldn't know what he was asking. I hardly knew myself.

He took a step forward. "I want you to help your people."

"You want me to become a traitor."

He snorted. "If not, you betray the Arnathim instead."

I shook my head. Realizing that I was pressed defensively against the door, I forced myself to relax.

"Need help with those?" he said, indicating the ropes at my wrists.

"No," I snapped. "I can do it myself." I looped the bindings off my hands and threw them onto the dressing table, then started on the knot of the gag that hung around my neck.

"Here, let me," he said. He picked at the knot with surprisingly nimble fingers. My mind raced—I had to get rid of him before the Gamo girls came down to change.

The gag came apart and I turned to face him. "I won't help

you," I told him, "so you might as well leave now. The less I know about you, the better."

He raised his eyebrows. His eyes were green, the exact color of the fog-jade vase in the palace entryway. I used to hate cleaning that vase—it always seemed ready to tip over at the slightest provocation.

"Interesting," he said smugly. "You're not planning to tell anyone about me being here. Not what I expected from a qodder willing to humiliate herself in a Qilarite pantomime."

That stung, though I didn't know what a qodder was, or why I should care what he thought. "What does it matter? In case you haven't noticed, the Qilarites are in charge."

"It matters," he said coldly, "because the rest of us don't have a choice about being humiliated for the pleasure of Qilarites. *You* do."

Suddenly I was irrationally angry. Who was he to judge me? "Get out," I spat. "I'll scream for the guards."

"No, you won't," he said, his lip curling, though his eyes darted to the door. "You'd have to explain why you were talking to me. I'll swear to Gyotia that you've been helping us."

"No one will believe that."

"Doesn't matter. It'd still be the end of your cozy life in the palace. Do you think the king doubts you'd betray him? You're Arnath, whether you like it or not."

I gritted my teeth. "I know what I am."

He leaned right into my face. I backed up until my hip banged painfully into the dressing table. "So you don't *care* about anyone but yourself. You don't mind if Arnath children are worked to death or Arnath women are raped by their masters or Arnath men die in the quarries, as long as *you're* comfortable in the palace. You don't care if the rest of your people die in ignorance. And you, born on the Nath Tarin." He shook his head. "The Learned Ones would be ashamed."

His words hit me like a slap across the face. Was he right? Would my father be ashamed if he saw me today? But my parents had sacrificed so much to keep me safe.

I planted my palms on his chest and pushed with all my might. He crashed backward onto the floor.

I forced myself to breathe normally, trying to regain control.

Someone knocked sharply on the door; we both froze. "Jonis?" said a voice.

"What is it?" said the young man quickly, planting himself behind the door as if ready to leap at anyone coming through.

The door cracked open and Kiti poked his head in. "Rale's on his last speech. You'd better get out of here." Kiti shot a shy smile at me. "Shinings, Raisa."

"Shinings, Kiti," I responded automatically, my mind reeling. Was Kiti helping the Resistance? Of course the other man—Jonis, Kiti had called him—couldn't have gotten past the guards without help.

Jonis nodded at Kiti, who withdrew his head and shut the door. Jonis grabbed my arm. I flinched. "You think the knowledge you have is a gift," he said. "But you wear shackles too, even if they're silk instead of iron."

He took my hand and traced something into it. As if his finger were a quill, I almost saw the symbol written there, a circle with two lines flying up on either side. *Freedom*. "We haven't forgotten what it means," he said in a low voice. "A messenger will come to you, and will say these words: 'The rains are coming off the ocean.' If you will help us, answer, 'Yes, from the islands.' If not . . . the gods help you."

He went to the door and knocked. When two knocks came from the other side, he dashed out. I caught a glimpse of Kiti's face before the door swung shut.

I grabbed my gown and slipped behind the changing screen in a daze. I could not afford to dwell on what had just happened or give any indication that anything strange had gone on.

The Gamo sisters spilled into the room as I was sitting down to brush my hair. Soraya dropped a condescending glance at me as she passed. "Well played, Tutor," she said, her tone balanced between respectful and sarcastic. I met her eyes in the mirror, pretending I had only heard the former.

"And you," I said, which was two words more than I'd ever said to her before. It was true; she'd played Lila, goddess of war, with haughty poise.

Caught off guard by my response, Soraya seized her gown and disappeared behind the screen. She clearly hated sharing a dressing room with an Arnath; Rale wasn't the only Qilarite who had a problem with the privileges granted to Tutors.

Alshara hurried away to change, but Aliana hesitantly returned my smile. I wanted to tell Aliana that she'd done well as Lanea, but for some reason I didn't want her sisters to overhear.

"Did you see the way Annis leered at me?" Soraya said to Alshara. "I can't believe he'd be so impertinent in front of the prince."

Alshara laughed. "Have you ever seen anything stop him being impertinent?"

"He'll never earn a seat on the council like that. And the way he shouted in the final scene! Even the king jumped!"

They went on, analyzing every detail of the performance. I quickly fixed my hair and escaped into the hallway.

Gyotia reached into the mountain and threw a handful of its fire into the sky, where it shone, fierce and bright. Then he bid it hide for part of each day, so that the earth made from his limbs would not grow too hot.

So it has always been with light, that it must coexist with darkness.

SIX

IN THE CARRIAGE back to the palace with Laiyonea, I dared a question: "What's a qodder?"

Laiyonea's attention snapped to me at once. "Where did you hear that? Did one of the others in the pantomime say it?"

"No, I just . . . overheard it, and I wondered—"

"Ignore it. Only a fool would call you that."

"But what does it mean?" I asked timidly.

"It is . . . a term used by those too ignorant to understand how things are, to belittle those of us who do understand. It comes from the use of qodal to dye one's hair black." She touched the ebony knot at the base of her neck. "As if any of us could forget our place."

I kept quiet after that.

Back at the palace, a luncheon for the players and their families waited in the garden. The poppies and blue lotuses were in full bloom, a spill of color under the bright sun. Laiyonea was immediately hailed by the Trade Minister, so I took a seat on the edge of the fountain.

I stiffened when I heard Mati and his cousin Patic, who had traveled from the Valley of Qora to play one of the ancient chieftains in the pantomime, coming along the path behind me. I had nearly convinced myself that I'd imagined that moment behind the stage. Here in the sunlight it seemed impossible that the prince would do something so rash. *Forget about it,* I told myself. It was nothing—it wasn't even the most shocking thing that had happened today.

"Bet you're glad the show's over, cousin," Patic was saying as they neared me. "You had so many guards around you couldn't even water the fields, if you know what I mean."

"Too bad they couldn't keep out the riffraff from the valley," Mati retorted, aiming a mock punch at Patic's arm.

Now that he mentioned it, I realized that the temple and stage *had* been unusually well guarded. "Why were there so many guards?" I asked.

Mati turned and met my eyes, then looked away quickly. "Oh, with me being on stage, the guard captain thought today was especially dangerous. There've been some escapes from the quarries, and attacks at the docks. Father thinks the Resistance is involved."

I nodded stiffly. Jonis had been right there in the temple. And Kiti had been helping him. The Resistance had gotten past the guards, and had gotten back out unscathed, by all appearances. I was glad they hadn't been caught, but . . . would they have hurt

Mati, given the chance? The thought turned my stomach to ice.

The luncheon bells rang. Mati shot me a swift, searching look as we joined the others on the path.

The Qilarite servants had set up round tables at the center of the garden, under a lacy roof of intertwined branches from the surrounding trees. I sat between Patic and Aliana, which, considering the possible alternatives, was a relief. I had a vague sense that Mati had arranged this, but I didn't dare speculate on what that might mean.

Aliana was practically mute for the entire meal. Patic, however, carried on a lively conversation with the War Minister's son on his other side. I picked at my food, my mind returning to the temple changing room. I'd told Jonis to leave me alone out of fear, plain and simple. I couldn't feel guilty for wanting to avoid the kind of horrible execution that Tyasha had suffered. Still, Jonis was right—I'd had no intention of telling anyone about his visit.

But the thought of Mati being in danger from the Resistance made me half want to report them to the guards. Then I wouldn't have to deal with Jonis or his messengers again, I thought, with mingled relief and self-loathing. But how could I report Jonis without getting Kiti into trouble, and without saying what he'd asked me to do? They had indeed trapped me neatly; I'd be accused of working with the Resistance. I hadn't called for help at once—that would be enough to condemn me.

"Mati's a good actor, isn't he?" said Patic.

I realized he was talking to me. "Yes, I suppose," I replied vaguely.

"Always has been." Patic's grin was impish, a bit like the

prince's. "When we were little, Mati would stay with us in the rainy season. He loved our cook's pomegranate tarts. Once he sneaked off and ate five before I found him. There he was, covered in sticky red filling, insisting with every breath that I'd eaten the tarts. My father believed him too."

I couldn't help smiling. "Well, he's the prince," I said.

"He was also very convincing in his indignation. I learned to watch my back with him." Patic nodded affectionately. "He's lucky my aunt married the king. He wouldn't last five minutes in the country."

"Oh, yes," I said. "He mentioned that you live in the Valley of Qora." With a pang, I remembered the day Mati had described the other players while teaching me the second tenset of the higher order symbols. His impression of Soraya Gamo's reaction to Patic's country accent had made me laugh so hard I'd nearly knocked over an inkpot.

"I run the operations for my father's olive farm, so I'm often back and forth to the city on business," said Patic. "Do a decent side business in message delivery too."

"That reminds me," said the War Minister's son, drawing Patic's attention back to himself. "I have a scroll for you to deliver on your way home."

I glanced at the prince as the conversation moved away from me. Patic was right—Mati was a good actor. The way he'd delivered his lines so naturally, the way he spoke deferentially to Penta Rale even though I'd often heard him mock the man in the Adytum. The way he laughed with the others now, as if nothing had happened behind that stage . . .

With sudden clarity, Patic's voice came to my ears.

"The wind has shifted. The rains soon will come from the ocean, I think."

I froze, my fork clanging against my plate. I forced myself to spear a piece of goat cheese and chew it, giving myself time to think.

But those weren't the words Jonis had said I would hear, were they? Not exactly right . . . but so close.

Beneath my fear fluttered something else, something that seemed to say, *"At least the Resistance is fighting back."* But what good had that ever done the Arnathim? My brother had fought back, and the raiders had skewered him.

All I had left of my family was my life and my heart-verse, and I wouldn't throw either of them away.

I swallowed the cheese and looked up. Patic was drinking from his goblet, watching me over the rim. I couldn't tell if his gaze was expectant or not.

"Really?" I said. "I didn't feel it."

*From time to time, the gods descended from the mountain to
visit the sea or hunt in the western forests. From their footsteps
sprang creatures like in form to the gods, but far smaller and
weaker. At first the gods paid no more attention to these mewling
pests than a rich man does to the dirt he tracks upon the floor for
a servant to clean.*

SEVEN

I ESCAPED TO the Adytum as soon as I could. Though
Laiyonea had canceled lessons because of the Festival of Aqil, I
still had to tend to the asotis, and afterward I relished the time
alone.

I pulled out my heart-verse and forced myself to examine each
character, but other thoughts kept creeping in. Jonis in the basement room, Mati touching my arm . . . his warm breath on my
cheek . . .

Stop it, I told myself for the hundredth time. It was insane
to think about it. Kissing the prince was a sure way to lose my
post, maybe my life. And even if, somehow, that didn't happen, I didn't need any distractions from my work. Being a good
Tutor would keep me alive; if I failed, there would be no going
back to my old life of cleaning, not with the things I knew. And
I had to keep learning, to figure out my heart-verse. That was

more important than anything else.

It was best, really, to forget about the prince's touch. It had been nothing—a slip resulting from the small space and the dark, and the energy of the pantomime.

And what about Jonis? I couldn't report him, and didn't really want to. But I didn't want him to approach me again either. If only I could go back to blissful ignorance of the Resistance and its doings . . .

Unbidden, his words came back to me: *"You don't mind if Arnath children are worked to death or Arnath women are raped by their masters or Arnath men die in the quarries, as long as* you're *comfortable in the palace."*

My fingers curled angrily around the edges of my heart-verse. What did he know? I'd been taking risks my whole life, just being alive as the daughter of a Learned One. And what could I possibly do to change all those horrible things? He was mad to think that learning to write would help the Resistance defeat anyone.

I returned my heart-verse to its hiding place and rearranged the flowers over the gap. A playful shout from the beach made me peer over the wall; a knot of young people lounged down by the water. Soraya Gamo stood in the shallows, smoothing her hair with one hand, watching Patic splash her giggling sisters. The others sat under the palms farther up the beach. I tried not to search for anyone in particular, but I soon found Mati, laughing at Patic.

I swallowed hard. And then there was Patic. I couldn't believe that Patic would harm Mati, or would help anyone who wanted to do so. Besides, the words he'd said at the luncheon weren't quite right—the more I thought about it, the more I was certain that I'd been imagining things. After all, he'd simply shrugged and gone back to talking to the others after I had answered him.

Fourth bell rang, and I hurried through the palace, intent on reaching the front corridor while the Qilarite servants were busy in the kitchens preparing for the night's banquet. As I passed the guards outside the Library, I kept my hand at my side, concealing the bread protruding from my pocket. Stung by Jonis's accusations, I had stolen a larger piece at the luncheon than I'd ever dared before. I smiled, imagining Linti's delight when she found it.

I slipped into the cavity under the stairs. As I didn't have a cloth to wrap the bread in, I started to leave it on the dusty stone floor. But then I noticed a white bundle in the corner. I crept closer to peek inside, and found three muffins, two teacakes, and a mound of dates. My hand hovered over the food as I realized that I'd told only one other person, besides Linti, about this spot.

I exhaled. It was all over. The easy days in the Adytum, talking to him like an equal. It had to be over, because the emotion that raced through me now was too dangerous, too close.

I closed my eyes. *Just forget it happened,* I told myself.

If only I could.

When I entered the banquet room beside Laiyonea that night, I couldn't help darting a look at the prince, sitting with his father at the head table. I hated how much care I had taken to dress—what reason was there to do so?—but I'd finally settled on a white dress with deep green sleeves.

The vibrant colors worn by the Qilarite nobles made my gown seem pale and drab. I hadn't had much choice, however, as everything the Tutors wore was white and green—white to show that we were handmaidens of the god Aqil, and green to show that we were still Arnath slaves, no matter how many palace functions we attended.

As Laiyonea and I took our seats, Prince Mati shot us an easy smile that encompassed us both. It was so exactly like the smile he would have given me the day before that I had to look down to hide the crashing disappointment in my chest.

All through the meal I distracted myself by going over the higher order symbols I had learned so far and tracing them in my palm under the table. It almost worked. I almost didn't notice the procession of completely useless Scholar daughters coming up to flirt with the prince. I couldn't tell whether he enjoyed it or not.

Gritting my teeth, I wrote *restraint* in my left palm.

Though King Tyno had responded with hardly more than a grunt to the Trade Minister when he praised Mati's pantomime performance, he laughed at the joking comments the western vizier, Del Gamo, kept making about the girls. I wanted to throw my goblet at both of them. Gamo's wife sat at another table full of veiled wives, but their three daughters sat with their father at the king's table, as even the eldest was not yet betrothed. Not many men would take pride in a houseful of girls, but the western vizier boasted about Soraya and Alshara and Aliana constantly. Of course, he had no need to worry about their dowries. Gamo's lands spanned the gold and silver mines around Pira, on the western coast of Qilara, and he was reputed to be wealthier even than the king. The golden necklaces and earrings the twins wore attested to this, as did the large purple jewel at Soraya's throat.

At our table, the War Minister boasted about capturing eleven Arnath slaves stowed away aboard a trading ship bound for heathen Emtiria in the east. I wondered uncomfortably if Jonis and Kiti had been involved in the escape attempt.

After the meal, Laiyonea pressed me to finish my fig cake, but I wasn't hungry. The bell dance began. For the first time, I would have liked to join the circle. It had nothing to do with the fact that there was an opening next to the prince. But Laiyonea said that dancing was not an appropriate pastime for a prince's Tutor. Soraya Gamo took the open place.

I didn't mind at all when Laiyonea said it was time to retire. Noticing my mood as we lit candles for evening invocations in our sitting room, she laid a hand on my forehead, then sent for sunamara tea for me to drink before bed.

After I had drunk every drop to appease her, she sent me into my room and locked me in. She must have gone back down to the banquet, as she didn't usually lock my door when she was in her room. I had to cross her bedroom to get to the sitting room, so she would have known if I left. I wondered if Laiyonea used to lock Tyasha ke Demit in at night, or if she locked me in because she *wished* she had done so.

Still, any foolish, fleeting thoughts I might have had of sneaking out were dashed when the heavy lock bar slid into place. I undressed awkwardly—the tea had left me sluggish—and slipped into my loose sleeping gown. The servants had already opened the willow shutters to the evening breeze, so the sounds of the celebration in the streets below wafted up to me as I blew out the lamp and lay down.

Be grateful, I told myself. I'd had two narrow escapes today—from the prince's heated touch, from Jonis's heated demands, both dangers that could have wrecked my world. Tomorrow I would go back to the Adytum and continue my lessons. Nothing had changed, not really.

Except that yesterday, I had wanted nothing more than to learn the higher order script and decipher my heart-verse. Now, I had let myself want something else, something I would never have, something I had no right to want.

I turned to find a dry place on my pillow, and was drifting into a restless half sleep when I heard a noise at the window.

At first I thought the shutter had banged in the breeze, but then a shadow dropped from the window ledge into the room. I sat up and took a breath to scream, but the shadow dashed toward me and, for the second time that day, a hand clamped over my mouth.

Gyotia fashioned a lamp from the sky-fire and carried it as he wandered the night philandering, though he veiled it when he visited the bedrooms of mortal women.

So regular were his wanderings that the mortals below began to order the year by the fourteen Shinings and fourteen Veilings of Gyotia's Lamp.

EIGHT

"IT'S ALL RIGHT," said a hoarse voice. I had rarely heard him speak that way, without humor. Maybe that was why my heart didn't start pounding until he let go and leaned over to light the lamp.

As Prince Mati's profile became visible, I clutched the blanket to my chest. He perched on the edge of the bed. "It took me ages to find you. I'd have given the western vizier's wife an awful fright if she hadn't already passed out from too much wine."

I stared at him in disbelief. "Why did you come?" I asked, my voice strained. I was overly aware of my bare arms, of my thin white and green nightgown, of his leg brushing mine through the blanket. Despite the sunamara tea I'd drunk, every part of me was almost painfully awake.

His face fell. "Don't be angry," he said. "I'm sorry about . . .

earlier. I shouldn't have—" He broke off and ran his fingers through his hair.

"I understand," I said woodenly. "It was a mistake. We should just . . . forget it happened." My fingers clutched the blanket so tightly that it hurt.

The softness in his eyes stole my breath. "But I can't forget it happened. I've been thinking about it all day. If you want me to leave, I will, and I'll never say another word about it. But . . . I had to come and see if maybe . . . you couldn't forget about it either." He watched my face, one hand tapping nervously against his leg.

Entire worlds of possibility blossomed before my eyes, and my skin went hot, then cold, then hot again.

Tell him to leave, said the sensible voice in my head, in Laiyonea's clipped tones. I tried to think of higher order symbols, and my father, and my heart-verse. But the truth was, more than anything I wanted Mati to touch me again, to kiss me as he almost had behind the stage.

And I was terrified, not of what might happen to me, but of the power of my own want.

"I haven't forgotten," I said faintly.

Mati's shoulders relaxed a fraction. "Do you want me to leave?" he asked.

"No," I whispered.

The night air was thick. My head spun as he leaned forward. He was so close that I saw his throat work as he swallowed and said, "I'd like to kiss you, Raisa. Would that . . . would that be all right?"

There were reasons I should say no, I knew, but I couldn't bring a single one to mind.

In answer I leaned closer. He let out a surprised exhalation and pushed my hair back from my face, his eyes closing as he leaned in to kiss me. His fingers touched my neck, my shoulders, my arms, leaving a trail of fire.

We were both breathing heavily when the kiss ended. Mati stroked my face and told me that I was beautiful, and I said some quite embarrassing things back. In the pale glow of the lamp, with his warmth beside me, it was difficult to hold on to any thought for long. We kissed again. This time he pressed me down to the pillow and I lay pinned by his half weight on top of me.

It was wonderful.

I couldn't think; feeling had replaced thought, and suddenly my heart seemed capable of holding more than my brain ever had. The noise of the revelers on the streets faded, replaced by Mati's soft murmurs in my ear.

Mati stayed with me for a long time—and yet not long enough—and eventually we broke off kissing and talked of the banquet, and lessons the next day. But these mundane topics seemed magical when discussed with Mati's head on my shoulder and his fingers twined through mine. I asked if he'd enjoyed the dancing. He laughed and looked sideways at me.

"Father'll complain that I didn't dance with the western vizier's daughters nearly often enough." He absently traced his finger over my palm. "I wish Laiyonea would let you dance."

A pleased flush spread through me. "So do I," I whispered. "She says it isn't our place."

"No one will find out," Mati said softly. "As long as we don't let Laiyonea suspect anything, she'll still leave us alone in the

Adytum sometimes. Besides," he added with a grin, "it's an easy climb to your window." He leaned over and kissed me again, and any nerves I might have had vanished into a sigh.

The knock on the door startled us both. Mati went still. I prayed to all the gods that we wouldn't be found out, not yet.

"Raisa," came Laiyonea's voice through the door. "Why is your lamp still lit?"

I couldn't think of a thing to say.

"Answer her, or she'll come in to check on you," Mati breathed impatiently into my ear.

I found my voice. "The noises outside frightened me."

Mati seemed impressed—he probably hadn't thought me capable of lying. Laiyonea obviously didn't either, because she laughed fondly and said, "Well, I'm back now, so blow out the lamp and go to sleep."

"Yes, Laiyonea," I managed to say, before Mati kissed me again.

"You have to go," I whispered when we broke apart.

He nodded and brushed his lips against mine before he rolled off the bed and stood up soundlessly. I watched him blow out the lamp. Even Gyotia in his chariot couldn't have been more beautiful than he was.

As he crept to the window and disappeared into the night, I bit my tongue against a crazy urge to call him back.

Rolling over, I squeezed my pillow—it still held his musky scent. When at last I fell asleep, I dreamed of asotis wheeling across the sky.

The seven gods breathed out the symbols of their power,
awakening root and stream and stone, bringing forth living
creatures—goats, cattle, oxen, small beasts of the fields. So the
language of the gods was written into the earth, astonishing even
the gods themselves as each day brought new creations.

NINE

THE NEXT MORNING in the Adytum, I was so dis-
tracted that Laiyonea actually rapped my knuckles with her quill
box to get my attention. "Honestly, Raisa! I'd planned to start you
on the higher order symbols today, but—"

I sat up straighter. "No! I'll pay attention, I promise. I just . . .
didn't sleep well. Because of the noise from the festival and . . .
the things the War Minister was saying last night." Even if that
wasn't why I was distracted, I didn't have to feign fear when it
came to threats from the Resistance.

Laiyonea smiled indulgently. "Raisa, you're safe here."

I looked down at my paper to disguise my confusion. I *did* feel
safe here, in the palace, in the Adytum, especially when I thought
of Mati's arms around me. But how could that be? Did the asotis
feel safe in their cage?

"Very well," Laiyonea said. "I suppose you're ready."

Fortunately, Mati had taught me the first three tensets by

then, so I didn't have to concentrate too hard on the symbols Laiyonea introduced. In fact, I did so well so quickly that Laiyonea commented on how unusual that was, and I purposely reversed the lines on the seventh and eighth symbols just to give her something to correct.

When we'd first entered the Adytum, I'd been nervous about how I would act when Mati arrived, but by the time he came at midmorning bells I was so enmeshed in my work that I'd forgotten to worry about him, about the Resistance, about anything but the curves and slopes of the symbols. His footsteps on the stairs set my heart pounding. I kept my eyes on my work, lest my expression betray me when I saw him.

Laiyonea greeted him as he crossed the courtyard. He looked over my shoulder at my paper. "Finally started her on the higher order?" he said to Laiyonea.

"Yes," said Laiyonea. "With things moving along as they are, it seemed prudent." I wasn't sure what she meant, but I glanced up in time to see Mati grimace and shrug as he sat down beside me.

"I'm surprised you didn't start torturing her with them sooner." Mati's eyes were on Laiyonea, but his hand found mine under the table and gave it a squeeze.

"It's only torture for lazy boys who don't pay attention," Laiyonea shot back.

"Laiyonea, you wound me!" said Mati, clutching his heart. I giggled, and even Laiyonea cracked a smile. After that she instructed Mati to review the first two tensets by showing them to me; the Trade Minister, Priasi Jin, wanted her to attend a meeting with the city's largest supplier of kirit, the plant used to make green dye for Arnath clothing.

As I watched her leave, I pondered how, even though people like Jonis might sneer at her qodal-dyed hair, Laiyonea had used her position as best she could. By staying on the good side of the king and most of the council, she probably did more to quietly help the Arnathim than the Resistance knew.

Such thoughts evaporated as the gate clanged shut behind her and Mati pushed his paper away. Before I had a chance to grow awkward around him, he kissed me. It was so different, kissing him outdoors in the ocean air, from the way it had been in my dark bedroom. We were under the canopy, so no one could have seen us from the palace windows or the guard towers, and the walls hid us from the beach below. I thought I felt the statue of Gyotia watching us. I tried not to care.

"I've been thinking of you all morning," said Mati softly.

"Me too." I ducked my head. "I was so distracted that Laiyonea got cross with me."

"And still she throws your work ethic in my face," said Mati. "I must do something to sidetrack you, to even the field." He kissed my palm, and moved his lips up my arm. I shivered at his touch, both liking and fearing how quickly it had come to feel natural. "Luckily you already know the first few tensets," he said conversationally, as he worked his way up my neck. "Gives us more time for other things."

A small noise of assent escaped my throat as I turned my head and met his lips.

All the rest of the dry, hot season of Lilana, Mati and I spent languid afternoons in the Adytum. Whenever his father called Laiyonea away, Mati excused himself from the proceedings and came to find me. He assured me that the king was used to his lack of interest in negotiations, and that he wasn't needed anyway.

Days in the Adytum fell into a dreamlike pattern: we talked, we kissed, occasionally we even did our work. And whenever he could, he came to me at night, especially when Gyotia's Lamp was veiled in the dark sky.

Even when palace business or Scholar functions kept us apart, I would see the packets of treats he'd left whenever I slipped into the cavity under the stairs, reminders of his kindness and the secrets that bound us together.

I'd thought my feelings for Mati would keep me from focusing on my work, but he knew how I felt about learning the higher order script, so he kept teaching me a few tensets ahead of where Laiyonea had left off. Learning the symbols with Mati's arm draped over my shoulders was much more pleasant than Laiyonea's teaching methods, even if it often ended in more kissing than writing.

It was fortunate I had his support, for I'd been wrong about the higher order symbols being easier, and though I had found more of the symbols from my heart-verse, I was no closer to decoding it no matter how long I pored over the faded paper. Once I had mastered the first twenty tensets, Laiyonea explained about the complicated determinatives used with the higher order symbols, which could change the meaning at least eight different ways. She showed me the higher order symbol *life* and all its determinatives.

I tried to imitate her quick, precise strokes, but within minutes I'd thrown my quill down in frustration.

The council was out of session for First Shining, and Mati had gone with his father to visit Del Gamo's mines near Pira, three days' ride from the city. Pira had been the site of a slave uprising the Veiling before, and Mati had told me, frowning, that his father planned to leave two hundred guards behind after visiting the mines; he plainly felt that the king showed too much favor to the western vizier. I worried about Mati's safety on the road, but he had only laughed when I'd said so, and pointed out that he would be surrounded by guards.

Ever since he had left, I'd thought I might burst out of my skin from missing him. But today I was glad he wasn't here—I'd never had so much trouble with any symbol before, not even *gift*, and I'd have been embarrassed for him to see it.

"I don't understand," I said grumpily. "Why does it need so many variations?"

Laiyonea tapped the paper. "Because the higher order symbols allow you to express more subtlety of meaning than the lower order symbols do." She pointed to the base symbol. "This means the basic act of living. Survival. With this determinative"—she added a swoop across the top—"it means living for a higher purpose. With this"—she added a curve at the bottom—"it means to live without fear." She continued to add lines, until they practically blurred in my vision. "With all of them in place, it means a state of being so fully engaged with life that one no longer fears death."

I stared at her. "How is that even possible?"

Laiyonea smiled. "Suffice it to say that the base symbol would be used for a creature that eats, sleeps, and breathes, while the determinatives describe a life lived more fully."

"So . . . the base symbol applies to animals, and you add the different determinatives to write about people?"

Laiyonea's smile froze. "Not exactly." She dipped her quill and sketched the symbol again without the determinatives. "The base symbol is used for animal life, yes. But . . . with the determinatives," she said without looking up, "it is only ever used to refer to Qilarites."

I swallowed, a vile taste in my mouth. So even the language of the gods—or, at least what I had learned of it in the Adytum— equated the Arnathim with animals, putting the lowliest illiterate Qilarite peasant above us. I wondered if Tyasha had taught the determinatives to the Resistance; I could only imagine what they would have said about this symbol. I was even more relieved, now, that Mati was away.

Reluctantly I tried the symbol again, but the lines came out all wrong. I wasn't sure I even wanted to get them right.

"You're doing fine," said Laiyonea in what was, for her, a patient tone.

"What does it matter?" I grumbled. "Who will know if any of the strokes are wrong? Everything I write will burn."

"It matters," she said crisply, "because you will train the future monarch of Qilara to converse with the gods. You cannot do that if you are too lazy to write the symbols correctly."

I had to look away from the harsh light in her eyes. It *was* important that I continue. It might be the only way to read my heart-verse, if I could just figure out how my father had used the symbols.

Laiyonea's voice, softer now, came to my ears. "It is an enormous responsibility. You are young, but many others have taken it on far younger. I was one of them."

I hadn't thought of that. I tried to picture Laiyonea as a child, three or four years old as most Tutors were when they began their study, and I could not.

Laiyonea took my paper and wrote something on the back. She held it up. I examined the symbols, but only recognized two: *palace*, and another that I thought meant *priest*, but it had a determinative I didn't recognize. "I can't read that," I said.

Laiyonea pointed to the first symbol. "This means priest. The determinative shows that it is the highest priest. The next symbol can mean either a person's face or a person's character, depending on context. See how the line shows that the first and second symbols are connected? Next is the palace—you should recognize that—and a crowd of people. Then the ground where they walk, and a compound symbol—*right*, with *everyday activity* on top. It means 'appropriate.' Next is the curved line connecting the face to the ground. What does it mean?"

I stared at the page, afraid to say what I thought.

"I know you're not stupid, so I assume you're just being timid," Laiyonea said. "'The high priest's face is like the stones beneath our feet.' In this case, the chief high priest, or Penta Rale."

I wasn't sure if laughing was allowed, but Laiyonea chuckled, so I let out a strangled giggle.

She leaned forward. "You could walk up to Rale, or any of the

Scholars Council even, and wave this paper in their faces, and they wouldn't recognize the insult. I know you couldn't really do that," she added impatiently, when I started to protest, "but the point is that you already have knowledge denied to most Qilarites. You know of the first Tutor?"

I nodded. One of the other girls in the Selection, a dark-haired, cocksure orphan from the city, had whispered the tale to the rest of us while we waited to be called to the council chamber. "King Balon taught his Arnath concubine the language of the gods so that she could teach his son. He feared what a priest or Scholar would do with the higher order symbols, so he entrusted them to someone who was . . . powerless."

Laiyonea lifted her chin. "That depends on what you consider power."

I pursed my lips, pondering her words. That was why we were kept away from the other Arnathim, and given so many apparent privileges—to keep us compliant. The phrase "shackles of silk" flitted through my mind. I pushed it away.

The knowledge I learned in the Adytum *was* powerful—it would help me unlock my heart-verse, if only I found the right symbols. That was what mattered.

"I'll try harder," I said.

Laiyonea smiled. She came around the table and fingered a lock of my hair, which I had not bothered to tie back. "We really ought to dye that," she said. "A bit of qodal would darken it. And cut it shorter too, in the Qilarite style, to get rid of the waves."

I remembered my mother's thick auburn hair, soft over my fingers when I used to touch it as a child. "No," I said.

"Hmm?"

"No," I repeated loudly. "I won't dye my hair. Or cut it."

Laiyonea went still. "I see," she said softly, but there was nothing gentle in her tone. "Braid it back then." She dropped my hair and returned to her seat; the other side of the table seemed farther away than it had before.

"*Life*," she said. "Write it."

"You didn't cut your hair," I said, and knew, by the patches of color in Laiyonea's cheeks, that she wore her hair in a knot because it waved, like mine.

Laiyonea cleared her throat deliberately. "Write it again. Do it correctly this time."

I bent over the paper and tried again.

Gyotia built a house of stone on the mountain high above the Olsunal, the sea-without-memory, and brought Lanea there to tend to him. The other gods and goddesses settled nearby. For a time, they lived in peace—or at least, not in open conflict.

TEN

WHEN MATI AND his father returned six days later, the royal household assembled to greet them. It was all I could do not to run down the steps and throw my arms around Mati's neck as he and his father climbed down from the carriage. I saved my welcome for when he came to my room that night.

We were both giddy, and once we'd had our fill of kissing, we talked too loudly and had to keep shushing each other so Laiyonea wouldn't hear. Mati sobered as he told me about the maimed slaves at the mines who had been allowed to live, as an example to the others of what happened when they rebelled.

See, Jonis? I thought. *See what your Resistance does?*

"It was horrible," Mati said, his hands clenching into fists. "I can't believe my father let that happen."

I touched his shoulder. "When . . . when you're king, things will be different."

Mati blinked. We never spoke of the future—it was too full of unknowns—but I was sure of his goodness. He gave me a grateful half smile and pulled me into his arms, and I let his kiss drive every worry from my mind.

On the Festival of Lanea, Laiyonea and I rode to the temple hill in an open carriage, seated behind the king and prince. It was a great honor for us to be there, but I saw now that, like many of the privileges granted to the Tutors, it was also the king's way of keeping us close. Laiyonea had told me that a slave trader had been found outside the city gates the day before, his throat cut. The council blamed the Resistance.

Mati smiled and waved to the people lining the streets, a perfect contrast to the way his father sat sternly surveying his subjects as though they were all slaves at a market. When the carriage approached the temples, King Tyno leaned over and spoke to Mati, low and sharp. The tips of Mati's ears reddened as he lowered his hand and faced forward.

At the Temple of Lanea, Obal Tishe led the invocations in a gentle voice, befitting the high priest of the goddess of the hearth. Then the banquet began. Though it was my first outside the palace, the faces around me were familiar—council members, high-ranking Scholars, here and there a wealthy merchant. The tables formed a horseshoe shape, with the high priests lined up in order of rank along one side. Even here in his own temple, Obal Tishe sat at the end of the line, with Penta Rale seated next to the king and Mati at the center of the arc.

To keep my eyes from lingering too much on Mati, I studied the temple alcoves with their friezes, automatically evaluating the difficulty of cleaning each one. Outside the temple, music started up. The fluting of a tin horn brought back a childhood memory—a young man in our village, with a red beard and merry face, who'd played for festivals. We'd seen his bloodied body slumped on the side of the road on the march to the raider ship.

I forced my mind to the present as the servants passed out packages. Gifts were traditional at this festival, because so many stories told of Lanea conveying anger, appreciation, or even desire through subtly given gifts. She was even said to send gifts to mortals occasionally; the previous High Priest of Lanea had made himself wealthy charging for his services interpreting "gifts of the goddess," ranging from birthmarks to oddly shaped yams to piles of stones.

The gifts given during the festival sometimes bore special significance too, as when the farmers in the Valley of Qora had presented the king with a fountain for the palace garden last year, to remind him of his promise to repair the aqueducts.

I started as a servant placed a long, shallow box on the table in front of me. Who would give me a gift?

"Who would give you a gift?" hissed Laiyonea.

"I don't know," I said, but my eyes darted to Mati. He was unwrapping a wooden box and laughing at something that the Trade Minister had said.

"Who sent it?" Laiyonea demanded of the Qilarite servant.

"A messenger delivered it this morning, Tutor," said the man around the stack of boxes in his arms. "Many council members also received anonymous gifts." He indicated the War Minister a few seats down, who was opening a tall bottle of oil.

"It must be for you," I said, pushing the box at Laiyonea.

"No, the messenger stated that it was for Raisa ke Margara," said the servant as he moved off to drop a package in front of the High Priest of Qora.

"Open it," Laiyonea said sharply.

I lifted the lid. Inside lay the most beautiful quill I'd ever seen—pure white, with just the barest touch of green at the core, and curled at the edges. The end had already been shaped to a fine point.

I had seen this kind of feather before, back on the Nath Tarin. My father had used one; he might even have written my heart-verse with it. Lifting the quill from the box, I trailed a finger over its impossibly soft edge.

"What kind of feather is that?" said Laiyonea.

I shook my head. "I don't know what it's called. . . ." I looked over at Mati again. He had noticed my gift now, and was wearing a puzzled frown.

So he hadn't sent it.

Suddenly Laiyonea touched my arm. "Put it away," she said. I followed her gaze and saw two council members with their heads close together, watching us. I dropped the quill into my lap.

One of the men tapped his neighbor on the arm and leaned over to say something to him, but before he got the chance, Penta Rale rose at his place beside the king.

"Your Majesty, the high priests wish to present a gift to you. With your leave?" The king nodded, and Rale clapped his hands. From the back of the temple came three men in green carrying a huge carving of a ship. The ship was four feet tall, and every bit of it, from deck to sails, had been hewn from glossy black stone.

"On this Festival Day," Rale said, "we honor our king with this token, to celebrate the good fortune of our nation under King Tyno's leadership." As the men heaved the ship past us, I saw how the carver had gotten every detail right, from the high prow to the chains across the hatches. It wasn't just any ship. It was a raider ship—a slave ship.

My stomach turned. I rubbed my wrists where the ropes and chains of the raiders had bitten into them so many years ago. Why would the priests give King Tyno something like that?

I looked away from the hideous thing, and my eyes fell on two temple slaves, an older man and a young woman, half hidden behind a pillar. Watching me.

All at once I knew who had sent the quill: the Resistance, reminding me of what they wanted me to do. And telling me that they would not leave me alone.

But I wouldn't help them. *It doesn't matter if they think I'm selfish,* I told myself uncomfortably. What choice did I have if I wanted to stay alive? And besides, one day Mati would be king and things would be better.

In the bustle of dinner, I shoved the quill back into its box and kicked the box under my chair. Afterward, I left it behind as I followed Laiyonea to the exit. The Temple of Lanea was celebrated for its delicious feasts, but even though I had secreted several small cakes in my pocket for Linti, I had hardly tasted a bite and was eager to return to the palace.

I was relieved to see two guards waiting for us at the door; the Resistance wouldn't be able to get anywhere near me. Four more guards hovered near Mati and his father as they came down the center aisle. The guards pushed the door open, and one of them preceded us through.

Though the sun was setting, the music was still going on outside. About twenty Arnathim in green, slaves attending those inside, had gathered next to the temple. Some were playing pipes and makeshift drums; others were dancing and laughing. Soldiers stood at intervals around the courtyard, but their stance was watchful, not ominous.

Laiyonea was climbing into the carriage, with me close behind, when it happened—the laughter turned to shouts and the music cut off. I turned and caught a glimpse of a familiar head of curly hair—Jonis, stepping between a little girl and a soldier. I saw the soldier's fist connect with his face, saw another punch him in the stomach even as he fell. Then there were soldiers everywhere.

As Lanea swept the hearth one fine morning, ashes swirled into the air and mixed with the goddess's breath, forming the first bird. Delighted, Lanea molded the ashes into birds of various shapes and presented them to the other gods. To Gyotia she gave the majestic golden eagle; to Lila the fierce falcon; to Aqil the shrieking crow; to Qora and Suna the gentle pheasant and swan. To Sotia she presented the first bird, gray as ash, and named it asoti in her honor. Gyotia laughed cruelly when he saw the small asoti beside his enormous eagle, but Sotia embraced Lanea, for she saw the value of this gift. Ever after, the gods wrote with fine quills of asoti feathers.

ELEVEN

"RAISA, GET IN the carriage!" shouted Laiyonea.

Only then did I realize that the guards were moving in closer to me. More were racing up the steps to protect Mati and his father.

Mati had stopped dead. "What are they doing? Stop them!" he cried. "That old woman didn't do anything!"

"Mati, hush!" hissed Laiyonea.

King Tyno grabbed Mati's arm. "Get into the carriage," he said in a low voice that nonetheless carried to where I stood, three steps down.

"But, Father, they—"

"Shut your mouth and get into the carriage," the king growled. Mati tried to pull away, but his father dragged him down the steps and practically threw him into his seat.

I clambered into the carriage next to Laiyonea. She exchanged a grim look with the king before they both turned to face forward, but Mati and I craned our necks to see the courtyard. Obal Tishe was making his way through the crowd, speaking to the soldiers. I watched, confused, as he helped an old woman in green to her feet.

Then the carriage started moving, and my gaze slid over the knot of priests standing on the temple steps. They looked relieved that the High Priest of Lanea was dealing with the mob—all save Penta Rale, who watched Tishe with a look that suggested he had just smelled something foul.

No one spoke on the trip back to the palace. The fighting had been all the more frightening for its suddenness. I hadn't seen how it started, but Mati had. He told me that night when he came to my room, still seething.

"Two soldiers just plowed into an old woman and hit her," he said. "At least, that's what it looked like. She must have done something before that, though. . . ." He trailed off uncertainly. "And he's not even looking into what happened!"

I didn't respond. If the people who'd been hurt were all slaves, it didn't surprise me that the king wouldn't pursue the matter. But I didn't like to say so to Mati. I took his hand, and he sat down on the bed beside me.

"He's more upset about that stupid carved ship the high priests gave him," Mati went on. "He thinks they're taunting him."

"Why . . . why did they give it to him?"

Mati paused, and I realized that I was rubbing my wrists again. I stilled my hands in my lap.

"They . . . want him to send raiders to the Nath Tarin," said Mati. "They think it'll be a message to the Resistance."

I stared at him in horror. Did Jonis have any idea what he and his people had done?

Mati swallowed. "He won't do it, though. He says it's . . ." He squeezed his eyes shut. "Wasteful. That there are . . . plenty of slaves here, and cheaper too. That breeding slaves here is more . . . economical. And he can't spare the men, with things so tense on the Emtirian border."

He looked so miserable that I took his hand. "But he's not sending them," I whispered. "That's the important thing."

He sighed, and we sat there in thoughtful silence until he said soberly, "Who gave you the quill?"

I tensed at his tone—did he suspect something? "I don't know. Laiyonea thinks it was Rale or one of the priests, playing some kind of joke." She'd said so when we'd gotten back to our sitting room, right after she'd said how stupid Mati had been to criticize the soldiers in front of his father.

Mati was silent. My stomach dropped a little—and then I realized what my own paranoia had been keeping me from seeing. "Mati," I said slowly, "are you . . . jealous?"

"No!" said Mati at once. But he looked away awkwardly and leaned back on the bed. I stared at him until he finally sighed. "Yes," he said. "*I* want to be able to give you gifts."

"But I can't give you anything either." I leaned over to kiss him. "Besides, you already gave me you." I nestled beside him, resting my head on his arm.

He winced. Remembering how his father had gripped him, I lifted his sleeve. Bruises blossomed on his upper arm—one ugly purplish-black mark for each finger. I kissed each one, thinking how different he and his father were, and how much better a king Mati would be because of that.

The next morning, Laiyonea told me that Mati was sitting in on an important negotiation with his father, and went to join them. She had me working on the *life* symbol with all its variants again; I was still struggling with it. Mati arrived in the Adytum an hour later, grinning giddily.

"Are the negotiations going well?" I asked as he put his arms around me. I didn't really care. I just wanted to hear his voice.

"Well enough," he said absently. "I have something for you." He blushed as he held up a small, flat beige stone, irregularly shaped, with a leather thong threaded through a hole at one end. "It isn't much, but I thought it was pretty. I found it this morning on the beach and I decided to make a necklace for you." He laid it in my hand, and I saw faint lines etched into one of the flat surfaces, lines that might have been deeper once, but had long since been made smooth by the ocean current. Mati ran one finger over the rock, then took my hand and sketched a shape into my palm. "It almost looks like a symbol. It's nonsense though. I don't know why, but it made me think of you."

I had to hold the stone right up to my eye to see the lines. I almost dropped it when I made out the shape—three wavy lines joined by a straight one. *Sa.* The first symbol of my heart-verse, which I had yet to find in the language of the gods. The second part of my name, as my father taught me to write it so long ago. It was a sound, but also a word unto itself: *light of wisdom.*

Mati didn't recognize the symbol—had said it was nonsense. It didn't mean *sa* to him; it didn't mean anything to him. Which meant that it couldn't be a higher order symbol.

It had to be part of the Arnath writing, because it appeared in my heart-verse. If it didn't appear in the Qilarite writing system, did that mean that learning the higher order symbols wouldn't help me read my heart-verse after all?

"Don't you like it?" Mati asked. "I know it isn't anything special—"

"I love it," I whispered quickly. I came so close to telling him about my father then, but I was afraid to—or maybe I didn't want to remind him how different we were.

Mati drew me closer and kissed my neck. "Tell Laiyonea you found it on the beach," he said, his words buzzing against my skin. "No one will know what it really is but us."

"What *is* it really?" I asked carefully. My skin seemed to dance up away from my bones, awaiting his answer.

He looked right into my eyes. I very nearly melted away into nothing. "It means you're mine, and I'm yours, Raisa. It means I love you."

I whispered it back, and smiled as he tugged my hair free of its braid and ran his fingers through it, his mouth bending to cover mine.

Mati had been coming to my room nearly every night during the dark Veilings. But after he gave me the stone, we were both eager for more time together, and so he risked the climb at the beginning of the next Shining too, when Gyotia's Lamp was not yet fully uncovered. That was probably why, five nights after Mati's seventeenth birthday celebration, one of the guards saw a figure creeping along the wall and launched an arrow at him. The arrow missed, but Mati had to explain away the sprained wrist he got on his hurried climb to a hall window.

The next afternoon, Mati couldn't write because of his injury, so he hovered and distracted me by clicking his tongue at my sloppy strokes and generally making a nuisance of himself. I wished he would stop; I didn't like the suspicious looks Laiyonea kept shooting at his bandaged hand. Clearly she didn't believe his claim that he'd injured it during a sword-fighting lesson.

"Enough, Mati," Laiyonea snapped, after he started flicking leaves at the asotis, causing them to gabble and shriek. "You might behave a little more seriously, with an intruder on the palace walls last night."

I dropped a splotch of ink on my list of the eighty-seven uses of the sunamara plant. "Intruder?" I squeaked. I had an image of Jonis on the outer walls with a knife in his teeth, before I remembered that it had been Mati climbing to my room.

Mati laughed. "Father's just worked up over nothing. The palace has been searched top to bottom. That guard was seeing things. Maybe it was a salamander."

Laiyonea frowned. "You know very well that your father

didn't imagine those attacks at the docks, or . . ." She pursed her lips. The fighting at the Temple of Lanea flashed through my mind.

Mati nodded, sobering. "I know, I know." He sighed. "Well, once the western vizier fills up Father's coffers with gold, he can hire all the mercenaries on the peninsula to clear them out." His tone was bitter.

I frowned. Mati had made it sound like King Tyno needed Del Gamo's money, but that couldn't be. After all, he was the king.

Laiyonea looked back and forth between us, her expression a mixture of pity and something else I couldn't name—anger, maybe? But she didn't leave us alone in the Adytum that day.

All that happened upon the earth appeared in the scrolls of the gods. Sotia gathered the scrolls and built a great library upon the mountain to house them.

When first the other gods stepped inside the library, Gyotia scoffed at her efforts.

Aqil looked around in puzzlement. "What is this place?" he asked.

"It is everything," whispered Sotia.

TWELVE

QILARA HAD ONLY two seasons: Lilana, when soldiers praised Lila, goddess of war, for the fine, dry weather that made for easy movement over land, and Qorana, named for Qora, god of the fields, wet and temperate and ideal for growing things.

When the rains of Qorana came, parts of the city flooded, and the king ordered the floodwalls raised partway as a precaution. The gray wall loomed up between the arms of the mountains on either side of the inlet, cutting off our view of the sea.

I worried that the rains would damage my heart-verse. I checked it daily when I went to the Adytum to tend to the asotis, but I still couldn't make sense of the way the symbols had been strewn together, even the ones I recognized. What did *cheese* have to do with *honor* beside it? But I didn't dare linger in the Adytum.

We could not study in the outdoor courtyard during the rains, of course, and as it was against the law for me or Laiyonea to write anywhere else, lessons were put on hold until the sun shone again. On rainy days, I was imprisoned in the sitting room, cutting endless piles of quills. I didn't know how I would stand not seeing Mati for days on end.

Mati, however, found something better than the Adytum, better even than late nights in my room. He crept into the sitting room on an especially miserable, gray day, grinning from ear to ear. Laiyonea had gone to speak with the king. I was happy to take a break—my hands were stiff from the knife, as I'd already completed an entire basket of quills.

Mati held one finger to his lips as he took my hand and led me down the deserted corridor. The lamps were all lit against the overcast afternoon. When I asked where we were going, he only shook his head.

At last Mati pushed open a door. I balked as I realized that he was leading me into the king's own chambers.

"Come on," he whispered. "It's all right."

He tugged me inside and shut the door, then led me across an anteroom and into the bedroom. Gold-threaded tapestries hung from the walls, and the high bed, piled with pillows and thick blankets, was as large as a temple alcove.

Mati opened a mirrored door, pushed aside his father's tunics, and opened another, smaller door at the back of the closet.

"Pull that other door shut," he whispered. He clutched my hand as he led me down a narrow staircase. We must have been close to the outer wall; I could hear rain pelting down as if it were right above my head, and murky light came in through windows—little more than vertical slits—set near the ceiling.

At the bottom of the steps, Mati pointed to a passage winding away to the left into the darkness. "That leads down to the dungeons and scribe rooms. There's a branch up to the council chamber too," he whispered. "But this is the best part."

He moved his hand along the wall before us. With a soft click, part of it swung open.

We stepped into the Library of the Gods—though I hardly recognized it. I had never seen it with the furniture and carpets in place, the high friezes, white and pure and clean, shining in the light of the central firepit. Linti and the other children must have cleaned recently, because there was not a speck of dust anywhere. With all its finery, the Library of the Gods resembled a temple—except that a Qilarite temple would never have letters openly displayed.

It flitted through my mind that this—a holy place full of writing—was exactly what a temple to Sotia would look like. But the goddess of wisdom would never stand for her gift of writing to be locked away from her people like this. And the Qilarites would never build a temple to a goddess who had been imprisoned by Gyotia himself since ancient times.

Mati put his arm around me. "Father showed me this entrance a few days ago," he said. "I'm not supposed to come without him." He didn't seem to regret his disobedience. When he nuzzled my ear, I didn't either.

He led me over to a soft bench near the firepit. A narrow desk stood nearby, and a pot of quills—which I'd likely sharpened myself—waited beside a fresh pile of paper.

A tall wooden case, adorned with a colorful tapestry, abutted the desk. As a child, I had polished that case countless times, but I'd never seen the tapestry before. I dropped Mati's hand and walked over to it. It showed the gods gathered on the mountainside in the very scene we'd played in the pantomime, Gyotia tall and regal, glaring down at Sotia on the ground before him. I imagined I could hear Gyotia's harsh voice telling Sotia that he had given her tablet of language to the chieftain who would keep it for the nobility only, that he had thwarted her plan to share the language of the gods with all people. Below the mountain, a line of ships tossed on a dark green sea, carrying away the banished followers of Sotia.

Mati touched my elbow. "Raisa?"

I turned to him. "What's in this case?"

"I'll bring the key next time," he said with a grin. "I saw where Father keeps it."

I cocked my head. "What is it?"

Mati kissed me quickly. "It'll be a surprise."

Annoyed at this response, I turned away, my arms folded.

"Raisa!" Mati touched my shoulder. "What's wrong?"

I turned, ready to snap at him, but then realized I was upsetting him.

I took both his hands. "Sorry," I whispered. "It's just . . . I've never seen the Library like this. It's . . . magnificent. A place the gods themselves would enjoy visiting."

Mati laughed. "Ah, but they do all their reading at third bell, while we're at luncheon. No chance of running into them." He pulled me close. "Or anyone else, if we're careful. It's safe here."

I started to protest, but he shook his head. "You're not the first Tutor to come into the Library," he said. "I'll show you." He went to the cache of letters on the wall by Gyotia's statue, pulled one out, and handed it to me. "Read this."

I stared at him, the memory of the last time he had held out a letter to me in this Library flashing through my mind. He didn't seem to realize how dangerous this was.

"Well, read it," he said, a bit crossly, then unrolled the scroll. He pointed to a line in the middle. "There."

It was a letter from a long-ago king, begging Gyotia's forgiveness for consorting with his son's Tutor in the Library and having her write his letters for him. The seal at the top showed a lion with ten lines across its face.

"My great-great-grandfather wrote that," said Mati. "And he wasn't the only one to do it. These old kings did all sorts of things to beg forgiveness for."

"What happened—"

"To the Tutor? Nothing." He took the letter and wrapped his arms around my waist. "No one will know we're here."

"As long as your father doesn't find us."

Mati's face fell. "My father will be in council all day. Laiyonea too. Don't you trust me?"

He touched the stone hanging around my neck, and looked so wounded that I kissed him right away. "Of course I do," I said softly. He drew me down onto the couch, the one that stood before Gyotia, ready to receive the god should he come visit the Library, and kissed me some more.

We went back three times that Veiling. Each time, Mati found amusing letters for us to read aloud to each other. It was fascinating to hear about the things past kings had done, things they believed no one would see but their heirs and the gods. Sometimes I felt guilty about going into the Library of the Gods at all, let alone raiding the thoughts of past rulers. But I also knew that I would go, again and again, when Mati wanted me to.

Not until our fifth visit to the Library was Mati finally able to steal the key to the wooden case. He made me cover my eyes while he opened the doors, then came to stand behind me. "You can look now," he whispered.

I opened my eyes and gasped. An enormous disc of yellowed stone, as wide across as my outstretched hands, stood upright inside the case. I recognized it at once as the tablet of the gods— the tablet that Sotia gave to the mortal Iano in the old stories, the tablet that Gyotia took back and gave to Belic, making him first king of Qilara in exchange for his promise to keep the language of the gods pure. I hadn't known until then that it truly existed, this tablet that the Qilarites had used to justify the enslavement of my people.

Mati's laughing voice faded behind me as I approached the case; I couldn't stop staring at the tablet. Our feeble imitation in the pantomime had not come anywhere near doing it justice. Firelight danced over the irregular cuts at the edges and the jagged gouge at the center, casting bizarre shadows over the symbols spiraling out upon it.

I touched the center of the tablet, where a chunk of stone was missing. My fingers tingled. The stone was rough, cold . . . my mind screamed with memories of terrifying nights of punishment in the Stander. The icy stone walls were too close—I couldn't take in enough air to fill my aching lungs.

Mati turned me around to kiss him, unknowingly pulling me out of the nightmare panic. I was in the warm Library again, safe in his arms, clinging to him as my breathing slowed.

"Not even the high priests know it's here," Mati said as his lips moved over my face. "Except my father, of course. You know, High Priest of Gyotia." He said this jokingly, as if that part of the king's office meant nothing to him, but I could tell that he liked the idea of taking on that title someday. I understood; it was hard not to be awed by the presence of the ancient tablet. He paused and looked down at me in mock alarm. "You won't tell anyone, will you?"

I smiled. "Of course not." Mati kissed me again, his fingers slipping down to the laces of my dress.

Perhaps I should have seen then where our time in the Library would lead. But all I knew was that I loved Mati with all my heart. We grew closer in every way in those quiet hours, whether it was reading letters, or lying on the couch sharing languid kisses, or just sitting together holding hands. We took more liberties there, our fevered fingers wandering as we kissed, until one of us—usually me—sat up breathlessly and suggested it was time to go. It would be treacherous to go any further down that road, no matter how tempting Mati's touch.

But then, one foggy afternoon half a year later, I didn't sit up, didn't protest, didn't stop Mati when he unlaced my dress and pushed it away from my shoulders, and pressed me back against the couch, his warm skin on mine. I knew what would happen next, and I wanted it—wanted Mati—more than I had wanted anything in my life.

So the last barriers between us fell, there in the Library of the Gods.

Aqil could not understand his mother's passion for the great library, and that made him restless and angry. He went to his father, trailed by the flocks of crows that were his only companions. Bowing low, Aqil said, "I have no place here. My mother walks with wisdom, my half brother serves the fields, and the others tend to memory, hearth, and war. I beg that you grant me a way to serve you."

Gyotia regarded his son's eager face and the cawing mob of birds that echoed his dissatisfaction. "Have patience," said the king of the gods. "I shall find a use for you."

THIRTEEN

IN THE ADYTUM the next day, hazy sunlight filtered down through gray clouds, and I couldn't breathe properly. Mati had barely looked at me all morning. I focused on the story of Lila's bow that I was writing, and tried not to cry. When Laiyonea asked what was wrong, I insisted that I was fine.

At length, she left us alone. I kept writing, afraid to say anything.

"Raisa?"

I looked up into a face so full of concern that I burst into tears from sheer relief. I wrapped my arms around his neck and sobbed into his tunic, and when I had gained control of myself I flushed with embarrassment.

Mati wiped my tears with his handkerchief. "What is it?"

I just shook my head. In the aftermath of what we'd done, I'd spent a sleepless, anxious night, cursing my own impulsive stupidity. What if there were consequences we couldn't hide, if it became clear that I was no chaste handmaiden of Aqil, as Tutors were meant to be? There were ways girls could prevent those things, I knew, but I had no way of getting them.

And then Mati had behaved so distantly this morning. I reminded myself that the distance was an act, and that Mati was a fine actor.

Still, it couldn't happen again, and I had to find a way to tell him so. I cleared my throat. "I . . . I love you," I began.

Mati smiled. "I love you too." Before I could say anything else, he kissed me so tenderly that it almost drove my fears away. Then he whispered, "I've got something for you." He pulled out a tiny vial and handed it to me. I turned it over in my hands.

Mati turned pink. "It's a tincture of silphium for . . . well." He gestured feebly at me. "You're supposed to drink it once a Shining, to make sure that nothing . . ."

I understood. Despite the fact that I'd been thinking about the same thing, my first, irrational reaction was shame. Was Mati ashamed of what we had done?

But I knew better than that. He was just taking care of me, of us.

I uncorked the vial and wrinkled my nose at the sharp, savory scent that wafted from it. Before I could think too much, I drank the contents; it was barely a mouthful, but the taste, like meat close to rotting, lingered on my tongue. "Thank you," I murmured. I wanted to ask what he was thinking, but I was afraid to hear his answer.

Mati touched my arm. "I can get more, if . . . if we . . . need it."

My heart swelled. "I think we might," I whispered, then buried my face in his shoulder, cheeks burning at my own audacity.

He sighed and put his arms around me. He kissed my hair, then reached down and tilted my chin up so that I was looking at him. "I love you, Raisa," he said. A shadow passed over his expression. "No matter what happens, I will always love you."

Seven days went by before the rains came back and we could return to the Library. I spent the time explaining to myself why it was a bad idea to go to the Library again, for so many reasons. Nevertheless when I woke to rain tapping on the shutters, my pulse sped up.

We didn't speak of it, but I knew Mati was burning for the moment as surely as I was. I didn't hesitate when he led me right to Gyotia's couch.

Afterward, Mati stroked my hair and murmured things that made me want to weep. I lay in his arms and contemplated the friezes I used to clean, wondering how so much had changed.

Mati asked what I was thinking about.

"I was so frightened when I first came here as a child," I said. Mati's fingers paused on my hair for the barest instant. I looked at him, afraid of what I'd see in his face. But he was only watching intently, waiting for me to go on.

I'd never really told Mati about my life before the Selection, but why hold back now? So I described the raid and the cages in the ship, the chains and the first, bewildering days on the platforms.

Mati listened carefully, occasionally kissing my shoulder or my hand. At last, my words spent, I lay on my back, fingers twined with his, and glanced sideways at his drawn mouth and furrowed brow.

"Do you remember your parents?" he asked quietly.

I tensed. I hadn't mentioned that my father was a Learned One, and only now did I realize that I didn't want to. That secret was so bone-deep that I couldn't share it, not even with him. Especially not here, in the Library of the Gods.

"Yes, I remember them," I whispered. I flicked through childhood memories like Laiyonea sorting through a pot of quills, searching for one that was safe to share. But so many memories of my father were wrapped up in the sight of his strong hand wielding a quill or his kind face bending near as he gave me my heart-verse. I landed on an image of my mother, singing as she spun by the fire.

"My mother . . . had a lovely voice. Our cottage was always full of her singing. She used to sing this little nonsense song to me—" Softly I sang a few of the lilting syllables, like I used to sing to Linti to soothe her to sleep in the palace slave quarters. I broke off with a laugh. "I didn't inherit her voice. Wilel always said I sounded like a strangled asoti."

"Wilel?"

"My brother." I paused. "He died in the raid too." I swallowed against the guilty lump in my throat; I was older now than Wilel had ever had a chance to be.

Mati touched my cheek. "I'm sorry," he whispered.

I shook my head. "You didn't send those raiders."

Mati looked up at the ceiling, his jaw tightening. "No," he said. "My father did that." Something grim and steely in his tone frightened me.

I pushed myself up on my elbow and kissed him, trying to pull him out of this dark mood. "It's in the past," I murmured against his lips. "At least . . . we're together now. Something good came of it." I couldn't decide if the idea of our love being born out of so much death was comforting or horrible.

Mati seemed to be thinking the same thing. He frowned. "Tyasha was right," he murmured.

I froze, then turned on my side so that he couldn't see my face, but I was still within the circle of his arms. "You cared for her," I said to the dim Library.

"Yes, of course I—Raisa, don't be ridiculous." He kissed my neck, working his way up to my ear, and when he got there he whispered, "I never have loved, and I never will love, anyone the way I love you." He pushed himself up and faced me, as though to make sure I believed him. I did. No one could doubt his fervent tone. It lit me on fire and made me forget what we were talking about, so that when he flopped back down and went on, it took me a moment to follow.

"Tyasha was like . . . a big sister, I guess," he said. "I was four when I started in the Adytum. She was eleven then. She loved telling me what to do." He barked out a laugh. "When I went to see her before she died, I asked why she'd helped the Resistance.

She said she did it because no one deserves to die in ignorance, without dignity or humanity. She said that most Qilarites are too weak to see that, and that . . . that I might be able to be better than that, to be less of a coward."

I pushed myself up and stared at him. "You're not—"

"She was right. I am."

If Mati was a coward, then what was I—I, who could not even bear to consider doing what Tyasha had done?

"Here I am," Mati went on, "making you sneak around, when I should be telling the world that I love you."

My heart thrilled at the idea, but I laid a warning hand on his chest. "Mati, don't be insane."

He took my hand. "I wouldn't put you in more danger, you know that. But I hate this hiding, and I hate—" He closed his eyes. "I wish I could just . . . just free all the Arnathim."

Would he? Could he, when he became king? Just like that?

He looked at me sadly. "I don't know if it's possible. But I'll try." He sat up and clasped both my hands. "And I promise, Raisa—no more raids on the Nath Tarin, ever. No more children will have to go through what you did."

I couldn't speak. I held him tightly, ignoring the pain as the stone around my neck dug into my breastbone.

Occasionally the gods turned their attention to the valley below. They saw how the mortals, weak and small, learned which of the plants and animals could be eaten without causing sickness, how they formed groups to protect one another. Mortal as well as godly deeds began to appear in the scrolls of the great library.

FOURTEEN

MATI AND I didn't speak again about my past, or the promise he'd made to do what he could for the Arnathim, but the knowledge hung between us, binding us even more closely together. We stole away to the Library whenever we could; I couldn't have stayed away from him if I'd tried. He showed me another passage into the Library from behind a hidden door in a kitchen storeroom, so that I could sneak away from the Adytum and meet him there. No matter that it was dangerous—when I was in Mati's arms I didn't care if the entire King's Guard came crashing through the doors.

The sunny days of Lilana returned, bringing the Festival of Aqil again. The Trade Minister, Priasi Jin, raised eyebrows at court by bragging as much about his granddaughter playing Sotia as he did about the girl's older brother playing Aqil. Minister Jin didn't seem to care that she was a girl or that she was playing the displaced goddess. The pride in his voice when he spoke of her always made me smile.

The day after the pantomime, Mati met me in the Library at fourth bell, bearing a large honeycake. He swept me into his arms, declaring, "Today is the anniversary of our first kiss."

"I thought that was yesterday."

"The Festival of Aqil was when I realized I was in love with you. I didn't do something about it until after eighth bell." He broke off a piece of cake and fed it to me. "This whole cake is for you," he said. "Linti got her own."

I kissed him. Though I had been seeing the packets of food he'd left under the stairs for the past year, this was the first time Mati had mentioned them.

I couldn't imagine ever loving him more.

We clung to each other that afternoon; Mati was leaving for a seven-day hunting trip with his father the next morning, and I knew that my days in the Adytum would be dull without him. At least I had my heart-verse to work on; as Mati had consumed more and more of my thoughts, I had spent less time on it than I should have, though I had now learned most of the higher order symbols.

When it was time to go, we scoured the carpet on hands and knees to pick up every crumb of cake—I was much better at this than Mati was—and shared one last kiss before I crept out through the kitchen storeroom and Mati left through the king's suite. I hurried toward the Adytum. I'd have to finish at least three pages before Laiyonea returned from the council meeting the king had asked her to attend, or she'd suspect something.

I was passing one of the smaller council rooms near the kitchens when a familiar screech cut the air. "This should have been done an hour ago!"

I hadn't heard it in over two years, but Emilana Kret's furious shout automatically made me scramble for a hiding place. I could guess the reason for the head servant's displeasure; that room's friezes were exceptionally detailed and held more than the usual amount of dust. Emilana had liked to press a white cloth into the tiniest crevices when we'd finished cleaning it; even a speck of dirt on the cloth meant no dinner for us. I'd lost more meals due to that chamber than the rest of the palace combined.

The corridor was still deserted. I crept closer to the door and peered in.

Emilana was shaking a white cloth covered in dust at a figure on the floor—Linti, looking dazed, as tiny at age eight as she'd been at six. Her white-blond hair fell in her face, but didn't disguise the red mark on her cheek where Emilana must have struck her. In the far corner, Naka and two other children I didn't recognize worked steadily, glancing uneasily at Emilana.

"It's the Stander for you tonight," screeched Emilana. "But first you'll finish this room."

My fear had turned to anger—how dare she treat Linti like that!—and I'd actually taken a step forward when I came to my senses. I was in a part of the palace where I was definitely not supposed to be. If I said the things to the Qilarite head servant that wanted to roll off my tongue—and I could picture with satisfying detail the expression on Emilana's face if I did say them—I could get myself banished, or worse. And I wouldn't help Linti at all.

In the time it took me to step back into the shadows, Emilana had hauled Linti up. Linti wobbled, and for the first time I had a clear view of her pale face and glassy eyes.

She's ill, I realized. How like Emilana to miss that, or to notice and not care. Hot, sick fury swooped through my stomach, and I stood frozen behind the door as Emilana shoved Linti back toward the others.

Unable to watch any more, I fled to the Adytum, where I collapsed onto a bench and caught my breath. I couldn't have intervened, I told myself. I wasn't just protecting my own secrets anymore, but Mati's too—

I sat up straighter. Mati! Of course, I would tell Mati what I'd seen, and he would find a way to help Linti!

But no—Mati and his father were leaving early in the morning, and there would be no formal dinner tonight, as many of the councilors had gone to their country estates for the Lilana break. I wouldn't see Mati for seven long days, and even if I told him, what could he do? Sneaking food to Linti was one thing—and for all I knew, he had his valet do that for him. But if he tried to interfere with the running of the palace, his father would be furious.

There's nothing I can do. This is how the world is, I thought. Besides, Linti was a tough little girl. Hadn't she and I hacked our way through a full Veiling of the coughing sickness when she was four years old? Sleeping beside her had felt like lying inside a firepit, but she'd come through it fine. Linti had been dealing with Emilana for years; the fact that I happened to witness this incident didn't make it any different.

Nevertheless, I couldn't sleep that night, picturing her leaning against the damp, dark walls of the Stander.

I worried about Linti nonstop, and didn't relax until I saw the children leaving the baths four days later. From a distance Linti seemed steady on her feet.

When Mati returned, I didn't mention it to him. What could he do? Besides, we didn't get to see each other much over the next two Shinings and Veilings, as the palace was consumed with preparations for Mati's eighteenth birthday celebration, his coming of age as heir to the throne.

At the ball, the viziers and ministers gave long speeches about how much Mati had grown, and what an inspiring king he would be one day. The eastern vizier did not come, however—I heard the War Minister tell Laiyonea that Emtiria's army had besieged our border city of Asuniaka.

"A minor matter," the War Minister insisted. "The Emtirian army is made up of castoffs and escapees and tialiks. Their discipline won't last long."

I flinched, but Laiyonea absorbed the casually dropped curse without blinking. I thought of waves pounding on stone, wearing it down bit by tiny bit.

So Emtiria was where the escaped slaves went. It made sense. Emtiria, the country just over the border, had no laws subjugating the Arnathim or anyone else. Indeed, from what Laiyonea had told me, Emtiria seemed to have few laws at all. But it was also desperately dangerous; the Emtirians believed in the pursuit of wealth above all else, and most would return an escaped slave for the reward without a second thought.

Later, Mati came to sit with us as the dancing started. He asked why Laiyonea hadn't given a speech. She shot him a warning look, and for once, I understood why: though the king and several ministers regularly sought Laiyonea's counsel, our presence was tolerated at these events because of tradition. They would never allow an Arnath, even an Arnath Tutor, a voice at such a gathering.

Mati continued grinning at Laiyonea, refusing to take the hint. Her expression softened. "There wouldn't be a point," she said. "No words could do you justice."

Mati blushed, but soon he was joking with her again. He took my hand under the table and sketched a symbol into my palm. I didn't need to see it to know what it was; his love was right there in the touch. I looked around at the Qilarite girls with their straight black hair and colorful gowns, and felt superior.

We'd only managed to steal away to the Library twice since First Shining, and it was painful to let go of Mati's hand when he had to go join in the dancing. Laiyonea sent me to bed at seventh bell, and I fell asleep hoping for an unlikely rainstorm the following day.

The next morning, the sun blazed down defiantly. I glared at it— no trips to the Library today. Alone in the Adytum, I pored over my heart-verse once I'd finished the work Laiyonea had assigned me. I still hadn't found nine of the symbols in the language of the gods, and had yet to make sense of the eleven I *had* found.

Laiyonea and Mati were with the king—another boring negotiation, some treaty or other. When they finally joined me that afternoon, I squeezed Mati's fingers under the table; he squeezed back, his face blank for Laiyonea.

We were settling in to go over the lists of kings when Laiyonea said, "Pay attention, Mati. You won't have much time to study once Soraya arrives."

Mati nodded and bent over his paper. I looked from him to Laiyonea. "Soraya Gamo?" I asked.

"Yes, Mati's betrothed," Laiyonea replied. "She will arrive tomorrow for the betrothal ceremony and stay until their wedding at First Shining."

*The gods saw the mortals huddle together in the driving rains
of Gyotia's anger, saw them starve when his wrath flooded the
fields and shook the earth. The mortals cried out in anguish, and
still the gods only watched.*

FIFTEEN

I FELT AS I had as a child, when my brother and I would jump
in the waves on the beach, and one would knock me down.

Mati met my eyes, his expression puzzled. A thousand questions wanted to tumble out of me, but before any of them did,
Laiyonea's voice cut through my thoughts. "Is something wrong?"

I shook my head, and the lesson continued, though I was
present only in body. Afterward, Laiyonea and Mati went to meet
with the king again. Instead of cleaning the Adytum, I sat staring
into space until the asotis' demanding cries roused me. I filled
their bowls, but couldn't bring myself to pluck their feathers, not
today. In the fading light, I shoved inkpots and quills into the
cabinet and went to my bedroom.

The rational part of me knew that I had no right to be shocked
or upset. Every moment with Mati had been stolen. I should have
realized all along that he'd be promised to another. I sat on the
floor against the bed, wishing fiercely that Mati were with me—
only I wasn't sure whether I wanted to hold him or strike him.

And then, as if conjured from my longing, he was there at the window. As he dropped from the ledge to the floor, silhouetted against the twilight, it occurred to me that it was brave of him to come so early.

He eyed me warily, as though I were a snake that might lunge. To think, Mati afraid of me! As if I could hurt him the way he'd hurt me.

I swiped furiously at the traitorous tears leaking from my eyes. He crossed the room and knelt, touching my shoulder.

"Why didn't you tell me?" My voice was toneless.

"I thought you knew. I thought we just . . . weren't mentioning it. You had to realize that . . . well. Obviously not." He gave a small laugh.

That laugh cut through me, transforming the emptiness in my stomach to a hard knot of anger. "I feel like a fool."

Mati sighed. "Don't be like that. It had to happen sometime, and now I'm eighteen, and with all that's going on with Emtiria and the Resistance . . . the treasury needs Gamo's money, and Father thinks the people need a reason to celebrate."

"Do you think she's pretty?" I choked out.

"I suppose," he said with a shrug. "She's the daughter of the western vizier."

I turned away. "Raisa," he said, stroking my hair. I tried hard not to let his touch affect me. "Come on, nothing has to change."

I gaped at him. How could he say that? I weighed my words carefully. "You'll be expected to produce an heir."

"Yes," he said, not seeming to realize why this bothered me.

All at once, he did, and he laughed. He *laughed*. He reached for my hand, but I flinched and pulled away.

"Damn it, what do you want me to do?" he said. "Give up the throne and tend goats in the mountains? I've made plenty of sacrifices to be with you. What more do you want?"

What did he know about sacrifices? Several angry replies came to mind, but I bit them back. "I wish you could," I said quietly.

"What?" he snapped.

"I wish you could tend goats," I said. "It would make things easier."

He stared at me. "Well, I don't. Look, when I'm king, I can do whatever I want. In the meantime, we keep it quiet."

"Laiyonea suspects something."

He sighed. "Of course she suspects something, the way you acted. Now I'll have to pay her more to keep her mouth shut."

"What?"

Mati shook his head. "Laiyonea's known for a long time. You're not exactly the best at hiding your feelings."

"And you are, I suppose," I said nastily.

His face darkened. "When I have to be, yes."

I thought of all the times he'd ignored me at banquets, all the times he'd looked right through me. How could he do that, if he felt the way I did?

He couldn't. And he couldn't ask me to share him—not if he truly loved me. I would never, ever ask such a thing of him.

"I think you should leave," I whispered.

"Raisa—"

"Leave," I told him.

"If you want me to, I will," he said slowly. "But I'll come see you tomorrow before . . ."

I laughed bitterly. "Before Soraya arrives? Don't bother." I looked into his eyes, then away. "Don't come back here. Don't find me alone. Don't come to see me anymore."

Mati's brows drew together, and for the first time, I was slightly afraid of him. I had just told the crown prince of Qilara to stay away from me; how many ways could he have had me executed, if he wanted to?

But his face fell into a frown—sad, not frightening—and he nodded. He pulled me into his arms, and I curled up against his chest, my throat dry and burning. Mati squeezed my shoulders and kissed the top of my head, then gently pushed me away and stood.

He didn't look back as he went to the window and swung out onto the ledge.

I don't know how long I sat there staring at the wall. The sky was dark when I stood and slowly took off the stone that Mati had given me. I placed it at the bottom of a box of hairpins on my dressing table. I didn't want to see it anymore.

Lanea, goddess of the hearth, slipped among the mortals and taught them to build houses of stone, protection against the winds and rains of Gyotia's wrath. Then Qora gave to them the knowledge of growing things. Soon the land was rich with olive trees, grain, flax, figs, and barley.

And then Lila went to them and gave them war.

SIXTEEN

WHEN I WOKE the next morning, I had a few blissful moments of forgetfulness before it all came crashing back. My hand went to my bare neck. I forced myself to go to the basin and splash water on my face, avoiding the mirror with its vision of my red, puffy eyes.

I'd told Mati to leave, and he had, without looking back. What had I done?

The door cracked open, and Laiyonea's face peered at me. She hadn't opened my door without knocking in a long time—because she'd known, of course. Did she know how things were now?

Laiyonea took in my disheveled state. "It's late," she said. "You must bathe."

I realized that the sunshine coming in through the window was midmorning light. Why had she let me sleep so long? I turned to ask, but the door had already swung shut behind her.

I dressed and followed Laiyonea to the stairs. I had no idea what I would do if I saw Mati. How could I sit beside him in the Adytum again, knowing that he was no longer mine—that he never really had been? I clutched the railing as tears threatened to blind me.

Two maids were carrying piles of pink linens up the steps. The one in front saw me and shared a look with the other, then both scurried up the stairs. I stared after them, puzzled, as I continued down the stairs. I often saw the Qilarite servants in the hallways, of course, but they usually ignored me.

Laiyonea veered off to the left, taking the corridor through the slave quarters instead of the main hallway. I paused on the threshold of my old rooms, wondering at this, but Laiyonea kept going, so I did too. The slave quarters were deserted. No doubt everyone was preparing for the future queen's arrival.

The passage gave out onto the rear of the palace, and Laiyonea led the way to the baths at the water's edge. She didn't stop until she stood in the cool shadows of the main pool. "The betrothal ceremony begins in less than an hour," she informed me. "You'd best hurry."

I forced myself to nod, and removed my clothes. I descended into the warm water and leaned back to wet my hair. The water was cloudier than I was used to; ordinarily Laiyonea and I bathed early, after the Scholars but before the Qilarite servants. By now all the servants and probably even some of the guards had bathed in the pool, and the tide would not bring clearer water until evening.

"Why did you let me sleep so long?" I asked as Laiyonea

handed me a slab of herbed soap.

"I was busy," she said stiffly. "King Tyno called for me early. Mati was seen leaving your room last night."

I froze.

She shook her head. "The idiot, to chance such a thing, practically in broad daylight!" She pointed at me. "At least one of you has sense. He told me that you broke it off. You'd have been wiser to do so long ago."

Broke it off. The phrase was apt. I felt as if a piece of my body, of my heart, had been broken off.

Then the full impact of her words hit me. King Tyno knew. I shivered despite the warm water. "What will the king do?" I squeaked.

Laiyonea tilted her head. "Nothing, for now. Nothing, if you do your work and keep away from Mati. Mati took the blame. He swore that nothing happened between you, that he went to your room to declare his love, and you told him to stay away from you."

I flinched. I *had* said that, hadn't I?

And still Mati had protected me. Again.

Had it been easy for him to lie, to say there was nothing between us? The very idea hurt more than turning him away had. I dunked my head under the water, squeezing my eyes shut to keep the soap out and the tears in.

When I surfaced, Laiyonea's low voice came to my ears. "Tyno is committed to making Del Gamo's daughter the future queen. You and Mati must both do as you're told. I know you realize this, but I have less faith in his sense."

I rinsed my hair and opened my eyes. Laiyonea regarded me

levelly. "It won't be easy for you," she said, her clipped tone at odds with her sympathetic words. "Especially since half the servants seem to know about you two. The guard who reported it gossiped with the kitchen maids before he was escorted out of the palace."

"Is that why you let me sleep?" I asked. "So I wouldn't have to face the servants?"

Laiyonea pursed her lips.

"Thank you," I said softly. I stepped out of the bath, dried off, and drew my dress over my head, then turned to face Laiyonea. "Did you really only keep our secret because Mati was paying you?" I asked. I suspected, from her behavior, that she felt more sympathy for us than I could have imagined.

Laiyonea looked up from the basket of combs she was sorting through. "He told you that?" she said guardedly.

I nodded.

She took a deep breath, nostrils flaring, then turned me around and combed my hair—something she'd never done before.

"I've tried to spare you as much as possible this morning," she said briskly, "but do not think to escape the betrothal ceremony today or the banquet this evening or the temple visits during the betrothal period. Now that Tyno knows Mati has had feelings for you, now that the servants are gossiping, you must be extra careful not to be like—"

She broke off, but I knew what she had been about to say. *Like Tyasha.* I couldn't show even a hint of disobedience.

The comb hit a snarl in my hair, and I cried out. Laiyonea worked through the tangle mercilessly, and braided my hair so tightly that my scalp hurt.

I ought to have realized on that first night that Mati could never truly love me, and that, even if he did, nothing would come of it. And now that we'd been found out, I couldn't even change my mind. Under the misery lurked an odd satisfaction that the choice had been taken from me. I feared my own weakness, and Mati was certainly that weakness.

When it was time for the betrothal ceremony, I followed Laiyonea to the front of the palace. My heart leaped into my throat at the sight of Mati with his father outside the doors, facing the distant gates.

The court was lined up in order of rank. Laiyonea and I stood below the councilors and Scholars ranged along the steps, but above the servants and slaves.

I knew I would break down if I looked at Mati, so I occupied myself trying to pick out Naka and Linti from the green-clad slave children in the distance by the gates. I spotted a tiny blond girl I thought must be Linti, but the way she stood wasn't quite right.

The gates opened, and I realized that the tall boy helping push them was Naka. He wouldn't be staying on the Library platforms for long. At least he would be safe in one of the temples soon.

A huge open carriage entered the courtyard, pulled by two black mares. People pressed back against the walls, and into the gardens and orchards on either side, to make room. Soraya sat in front with her parents, smiling already like a benevolent queen surveying her subjects. Alshara and Aliana, dressed in identical blue silk, sat behind them.

Out of the corner of my eye, I saw Mati straighten his shoulders. My heart ached.

The carriage stopped at the steps. Two servants helped the family down, and Del Gamo led Soraya up the steps to the king. Soraya wore a peach gown, with a matching scarf over her hair. She would wear her hair covered until First Shining, nearly a year from now, when she and Mati would make the final vows and she would take the full-length veil of a Scholar wife.

Del Gamo solemnly placed Soraya's hand in the king's. I tried to look away, but couldn't. Even I had to admit, Soraya Gamo was beautiful, her cheeks flushed, her smile radiant.

The king smiled and spoke in a low voice to Soraya. She laughed shrilly. King Tyno placed her hand in Mati's.

I had steadily avoided looking at Mati so far, and I didn't mean to look at him then. I couldn't help myself, though, and he flashed me one quick look as he bent to kiss Soraya's hand.

He didn't so much as glance my way during the luncheon that followed, or during the endless rounds of the temples that afternoon, where he and Soraya received blessings from the gods.

The banquet that night was interminable, but Laiyonea let me leave before the dancing began. She informed me that she would work with the prince in the Adytum for two hours each morning; I would spend that time in my room. She didn't say whether this was her idea or the king's—or Mati's—but I was grateful for it.

Time passed in a blur. I rose, I bathed, I studied, I ate . . . but I did not feel. I didn't let myself. I shut my ears to the talk at banquets. I didn't care which side was winning in the conflict with Emtiria or about the constant clashes with the Resistance. I only knew that I had lost.

But each time I sneaked under the stairs to leave food for Linti, I found tidily wrapped parcels of biscuits, or cakes, or fruit. These reminders of Mati's kindness hurt most of all.

It means nothing, I told myself each time. I would not let myself be fooled by the warmth in my chest, the false sense of closeness. He was out of my reach and always had been.

I threw myself into my lessons. I penned lists of ministers, rewrote tales of the gods, copied heathen treatises from Emtiria, labeled maps of the peninsula from the City of Kings to the southern coasts of Galasi. Whatever task Laiyonea gave me to practice my writing, I took up eagerly, and watched my hours of work consigned to the flames each afternoon. Odd that the sight should still affect me so after years of watching my work burn, but it did.

Whenever Laiyonea left me alone, I pulled out my heart-verse, but even that did little to stir me. I recognized most of the symbols now, but they didn't have any determinatives, and their order still made no sense.

One overcast afternoon, twenty days after Mati's betrothal, Laiyonea finished introducing the higher order writing. I fought back tears as she wrote the final symbol—a set of curving lines that meant, in the determinative-free form, "dare." I'd always imagined that it would be Mati showing it to me.

When Laiyonea left me alone to practice, I went directly to the poppies and pulled out my heart-verse. Surely, now that I knew all the higher order script, my father's message would make more sense.

Only it didn't. Some of the symbols were close to what I had learned in the Adytum, but not the same. I let out a long sigh. What if all my efforts had been for nothing?

I traced the last symbol of my heart-verse. It looked a little like *life*—only it was simpler than that complicated monstrosity, as if the various determinatives had been incorporated into the primary symbol. *Koros*, whispered my father's distant voice, and my finger froze over the paper.

Of course. The symbols didn't just have different names in the Arnath writing; the whole *system*—the order of the symbols and the way they were grouped together—was based on sound. Maybe some of the symbols were the same as those I'd learned here in the Adytum, but they weren't *used* the same way. So often my father's voice had whispered sounds to me as I learned a symbol . . . why hadn't I paid more attention?

The Arnathim and Qilarites spoke the same tongue, and had, perhaps, started out with the same writing system. But the Arnath writing had changed over the years—had come to represent sounds instead of concepts; had, it seemed, dropped some symbols and simplified the connectors. The Arnath writing in my heart-verse was far simpler than what I had learned in the Adytum, but also more elegant—exactly what might happen if writing were a shared endeavor, meant to connect people instead of being hoarded as a tool of power and privilege.

I scrambled to the table, so abruptly that the asotis shrieked at the burst of movement, and pulled paper from the pile. I dipped my quill into the ink and let it sit there, thinking hard.

I needed to record those memories, to sort out the differences between the Qilarite writing and my father's. Only how could I write these things down, when Qilarite symbols had nothing to do with sounds?

I puzzled over this question for more than an hour, wasting page after page as I attempted various ways of recording the sounds. At last I settled on using higher order symbols combined with my own code to show which part of the word the Arnath symbol represented. For the sound "rai," I drew the traitor symbol, and after it the symbol *pray*. Next I drew two boxes, with the second filled in to show that the second sound in the word *pray* went with the first symbol in the line.

I sat back and smiled. Even if Laiyonea found the page, it would look like nonsense to her.

I allowed myself another quarter of an hour to encode the sounds of as many symbols as I could recall, but I barely filled one page. When I compared it to my heart-verse, I sagged in disappointment; I had only discovered sounds for three of the symbols there. No matter, I told myself—I would go through the language of the gods, symbol by symbol, lower order and higher order alike, and encode every symbol that reminded me of the ones my father had taught me, until I had identified every part of my heart-verse.

I stole drying powder from the chest—we rarely used the stuff, as it mattered little whether our pages dried before they burned—and sprinkled it over the gleaming lines of the page. My heart raced as the utter foolishness of what I was doing hit me, but the feeling was more elation than dread.

Carefully I rolled the page and slid it into the gap in the wall with my heart-verse. It looked just like a letter in the Library of the Gods, tucked into its slot.

When Laiyonea came back to check on me, I realized that I had gone almost an entire afternoon without thinking of Mati.

From then on, each time Laiyonea left me, I wrote more pages. Soon I had so many that they no longer fit in the hole in the wall, so I found more hiding places. I laid some flat under paving stones, and scaled the back of the writing cabinet and hid more in the fluted wood that adorned the top.

And still there were thousands of symbols left. But I would make the language of the gods give up its secrets to me.

Sotia was moved to give her own gift to the mortals. She fashioned a disk of stone and exhaled the symbols of the language of the gods upon it. But when she descended the mountain to give it to the people, the eyes of Gyotia, often suspiciously upon her, saw what she planned.

SEVENTEEN

WHILE I WAS in the Adytum working on my project, the emptiness seemed to abate. But each time I heard the servants gossiping about wedding plans or saw Soraya on Mati's arm, the pain returned.

One day was especially brutal—Karita Jin, the Trade Minister's wife, had organized a luncheon for Soraya, and asked Laiyonea and me to be present for the invocations for the health of Soraya's future son, the boy I would one day teach. Afterward, Lady Jin insisted, in what she clearly thought was a kindness, that we stay for the meal. I pushed fish around on my plate and tried to tune out the laughing advice the other women offered Soraya for her wedding night.

Laiyonea pulled me away for lessons as soon as was decent.

In the Adytum, I sat down heavily and rested my forehead on my arms. My tears had long since been spent. The pain was a dull ache now, a vast, perennial emptiness.

Laiyonea rubbed my shoulder. She wasn't one to fill up silences with chatter or to offer meaningless comfort.

At length she gave me a project—busywork to keep my quill moving and my mind empty. I don't think she meant to leave me that afternoon, because she looked at me regretfully when a summons from the king came.

It didn't matter. I'd have been equally miserable with or without her there. I tried to distract myself with my encoding project; I'd gotten through the thousand higher order symbols by that time, and was ready to begin the lower order.

I dipped my quill into the ink, but my heart was too heavy to focus on symbols or sounds. I thought of how the kings wrote to the gods when they had a problem or a request—that was the sole purpose of the higher order writing, after all.

One does not entreat the gods through shouted prayers or offerings, my father had told me when I was a child, *but through their greatest gift to us, writing.*

I was a child of the islands. The gods who listened to the Qilarite kings surely would not listen to me.

But the caged goddess might.

My quill shook as I set it to the paper. *Most Honored Sotia,* I wrote, and I poured out my emptiness and anger onto the page. Surely Sotia, even if she could receive this message in her imprisoned state, would care little for my sorrows, but my heart lightened as I unburdened myself. I wrote of endless nights in the banquet room, of Laiyonea's brittle kindness and Mati's uncaring coldness. And somehow, as the feelings transformed themselves into the geometry of symbols and lines, I felt less alone.

When I was done, I held the letter over the firepit for a long time. These words were completely mine, unlike anything else I had written, and harder to give up.

But I wasn't stupid, so I did drop it into the flames in the end. I imagined the smoke lifting my misery to the sky, carrying my words to the goddess, wherever she was.

After that I often wrote to Sotia, and then I imagined my grief turning to ashes along with the pages in the firepit. Most days I wrote no more than a page, but that page helped me bear the sight of Mati in the corridors or laughing in the garden with Soraya. Slowly, I began to feel myself again.

Laiyonea approved of the change. She didn't say so, of course, but I sensed it as I sat by her at banquets, pretending all was well. I even answered the kindly Trade Minister, Priasi Jin, with more than two words when he asked about my training, and did not flinch when he told Laiyonea boisterously that I would be more than ready to replace her in a few years when Mati's son was born.

Now that I was emerging from oblivious misery, I realized how much I had been missing in the palace while Mati had consumed my thoughts. Ambassadors from drought-stricken Galasi had come to ask for aid, which the king had refused—perhaps because the conflict with Emtiria had gotten worse. Everyone on the Scholars Council seemed to have a different opinion of King Tyno's decision to send soldiers to Asuniaka to break the Emtirian siege, but all agreed that it wasn't going well.

Far more interesting to me, though, were the rumors of the Resistance in the city. I overheard two guards muttering about a massive slave escape at the quarry, until they saw me lingering and sped off in different directions. Later I heard that two Arnath boys had been killed in the market for stealing swords from a blacksmith. Scholars now went about the city with armed guards in their carriages.

Perhaps that was why the king ordered the palace gates shut at the Festival of Qora, and the fair took place in the front court-yard. Laiyonea told me that many Scholars now refused to set foot in the market, so the council had convinced the king of this measure so that the highborn ladies could purchase dress materials for the wedding, which was now but a season and a half away.

I forced myself to watch dispassionately as Mati and Soraya opened the fair, and was rewarded with a nod from Laiyonea as she bid me take the afternoon off, and even dropped a few coins into my palm.

I walked down the lanes of merchants, enjoying the unaccustomed leisure. Scholar ladies gathered around a silk merchant's stall, arguing the merits of various colors. I hurried away and bypassed the next two aisles full of milliners, seamstresses, and jewelers shouting suggestions for wedding gifts for the royal couple.

I spent most of my coins on a roll stuffed with shredded lamb, and devoured it, grease dripping down my hands, as I wandered the next row of stalls. This row featured exotic items: carved scroll stands from Emtiria, heavy woven scarves from mountainous Pyla, fat-bellied inkwells from Galasi in the south. I wiped my hands on my skirt and examined a pot of quills with pale green cores and white, curling feathers. My fingers tingled as I recalled the softness of just such a feather, given to me at the Temple of Lanea.

The stall's owner, a powerfully built man with a clump of dense black hair right in the middle of his head, approached me. "Many Shinings, Tutor," he said; my white and green dress had given me away. "Horel Stit at your service. I see that you are admiring my quills—"

"No, I have quills enough, thank you," I said quickly.

"Ah, then perhaps I can interest you in my Silkstone Pendant. This is one of several pieces I brought back from Illana in the far north." Stit indicated a pendant carved from stone so thin that it let light through.

"I thought Illana was deserted." And had been, for hundreds of years.

Stit smiled; three of his front teeth were missing. Most people looked friendlier when they smiled, but he looked somehow less so. "Caches of treasure wait in the mountain caves for those who wish to find them."

He meant the ancient tombs hidden in the frozen mountains, filled with offerings left by the long-ago inhabitants. His oily smile made me feel a little sick.

"Such an item would be a lovely wedding gift for the prince's bride," he went on.

Someone snorted. I turned to see a familiar figure at the other end of the stall, measuring out powdered herbs for a girl in green.

Jonis flashed me a nasty look before turning back to the scale. The girl, who looked about my age, whispered something to him and glared at me. Thick black hair hung straight to her shoulders, but her skin was pale. I thought I'd seen her before, but couldn't place her—and I had no idea why she would look at me like that.

When I turned back to Stit, he was watching Jonis, his eyes narrowed.

I cleared my throat, inexplicably frightened for Jonis, and horrified at the risk he must have taken in stealing the white quill from his master—the quill I had kicked under the chair and left behind. "My gift is dictated by tradition," I said to Stit, to draw his attention back to me. "I will present the next Tutor." I was proud of myself for saying this so dispassionately. The presentation was one of many parts of the upcoming wedding I dreaded.

Stit nodded. "Of course. Have you seen these exquisite inkwells?"

I shook my head. "My coins have gone to fill my stomach today," I said cheerfully.

Stit's interest in me evaporated with comical speed. I hurried away, not daring to look at Jonis or the girl. My path took me to the temple tents at the corner of the courtyard, a convenience for Scholars during the festival days. I sighed and fingered my last two coins, knowing that a good Tutor, as a handmaiden of Aqil, would make an offering to the god; that was probably why Laiyonea had given me the coins anyway.

The red silk tent was quiet inside, with two alcoves closed off by curtains. In the small central space, Kiti perched on a stool, carving a small wooden figure.

He leaped up at my entrance. "Raisa!" he said warmly.

I glanced meaningfully at the partitions.

"It's just me here," he said in a softer voice. "The priests are all at council and no one's at the altars."

Kiti was taller than I remembered, and he smiled with a quiet confidence I could hardly reconcile with the serious boy who'd cleaned the palace beside me. I felt gangly in comparison. "I need to make an offering, I suppose," I said.

Kiti nodded and opened one of the curtains. I went in and knelt before the narrow altar, which held a golden statue of Aqil—standing over Sotia, of course—and a handful of earrings, coins, and other trinkets. I placed my coins on it and pressed my forehead to the prayer rug, feeling stupid doing this without Laiyonea beside me.

"Bowing down to her Qilarite captors. Unsurprising," said a voice behind me. I sat up so quickly that my head spun. I hadn't heard him come in, but Jonis stood behind me. Kiti, holding back the curtain, smiled apologetically.

"What are you doing here?" I hissed, tripping over the hem of my dress in my haste to get to my feet.

"I'm wondering that myself," he said darkly, crossing his arms and glaring at Kiti.

Kiti held up one finger and peered out into the tent, then dropped the curtain and stepped closer. Jonis, however, backed up right to the tent wall, as if trying to get as far away from me as possible.

"Raisa," Kiti said solemnly, "you and I have known each other a long time. You know you can trust me."

I looked back and forth between the two of them. "What is this?"

"You're wasting your time, Kiti," said Jonis. "She's a qodder through and through. In bed with the Qilarites all along."

I flushed. Of course the Resistance would have gotten wind

of the palace rumors about Mati sneaking out of my room. *But Jonis can't possibly know the truth about us,* I reminded myself.

"Stop it," said Kiti sharply. He turned to me. "Raisa, I know you. You would have done anything to protect the rest of us children. Well, now you have a chance to help even more people. I know it's dangerous. But you've survived worse." Jonis snorted, but Kiti ignored him. "The Resistance is real, Raisa. Hundreds of Arnathim in this city are sick of being slaves. Aren't you one of them?"

I had to look away. "I knew you were with them, after the pantomime," I said. "Is that how it's to be? You'll recruit all the palace children into the Resistance, put them all in danger? Naka and Linti and all the others too? You've already annoyed the council so much that they want to send—"

"Not Linti," Kiti interrupted quietly. He paused long enough that I opened my mouth to ask what he was talking about, but he spoke before I could. "Linti's dead. Didn't you know? She fell from a platform in the Library and cracked her skull."

Gyotia summoned all the gods and goddesses to him and demanded to know what Sotia intended to do with the tablet. When she declared that she would give the gift of writing to the people below, Gyotia's fury rose. "It is not yours to give," he roared, lifting a hand to strike her.

EIGHTEEN

THE WORLD ROCKED around me, and then I was sitting in a heap on the prayer rug. Sweet little Linti . . . I had a horrible image of her laid out on the Library floor, her fair hair fanned out around her, stained with blood.

Slowly I became aware of Kiti kneeling beside me, shaking my shoulder. "Are you all right?"

I couldn't look at his face. "When?" I choked out.

"Sometime during First Shining," said Kiti. "Naka told me. He's at the Temple of Lila now. He said . . . the rest of the children had to clean the floor."

My stomach turned. But the food I'd been leaving under the stairs, and the food that—I pushed away the thought of Mati before it could hurt me. The food had been disappearing. Surely that meant Kiti was mistaken, that Linti was fine?

No, I realized at once. No, it only meant that Linti, always kinder than I was, had told the other children about the hiding spot.

Sometime during First Shining. That meant she had died not long after the incident with Emilana. Had Linti's illness contributed to her fall? Why hadn't I been brave enough to confront Emilana?

Ashamed at the sympathy Kiti was showing me, I looked past him at Jonis's disgusted scowl. For the first time, I agreed with Jonis's assessment of me.

I pushed Kiti's hand away and got shakily to my feet. "I'm sorry. I . . . I didn't know."

"Obviously," said Jonis. "You've been busy with other things." He turned to Kiti with a sneer. "You wanted to do this, so get on with it."

Kiti turned back to me. "I know it's dangerous for you, but what if you could help the Resistance without doing what . . . the other Tutor did?"

"Her name was Tyasha ke Demit," said Jonis testily. "Don't be a mouse, Kiti."

"I can't pretend to know what it's been like for you, being Tutor," Kiti went on. "But if you could help Arnath children—like Linti—wouldn't you?"

I nodded slowly. Jonis turned away, but from the set of his back I knew he was still listening intently.

Kiti smiled. "The Trade Ministry's got a shipment from Lilano coming in ten days—cloth and some other goods, but mainly slaves. A hundred, mostly children. We can get them out of the city, but it would be a lot easier if we had someone inside the palace who could alter the scribes' records. Then those children could just . . . disappear. We can't move fast enough in the mountains to evade pursuit, but if the guards weren't even alerted . . ."

"But I can't go into the scribe rooms," I said, even as I realized that Mati had shown me exactly which passage would lead me there.

Jonis turned and glared at me, but spoke to Kiti. "See? I told you this was a waste of time. You're lucky she hasn't called the guards yet."

"You can't *not* do it, Raisa," said Kiti gently. "I've been a slave as long as I can remember. You have for most of your life. You can make sure these children don't have to go through that. Don't you think our parents would have wanted us to help each other?"

I thought of my parents, realizing how often I had used their sacrifice as a reason to avoid acting, how often I had told myself that they wouldn't want me to risk my life. I cleared my throat. "But won't it attract attention if a hundred slaves disappear?"

Jonis rolled his eyes. "That's why you won't remove all of them from the list. Only half."

"What about the other half?" I asked. "Won't they go to the platforms?"

"Listen to her, now she's criticizing us," said Jonis. "We do what we can, but we can't afford to have the guards scrutinizing too much right now."

"We'll attack on the road and get the younger ones out," said Kiti. "We hope the older ones will join us."

"And this plan depends far more than I would like on the cooperation of one *qodding* Tutor," said Jonis, taking a threatening step toward me. "Kiti trusts you. I don't. In case you hadn't noticed."

"Jonis," said Kiti mildly. He looked at me. "So that's the question, Raisa. Can we count on you or not?"

I hesitated. I'd had plenty of reasons to ignore the Resistance for a long time—keeping myself and my identity safe, and my loyalty to Mati. But I didn't owe Mati anything any longer, and besides, they weren't asking me to teach the language of the gods to others. Just to change a few records and save some children's lives—as I hadn't saved Linti.

Guilt rolled over me. Was that why I was so tempted to help them? But Linti's death was utterly unremarkable in Qilara. Arnath children and adults died every day in horrible ways, without dignity or freedom. That was what Jonis had been trying to tell me all along. How selfish I was, that it had taken the death of someone I cared about for me to understand it!

All my life, I'd made choices based on caution. But I saw them now for what they really were: cowardice.

"Yes," I said humbly. "I'll help you."

Kiti smiled. Jonis whipped back the curtain and disappeared. I barely had time to shoot Kiti a questioning look before Jonis was back, carrying ink, a quill, and a roll of brownish paper.

"This, Tutor, is the first test of your loyalty," said Jonis acidly. "You will write a letter from Roa Alton of the Lilano City Trade Ministry explaining why the shipment contains fewer slaves than promised, to keep the scribes at the checkpoints from getting suspicious." Sweeping the offerings off the altar, he plunked coins at the corners of the paper to weight it down. Challenge in his eyes, he held the ink bottle and quill out to me.

I took them. I wasn't nervous, exactly, but I hadn't expected to be committing treason quite so soon. I bit my lip, thinking. For a letter from a Scholar, I could use only lower order symbols.

"Have you only the one piece of paper?" I asked.

"Yes," he said, his tone verging on belligerent.

I ignored this and knelt before the makeshift desk, composing the letter in my head. I had to decide exactly what to write before I even dipped my quill. There was no room for mistakes.

A low whistle sounded outside. Jonis and Kiti tensed.

"I'll take care of it," said Kiti. He disappeared through the curtain, and spoke in a low voice, directing whichever Scholar had entered to the other alcove. Jonis moved to the curtain and peered around the edge.

I dipped my quill, then shook away the drips and began to write—but not too slowly. No Qilarite would put too much care into writing about Arnath slaves, and Lilano was a much smaller city than the City of Kings; I'd heard the Trade Minister himself complain about the sloppiness of its scribes.

"What does that mean?" said Jonis, leaning over me and pointing to a symbol. I started, sending a droplet of ink onto the next line. I hadn't heard him approach. Quickly I turned the droplet into a connecting line before it dried.

"I thought that . . . Tyasha taught you to write," I said. No matter how I tried, I could not seem to make my tone anything but defensive when I spoke to him.

His lips pressed together tightly; I suspected that he approved of the fact that I'd said Tyasha's name out loud, but he didn't like to approve of anything when it came to me. "Some," he finally said. "But there was never enough time. None of us learned all of it." The admission seemed to cost him something. He pointed to the page again. "So what does it mean?"

"Illness," I replied. "I wrote that the coughing sickness has been running through the slave population and that many children died before they could be rounded up. The Trade Minister told me that Lilano has been having the same coughing sickness we had here a few years ago."

Jonis stared at me with a mixture of revulsion and respect. I went back to writing.

"Why was the prince in your bedroom?" said Jonis.

My quill stilled on the page. "He wanted to talk to me."

"About?"

"That is my business, and his." I forced my quill to move, penning the last lines with a flourish. "Actually, I rarely see the prince. He is far too busy with wedding plans." My voice betrayed no pain; the fact of Mati's impending wedding had become an ever-present looming melancholy.

Jonis made a sound I couldn't decipher, then knelt and examined the letter skeptically. His brow furrowed, his lips moving as he worked out some of the symbols. He looked up at me. "What proof do we have that it says what you say it does?"

I glared at him. "You'll just have to trust me."

He shook his head. "But I don't. Trust is something earned. Know this—" He leaned closer. "If you betray us, I'll kill you myself."

I had no doubt he meant it. I should have been terrified, but his words only angered me. Who was he, to demand my help and threaten me when I gave it?

I shoved the stopper into the bottle and stood abruptly. "I'll do this, but only for those children. Not for you. Be perfectly clear: I wouldn't help *you* if you were on fire and I were the ocean." I whirled and ripped back the curtain, startling Kiti.

I caught a glimpse of my ink-stained fingers. Muttering a curse, I shoved my hands into my pockets and headed back toward the palace. I would have to spend some time in the Adytum today after all, to have a reason for the ink on my hands.

Sotia trembled, for Gyotia had overpowered her once, and she could not help fearing him. She knew that Qora and Lanea supported her, though both feared Gyotia too much to speak in her defense. Lila stood at Gyotia's side, her hand upon her bow, ready as always to do his bidding. Suna stood aloof, absently stroking her own scarred cheek. Aqil, Sotia's own son, stood behind Gyotia, watching his father like a dog waiting for scraps to fall from his master's table.

NINETEEN

I WAS TERRIFIED the first time I went to the scribe rooms that housed the various ministry offices, but sneaking in turned out to be almost laughably easy. Early the next morning, I slipped into the Library of the Gods from the storeroom entrance. Not allowing myself to dwell on the image of Linti sprawled on the floor, I raced across the silent Library and entered the passage that led to the king's bedroom, feeling along the wall so I wouldn't miss the turnoff to the pitch-black lower level. I hadn't dared to bring a lamp. At the bottom of a shallow stairway, I stood behind a tapestry, gathering my nerve.

I peeked out. A lamp shone dimly away to my left, and the hallway curved into the darkness to my right. My palms began to sweat as I realized I had no idea which way was the dungeon and which the scribe rooms. Suppose I walked straight into the guards?

Use your brain, I told myself. I had seen the long rectangular windows, adorned with flower boxes, at the edges of the garden. Would such a view be afforded to prisoners? Of course not. I turned right.

The scribe rooms turned out to be large open spaces grouped around a central hallway. On pure instinct, I went to the largest—surely that would house the Trade Ministry records. I slipped in, both glad for and dismayed by the weak sunlight peeking in through the high windows. Not much time left.

Wooden tables lined the walls, with papers and quills scattered about. A glance at the open scrolls there—all shipping lists and schedules—showed I had come to the right place. I smiled to see how carelessly the scribes left their papers lying about, when they held them so close in public, as though afraid some errant Arnath might snatch them. All scribes were of the Scholar class, of course, but the palace scribes fancied themselves far above the others in the city, as they at least did not have to hire themselves out to merchants and traders. Plenty of second and third sons, and even daughters, of noble families had to turn to their quills to earn their bread by working for the lower classes.

In another world, that might have been an option for someone like me, too. Years of habit started to push the thought away, and then I realized: that freedom was exactly what the Resistance was fighting for.

My stomach fluttered. What if I couldn't find the record?

I made a careful circuit of the room, taking in the baskets of scrolls next to the desks. A narrow door at the far end led into a large chamber filled with shelves of scroll baskets. I seized a yellowed tag hanging from the end of a scroll, and, by comparing it to the others in the basket, worked out that the records were stored chronologically along the top row of shelves. More baskets lined the bottom row, but I couldn't see how they fit into the pattern. I worked my way down the top row, following the timeline until I found the most recent scrolls by the door. But even those were over a season old.

Which meant that the newest entries were out in the scribes' area. I stepped back through the doorway and located a half-full basket—and on the desk nearby, a stack of scrolls. I opened each carefully, trying to remember exactly how it had lain on the desk so I could replace it.

The sixth scroll was the one I sought. It listed the items in the shipment from Lilano: fifty sacks of grain, forty bolts of cloth, two hundred swords, three hundred jugs of lamp oil, and one hundred slaves. I grabbed ink and quill from the desk and quickly applied the lines that would halve the number of slaves, then closed the ink bottle and wiped the quill on the much-stained blotter. I hovered as the ink dried—far too slowly—and blew on it for good measure, until my lines were virtually indistinguishable from the original scribe's. I replaced the scrolls and, satisfied that the room looked untouched, I crept back the way I'd come.

It went so well that I didn't hesitate when Kiti whispered my next assignment to me through the screen as I knelt in a temple alcove on the final day of Qora's festival. Now the Resistance needed food for the children we had freed before; a shipment from the Valley of Qora was the target.

"It'd be best if you destroy the whole record," he whispered. "The more we can take at one time, the less often we'll have to do this."

I bent forward to feign prayer as someone passed by the door. "Won't they notice if the record goes missing?"

He laughed softly. "You'll figure it out. I trust you." The way he put the emphasis on "I" reminded me of exactly who *didn't* trust me. I thought I'd proved myself, after the first time.

"I'll do it tonight," I told him.

But I wondered about the wisdom of that promise when I crept out of the banquet late that evening, finally having been excused. In the kitchen storeroom I felt around for a candle and matches, then flipped the hidden latch to the passage.

When I reached the Trade Ministry office, I stopped short, realizing that I had concentrated so hard on getting here that I still hadn't decided how I would make the record disappear. Assuming I could find it, of course. I raised my candle, peering into the shadows, then moved along the desks, using one finger to slide scrolls open, looking for any mention of the Valley of Qora.

I found the scroll on the third desk, no unrolling necessary; the paper lay flat, weighted by stones at each corner, with a fresh page next to it where the scribe had half finished a copy. I chewed my lip. Removing it would raise suspicion; a scribe in the midst of copying the supply list would certainly remember its existence.

My eyes lit on the unstoppered ink bottle at the next desk. I looked back at the supply list. A stoppered ink bottle stood a hand's length from the paper. But as I looked more carefully, I saw that the stopper was loose, not fully inserted into the neck of the bottle. A strong wind or a mouse scurrying across the desk might topple it. . . .

I tilted my head, calculating at exactly which angle the ink might spill in a flood over both copies. I nudged the bottle closer to the weighted letter, then carefully loosened the stopper even more and knocked the bottle on its side, jumping back as bitter black ink soaked the supply list and ran over the copy. Ink streamed to the edge of the desk and splashed onto the braided rug and scroll basket below.

The original was completely illegible, the copy mostly ruined, with only the shipment's origin and the first line ("seventy-five iron pikes") visible. I took a quill and spread the ink until the words were obscured, then wiped the quill on the blotter and replaced it on the desk.

I stood back and surveyed the scene—it was quite convincing. And if I knew anything about scribes, it was that they were proud. The scribe who'd been copying this would probably burn the inky remains rather than draw attention to his own carelessness with his ink bottle.

Smiling, I crept back along the corridor.

The next time Laiyonea left me alone in the Adytum, I wrote of my doings with the Resistance, giddy at seeing the deeds on the page. It made them feel more real, somehow—so much so that I hated to burn the letter. But burn it I did.

I continued my encoding project too, and managed to work my way through the first five tensets of the lower order symbols before the rains drove us out of the Adytum for a solid Shining and a Veiling, and the raised floodwalls blocked the sea.

I was eager for another assignment from the Resistance, and one finally came at the Festival of Suna. Laiyonea bid me wait in the carriage until called for the service; the king had ordered her to keep me out of the way except when the presence of both Tutors was explicitly required. As this meant I was also spared the sight of Mati and Soraya socializing with the other nobles before the service, it suited me fine.

No sooner had Laiyonea disappeared into the temple than the other door slid open and Jonis slipped inside the carriage.

"How did you do it?" he asked.

"Do what?" I whispered defensively.

"Make that shipment disappear. We've been listening around corners for two Shinings, and no one even seems to remember that there *was* a shipment due from the Valley of Qora."

"You got it all?" I sat up straighter. Those children would eat well, because of me.

"Yes." Jonis's mouth twisted begrudgingly. "What'd you do?"

"If you think I'm so incapable, why did you ask for my help?" I said, more loudly than I should have with the guards and driver just outside.

Jonis tensed, then relaxed when no guards slammed the doors open. He glared at me. "Oh, you're very capable, I think. Capable of betraying us in an instant if it suits your mood."

"My *mood*? If that were the case, I wouldn't have helped you at all, the way you keep insulting me."

Jonis's nostrils flared, and then I saw him make the decision to calm down. His entire demeanor changed, a veil dropping over the anger in his eyes. Was this the face he showed his master?

"So, how did you make every Scholar in the city forget that shipment?" he said.

I might not have heard the forced humor in his tone had I not seen his anger just the moment before. Blushing, I told him about the ink bottle.

He shook his head. "All right, to business. This job's a little different." He leaned forward and dropped his voice. "You need to alter the record of an Arnath named Ris ko Karmik. As soon as possible."

"Why?"

Jonis gave me a hard look. "Ris is taking on an important mission. He agreed to do it only if we guarantee protection for his family. You'll remove the record of his wife and son, so if Ris is captured they can't be tortured to make him speak."

I gasped. "Would the guards really—"

He stopped me with a glare. "In a heartbeat. We're nothing to them. You think Qilarites would hesitate to torture an infant? Your friend the prince wouldn't even blink."

I looked away. "He's not my friend." It was true. He wasn't anything to me anymore. The thought didn't even hurt, not really; there was just a hollow where the warm glow that was Mati used to be. I took a deep breath. "This man is willing to abandon his family?"

Jonis snorted. "His master sold him to an olive farmer in the Valley of Qora not ten days after the baby was born. He'll be lucky if he ever sees that child again. That's how life is for slaves, Tutor.

Most of us have nothing left to lose."

I nodded. "I'll go today, after the service."

"Good." Jonis reached for the door.

"My name is Raisa," I said.

He looked at me. "I know."

"You always call me Tutor. My name is Raisa."

Jonis paused. "Good-bye, Raisa. Don't fail us. A good man's life depends on you." And then he was gone.

I sat formulating a plan, and presented a calm facade to Laiyonea when she came to fetch me. That afternoon, in the scribe rooms, I was less calm. Getting there had been easy enough—all the scribes were at an open council meeting, and Laiyonea too. But I had no idea where to find the record of a particular Arnath. I'd only dealt with shipping records so far, in the Trade Ministry office. I poked around the other rooms, and even spent a good ten minutes unrolling census scrolls, before I realized: slaves wouldn't be counted in a census, like people. Slaves were property. *We* were property, to Qilarites.

A sour taste in my mouth, I hurried to the Trade Ministry office. I examined the scrolls on the desks and found a few slave records, but nothing about Ris ko Karmik.

I stepped into the storeroom and studied the baskets lining the shelves. Remembering my puzzlement over the bottom row of baskets, I examined one of the tags. It held the name of a Scholar, and underneath, *City of Kings, east.* Unrolling the scroll, I found a list of the Scholar's property, including information about all his slaves. No names, of course; only descriptions of age, appearance, and family members. The language of the gods only allowed for symbols to name Qilarites.

My heart sank. How was I to find Ris ko Karmik, when all I had was his name? I didn't even know who his master was—I hadn't known enough of the record system to ask for it.

I sorted through the other scrolls in the basket, pausing when my hand brushed a tag that said *Horel Stit, City of Kings, east.* I knew that name—Jonis's master. Remembering the man's oily smile, the way he had pinned his cruel eyes on Jonis, I unrolled the scroll and found a long list of property, ships, and a home by the docks, and, at the bottom, an inventory of slaves. Stit kept three household slaves: an older woman who cooked and cleaned, a young boy for errand-running, and a young man for everything else. I read the description of the third: *tall, curly sand-colored hair, typical Arnath complexion, by nature stubborn. Original owner: Kladel Ky. Came to Stit at age fourteen as part of the dowry for Ky's daughter upon her marriage to Stit. Mother and sister remain in Ky's possession.*

Jonis would hate that I was reading this—and would hate that, even if he stood right beside me, he *couldn't* read it.

I replaced the scroll and forced my mind back to my task. I didn't have much time; if Laiyonea came to look for me in the Adytum, I'd best be there.

If only I'd thought to ask for Ris's master's name!

But wait—Jonis had said that Ris's master was an olive farmer in the Valley of Qora. And the records seemed to be arranged geographically. . . .

Luckily there was only one basket for the Valley of Qora; that area was mainly inhabited by peasant farmers who turned most of their crops over to the Scholar landowners in exchange for the right to work the land. I found one slave with a young child, but he had grown up in the Scholar's household, and Ris had been sold there recently. I shoved the scroll back into the basket and reached for the next.

The edge of it caught in the weave of the basket as I pulled it out. I worked the scroll back and forth, trying to loosen it. I tugged, and heard the heart-stopping sound of ripping paper. Kneeling, I reached both hands into the basket and forced the scroll out, cringing as another rip sounded.

At last the scroll was free, but the bottom dangled like a half-severed limb, torn edges crinkled where the weave of the basket had chewed it like tiny teeth. The rips, though they had thundered in my mind, were tiny compared with the crushed portions that had caught in the basket.

I stared at the scroll, which listed the holdings of an olive farmer named Eral Kone, and found a note at the barely connected bottom about a recently purchased male slave with a wife and young son back in the City of Kings.

I'd found the scroll I was looking for.

There was no way to hide this. I could steal the entire page— but when the Trade Minister next levied taxes, its absence would be noticed. Even more scrutiny might descend on Ris and his mission, whatever it was.

And then, a sound even worse than tearing paper: voices in the hallway.

*Gyotia's blow sent Sotia crashing to the stones, but she would
not give him the satisfaction of hearing her cry out.*

TWENTY

FRANTICALLY I RIPPED off the bottom of the scroll
and shoved it into my pocket, then rolled the mutilated top half
and stuck it in the basket. I dove into the corner behind the
shelves and held my breath.

At first, I couldn't hear anything over my pounding heart, but
then the voices came again. Two men, out in the main room—
arguing.

"It was right on my desk! Why'd you move it?"

"I told you I was filing anything already rolled," said a second
voice, deeper and milder than the first. "Don't blame me if you
can't keep track of your scrolls. Let's just find it and get back."

The first man sighed. His grumbling grew closer. I shrank
against the wall as he entered the records room. My heart nearly
stopped when he crouched and started going through baskets on
the bottom row of shelves. I prayed to every one of the gods that
the shadows of the corner would hide me, my panicked mind slipping into the litany recited on the festival days: *Gyotia, greatest of
the gods, lend me your might. Aqil, patron of Scholars—*

An angry cry cut through my thoughts. I braced for discovery, but heard only shuffling paper and an impatient sigh. I peeked out to see the black-haired Scholar carefully lifting the tattered scroll from the basket where I had so hastily placed it.

"Mice again! Jin will have our heads. Aqil have mercy on a Scholar." He replaced the damaged scroll and poked around at the others in the basket.

"Terin!" The second man appeared in the doorway, dangling a scroll from his fingers.

Terin looked up. "You found it?"

The second man nodded. "Old slave, no children, originally from Asuniaka? Master's name is Botai?"

Terin shoved the basket back onto the shelf and snatched the scroll. "That's it! Anything about Resistance ties?"

"Nothing specific. Looks like he's had plenty of whippings, though."

Terin snorted. "That's nothing to what he'll get when the guards recapture him. Let's get this to Minister Jin before he makes an example of us."

The second man followed Terin out. "Us? I had nothing to do with it. I was merely helping."

"Oh, be quiet."

Their banter faded down the hallway. I stayed still for a full count of one hundred, hardly daring to breathe. Then it hit me that, somehow, impossibly, I hadn't gotten caught.

The Scholar had thought mice destroyed the scroll. I unfolded myself from my hiding place, my hands moving to the basket before my brain had fully caught up with their plan. Deliberately, I rubbed another scroll against the weave of the basket, letting the edges crinkle and tear. I damaged a few more, then fled to the Adytum, where I burned the scrap of Ris ko Karmik's record and watched the smoke rise up to the gods.

I threw myself back into my work with the fervor of one with something to hide, but Laiyonea seemed to attribute my enthusiasm to her teaching methods. Three days after my close shave in the records room, she looked over my afternoon's work and, for the first time, found nothing on which to comment.

"It's well you're done learning the higher order script," she said as she slipped my pages into the firepit. "You really must start planning for the Selection. The wedding is less than five Shinings away."

I focused on the quills I was laying in their box. "I thought that the Selection would happen closer to the . . ." I couldn't bring myself to say "wedding."

Laiyonea shook her head. "No later than Fourteenth Shining. Emilana Kret may grow fangs if she has to host a pack of young girls too close to the wedding. Once the new child is selected, your training will shift to focus on teaching methods."

I didn't answer. The last thing I wanted to do was round up Arnath orphans for the Selection of the next Tutor, whom I would present to Mati and Soraya as a wedding gift. The thought of doing anything at Mati's wedding other than curling up into a miserable ball was difficult for me.

Laiyonea sighed. "I've already made inquiries, and none of the palace slave children are the right age—the youngest is six." I still didn't respond, and she went on, "The quickest way would be to go down to the market. Arnath orphans run wild there, those too young for the platforms."

Silently I closed the quill box and placed it in the cabinet.

"Raisa!" Laiyonea's tone made me look at her at last, but her face softened as she took in my expression, and she held in whatever she'd been about to say. She walked over and placed her hand briefly on my hair. "Just . . . take care of it soon."

I spent the next few days in the Adytum, puzzling over my heart-verse and thinking what a shame it was that I had no missions to take me to the scribe rooms, since the full Scholars Council was in session and the rooms stood empty most of the day. But I wouldn't dare visit during daylight hours again. I wondered if, perversely, it would prove something to Jonis if he knew I'd almost been caught.

I had no chance to tell him. I listened hard at every banquet over the next Shining and Veiling, even forcing myself to eavesdrop one night while Soraya had a long conversation with the Finance Minister about council doings at the next table, trying not to dwell on Mati's worried frown as he spoke to the War Minister on his other side. I heard no more than the usual whispers of fear about the Resistance. Nothing of Ris ko Karmik's mission reached my ears, and there was no more talk of escaped slaves or disrupted shipments. In fact, the Defense Minister boasted one night that he thought the "slave problem" was completely under control, and that the guard captain had personally killed several Arnath conspirators in a raid a few days earlier. My heart twisted.

Was that why I hadn't heard from Kiti or Jonis?

I deliberately wandered into an alcove at our next visit to the Temple of Aqil, and even begged to take a walk in the gardens at the Temple of Lanea two days later, but no one approached me. I had no way to contact them.

So I waited. At Eleventh Shining, when Laiyonea and I visited the Temple of Aqil to make our offerings for the royal couple's health, I almost cried out with relief when we found Kiti sweeping the floor in an alcove. Kiti bowed and hurried off without even looking at me. When we finished the offering, Laiyonea went to speak to the priest and I stayed in the alcove, waiting.

Kiti didn't come.

I squeezed my hands together in my lap and fought back tears. Mati was gone, my heart-verse remained an indecipherable mystery. Working with the Resistance had been the one thing that had given me a sense of purpose. I knew I could help them—help my people—if they only let me.

Gyotia lifted his hand to strike Sotia a second time, but Aqil spoke, distracting him. "How can they worship their gods, without the language to do so?" Aqil asked. "Perhaps the noble among them should receive this gift, so that they can instruct the others to worship you properly, mighty Father."

Gyotia looked over his shoulder, considering.

"It is a reasonable compromise," said Lanea. Her words seemed to be directed at Gyotia, but the warning look she shot at Sotia made it a plea for her to stop provoking Gyotia's fury.

TWENTY-ONE

AS THE DAYS grew warmer, the Scholars visibly relaxed. Why shouldn't they? The rumors of rebellion had faded, and the royal wedding was only three Shinings away.

On the first day of Lilana, the Scholar men of Qilara gathered in the palace courtyard for Mati's eland hunt. Any man who killed an eland during the hunt would earn a place of honor at Mati's wedding. The hunt was held now because the female elands were in heat, and so more dangerous. Mati himself would kill a large horned female and present the bloody knife to Soraya upon his return, a symbol of the bridegroom's passion for his betrothed.

I told myself that it had nothing to do with me, and yet, standing with the entire court to see them off, my hands went cold. Mati knew how to hunt, of course, but suppose one of those wild creatures hurt him? The hunt seemed pointless, danger for danger's sake—it could only have been devised by men.

The High Priest of Lila blessed the men's weapons; Penta Rale insisted upon giving a benediction as well. When his droning voice finally fell silent, the men climbed into the carriages. I let my eyes linger on Mati where he sat between Annis Rale and his cousin Patic. When the gates closed behind the carriages, the women went inside, where they would spend most of the day embroidering and gossiping until the men returned for the night's feast. Laiyonea sent me to the Adytum, with a stern reminder to meet her in the garden for the women's luncheon at third bell; she knew how I longed to skip it, but the Trade Minister's wife had again made a point of inviting us, and failing to appear would both dishonor her and insult the prince's betrothed.

The sky above the Adytum was perfectly blue and cloudless, the ocean breeze balancing the sun's warmth. Quickly I finished the tasks Laiyonea had set me, and worked on my encoding project. I still had almost three thousand lower order symbols to go through, but I was beginning to wonder if it would ever help me figure out my heart-verse. I considered writing another letter to Sotia, but found I had nothing to say.

At third bell, I headed to the garden. Laughter and chatter drifted over the hedges, but my mood was dark as I stepped off the path—and nearly collided with Soraya Gamo.

She was beautiful, as usual. Shining black hair flowed down her back, under a spangled scarf of brilliant blue. Her silk dress matched exactly, bound with gold cord at her waist.

How little I had to offer Mati, compared with her. No wonder he'd left me without looking back.

Soraya stopped short when she saw me, hesitation clouding her eyes before her familiar haughtiness slipped into place.

I bobbed an awkward curtsey, hoping that I would not have to speak to her; my throat was too tight.

"Pardon me," she said. Was I imagining the frost in her tone? Her eyes ran over my plain white and green dress, her face falling into a delicate frown. Surely she'd heard the rumors about Mati coming to my room the night before her arrival. Dread flashed through me—had Mati told her what had really gone on between us? Did they laugh together over the silly Tutor who had thought the prince in love with her?

I considered a new, horrible possibility: that Mati might have given his heart to Soraya Gamo. It had been bearable—if only just—when I'd thought he was marrying Soraya to please his father. But to think that he loved her . . .

What difference does it make? I asked myself bitterly.

But oh, it mattered.

Soraya turned away. She hadn't gone more than a few steps, however, when the wild clatter of a carriage came from the front of the palace.

My heart constricted. *Mati.* I turned and raced to the courtyard, reaching it in time to see a carriage lurch to a halt by the steps, the driver shouting as guards and servants scurried around in confusion.

The palace doors opened and more people spilled out to see what the noise was about. The women arrived a few minutes later from the garden.

"Get the doctor!"

"Out of the way!"

"Now—"

"Keep the women away!"

I caught sight of Laiyonea at the back of the crowd, straining to see. Her panicked expression broke the unreality of the scene for me. I ducked under the outstretched arm of a servant and hurried to the carriage. A moment later I realized that Soraya was beside me, having done the same.

We both jumped back as the carriage door banged open and Mati stood before us, his golden tunic spattered with mud and blood. He clutched a bloody knife.

"Call the doctor!" he cried. He looked down and saw Soraya and me, and held out the knife. "My father—I need help." I wasn't sure if he was speaking to her, or me, or both of us.

Soraya looked into the carriage. Suddenly she covered her mouth with her hands and turned and ran into the palace.

"Help me," Mati pleaded. He thrust the knife at me, and I took it automatically, realizing that the crumpled, bloody heap behind him was his father. I dropped the knife and rushed to help him, but I did little good. I clutched at the king's cold shoulder, gagging a little at the sight of the jagged hole in the front of his tunic and the blood spreading from it. King Tyno's eyes were closed. I couldn't tell if he breathed.

"It's all right, Father," Mati said, his voice hollow and distant. "We'll get the doctor . . . you'll be fine." The king gave no indication of having heard him.

Two servants pushed me aside. They heaved the king onto

their shoulders and carried him into the palace, Mati trailing behind them. The women on the stairs went silent as they passed, and wailing started up once they'd gone inside.

One voice rose above the others. "The king is dead! Gyotia save us! King Tyno is dead!"

In the crowd I found Laiyonea's face, white as ash.

Gyotia lowered his hand. "Very well," he said to Sotia. "You may give the language of the gods to the leaders of the valley people only." His lip curled as if he knew that this stipulation would hurt her far more than another blow.

Sotia struggled to her feet and walked down the mountain, her heart as heavy as the stone tablet in her hands.

TWENTY-TWO

"THE KING LIVES, but just barely." Laiyonea sat down heavily next to me in the sitting room, where she had sent me after we'd been turned away from the king's chamber an hour before. Laiyonea had been so pale that I hadn't wanted to leave her, but she'd insisted on staying by herself to argue with the guards.

"Did you see him?" I asked timidly. I couldn't shake the memory of King Tyno's prostrate form, the hole in his chest. Or of Mati's face, terrified but determined. I ached to be near Mati, to take his hand and offer what comfort I could.

Laiyonea shook her head. A tendril of black hair had come loose from its knot and lay curled against her neck. "Mati won't let anyone in. The doctor sent me word."

I laid my hand over hers on the armrest. "What happened?" I whispered.

"Gored by an eland. The gash goes clean through—" Laiyonea

broke off. I squeezed her hand. She took a deep breath. "Rale is preparing for Mati's coronation, likely within the next few days."

I blinked, thrown off by the seeming change of subject, but then I realized what she was saying. King Tyno would die, soon, and Mati would become king.

Laiyonea eyed me critically. "Change your dress. Burn that one."

I looked down at the streaks of dried brown blood—the king's blood—across the front of my dress. I nodded and stumbled to my room to change. At the threshold I turned back to see Laiyonea sagging wearily in the chair with her eyes closed.

Later that evening, Mati sent for Laiyonea. Soon after she left, the palace bells began tolling. They continued for a solid hour, announcing King Tyno's death. Laiyonea told me later that Mati had refused to allow anyone except the doctor and his assistants into the chamber, and had only called for Laiyonea when the king had asked for her at the end. Laiyonea wouldn't say anything else, but I knew that her sharpness with me hid her grief.

I lay awake half the night, yearning to go to Mati. Twice I even crept to the doorway, intending to do so, but Laiyonea was sitting up in her room, and ordered me back to bed. The second time she pointedly left the door between our rooms standing wide open.

Mati's relationship with King Tyno hadn't been warm—how often had he told me of his father berating him for being soft and foolish? The king hadn't understood Mati at all. But still—I knew the pain of losing a father.

Mati would be crowned king the following day. What must he be thinking?

Unbidden, his words came back to me. *"When I'm king, I can do whatever I want."*

Could he? Could he refuse to marry Soraya?

I turned on my side, chiding myself. Mati's father had just died. This wasn't about what I wanted.

Then I sat straight up in bed as another memory came back to me. Mati, lying on the couch in the Library after I'd told him about my childhood. *"I wish I could just . . . just free all the Arnathim,"* he'd said. *"I don't know if it's possible. But I'll try. And I promise, Raisa—no more raids on the Nath Tarin, ever."*

Would he—could he—keep that promise? Even now, after I'd turned him away?

The next day dawned bright and clear, but the mood in our carriage was somber as we clattered through the streets. Mati rode at the front of the procession with his father's body. I had caught a glimpse of him in his purple tunic as we had climbed into our carriage, but I hadn't seen his face.

Laiyonea had kept me close all morning; I knew she suspected that I would go to Mati the first chance I got. And she was right. All that had happened between us no longer mattered. Mati was hurting; I had to go to him.

The carriages let us out at the Valley of Tombs, and we processed silently between rows of livery-clad guards to the open space before the Royal Tomb. The long, low structure had been built right into the side of the mountain, and held the remains of every member of the royal family for twenty generations, but was so large that it would hold twenty generations more.

Laiyonea remained dry-eyed through the funeral. I stood beside her, sweating under the glaring sun, as Penta Rale recounted the life of King Tyno in a singsong voice, and ten tall Scholars carried the king's body into the tomb. Priests from all the temples chanted incantations over the door, then Mati said the final words to send his father's spirit on to the afterlife. Mati pushed the door closed; stone met stone with a dull thud.

The mood shifted. Penta Rale stepped forward and held up the crown. I let his droning voice fade into the background as I studied Mati. Something in his face had changed. I couldn't identify exactly what, but I realized that I didn't know him anymore. For almost a year I'd been longing for the boy I had known, but the man before me wasn't that boy any longer. He was a king now.

He had turned to me in panic yesterday in the courtyard, but that was all it had been—panic. I had let those few moments of false closeness lead me into foolish dreams that something might change, that he needed me.

Penta Rale lowered the crown onto Mati's head. Mati stepped forward, and the assembled people cheered. Mati lifted his hands to quiet them.

"My father died a heroic death," he said, the hollow echo of his voice bouncing off the walls of the surrounding tombs. "The eland that gored him had leaped at me. He jumped into its path and sacrificed himself to save me. That is how he must be remembered, from now until the gods read out the scrolls." Mati's face was blank, his voice even. My heart lurched at the thought of

Mati in the beast's path, and I thanked all the gods that he stood safe before me now. Even if he hadn't acknowledged me since the day before, in the carriage.

The crowd was still. Rumors had circulated about the king's death, but this was new information.

"I am not my father," said Mati. "But I will try to be a just ruler for Qilara and its people." He looked around, his eyes lighting on me for the barest second. "Some have suggested that I move my wedding up in light of my father's untimely death. However, my father chose First Shining because of its sacredness to Gyotia. The wedding will go on as planned. We welcome this union with the house of Gamo." Mati nodded first at Soraya, then at her father beside her. Del Gamo bowed.

I lowered my head, swallowing hard against the lump in my throat. Had I really thought anything would change? And those things he had said to me in the Library . . . why would he free the Arnathim? Why would any Qilarite care to?

"Long live Qilara," said Mati, and then he stepped back abruptly and led the procession out. I trailed Laiyonea and watched dully as Mati helped Soraya into the carriage in front of us. He smiled at her, and I could no longer tell whether it was a true smile or not.

A Shining and a Veiling passed. In the corridors, scribes complained about adjusting to the new dating system, arguing about whether the new era began on the day of King Tyno's death or the day of King Mati's coronation. I wondered why Mati didn't just silence the matter with a decree. Perhaps he wanted to give them something trivial to argue about, to keep them out of trouble.

I was back to spending long days in the Adytum, now that Laiyonea no longer worked with Mati. He was far too busy, she said, and anyway she couldn't teach him anything more to help him. She seemed to feel sorry for Mati; when I saw how tired he looked, I could not help feeling the same. He hadn't been ready to become king. The Scholars Council seemed to see that too, especially when Asuniaka fell to Emtiria ten days after the coronation. The murmurs at banquets grew less guarded, less respectful, and I grew annoyed on Mati's behalf even as I told myself that the whole matter had nothing to do with me.

"You really can't put it off any longer," said Laiyonea one morning as I took my seat in the Adytum.

I didn't have to ask what she meant. Mati's wedding would take place in sixty-two days—I wished I didn't know that number so exactly, but it had become a daily countdown I couldn't ignore. And I hadn't done a thing to find girls for the Selection.

Laiyonea had told me that, in days past, Scholar families had raised young Arnath girls to take part in the Selection, sometimes even doing away with their parents to meet the orphan requirement. The resulting patronage battles had nearly destroyed the council more than once, so now it was up to the Tutors to find girls with no ties whatsoever and submit them for the king's approval.

It was a responsibility I definitely didn't want.

"I'll work on it," I said, playing with my quill.

Laiyonea sighed. "This wedding is going to happen, Raisa."

"I know that."

"So stop feeling sorry for yourself and do what you must."

"Fine," I snapped. "I'll go to the market, like you said."

Laiyonea gave me a stern look, but let my tone pass without comment. "Very well," she said. "I'll talk to the king and get it approved."

It took me a moment to realize that "the king" meant Mati.

Sotia appeared to Belic, the leader of the valley people, and showed him the wondrous tablet that held all writing. "How will you use this gift?" she asked.

Belic bowed low. "I shall keep this gift holy and precious, and only the noblest of birth shall learn its secrets."

TWENTY-THREE

THE WEDDING PLANS went on, despite the interruptions in trade stemming from Emtiria's army pushing south from Asuniaka and clashing with the king's South Company. Linens and decorations arrived daily after being diverted through other trade routes.

An entire house on the harbor had been set aside for the creation of the future queen's wardrobe. Scholars from all over the city sent slave women there to assist with sewing, but Soraya seemed more interested in sitting in on council meetings than trying on dresses. I heard two servants in the baths speculating on her ambitions one day as they waited for me and Laiyonea to finish. I ducked my head underwater and tried to ignore them.

I had thought that, with the battles in the south and the focus on the wedding, the Festival of Aqil at Thirteenth Shining might be muted, but it was just as lavish as ever, as though Mati were trying to prove something to the Scholars. The entire court attended the pantomime; Mati sat in the front row, where his father had once dispassionately observed him in the part of Aqil. I rarely saw Mati these days except at functions like this. I suspected that he was avoiding me as much as I had been avoiding him.

I looked away from Soraya, who was leaning over to whisper something in Mati's ear, and focused on the pantomime. Had it really been only two years since I stood on that stage? Now all the players seemed childlike to me. I had to look away when Aqil threw the tiny girl playing Sotia to the ground. I caught a glimpse of green in my peripheral vision, and turned to see Jonis standing beyond the guards. He'd obviously been waiting for me to look in his direction. He raised his eyebrows meaningfully, then turned and disappeared into the crowd.

I had long since stopped looking for the Resistance to contact me; indeed, no rumor of their actions had reached my ears since well before King Tyno's death, and I had resigned myself to the idea that I had helped them all I could. Now my pulse quickened with dread and wild curiosity.

I tugged Laiyonea's sleeve. "I need to use the toilet," I whispered.

"Not now," she mouthed back impatiently.

"I can't wait," I whispered a little more loudly. I held her gaze, and finally she leaned over and spoke to the nearest guard. He led me through the crowd and into the temple, then pointed me toward the toilets and took up a position at the bottom of the stairs.

The toilet room was long and narrow, with stone benches lining the sides, rows of holes cut out for sitting on. The smell was not as foul as it might have been; the pipes below had probably been cleaned out before the festival. I perched on a solid corner of bench and wondered how Jonis would get past the guard.

I didn't wait long before a figure appeared in the doorway—but it was Kiti, not Jonis.

"We need you to destroy another record," he whispered without preamble.

"I'm being spoken to again, am I?" I said.

"Shh! Don't be stupid. We had something going on. We stayed away to keep you out of it." Kiti peered at me, an unfamiliar hardness in his eyes. "You're in the most danger of getting caught—we're only coming to you when there isn't any other way. This one's important."

I sighed. "All right, what is it?"

Kiti smiled. "A shipment in four days. Grain and some other supplies . . . we need food for those children, and we've freed more, so it's a big group. . . ."

I nodded. "Four days. All right. Do you know anything else?"

"It's coming through the mountain pass. If we can attack on the valley side and you destroy the records, we might get the whole thing."

I paused. If the entire shipment were to disappear, that meant that the men transporting it would disappear as well. Would the Resistance give those men a chance to join them, or simply ambush them? And should I even be worrying about that, if it meant keeping those children alive?

"I'll do it at first light tomorrow," I said.

Kiti took both my hands and pulled me up from the bench.

"I knew we could count on you. Thank you." He leaned forward and kissed my cheek, but I thought I saw something troubled in his face. I didn't get a chance to ask about it though, because the next moment he was gone.

By the time I got back outside, I'd missed the rest of the pantomime. Laiyonea was cross, but I pretended to have an upset stomach, and she calmed down. It even gave me an excuse to leave the banquet early that night, and I lay in bed planning my next venture into the scribe rooms.

It was gratifying to know that Kiti and Jonis had been ignoring me for good reason—not because I was useless. I wondered what Kiti had meant by "something going on," and then I remembered—the guard captain had killed some of the Resistance a few Shinings back, and then the rumors of rebellion had stopped. Maybe the Resistance had foundered—not a comforting thought. But Kiti had seemed confident, not like a member of a failing movement at all.

I was so anxious that I almost decided to go in the middle of the night, but I remembered how long it had taken me to find the document I needed last time, working by the light of a single flame.

And then, an insane thought: *I could burn all the records.*

But destroying the Trade Ministry, even if I dared, might bring more scrutiny to the fragile Resistance. And it wouldn't change the cruelty of men like Horel Stit. Most slaves weren't bound by chains or guarded constantly. They were like the asotis in the Adytum, caged by fear—fear of what would happen to them or their families if they ran. I thought of Ris ko Karmik's

insistence on severing all ties with his wife and child before helping the Resistance. I thought of Kiti with his newly hardened
eyes. And I thought of Jonis, eschewing every chance to run, staying instead to make the Resistance work.

I should be doing more, I told myself. Jonis was right—I'd had
an easy life as Tutor, so easy that I'd almost forgotten that I was a
child of the islands.

These thoughts gave me new purpose as I crept along the
corridor toward the scribe rooms the next morning. I imagined
the conversation I would have with Jonis when next I saw him. I
would tell him that I was ready to do more to help the Resistance,
that I would even follow in Tyasha ke Demit's footsteps and teach
them the language of the gods.

Then I turned the corner and tripped over the guard setting
mousetraps in the hallway.

Though Belic's vow to keep the language of the gods for the nobility would please Gyotia, it tore at Sotia's heart. Her eyes fell upon the frowning face of Belic's attendant, his younger brother Iano. "You do not agree?" she said to him.

Iano lowered his head respectfully, but his voice was strong and sure. "Such a gift should be shared with all your people, my lady, so that all may know the glory of the gods."

TWENTY-FOUR

I SQUEAKED AS I landed in a heap. Swearing, the guard leaped up and drew his sword. With its point at my chest, I didn't dare move.

He squinted at me in the dim light. He was a few years older than I was, with close-cropped black hair and a large Qilarite nose. His youth was hardly comforting though, as his sword was sharp and steady.

My mind raced as quickly as my heart. I had no excuse for my presence here, or for how I'd gotten past the guards. I had never prepared one; I'd always known there would be no surviving discovery.

The young man's eyes ran over my white and green dress, and I saw him realize who I was. "What are you doing here?" he demanded.

No brilliant answer came to my lips, so I pressed them closed. This seemed to unnerve him; he motioned me to the wall. I scrambled over to it, and he followed with his sword.

I looked past him at the Trade Ministry office. Was there any way to warn Jonis and Kiti that I'd failed?

Not likely from the dungeons.

My captor called to another guard down the hallway. The other didn't want to come at first, but as the younger guard's voice grew more insistent, the other guard came into sight, grumbling, "This had better be important, Kirol. If the captain finds out I left my post—"

The younger guard, Kirol, stepped aside, revealing me behind him. I looked up into a weathered face, and recognized Peron, the lead guard from the day I'd knocked the letter out of its slot in the Library, a lifetime ago. He gasped.

"She just came down the corridor," said Kirol, his voice rising.

I looked away, determined to reveal nothing. My stomach lurched—what if they suspected why I was here? Would they torture me if they thought I could tell them about the Resistance?

They muttered to each other. Kirol's swordpoint dipped as he listened, nodding, to Peron. "I think you're right," he whispered back. "I've seen it too."

I swallowed hard. What had they seen? Did they suspect that I'd been here before?

Kirol handed his sword to Peron, who pointed it at me. I cringed against the wall as Kirol bound my hands with a leather strap. *So this is it*, I thought. At least it wasn't a long walk to the dungeons.

Kirol took his sword back and sheathed it, and they each grasped me by an arm and dragged me toward the stairs—not the dungeons. I balked in confusion, so that they had to haul me up. Neither spoke as they pulled me up two flights of stairs. My feet stumbled on the soft carpet of the upper level of the palace—were they taking me back to my own room?—but they turned right instead of left, and stopped in front of a white door. Peron knocked and spoke to someone inside, then they pulled me through. I caught a glimpse of a small anteroom before I was dragged through another door and deposited in front of a huge desk of gleaming blackwood.

Mati sat behind it. He'd been writing something, but now he laid aside his quill. His eyes went from my face to my bound hands, then to the two guards who had stepped away from me as though I had the coughing sickness.

"What is this?" he demanded, sounding like the boy I'd known, not the king making a proclamation. I hadn't heard that voice in so long that it made my knees wobble.

As Kirol explained, I flushed; Mati would know immediately how I'd come to be in the scribe rooms, as he himself had told me how to get there. How was it possible that, after everything that had happened, I felt guilty at betraying his trust? I studied the flowers on the carpet, trying to think of an explanation, any explanation, for my presence in the rooms below. Maybe it was the way Mati's voice had sounded when he'd first spoken, but I hoped that if I *could* explain it, he might believe me. After all, the boy I'd loved had despised violence. He'd visited Tyasha ke Demit before her execution. Maybe he would be lenient, even if he no longer loved me.

Kirol's words trailed off, and Peron cleared his throat. "We thought it best to bring her to you directly, Your Majesty."

I peeked up at Mati, feeling much like I had as a terrified fourteen-year-old. Mati had saved me then, I told myself, and he hadn't even known me.

"You were right to do so," he told the guards as he sat back and rubbed his eyes. His tunic was unlaced and his hair untidy, as though he hadn't bothered to dress properly—or as though he'd never gone to bed last night. He sighed. "Peron, Kirol, wait outside."

The guards bowed and left. I kept my gaze on the desk as Mati stood, and I made out the lower order symbols *tax* and *slave* on the page he'd been writing, before he walked around the desk, blocking the paper. He regarded me for a long moment, then leaned back against the desk. My wrists smarted where the strap cut into them.

"Obviously you've been using the secret passages," he said. "I'm not an idiot, so I thought you might. But what were you doing in the scribe rooms?"

I swallowed. "Looking for orphans for the Selection," I said, the lie popping out fully formed. "Girls in . . . bad situations."

Mati looked away. "I can understand that," he said softly. "It was stupid, though. You could have just asked me."

My face must have said what I was thinking, because he laughed. The sound melted away the last of my fear. I knew now that I was not headed for the dungeons.

"All right, maybe not," he conceded. "But I need you to be

more careful, Raisa. Things are touchy right now. If the council knew about this, I don't know if I could protect you."

"But you're the king," I said, proud that my voice didn't even shake.

He gave a humorless laugh. "So was my father. Look where that got him."

It was a strange thing to say; I stared at him. Mati sighed. "My father's death was not an accident. He was assassinated. Likely someone on the council is behind it."

I gaped at him. "But . . . the wound was . . ." Horrible. Bloody. Obviously from an eland.

"Oh, he was gored by an eland, that's true. But not because he jumped in front of me. We'd been stalking that eland all morning. We were waiting it out in the bushes. Suddenly Father started twitching and gasping. He staggered out and fell practically at its feet, and it gored him. I went after it with my knife, to get it off him, and it ran away."

"You think he was poisoned?"

"I'm sure of it. His canteen disappeared in the confusion, and no one else was nearby when it happened, so I can't prove it. But I know what I saw. I just don't know who, or why."

I nodded slowly. "That's why you wouldn't let anyone in to see him."

"Yes. I still don't know who I can trust."

I took that in. "Why are you telling me this?"

Mati's eyes were soft. "Because I trust *you*, Raisa." His words hit me like daggers. Blood pounded in my ears so loudly that it almost drowned out what he said next. "And with the other things going on right now . . . I need you to be careful. Don't give them a reason to accuse you of anything. I couldn't bear it if they got you too."

He stepped closer. Instinctively I lifted my hands to stop him. He frowned. "Oh, sorry. I forgot." He closed the distance between us and unbuckled the strap from my wrists.

"Thank you," I said, rubbing my wrists to get the blood going. His nearness made it difficult to think. His familiar scent hit me, musky and sweet, and my body responded of its own accord, my pulse racing.

Mati took my hand. "Gods, I've missed you," he whispered. In his eyes was the same longing that had been in my heart for nearly a year. He touched my cheek. My breath came in little gasps.

I turned my head and forced myself to inhale and exhale properly. "What other things?" I asked, my voice strained.

Mati dropped his hand from my cheek, looking at me quizzically.

"You said 'the other things going on right now,'" I clarified. "What do you mean?"

Mati laughed. "Oh, some nonsense with the Resistance. My guard captain's set a trap—he's planted rumors about a weapons shipment coming through the mountain pass in a few days. They've obviously been stockpiling weapons—half the time they don't even touch anything else." He shook his head. "They don't help their cause by doing that. It angers the council, and frightens people, and makes real change more difficult. Dimmin will have a squad waiting when they come for those weapons. He wants to take out the leaders before the wedding. . . ."

He trailed off and looked at me apprehensively. I had let go of his hand, and obviously he thought it was because he'd mentioned the wedding. But I had realized two things simultaneously. First: Jonis and Kiti were walking into a trap, and even if I'd destroyed the shipping record, it wouldn't have saved them from it. Second: they had lied to me. *We need food for those children*, Kiti had said. And Jonis, harping on rescuing young ones with each raid . . .

Of course, I realized. Of course they'd taken that tack, when they'd seen my reaction to Linti's death. I'd seen those shipping lists myself, seen the numbers of swords and pikes listed there. How could I have been so naive?

I couldn't properly process my anger, not with Mati standing two feet away watching me anxiously. Then I realized—I was angry at him too. How dare he hold my hand and touch my cheek, and bring these feelings up in me after all this time?

It wasn't rational. I had just escaped punishment and should have been grateful, but all I felt was anger—at Mati, at Jonis, at my own folly. No matter what I did now, I would betray someone's trust.

Mati reached for me again, but I stepped back. "Don't," I pleaded in a whisper. "We can't. You know that. Thank you for helping me. I'll be more careful. But we both need to . . . remember who we are." I turned away.

Mati seized my arm, and when he pulled me back around, his face wore an aristocratic blankness. "It seems that you *have* forgotten just who I am," he said coldly.

I stared at him in shock. A moment before he had been my

sweet Mati, but now he had become someone I didn't know. "Don't touch me," I spat, shaking his hand off my arm. I whirled around and wrenched open the door.

The two guards in the anteroom jumped to their feet as I stalked past. "Let her go," said Mati's voice quietly behind me. I paused for only an instant, but didn't look back.

I charged into the sitting room to find Laiyonea calmly sipping tea. I dropped into a chair next to her, still seething. My anger was masking fear, disappointment, and relief, I knew, but somehow the anger felt more comfortable, more righteous. So I clung to it.

"Have you gotten permission for me to go to the market?" I asked.

Laiyonea nodded, studying me over her teacup. "Just speak to Captain Dimmin when you're ready."

I laughed, thinking how close I'd come to having an entirely different encounter with the guard captain. "This afternoon," I said, grabbing a roll from the table and taking a savage bite.

Belic rebuked his brother sharply for his insolent words to the goddess—how dare he suggest that the language of the gods should be written by any but the noblest hands?

Sotia held her tongue, and presented the tablet to Belic, as the gods had willed.

TWENTY-FIVE

THREE GUARDS ACCOMPANIED me to the market later that day; thankfully, the two from my morning's misadventure were not among them. I explained that approaching an orphan with royal guards in tow would only frighten a likely candidate away, so they let me walk alone and question the merchants about where they might have seen children, as long as I stayed in their sight.

The market was a large amorphous space in the depression between the temple hill and the mountain that formed the city's southern border. Rows of stalls stretched off in every direction— though to call them "rows" was generous. They were more like meandering clumps, set up wherever sellers had decided to drop their wares. Often this was in the middle of an already established aisle, which forced shoppers to stop and wait for others to come through the narrow opening. And of course they browsed the wares in that stall while they waited.

I hadn't entered the market since my days running errands for Emilana Kret as a child. It hadn't changed much, but I had. I turned my back on the three rotting heads on pikes next to the arched entryway. Enough hair still clung to the misshapen forms to recognize them as Arnath—most likely the conspirators captured a few Shinings back.

Near the entrance, a smooth-faced young Qilarite on a raised platform hawked the virtues of the slaves tied up behind him. The eyes of passing Arnathim darted to those on the platform and away, any expression quickly disappearing as they hurried back to the tasks set to them by their masters. They moved about freely, and those on the platform would too, once they showed their new masters that same blank, passive look.

I could see that those on the platform already knew this—the raid that had brought me to the city had been the most recent, which meant that these slaves had all grown up here in Qilara and were being resold. Those of us from the islands had fought at the slave market. Margara had wailed and scratched the slaver's face when he'd sold her oldest daughter to a leering blacksmith. The slaver had raised his arm and sent her sprawling, her head hitting stone with a sickening crack. She had limped dizzily back onto the platform, and had been thrown over a servant's burly shoulder when some Scholar's representative had purchased her and the other women from our village.

Only the children had been left, and we were speedily divvied up among the buyers, with Emilana Kret claiming the smallest of us for the palace: Kiti, me, a seven-year-old girl called Elna, and Deri, Margara's five-year-old son. Deri had been sick on the voyage, and died a few days after we came to the palace. Elna cried constantly; she was terrified of the platforms, and so it was perhaps inevitable when she fell and broke her leg. It never healed properly, and she was sent away—no one ever said where, and she never came back.

I turned away from the slaver and started along the meandering pathways, paying close attention to the children creeping under carts and hiding behind pillars. I approached two girls playing with stones in the dirt, but they scuttled away, and I lost them in the crowd.

I arrived at the market center, and turned back to make sure I was still in the guards' sight. One of the guards raised a hand in acknowledgment. I decided to head to the fountain. The crowd melted away in front of me; with my white and green dress, I had, of course, been recognized. I hurried on, my cheeks burning.

At the fountain, I found what I'd come for—with their scruffy clothes and underfed faces, these children had to be orphans. I smiled and walked toward them—seven children total, the oldest not more than six. I couldn't tell which were boys and which girls, for they all had long, unkempt hair and skinny arms poking out of their filthy rags.

"Hello," I said gently. They fled in all directions. One small girl who had been bathing her feet in the fountain splashed me in her haste to get away.

By the time I had wiped the water from my face, the children had all disappeared. One of the guards hurried over. "Are you all right, Tutor?"

I tucked a sodden strand of hair into my braid. "Fine, just wet."

"We could round them up for you."

"No," I said quickly. "I'd rather do it this way."

The guard shrugged and took up a post near the fountain. I moved down the adjacent row, peering between stalls. I reached the end without spying a single child.

"You'd have better luck," said a voice in my ear, "if you shop at the stalls for a bit. They'll come back. You're a curiosity."

I turned, but a warning pinch on my arm stilled the movement. Anyway, I knew the voice. Jonis's superior tone infuriated me—not least because his suggestion was a good one.

I caught the guard's eye and gestured that I was going to visit the vendors, then approached a busy glassblower's stall.

I wasn't surprised to find Jonis next to me, idly turning over a dish as though inspecting it for flaws.

I leaned closer, pretending to look at the dish he held. "The shipment from the valley is a trap," I whispered. "Don't go after it."

The dish lay still in Jonis's hand for a fraction of a second, and then he set it down. "How do you know that?"

"I just know. They made it weapons specifically to tempt you." My fingers curled into my skirts. "Did you even save any of those children, or has it always been about stealing weapons?"

"I don't know what you're talking about."

"I've *seen* the supply lists," I shot back, leaning forward to inspect a bowl. "I'm not stupid. If you ask me to risk my life to help you, you could at least tell me the truth."

Jonis looked sideways at me. "Would you have agreed to help us if I had?"

I didn't answer. Jonis nodded as if he had scored a point, then moved to the herbseller's stall, swinging the market basket in his hand. I waited a few minutes, then followed as though the herbs were fascinating. "You're going to get a lot of innocent people killed," I told him in a low voice.

"What're we supposed to do?" Jonis shot back without looking at me. "Wait for the benevolent Qilarite king to give us our freedom?"

"He might, if you'd stop scaring the rest of them," I said, and though I no longer knew whether the first part of that statement was true, I understood that the second part was what Mati had been trying to tell me that morning.

Jonis snorted. "If you believe that, you deserve to be lied to."

"Did you know that the council wants to send raiders to the Nath Tarin, because of you?" I said through gritted teeth.

"Do you really think they wouldn't send them anyway?"

I pressed my lips together and nodded to the herbseller as she approached. Mechanically I sniffed the sirret that she held out to me, asked her to send a packet to me at the palace, then trailed Jonis to the other end of the stall. "But untrained slaves against soldiers?" I whispered angrily. "Those lives are on your head. How many children have you sucked in?"

Jonis looked at me quickly, and I gasped as I saw his face. His right eye, bruised and blackened, was nearly swollen shut. "What—" I started to ask, but Jonis touched my wrist and surreptitiously indicated the oilseller's stall nearby.

"See that tall man with the brown hair?" he said. I looked, and located an Arnath with a laughing face, deep in conversation with the oilseller, whom he towered above. I nodded. "That's

Ris ko Karmik," Jonis said. "It's thanks to you that his head is attached to his shoulders, instead of on a pike over there, and his wife and child are safe."

"His mission was successful?"

"Yes." Jonis looked sideways at me again. "I don't take stupid risks with people's lives. We only do what we have to do." He paused. "Just like you. You're here to gather girls for the Selection, aren't you?"

"Yes," I whispered.

Jonis was silent. Remembering my pretense, I lifted a plate of herbs and smelled it. The stinging scent of nettleblossom made my eyes water.

"How many do you need?" Jonis asked at last.

"At least twelve. Orphans, no older than five."

Jonis nodded. "I can help you, but you have to make sure a certain girl is chosen."

"That's not how it works."

But Jonis wasn't listening. He turned and walked away; I was clearly meant to follow. I waited a few minutes, then gestured to the guard to tell him where I was going. I stayed far enough behind Jonis to avoid arousing suspicion, but when he turned and disappeared between two stalls, I stopped, at a loss.

A weaver's cart stood in this less-crowded corner of the market, and the woman in green behind it called out to me. "Tutor," she said, "come see these fine new fabrics from Master Ky."

I stepped closer. "I am not shopping for cloth today, I'm afraid," I said. I looked behind her to see Jonis seated on the ground beside a tiny girl wearing a man's faded green tunic as a dress. A half-finished cloth waited on a handloom behind the woman, and the girl sat patiently with the thread from the loom spooled around her raised hands.

I glanced at the guards. From their vantage point, they wouldn't be able to see Jonis or the little girl. I angled my body so they couldn't see my face either, and pretended to examine the length of fabric the woman held out to me.

Jonis laid a hand on the girl's dark hair. "This is my sister, Jera," he said. "She'll be five at Second Shining, the right age for a Tutor."

The woman turned her head away and folded her arms.

I stared at him, my fingers stilling on the fabric. "You want me to take your sister?"

Jonis looked up at me, resigned. "No Arnath has the opportunities a Tutor has."

Perhaps so, but he obviously didn't understand the dangers. "I'm . . . supposed to find orphans," I managed to say.

Jonis and the woman looked at each other. She was his mother, I realized. How had I not seen the resemblance immediately? She had the same green eyes, the same sandy curls pulled back under her scarf. Jera's dark eyes were the same shape, but her black hair flowed straight down her back like a Qilarite's, and her skin was darker than theirs.

Jonis and his mother seemed to be having a silent conversation, and after a moment they both looked at me. The woman's shoulders slumped. "She may be an orphan soon enough," she said in a hoarse whisper. "She'll be safer with you."

I didn't understand her meaning at first, but then it dawned on me that she was referring to whatever the Resistance had planned.

I bit my lip. "I—I can't promise she'll be chosen."

Jonis just looked at me steadily.

"It's not under my control," I said, my voice rising.

Jonis slid the thread from Jera's hands and draped it carefully over the loom. "Turn around, Jera," he said. The girl turned obediently, and he lifted the back of her tunic-dress. My hand rose to my mouth when I saw her back, crisscrossed with thin white scars. I knew it was common practice in the city to whip disobedient slaves, but what could this tiny child possibly have done to earn that?

Jonis dropped the edge of Jera's tunic and pulled her onto his lap.

Part of me understood that he was playing on my sympathy for children just as he had all along . . . but that didn't matter. Jera couldn't stay with such a cruel master.

I swallowed hard. "You won't be able to see her again. I'll have to pretend she's an orphan."

The woman's eyes tightened, but Jonis nodded somberly. "We know. It'll be better that way."

Jera had watched our exchange seriously. I had the impression that she knew what was happening, despite her age. She didn't cry or make a sound, though—she'd probably been well trained not to give away secret hiding places and clandestine meetings.

The woman knelt beside Jonis, and he handed Jera to her. She held the little girl close and spoke to her softly. I had to look away.

"We won't ask anything else of you after this," said Jonis. "Just take care of her, Raisa."

"But I can't promise that . . ." My voice trailed off as he frowned at me. "I will," I said, though I had no idea how to make that statement true. "Won't her master notice if Jera disappears?"

Jonis shook his head. "They'll both disappear. My mother isn't staying with that—"

"Not here, Jonis," said his mother mildly. He shot her an incredulous look.

I glanced nervously down the line of stalls. Two of the guards stood together at the other end, talking as they watched me. I knew they couldn't see Jonis or Jera behind the stall, but still, I had lingered far too long.

"You'll have to send her out to me," I whispered urgently, folding the fabric and setting it on the cart.

"Yes," said Jonis. "Go sit by the fountain. The children will come to you."

I forced myself to wander casually down to a silk merchant's stall closer to the guards. I made a point of speaking to the owner, an elderly half-deaf Qilarite, for even longer than I'd spoken to Jonis and his mother. I questioned him loudly about whether he'd seen any children.

He didn't understand, so I repeated myself, but a louder voice than my own made me stop and look around.

"There you are, you useless tialik. Dawdling again, are you?" The harsh voice came from a brawny Qilarite; as he turned, I recognized Horel Stit from the fair at the palace. Jonis's master. He stood in the pathway, gripping Jonis by the chin, and shook him as he spoke again. "Don't you keep Mistress Kelia waiting. And I want all that wood chopped before I leave tomorrow morning, or your face won't be the only thing smarting." A second Qilarite stood a few feet away, watching unconcernedly. The few other shoppers nearby passed without even glancing their way.

"Yes, master," said a meek voice. It took me a moment to realize that Jonis had spoken, so different was it from any tone I'd ever heard from him. His arms hung at his sides, and he seemed to have shrunk a few inches.

Most disturbing of all, I doubted it was an act. Jonis truly feared his master; it was easy to see why he also hated him, and all Qilarites, so much.

Of course he did. Hadn't I felt that same helpless fury, whenever the guards shook the Library platforms or Emilana Kret locked me into the Stander?

I forced my fingers to unclench, then casually touched a length of silk. The old Qilarite smiled sympathetically, as if to remind me that they weren't all like Stit.

"I can send one of mine over to help this afternoon," offered Stit's companion.

Stit laughed nastily. "Oh, no, this one's got to learn his lesson. If he dawdles, he stays up all night finishing it. Simple as that. Don't worry, we'll have that wood before we sail, one way or another. Come on." I watched out of the corner of my eye as Stit shoved Jonis aside.

The other man laughed as they walked away. "Don't you ever worry, leaving him here with Kelia when we're at sea?"

"Oh, no. He knows what would happen to him if he acts up. And it's not a whipping, I tell you."

The two men passed behind me and down toward the

fountain square. The instant Stit disappeared through the gate, Jonis's expression switched from battered subservience to vicious hatred. It made the fiercest glares he'd ever given me look like warm greetings to a friend.

Jonis's gaze shifted to me, and his face went blank. He looked away and marched past. "Wait by the fountain," came his crisp whisper.

I turned back to the silks and forced myself to wait for a count of one hundred before I thanked the old man and walked back to the guards.

When I reached them, I shrugged. "The woman in the weaver's stall told me there are at least fifty urchins running around here most days." I sighed and pinched the bridge of my nose. "Maybe I ought to see if they'll come to me. If I sit near the fountain, can you stay nearby without being obvious?"

"Of course, Tutor," said the nearest guard, and the unconcerned way he said it told me they suspected nothing.

I sank onto a stone bench beside the fountain. The guards fulfilled my request well; I saw none of them, but I didn't allow myself to think that they weren't watching.

After about ten minutes, two children emerged timidly from between the stalls across the fountain. One was Jera, though I hardly recognized her. Dirt stained her face, her bare feet, and her now-ripped tunic. She clutched the hand of another little girl who was perhaps a year older, and the two of them came to sit on the ground by me. I don't know what made me do it, but I started singing softly, my mother's old nonsense song from the Nath Tarin. More little girls came and joined the group at my feet. When the group numbered fifteen, rounded out by a chubby little thing who wobbled on her feet, I stood.

Immediately the guards appeared in the fountain square.

"It's all right," I told the girls with a smile, feeling like an evil spirit in a children's tale. "Would you like to visit the palace?"

After she gave the tablet to Belic, Sotia returned to her home
under the willows and found Lanea waiting for her.

"It was a good compromise," said Lanea.

"You did not speak in my defense," said Sotia disdainfully.
"Why are you here now?"

Lanea stuttered out an apology, for she had never had Sotia's
grace with words. But Sotia cut her off with a cold gesture.

"See that your husband goes wandering tonight," Sotia
demanded, not caring how the reminder of Gyotia's indiscretions
would wound his wife. "For I also have visits to pay."

TWENTY-SIX

"FIFTEEN AT ONCE!" said Laiyonea. "Well done."

I blushed and toyed with my quill. I'd been so relieved to return to the palace and turn the children over to the elderly servants who would look after them until tomorrow's ceremony that I hadn't thought about how it would look, the children having come to me so easily. When I confessed that I'd done it by singing a tune from the islands, Laiyonea's mouth became a thin line, and she told me not to mention that part to anyone else.

As if I didn't already know that. "Is it really necessary to keep them from eating?" I said, to distract her. "Most are already half starved."

Laiyonea nodded. "I know. Likely Arlin and Mala will slip them some food before sunset. The potion they drink before the ceremony will keep hunger pangs away."

Well did I remember that haze-inducing potion. My own Selection had been a blur because of it—a whirl of symbols and ink, in which we were to copy whatever Laiyonea wrote, though none of us knew how, and Laiyonea kept sending girls out until only three of us remained. I wrinkled my nose at the thought of those tiny children drinking that clear, deceptive liquid.

Laiyonea seemed to have read my thoughts. "They'll only have a little. It will help them relax and focus."

I nodded, thinking through the steps about which Laiyonea had been drilling me. Once I selected the three most promising girls based on the writing tasks, I'd have to ask the gods to make the final choice. I had clearer memories of that part—Laiyonea, her face lit from below as she stood over a firepit, holding a bone to the flames, the eyes of the silent council upon her. At last she'd looked at the bone, then at us. "The choice is made," she'd said quietly to the king, her words a question, which he'd answered with a nod.

Then someone had pulled me to my feet and Laiyonea had tied the green sash around my waist.

"I understand the ceremony," I said slowly. "But how exactly does the oracle work?" My heart fluttered. Jera might do well enough on the writing tasks to justify my leaving her in until the end, but the oracle was another matter.

Laiyonea smiled. "Sometimes it is clear, sometimes not.

When it is not, you must use your discretion."

I absorbed that. No one but Laiyonea had examined the oracle bone at my Selection, I realized. Perhaps I could keep my word to Jonis after all.

"With you, for example, it was quite clear." Laiyonea pulled a sheet of paper to her and wrote something. "You must carve the lines of the question carefully at the top. Once the fire cracks the bone, the lines will extend into the answer." She pushed the paper toward me.

It held two exquisitely written characters. The top one, with *quill* above and *slave* in the subordinate position, was the symbol *Tutor*—the question I would scratch into the bone. The lines of the quill extended down the paper, curling into four small spirals. I turned the paper sideways and saw the symbol they formed. *Library.*

Laiyonea smiled. "Given how you came to my attention, the meaning seemed clear."

"What about . . . your other Selection? Was that also clear?"

Laiyonea's smile evaporated. "No. As I said, sometimes you must use your best judgment."

I nodded thoughtfully. Laiyonea obviously blamed herself for Tyasha's fate. It was an uncomfortable thought, especially when I considered that the futures of fifteen little girls hung on my own actions. At least, I told myself, the girls who weren't chosen wouldn't be going to the platforms, but instead to the olive farms in the Valley of Qora. It had been my suggestion; Laiyonea had taken it to the king herself.

The next day I nervously entered the council chamber at midday bells. The council was already assembled. Soraya Gamo sat in the back row, next to the Justice Minister, projecting an air of deliberate boredom that didn't fool me. She was probably just waiting to laugh when I made a mistake. All the high priests were there too, lined up in order of rank along the front row, with Penta Rale beside Mati, and Obal Tishe, the High Priest of Lanea, at the far end.

That didn't help my nerves any more than the scribes seated by the door, scratching notes. Even the slightest misstep on my part would be noticed and recorded.

Laiyonea sat off to one side; I was grateful for her quiet support. I threaded my way through the rows of goblets set at intervals along the tiles, to the king's raised seat at the center of the semicircle of councilors.

I curtseyed, then had to begin twice before my voice was loud enough. "The girls are assembled, Your Majesty."

"Bring them in," said Mati, his voice carrying easily to every corner of the room. I took the stool below Mati's chair, smoothing my skirts unnecessarily. The doors opened, and the children filed in.

When each girl was kneeling before a goblet, I stood and told them to drink. They did, most greedily, and it was clear when the quick-acting potion made its way into their blood; they looked around in confusion. One girl examined her hands as though she'd never seen them before.

I passed out paper and quills and ink bottles, the only sound the click of my heels on the tiles. A few of the girls held up the paper curiously, or played with the quills, but most—including

Jera—waited solemnly to be told what to do.

I explained the tasks, then scrawled the first symbol. I held it up and the girls copied it, half clutching the quills with chunky fists, only one or two holding them anywhere near the correct way. But I wasn't to instruct them in the details—that was part of the test.

I continued, making the symbols more complicated. Jera and a few others shifted their grips. I smiled.

After twenty symbols I walked around the room, examining their work and touching some girls on the shoulder. Silent servants came and led these away—or carried, in the case of the tiniest girl, who'd given up the exercise halfway through, curled up on the floor, and begun snoring gently. I happened to glance up at Mati as I came to her. I bit back my own grin as I saw him trying to suppress a smile.

With nine girls left, I began the second set of symbols, more complicated now, with connecting lines. Four girls were cut easily, their symbols degenerating into meaningless scrawls.

I maneuvered the remaining five into a line and began on the last set. Fortunately Jera had kept up. I realized, in the midst of laying out the complicated symbol *family*, that she'd probably already been taught some writing, just as I had. I thought, with a pang, of my heart-verse, and wondered if Jonis or his mother had slipped her some similar keepsake before sending her out to me. If so, I hoped she had the sense never to show it to me.

Fifteen symbols later, I was left with Jera just in front of me, a girl with vibrant red hair on one side, and a skinny blonde on the other.

I cleared my throat. "Three remain, Your Majesty," I said, striving to keep the right cadence to the ceremonial words. "The gods shall decide it now."

Penta Rale rose from his seat at Mati's right and held out the ox bone, taken from last night's sacrifice to Gyotia, for Mati's inspection. Mati nodded. Rale handed the bone to me.

I went to the firepit and used the knife waiting there to carve the question, mindful of Laiyonea's admonitions about care and straight lines. It took longer than it should have; the councilors stirred impatiently before I finally laid down the knife.

Rale stepped forward and moved the striker in the firepit, murmuring an invocation to Aqil as flames shot up inside it. He seized the stack of papers, both mine and the children's, and fed them to the fire. Smoke tickled my nose so that I had to step back to prevent an undignified sneeze. The three girls watched all this with somber interest.

Rale bowed to me—too deeply to be anything but insulting, I realized as he sat back down. I glanced at Laiyonea. Her pursed lips told me to keep going, so I stepped forward and held the bone over the flame.

Fire licked the bone, and it seemed ages that I stood there, waiting. At last a gentle pop broke the silence. I watched the cracks of the symbol widen and lengthen, and two side-facing triangles appeared, one lower than the other. *Red*.

The girl on the left had copper curls. *Red*. The oracle had been more than clear this time.

I looked back down at the bone, not considering what to do,

but steeling myself to do it. If the oracle was truly the word of the gods, then how would they react if I ignored their word?

At last I spoke. "The choice is made," I said, turning my head nominally toward Mati. I caught his nod out of the corner of my eye, and I dropped the bone into the fire and swept up the green sash from the table as I stepped in front of Jera.

The roof did not fall in. Lightning did not strike.

But a mild voice to my right said, "If I may speak, Your Majesty?"

I turned to see Penta Rale standing at his place.

"Go on," said Mati warily.

The priest spread his arms and addressed the council, his voice a monotone, but loud enough to carry. "This Tutor has trained for merely three years. How are we to trust that she is proficient enough to read the oracle?"

A few of the Scholars stirred, and I sensed that they agreed with him. I longed to look to Laiyonea, but knew this would be considered a sign of incompetence. So instead I faced Rale and weighed my words carefully. "I have been taught everything I need to know"—*more than you,* I tried to imply with my tone—"and by an excellent teacher."

"Nonetheless," Rale said, in a tone of elegant doubt, "I call upon the king to verify the Selection." He turned to Mati, who narrowed his eyes. I recognized that look; Mati was trying to figure out Rale's motives.

"Certainly," said Mati pleasantly. He paused, then stood and went to the basin. I realized belatedly that I ought to have taken the bone to him, and flushed. But Mati gave no sign of my lapse, only took up the tongs from the table and lifted the bone from the flames.

I held my breath as he looked down at it. His eyes flicked to the three girls, then to my face, his expression inscrutable. I lifted my chin and looked right back at him, my fingers tightening around the sash.

"The choice is made," said Mati, inclining his head toward me. He dropped the bone face down in the basin.

The crackle of rising flames met my ears as I turned back to Jera. The servants at the back of the room came forward and helped the girls up, and I knelt and tied the sash around Jera's waist. Then I curtseyed to Mati and the council and led Jera away to our rooms.

I helped her into my bed and pulled the blanket over her. Within three breaths she was asleep. She would sleep off the effects of the potion for the rest of the day, and part of the next. When she woke she would be ravenously hungry.

I went into the adjoining room and lay on the bed, exhausted. Laiyonea had removed to a room at the other end of the palace that morning, leaving the Tutor's suite for me and Jera, so this would be my room from now on. Laiyonea would continue to work with me in the mornings, advising me how best to teach Jera.

When a tap on the door awakened me, the indigo light of evening shone through my windows. It took me a moment to orient myself—my new room faced the front of the palace, instead of the gardens. The door opened, and Laiyonea's head appeared. "Dinner is laid out in the sitting room," she said.

I stood and straightened my gown. I was glad Laiyonea would

continue to join me for meals—it lessened the unreality of the day somewhat.

Laiyonea was quiet, though, as I buttered my bread and started on my soup. I swallowed a mouthful of wine and looked at her, waiting.

"You did fine, Raisa."

"So why did—"

"Penta Rale make an ass of himself?" said Laiyonea drily. "I suspect that had more to do with me than you."

I frowned. "Because he doesn't like Tutors?"

Laiyonea clicked her tongue. "Perhaps. Rale and I have never gotten along, and he's gotten worse these last few years."

Since Tyasha. That was what she meant. Surely Rale had tried to discredit Laiyonea after Tyasha's betrayal, but King Tyno, and now King Mati, regarded her too highly. So he had gone after the weaker Tutor—me.

Laiyonea waved a hand. "He's harmless enough, I suppose. Let him hold his grudges. You were able to read the oracle easily?"

I nodded. "It was very clear. *Black*," I lied. "And only one girl had black hair." As I met her eyes, I sketched the rounded symbol in my mind, as though by doing so I could make the lie true.

Laiyonea nodded and chewed her bread thoughtfully. "You won't work with Jera in earnest until after the wedding, of course," she said. "But start familiarizing her with the Adytum and the tools. Begin the first tenset, perhaps."

I nodded. Jera's training would follow the usual slower course for young Tutors; mine had been accelerated because of the need to catch up to where Tyasha had been. I was actually looking forward to putting to use the skills Laiyonea had taught me—seeing Jera learn would be a nice change from burning all my work. But the thought of what was to come before that—presenting Jera at Mati's wedding—made my stomach swoop. Against my will I remembered the way Mati and I had laughingly shared a look when the littlest girl had fallen asleep, and the way he had backed up my lie. And then I remembered his distant, kingly manner yesterday, when he'd spoken to me like I was—I forced myself to finish the thought. Like I was a slave.

Well, I was, wasn't I?

We finished dinner and lit the candles for evening invocations, and Laiyonea left soon after. I lit the lamp in my room, then checked on Jera.

She had kicked off the blanket, and lay curled up on her side, her mouth hanging open and her fine dark hair tangled on the pillow. I tucked the blanket in around her, then gathered those of my things that the servants hadn't already moved and slipped back into my new room.

Mati was waiting by the outer door.

*That night, Sotia crept back to the valley while Gyotia's
Lamp was veiled. She took the tablet from Belic and appeared to
Iano. "Share this knowledge with all your people," she told him,
"and find wisdom in the sharing."*

*Iano bowed low in gratitude. "I shall speak to my brother and
help him understand your will, great one," he said.*

*"I advise you to proceed carefully," replied Sotia. "For I, too,
have a brother."*

TWENTY-SEVEN

I STOPPED SHORT, and two small boxes of hairpins and
ties tumbled from the stack in my arms, spilling open on the rug.
I followed Mati's gaze to the floor. My face grew hot when I saw
the stone he had given me lying amid the jumble.

A crease appeared between his brows. Silently I went to the
dressing table and deposited my load, then bent and gathered up
the hairpins and ties and the stone, and shoved them back into
the boxes. I took my time setting the boxes in place, to put off the
moment when I'd have to face him.

Finally I turned around. Mati hadn't moved. The memory of
the last time we'd been alone hung in the air between us.

"So," Mati said at last, "are you going to tell me why I lied for
you today?"

Of course—why else did I think he had come?

"I told you I wanted to find girls in bad situations," I said. "All I can say is . . . it had to be Jera."

He nodded slowly. The six feet between us felt like an uncrossable ocean.

He reached into his pocket and held something out to me— the burned and blackened ox bone from the ceremony. "I thought you'd want to destroy it," he said, turning it over. The original lines had split again and again in the heat of the flames, but I could still see the triangles if I looked hard. When I made no move to take it, Mati laid the bone on the bed.

"That's twice in two days that I owe you thanks," I said. "I am sorry if I've . . . caused difficulties for you, Your Majesty."

He took three steps toward me, bridging half the distance, and held up a hand. "Don't . . . do that, please. I can't stand it, not from you."

I stared at him. "I haven't forgotten who you are, or who I am."

Mati groaned and sank onto the bed, his head in his hands. "But that's just it," he said, his voice muffled. "I have. Forgotten who I am, that is." He looked up, searching my face. "I was an ass yesterday. I . . . I'm not myself without you. I'm sorry. For . . . everything. Maybe you can't believe that, but it's the truth."

I had to look away. "I can believe it," I said softly. It had been so easy to storm out the day before, when his face had been haughty and so utterly foreign to me. But now my own sweet Mati was looking up at me, his expression begging me to forgive him, and my heart's desire to do so warred with the knowledge of the lies I had told him. If he knew the truth about why I'd been in the scribe rooms, would he still be here?

Does it matter? whispered my heart. *He's here now.*

"You don't know how often I've stood out in that hallway," said Mati. He studied his hands. "But I thought you wouldn't want to hear it." He sighed. "I shouldn't have come. This only makes it harder. I miss you, Raisa, more than you can imagine. I just . . . thought you ought to know that."

He pressed his hands down on the bed next to him and began to rise. Within an instant, I was beside him, my hand on his shoulder. My heart, so long tamped down, would not allow me to let him leave.

Mati took in my expression, and a moment later I was in his arms. His kisses washed over me like floodwater over parched earth. I clutched him helplessly, tears falling down my face and mingling with his as he whispered my name.

A small voice in the back of my mind warned of all the reasons why this was wrong, but it was quickly drowned out in the roar of emotion and desire, and the pounding of my long-denied heart. The kisses grew more insistent; our hands wandered, relearning each other's bodies. There were no more apologies, no explanations, only whispered words of love as we fell onto the bed and fell back into each other's hearts.

A sound made me look up from the letter, my quill suspended over the page. I sat at the desk in the Library of the Gods, and a dark-haired woman with a heart-shaped face stood nearby, one hand on the huge wooden case that housed the tablet of the gods.

She was sobbing. I looked around, bewildered, wondering how she'd slipped into the Library without me knowing it.

I opened my mouth to speak to her, but no words came out. I looked back down at the letter. Ink had spilled over the parchment, blotting out the symbols. Only one—*traitor*—was visible, still shining wet and dark.

I sighed and crumpled the paper in my hand; ink streamed like blood from my fist. Dropping the quill, I tossed the ruined letter into the firepit, where it flared with a dull orange glow. I stood and wiped my hands on my dress; they left long reddish-brown stains.

Distant laughter echoed. I started as a panel between the statues of Qora and Lanea opened. A young woman and man spilled into the room, giggling and holding hands.

The woman by the tablet noticed me for the first time. She nodded toward the young couple, smiling fondly, and pressed a finger to her lips. They had paused for a kiss, and the young man reached behind the young woman to free her hair from its braid. It shone, reddish and wavy, in the firelight, as he sighed and ran his fingers through it.

The young woman whispered something that I couldn't hear, and he lifted his lips from her neck and grinned. He took her hand and pulled her toward the couch. I caught a glimpse of an unadorned beige stone, irregular in shape, swinging from a thong around the young woman's neck.

The woman by the tablet case stared at the couple, her hands in fists at her sides, a mixture of longing and sad determination on her face.

As they passed the tablet case, the young woman paused—obviously not seeing me or the other woman at all—and her free hand touched the stone around her neck, her head tilted as if she'd heard some distant music and was trying to make out the tune. The young man spoke to her, and she tore her eyes away from the case, melting into his embrace.

The woman beside me sighed sadly. "It is all I can do," she murmured. "Never enough."

I woke slowly, with the sense that there was something important I was supposed to remember, but it fled as soon as my eyes opened. I blinked, taking in the unfamiliar angles of morning light in the room. When I recalled where I was and what had happened the night before, I sat up straight in bed.

I was alone, I registered with disappointment and relief. But on the pillow beside me lay the stone on its thong. I turned it over, tracing the faded carved lines. It was a question, I realized, like the one I'd carved in the bone. I could put it away, or destroy it—or I could wear it, as I had before. No one else would know what it meant, but Mati would. If I chose not to wear it, I knew he wouldn't seek me out again. He was giving the choice to me.

Only it wasn't a choice any longer. My heart had made its decision last night. Going back to being without Mati was simply too painful to contemplate. I was not foolish enough to think that the situation had changed; Mati would still marry Soraya Gamo in fifty-eight days. But *I* had changed. I knew how it felt for my heart to lie dormant, and now that it had been reawakened it would not go silent again.

So I hushed the doubting voices in my mind and slipped the thong over my head, gripping the stone like a long-lost friend.

I sang my mother's nonsense song as I dressed and straightened the room. I found the ox bone on the floor and slipped it into my pocket, deciding to take it to the firepit in the Adytum to destroy it.

Jera finally woke just after lunch. I had to send for three plates of eggs, fruit, and bread to satisfy her hunger. Not that she asked for more, of course; she was clearly used to accepting whatever she was given. But I remembered the effects of the potion and kept offering more until she shook her head.

That night a banquet was held to see the council members off for the Lilana break. I dressed with care, choosing a wide-necked gown that would show my necklace without emphasizing it. After helping Jera into a white gown with a green underskirt, I brushed out her straight black hair so that it gleamed upon her shoulders. Save for the green in her dress, she might have been a Qilarite princess.

When we walked into the dining room, conversations sagged as people saw us. Priasi Jin hailed us over and greeted Jera warmly.

"What is your name, little one?"

Jera looked at me. I nodded. "Jera," she said, her voice timid but clear.

Jin smiled—I knew he was thinking of the new baby granddaughter he was always going on about—and asked her the next polite question. "And your mother's name?"

"I don't know," she said matter-of-factly. "My mother died when I was a baby."

Had Jonis rehearsed her?

"Well, here you are in a palace now, " said Jin, leaning forward. "Perhaps you will dance with me in the bell dance? Such a pretty partner you'd be."

Jera looked to me. I cleared my throat. "Laiyonea feels it's not our place to join in the dancing, Minister."

He waved this off. "Oh, goat piffle. Her predecessor adored the set dances. Laiyonea herself was a fine dancer in her younger days."

I stifled a laugh at the image of Laiyonea mincing her way through one of the dances. "Perhaps another evening," I said. "Jera is still recovering, after all."

Minister Jin ruffled Jera's hair. "Another time, then. Jera, you work hard and be a good girl."

"Oh, no doubt she will," said another voice, and I turned to find Penta Rale settling into his seat next to the Trade Minister. A smile transformed his flabby features as he reached across the table and pinched out the candle at its center. He drew his fingers together, as if kneading the flame into them, and then held his flat palm out to Jera. A red kuri blossom lay there.

It was simple sleight of hand, but Jera laughed with delight. Rale tucked the blossom behind her ear. I realized that my mouth was hanging open, and I gathered my wits. "Say thank you, Jera," I said.

"Thank you," she said obediently, and giggled when Rale pulled a silly face at her. The Trade Minister laughed. I might have too, if the situation had not been so absurd. They had never treated me like that, when I had started as Tutor. But then, I wasn't young and sweet—and I didn't look like a Qilarite.

The heralds announced the king's entrance, so I hurried Jera off to our seats, my palms suddenly sweaty. Mati entered the room, stopping here and there to greet various Scholars. His gaze swept over me as he passed, and only the joyous crinkling of his eyes told me he had seen the necklace.

Fortunately I was able to escape after dessert; the strain of not looking in Mati's direction was almost impossible to bear. I dared one glance as I led Jera out of the dining room, and saw by the subtle shift of his shoulders that he was aware of my presence, though his attention did not waver from his conversation companion. My heart thrilled with delicious intimacy. I knew he would come to me as soon as he could.

I settled Jera into bed and bolted the door in case she turned out to be prone to nighttime wanderings. This time, when Mati came just after seventh bell, we held each other and spoke of love. He told me how dull his days had been without me, and I told him how I'd longed to go to him after his father's death.

"When I opened that carriage door and saw you standing there," he said, "it was as if the gods were providing just what I needed." He paused, his fingers drifting over my stomach. "I thought things would change when I became king, that I'd finally be able to prove my father wrong about me, do what I wanted." His mouth skimmed my neck. "It's not that easy though."

I tensed. We were skirting dangerously close to reminders of our different stations, and though my head knew they wouldn't go away, my heart was reluctant to deal with them.

I touched his face. "You've looked tired ever since you took the crown."

He smiled. "Half the councilors are like feuding children, and the other half are either imbeciles or are plotting against the others. I have new respect for the way my father managed them all." He paused. "Rale . . . keeps bringing up a proposal to send raiders to the islands. But I won't let that happen, Raisa, I promise. No matter what they do."

I traced the planes of his back with my hands, my throat too tight to speak for a moment. "But you have the final say," I said at last.

"Not always. A king whose own council won't back him doesn't last long in Qilara. My father always said that. I'm learning that he was right. I can force decrees out, but unless I have the council's support they won't be enforced."

"Have you?" I asked. "Forced decrees?"

Mati rolled onto his side, propping himself up on his elbow. He played with my hair as he spoke. "Well, I wanted to start with something small. I tried to reverse that ridiculous law about the Arnathim wearing green. I thought the merchants and farmers would support it—after all, kirit dye isn't cheap. Even Soraya thought it made financial sense."

I stared at him, unable to shake the image of him closeted somewhere with Soraya Gamo, talking over council matters, maybe as intimately as we were now. . . .

Mati shook his head. "She said so in council," he said, his tone a gentle reproof. "She may be annoying, but she knows money."

I flushed, knowing I had no right to feel jealous. I knew I

ought to say something lighthearted or clever, to show that I had accepted the situation for what it was, but I couldn't.

Mati gave me an apologetic half smile and went on. "But it didn't work anyway. The high priests banded together and talked it down. It happened so quickly I didn't even know they'd taken over until Laiyonea explained it to me." He laughed bitterly. "I'd hoped that repealing that law would lead into raising taxes on slave owners, but now . . . well. Maybe my father was right. Maybe I'm not cut out to be king."

His discouraged tone pulled me out of my own gloom. I touched his cheek. "Your father never would have tried to repeal that law," I said softly. "You're a better king—a better man—than he ever was."

I saw in his eyes how much my opinion meant to him. He bent down and kissed me, and there was no more talk of councils or laws that night.

Iano took the tablet to his brother Belic and spoke of a world
where the wonders of knowledge were available to all. Iano's words
wrapped around his brother's mind like the symbols unwinding
upon the tablet of the gods, and Belic's heart weighed his love for
his brother against his fear of the gods.

TWENTY-EIGHT

THE NEXT MORNING, I took Jera on a tour of the palace, ending with the Adytum. I saw it anew through her amazed eyes as she learned how to strike the surface of the firepit to kindle the sacred stone, as she ran her fingers over the quills and ink bottles in the writing chest and giggled with delight when the asotis nibbled seeds from her palm.

I was showing her how to run the metal comb through the sand to remove the hardened droppings when the gate opened below—Laiyonea, checking up on me, I thought.

But it was Mati who emerged at the top of the stairs. "I thought I'd find you here," he said. He smiled at Jera, and she ducked behind me.

"It's all right," I whispered to her. To Mati I said, "Yes, Your Majesty, I was just showing Jera around the Adytum."

The corners of his mouth quirked. "I have a bit of a dilemma. I have this lovely ball, but I cannot find a child who might like it.

Can you help me, Jera?"

Jera poked her head out curiously as Mati held up a little ball of silver. He tossed it, and it sparkled in the sunlight.

Mati knelt and held it out to her. "Would you like it?"

Jera nodded shyly, but wouldn't move until I took her hand and went with her. Finally she accepted the ball, examining it seriously.

"Say thank you, Jera," I prompted.

"Thank you," she whispered. She bounced the ball experimentally, squealing with delight when it spun across the stones.

As she dashed after it, I held out my hand to Mati and he took it, standing. "Thank you," I said. "That was very kind."

He shrugged. "It gave me an excuse to visit you."

I dropped his hand. Jera was entranced by the ball, but still . . .

I went back to the asotis, taking up the comb and smoothing the sand, mostly to have something to do with my hands. Mati shot me a knowing smile and stepped out into the sunlight. "Throw it here, Jera," he said.

She did, and a spirited tossing game ensued. Jera missed the ball most of the time, but laughed as she went tearing after it. Twice it landed in the flowers, and she came out with leaves in her hair.

I combed the sand mechanically as I watched Mati gently teasing Jera, and couldn't help thinking that he would be a wonderful father someday. As this was decidedly in the category of things I would not allow myself to think about, I pushed it away immediately. But a voice in my mind asked how this could end in anything other than more heartbreak.

"She's lively, once she opens up," Mati said, laughing, coming to stand next to me. He glanced at Jera, who was chasing the ball across the courtyard, and put his arm around my waist, dropping a quick kiss onto my cheek. I sighed, accepting my own inability to resist him.

"Yes," I said. "I think she'll do well."

Mati bent his head and murmured in my ear. "I'm to go hunting with the western vizier this afternoon, but I fear a horrible headache will prevent it. Meet me in the Library at midday bells?"

"I'll be there." It would be easy enough to draft Arlin or Mala to watch Jera for me—both the elderly servants, like everyone else in the palace, adored her.

"Oh!" came Jera's voice. Mati and I sprang apart. I turned to find her standing by a certain spray of red poppies and chamomile, clutching a beige square of paper in one hand and her ball in the other. I dashed forward and tugged the paper from her hand, babbling about how the paper must have blown into the flowers and been left accidentally. Jera seemed to want to say more—no doubt to tell me about the wad of such pages pushed in between the stones behind the plants—but I talked over her, chattering on about how important it was that everything the Tutors wrote was burned. I hurried to the firepit and stoked the flames, then dropped the paper in, watching it curl into ashes. Blood pounded in my head so hard that it blurred my vision. My codes would have meant nothing to anyone else, but still I hovered by the pit until every bit burned to ash.

When I turned from the fire, Mati was watching me, his brows lifted in amusement. I hurried forward and snatched the ball from Jera's hand. "Come, let's all play," I said, my voice falsely bright.

"Yes, Jera, let's see if Raisa can catch the ball as well as you," said Mati. I was tense for the rest of the morning, but Jera and Mati laughed and played until the luncheon bells rang and I set to cleaning up.

"I'll see you later," Mati said with a meaningful look at me. Then Jera surprised us both by wrapping her arms around his waist before dashing around the asoti cage to hide behind me.

I opened my mouth to scold her, but Mati's pleased smile stopped me. He reached behind me to tousle Jera's hair, and then left the Adytum.

At lunch, I explained to her how inappropriate such behavior was, and she sank back into meek silence. I was too distracted to make my words gentle. Mati obviously knew I'd kept papers, and didn't seem to mind. But if anyone else were to find them . . .

I knew what I had to do. I raced back to the Adytum after lunch, having seen Jera off for a walk in the garden with Mala. I snatched the coded pages from the hole by the poppies and laid them in the firepit, then whirled from cache to cache, pulling up pages from under stones, retrieving letters from the loose panel of the writing cabinet and the ridge at the top. I fed page after page into the flames, praying that none of the guards in the watchtowers would question the smoke rising, black and choking, over the Adytum. Midday bells rang, but I kept burning pages. My heart ached—I had barely gone through a third of the lower order symbols to look for those that translated to Arnath sound-based symbols. Maybe, I told myself, I could start again later, when it was safer.

I couldn't imagine it ever being safer.

Finally I came to the very last page: my heart-verse. It hung limp from my fingers as I held it over the flames for a moment that stretched into an eternity. Keeping it was too dangerous, I told myself. It always had been, but now that my writing had been found, I'd be insane not to burn it.

I dropped to my knees and smoothed the fragile paper in my lap, intending to look at it one last time. But even as I traced the symbols that my father had written so long ago, I knew that I wouldn't burn my heart-verse. I couldn't. I would have jumped into the fire myself first.

Still, it couldn't stay in the Adytum any longer. I folded it into a tiny square and shoved it into the toe of my shoe. It couldn't stay there either, but it was the best I could do for now; I didn't trust any of my former hiding places. I resolved to sew it into the lining of my shift as soon as I found myself alone with needle and thread.

Exhausted and reeking of smoke, I left the Adytum and darted down the corridor to the storeroom, wondering what I would say to Mati. My fingers found the hidden latch easily now, and it was only few seconds before the door to the Library swung open.

Mati, who'd been sitting at the desk, leaped up and came to swing me around. "I thought you weren't coming," he said into my neck, and then he was kissing me, and I was kissing him back.

He didn't bring up the incident in the Adytum until later, when we were entwined on the couch, talking between lazy kisses. "I know you were upset this morning, when Jera found—"

"Have you noticed how dusty it is in here?" I asked quickly, pointing to the frieze above us, as if I could somehow distract him from what he had seen.

Mati frowned. "I changed the Library cleaning days. It's only First and Eighth Shining now."

This startled me, and I met his eyes. "You did?"

"Of course. I wish I could do away with the platforms altogether, but . . ." He spread his hands in a helpless gesture.

But the council would use it against him. Just as they'd use it against him if they found out how he'd helped me.

My throat was tight. I almost told him then, about Linti's death, about the Resistance. But what would the softness in his eyes turn into, if he knew?

Mati will never have to know, I reminded myself. *Jonis said they wouldn't ask anything else of me, after taking Jera.*

Mati touched my cheek. "It's all right, about the papers. Just please, hide them better." He smiled wryly. "You could—"

I lifted my chin. "I burned them all," I lied. He didn't need to risk himself any more for my sake.

He visibly relaxed. "Well, then," he said, kissing my shoulder. "Nothing to worry about."

Headaches plagued the king over the next twelve days, forcing him to cancel more hunting parties, an audience with the High Priest of Qora, even a picnic with his fiancée. I claimed to spend afternoons in the Adytum, readying for Jera's lessons, while Jera romped in the gardens under Mala's supervision. Mati and I both knew we couldn't continue the afternoons in the Library once the council went back into session. But he worried about the secrecy of our nighttime meetings—though he trusted his valet, Daki, to keep his mouth shut, there was always the risk that someone else would see him. I think the deeper truth was that being together in the Library was so much like the old days, before everything had grown so complicated. He wanted to keep those fragile moments as much as I did. We even went back to reading letters together, anything to extend our time by each other's sides.

I was lucky that Jera had become so beloved in the palace. Emilana Kret didn't mind sparing Mala, when I told her it was for Jera, and I often found Priasi Jin visiting with Jera when I returned to the gardens. Once he brought his daughter and baby granddaughter to play with her. Jera was so gentle with the baby that everyone fawned over her. Jera even told me that Penta Rale came to see her sometimes, and she showed off the green hair ribbon he'd given her. So long as Jera was available to coo over, no one seemed to mind my disappearances.

One day I returned from the Library to find Laiyonea by the fountain, watching Jera digging in the dirt with Mala. Laiyonea's lips compressed as she took in my dress—I looked down and found my laces askew, and straightened them hastily.

Laiyonea stood. "Mala, stay with Jera. I need to speak with Raisa."

"Yes, Tutor," said Mala. Jera didn't even look up from her digging. I winced as I saw the mud on her dress. No doubt Laiyonea had seen it too.

Laiyonea swept past me. She didn't speak until the Adytum

gate had clanged shut behind us and I had slowly followed her up the stairs.

"I thought this nonsense was over with," she said, anger and exasperation dripping from every word.

I lifted my chin. "I don't know what you mean."

Laiyonea snorted. "You'll have to lie better than that when the council questions you."

"How does the council—"

She shook her head impatiently. "They don't, not yet. But it's only a matter of time, isn't it, with the way you two are going on. I thought *you* at least had some sense."

"I've been careful!"

Laiyonea's dark eyes narrowed. "You've been neglecting your responsibilities. Or do you think that letting her roam all over the palace gardens is proper training for a Tutor?"

"I've made sure Jera is taken care of."

"You haven't given a single thought to what that little girl needs. You've been too wrapped up in yourself."

I knew she was right, knew that the anger welling up inside of me was at myself, not at Laiyonea. But it was easier to direct it at her, since she was the one telling me that my heart's desire was selfish and wrong.

"So what will you do, report me?" I said, shocking myself with the contempt in my tone.

Laiyonea slapped my face. As I buckled onto the bench, eyes stinging with tears, I knew I had deserved it.

"Get your head out of the clouds," said Laiyonea in a low voice. "Mati needs this alliance with Gamo—or at least with his money—if he wants to keep a rein on the council. He doesn't have enough goodwill to push new ways through, not when most of the councilors still think raiding the islands every ten years is a grand idea."

"But . . . Mati said there would be no more raids."

A gleam of sympathy pierced Laiyonea's impatience. "Don't you understand, Raisa, how dangerous this is for Mati?"

I was silent as her words sank in. Our relationship had been dangerous from the beginning, but I'd always imagined that the consequences would fall on me if we were found out. It was a new and frightening thought, that Mati might suffer.

Laiyonea sighed wearily and waved me away. "Go get Jera cleaned up before dinner. And for Gyotia's sake don't let her roll in the mud anymore, or half the council will be talking about the disgraceful Tutors."

I nodded and left the Adytum.

When Gyotia learned how his sister had defied him, he smote the mountains in his anger, turning the great range south of his home to sand. And yet he relished her disobedience, for had he not goaded her to do just this, to give him righteous reason to bring the might of all the gods against her?

Gyotia called Aqil to him, saying, "Serve me well and you shall have a place high among the gods."

Aqil fell to his knees. "Whatever you ask, I shall do, mighty Father."

Gyotia smiled grimly. "Bind your mother, the traitor, and bring her to me."

TWENTY-NINE

"I WISH I could cancel this stupid banquet and carry you off to the Library right now," Mati murmured as his mouth made its way down my neck.

"We can't," I said breathlessly. "The council—"

Mati gripped my waist and pulled me closer. "Hang the council," he growled. His hand slid lower. I tensed, but no crinkle gave away my heart-verse, sewn into my shift near my right thigh. That was one advantage of paper so old and soft.

It had been four days since our last visit to the Library. Mati hadn't been able to slip away to see me at all since; the dinners, card parties, and other entertainments put on by the returning councilors over the past several days had kept him busy. I'd told him about Laiyonea's warning; he had reluctantly agreed that the headache excuse would no longer work, though he thought she was overreacting. Laiyonea herself had been frosty with both of us.

So tonight we'd met briefly in this small chamber off the main hallway; the very room, in fact, where I'd seen Emilana Kret scolding Linti. Mati had no idea how much I despised the room.

I broke away from his lips. "I have to get back. Laiyonea will never believe it took me this long to get hairpins."

Mati sighed and kissed my forehead. "Why couldn't it be Rale or Sarin retiring tonight, instead of Hait? The speeches will be *endless*. I have a surprise though—I've picked Hait's replacement." Mati tapped my cheek. "But you'll have to wait to find out, just like everyone else. You don't receive special treatment just because you're irresistible." He nibbled at my neck, making me squirm.

I gently disentangled myself from him. I pulled out the extra hairpins I'd hidden under my braid, then shook my hair out and rebraided it quickly. Tucking in the pins to flatten the waves, I turned to him.

"Do I look all right?" I asked, smoothing my dress.

"Beautiful," he murmured. My heart fluttered at his tone—how was it possible he still had that effect on me?

Mati went to the door and spoke to Daki, who confirmed that the corridor was empty before I slipped out. I didn't look at the valet as I passed—Mati trusted him, and his bland expression never betrayed a thing, but I couldn't help wondering what he thought of me.

I crept down the hall. Music and laughter spilled out of the open banquet room doors ahead, where guests were catching up on all that had happened during the council break. The corridor was quiet, only a few late arrivals hurrying into the banquet.

I slid along the wall, and, because I was sneaking, I noticed them, also sneaking. Two men, one thickset, dark-haired, and olive-skinned, wearing the fine woven tunic of a Scholar, the other thinner and taller, wearing a simple green tunic and trousers. The Scholar led the slave away from the banquet room, toward an alcove by the front doors. As he looked around, I recognized Mati's cousin, Patic. I stepped back into the shadows, something about Patic's manner making me curious. But though I strained to hear their conversation, the chatter from the banquet room blocked it out.

I'd just given up and stepped out into the light when they emerged from the alcove. "Everything is going as planned," Patic was saying cheerily. "Tell my mother I'll send word as soon as the announcement is made. Who knows? Maybe tonight."

Then the other man—a familiar, tall figure with brown hair—nodded and said quietly, "Yes, master," before leaving through the front doors of the palace.

Ris ko Karmik.

I stood rooted to the spot. Patic turned and found me there. "Tutor, are you well?" he enquired politely.

"Yes, I . . . hairpins," I squeaked, gesturing lamely at my braid. I scooted into the banquet and floundered into my seat beside Jera. Laiyonea gave me a disapproving look, but I couldn't care.

I hardly noticed anything during the meal. Eventually my jumbled thoughts resolved themselves into two solid facts:

Patic was Ris ko Karmik's master.

Ris ko Karmik had performed a special mission for the Resistance.

So did that mean Patic *was* working with the Resistance? What had he meant by "everything is going as planned"?

I chased these thoughts around and around like Jera chasing her ball, and not until the spiced oranges were served did I realize how thoroughly I had missed the key question: what exactly *was* Ris ko Karmik's mission? I'd assumed it had to do with stockpiling weapons, but now I remembered the long periods of silence from Jonis and Kiti, the troubled look in Kiti's eyes when he'd said, *We had something going on. We stayed away to keep you out of it.*

More important, I remembered *when* those periods of silence had been: around the time of King Tyno's death.

And Patic had been right there beside Mati when the hunters had left the courtyard.

Mati thought someone on the Scholars Council was behind his father's death, but what if the Resistance had done it?

I'd been automatically eating my orange, and upon this realization I inhaled sharply and choked. Laiyonea pounded my back as I gulped wine, my eyes streaming. When I was finally able to breathe, I mopped at my face with my napkin.

"Are you all right?" asked Laiyonea.

I nodded absently, my mind racing as I turned and found Patic sitting at Mati's table, laughing with Alshara Gamo. He met my eyes, then looked away.

My stomach turned to ice as I realized what he must know: that I, too, had helped the Resistance. Would he tell Mati?

Of course he wouldn't, not if he was with the Resistance himself. And what had he said in the hallway, about an announcement tonight?

I've picked Hait's replacement, Mati had said.

Of course, I thought. Of course Mati would choose his cousin to be on the council. He wouldn't care that Patic came from an olive farm instead of a country villa.

But Patic, or Ris ko Karmik with Patic's help, had killed Mati's father. No doubt they would do the same to Mati if they thought it would advance their cause. I closed my eyes, remembering Jonis's resolute face as he'd sent his sister away, as if he'd been preparing for something, ensuring her safety just as Ris had done for his family.

Mati had no idea, of that I was certain. He smiled and joked with his cousin, and the way his eyes sparkled told me he was excited to announce Patic's appointment.

I had to stop him. But how, in a room full of Scholars, with Laiyonea watching me like a hawk?

The servants began shifting tables to make room for the bell dance. My hands went cold. Hait would make his farewell speech during the desserts, after the first round of dancing. Surely Mati would make his announcement then, after Hait had been properly feted.

Priasi Jin approached Jera and took her hand. "I believe you owe me a dance, my dear."

Laiyonea's face said quite eloquently how she felt about Jera dancing. Nevertheless I seized the opportunity. "Of course, Minister," I said sweetly. "We'll both dance, though you must excuse my clumsiness, as it's my first time."

Jin nodded—I really did like that old man—and Jera looked back and forth between us as I steered her into the circle. I only had a few seconds to be embarrassed before the bells started up and I was busy trying to mimic the steps of those around me. The circle moved into two undulating lines; the Finance Minister's son became my partner. I took his hand and watched his feet, my kicks coming a fraction of a second later than anyone else's. Minister Jin had pulled Jera up so that her feet rested on his shoes, and was doing the steps for both of them as she giggled. I glimpsed Soraya Gamo's smirk as she danced by with Mati, and my face burned. Mati shot me the slightest puzzled look. I tried to convey with my expression that I had joined the dance for a reason other than humiliating myself.

Then we were back in the circle and the roundabout began. I gripped the hands of the pudgy Scholar to my left, stepping away and back, away and back, then turning three times before being passed off to the next. I had to work so hard to follow the turns that I almost didn't realize when I came to Mati. I grabbed his hand as my feet performed the repetitive steps, and began to write in his palm with my finger. Mati's eyes flicked to mine in surprise, then he stared at the wall over my head, his face relaxing into a bored, aristocratic frown. I traced the symbol "warning" into his hand. Just before I twirled away, I added a curved line across the top, the determinative that made it a command for attention.

Two partners later, I was back in my spot in the circle, Jera bouncing beside me, and it was the men's turn to do the roundabout. I focused on the steps, not allowing myself to look to the line of partners coming from the right, but I was ready when Mati got to me, and so was he. He cupped my hands loosely instead of gripping them. Immediately I launched into the next symbol: *announcement*. This was more complicated, and I hoped that the curving lines would be as clear through touch as they would have been on paper. I fervently placed the last line in place—the strike that would negate the concept of announcing—just as we came out of the third twirl. Mati moved on to the next partner. As I turned with the War Minister, Mati caught my eyes and gave a tiny nod. He'd understood.

Laiyonea's lips were pursed when Jera and I returned, breathless and sweaty, to our seats, but she said nothing. I watched the set dances, for the first time without envy. But I let Jera dance again at the women's dance, and the veiled wives helped her through it.

The speeches were just as boring as Mati had predicted. Everyone had fallen into a stupor by the time Mati rose and praised Hait's long service to Qilara—except for Patic, who perked up as Mati finished. But Mati simply ended with a blessing and bid the musicians to start again.

Patic's perplexed expression slid away as he turned back to joke with Alshara—but he left with the first wave of Scholars soon after. Relieved, I said good night to Laiyonea, ignoring the furious set of her shoulders. She must have thought my dancing was a deliberate affront to her authority or a ploy to get close to Mati. Either way, I didn't care.

I led Jera upstairs and helped her into her nightgown. Since the day Laiyonea had accused me of selfishness, I'd made a point of spending time with Jera at bedtime, talking over the day's events. Tonight, however, she was so exhausted that she fell asleep almost immediately. I blew out the lamp and crept to my room, where I changed out of my sweaty gown. Mati would come, I knew, even if it was past eighth bell before he got away.

But what could I say? More lies? He'd trusted me, but now he'd want to know why Patic was a danger.

I stared out the window, thinking hard, and still wasn't ready when he knocked an hour later. I opened the door and Mati entered. He took my hands and pulled me down to sit on the edge of the bed.

"Tell me," he said.

"Patic is working with the Resistance. I'm certain of it. And . . . he may have had something to do with your father's death."

Mati stared at me. Then his breath came out in a huff. "Those are serious accusations, Raisa. What makes you think—"

"The Resistance approached me," I whispered. "Ages ago. At the pantomime, in the basement before the other girls came in. And Jo—the man said that if I would . . . join them . . . I had to respond a certain way when someone said a phrase to me. And later, at the luncheon, Patic said the words—or something like them. It wasn't exactly the same, so I wasn't sure—"

"And how did you respond?" said Mati sharply.

I darted a look at his closed, cold face. "I pretended I didn't know what he was talking about," I confessed. "I didn't know what else to do."

Mati nodded slowly. "You could have told me about this then," he said evenly.

I hung my head. "I was afraid to. I didn't want you to think . . ." *That I was a traitor.* Hot tears stung my eyes, but I fought them back.

Mati took my hand. "I wouldn't have blamed you for those tialiks trying to use you." My skin crawled at the curse, but I tried not to let Mati see. He frowned into the distance. "But Patic? I never would have thought . . ."

I nodded miserably. "I know. That's why I didn't believe it. But he was right there with you on the hunt, Mati. It would have been easy for him to poison your father."

"Still . . . there's no proof."

I looked down, choosing my words carefully. Did Mati know that I did that when I lied? No time to worry about that now. "I saw him tonight with a man from the Resistance—one of his slaves. They sneaked into an alcove, and when they came out, Patic was saying how everything was going as planned, and talking about you announcing the council position. He's still working with them. And now they may be after you."

Mati shook his head. "Patic wouldn't—"

"Would you have suspected him capable of assassinating your father? Or joining the Resistance in the first place? I know you grew up admiring him, but you can't let that blind you to the danger."

Mati stood and paced to the window and back. He stopped and looked me in the face. "How could you have known this for so long and not told me?"

"I hoped it wasn't true . . . but when I saw him tonight, I knew it was."

Mati let out a growl of frustration. "The gods-damned Resistance again. First Tyasha, now Patic, and if they killed my father . . ." He shook his head. "But when I think of those tialiks trying to get their claws into you—"

"Stop using that word, Mati." I clenched my hands in my lap. "Or have you forgotten that I'm Arnath too?"

Mati stared at me. "You tell me they killed my father, and you want me to speak *kindly* about them?"

"Maybe . . . maybe they're doing what they feel they have to. Did that ever occur to you?" I looked down at my fists, my words coming low and fast. "I told you what it was like for me here in the palace. Think of the slaves out there. They can have their families taken from them at any time, or be whipped for just looking at someone the wrong way. Jera has scars all over her back, Mati. Tell me, what could that little girl have done to earn that? And the man who did it was perfectly within his rights, because she was his property."

He looked at me thoughtfully. "You sound like Tyasha," he said at last, his voice so neutral that I couldn't tell whether this was a good thing, in his mind, or a bad one.

I sighed. "I know this is hard for you—"

Mati gave a hollow laugh. "Hard? You have *no* idea." He flopped onto the bed. "At least for the slave I can arrange for it to be quick. The council will demand blood—in public—for a Scholar though."

My stomach turned. "Mati, I know you're angry and you want to . . . but can't you just . . . banish them?"

"This has nothing to do with what I want! I *want* my father to be alive so I don't have to deal with any of this. I *want* Qilara's treasury to be stable enough that I don't have to marry Soraya. And I *want* the woman I love to trust me enough to tell me the truth. But I don't get to have any of those things, do I? If I don't make an example of Patic I'll have ten assassins a Shining after me, and the Resistance will only gain more supporters." He sighed and rubbed his forehead. "You know I have no heart for violence—everyone knows, thanks to my father complaining about it all the time. But what I want to do isn't always what I have to do."

I nodded silently. That was what Laiyonea had been trying to tell me: Mati no longer had the luxury of following his heart. No matter how much I deluded myself in the meantime, I'd be watching him marry Soraya Gamo in forty-two days.

Mati touched my shoulder. "I'm sorry I let loose on you like that," he said quietly. "It's not your fault. It'll be all right." He took me in his arms, and I did my best to believe him.

And it did seem that it would be all right. The guards who were sent after Patic and Ris came back with the news that both had escaped, likely to Emtiria. Mati came to me at night, and we focused on the present time together, and didn't talk about what was to come.

So I was unprepared when, three days later, six guards dragged me before the council to answer charges of treason.

Much as he burned to please Gyotia, Aqil feared his mother's power. So he sent his crows to her, for she had always treated them kindly. But when she reached out to stroke them, they struck at her and bound her hands with cords they had hidden in their black plumage. Aqil dragged her before the assembled gods and stood triumphant, one foot upon her back.

Gyotia lifted the tablet. "Aqil, I name you god of sacred learning, in place of Sotia the traitorous. You shall present this tablet to Belic, who has banished his brother and pledged to revere the language of the gods evermore."

Aqil stepped forward. The moment he removed his foot from her back, Sotia leaped at Gyotia and knocked the stone tablet from his hands.

THIRTY

I WAS IN the garden with Jera when they came. My body seemed to understand before my mind did—my heart started racing as soon as I heard the clump of booted feet on the path. Then the guards emerged into the clearing, led by Captain Dimmin.

The guard captain was young for his post, and supposed to be quite handsome, but I took one look at his unsmiling face and swallowed hard. "Jera," I said, trying to keep my voice light. "Run up and see Laiyonea."

She scurried out of the garden, and the guards let her go without a glance.

"Tutor," said Dimmin, "you are summoned before the Scholars Council on charge of treason against the crown."

"I—"

Dimmin continued as though I hadn't spoken. "You will first be searched."

I felt as if I were outside my body, watching someone else rising from the bench and squeaking, "Searched?"

"Unfasten your hair," said Dimmin in a clipped voice. He motioned two of the other guards forward—there were six altogether, I took in with distant wonder. How could they think they needed six guards to control me?

Slowly I slipped the bands from my hair and shook out my braid. One of the guards seized my head and pulled roughly through the strands, and I cried out in pain.

"Nothing," he said gruffly, pushing me away.

Angry tears sprang to my eyes. What did they think would be hiding in my hair?

Dimmin gave a businesslike nod. "Now unfasten your dress."

I lifted my chin defiantly, but before I had a chance to protest, Dimmin gestured to the two men. The shorter one, leering, untied the laces of my dress in a single swift movement and pushed it off my shoulders. It puddled at my feet and I stood before them in only my shift.

Fear sliced through my anger now. *Stay calm*, I told myself. They had no way of knowing what was sewn into my shift. And surely they wouldn't expect me to strip naked. Surely, even though I was Arnath, my post as Tutor would protect me from that humiliation.

"Continue," said the guard captain in a hard voice. Instinctively, stupidly, I fought the firm hands that raised my shift over my head, trapping my arms inside. My stomach lurched with hot humiliation as I heard a rude comment from the shorter guard and guffaws from the others. I struggled harder, and heard fabric ripping.

They pulled the shift over my head, leaving me completely naked. My cheeks hot, I grabbed the dress at my feet and held it over myself. I wanted to curse at them, but I didn't dare utter a word.

Then my gaze fell on the torn shift in the shorter guard's hand and my breathing stopped. The careful stitches of my added, hidden pocket might have gone unnoticed—if the garment's side seam had not split in my struggles, leaving a soft edge of pale paper protruding from the tear.

"Give me that," said Dimmin sharply. "The council will want to see this. Bring her along."

Silently I drew my dress over my head and let the guards lead me back to the palace.

It was over, all over. I had told Mati that I had burned all my writing. How could I explain this?

We arrived before the closed doors of the council chamber. Dimmin knocked and spoke to the servant who answered.

I heard Mati's voice from inside the room. ". . . outlaw such methods as inhumane and—" The words were cut off as the door clicked shut.

The doors reopened a moment later and I was thrust inside. The guards deposited me in the middle of the floor, then stepped back, pointing their swords at me.

"What is the meaning of this?" said Mati sharply. I couldn't look at him.

Penta Rale rose lazily from his chair. I darted a glance around the room and saw the other councilors whispering and sharing looks of consternation. Soraya Gamo, in her spangled scarf, watched me with narrowed eyes.

Rale lifted his hands, and the whispers ceased. He produced a bundle of cloth—my shift—from which he withdrew a folded sheet of paper. I gritted my teeth at the sight of my heart-verse in those fat fingers.

"I submit evidence of treachery from this . . . Tutor." The word was an epithet in Rale's bland voice. "This page was found in her undergarment."

Mati's eyes ran over my rumpled dress and disheveled hair, and he rose angrily. "And who ordered such a search?"

"Why, I did, Your Majesty," said Rale. "You see, it was something that dear child Jera mentioned that first raised my suspicion. She told me of finding papers hidden in the Adytum, and asked me, as innocent children will when bewildered by the actions of their elders, why pages would be hidden there when everything written in that space is to be burned." He aimed a poisoned smile at me. "Why, indeed, Tutor?"

The eyes of the entire council turned on me. "Perhaps they were left by accident," I said, my voice like a creaky door.

Rale raised his eyebrows. "And this sheet *accidentally* fell into your garment? Do not insult this council with lies." He turned to the others with a sweeping gesture. "When I searched the Adytum and her rooms and found nothing, I concluded that she had secreted the pages on her person."

"You overstep yourself," said Mati, voice even but hands clenched into fists at his sides. "The Adytum, the palace, and the Tutors are all the property of the crown, and you had no right to search any of them." I flinched at his choice of words. *He's a fine actor*, I reminded myself.

Rale smiled unpleasantly. "Why, Your Majesty, this offense is an affront to the gods themselves. As High Priest of Aqil, I felt it my duty to investigate. My responsibility to the god outweighs my adherence to mortal law."

"Convenient, that," remarked Mati drily.

Out of the corner of my eye, I saw Minister Jin give a tiny shake of his head. Mati must have seen it too, because he looked around at the faces of the councilors and fell silent.

"It puzzles me, Your Majesty, that no one asks about the *content* of the page," Rale said.

Mati inhaled sharply, as though he had realized that ought to have been his first question. I flushed, Laiyonea's warnings whispering through my mind. Had I given Rale the ammunition with which to ruin Mati? I fiddled with the thong at my neck, twitching the stone under my gown. Mati noticed, and sent me a swift look that told me to keep quiet.

"Well, what of the content?" said the High Priest of Qora. "Its mere existence is enough to condemn her, yes?"

"Indeed," said Rale. "However, the Tutor appears to have

written in *code*. Suspicious, yes?" He held up my heart-verse, the corner tearing in his rough grip. I suppressed a whimper.

Mati drew himself up and spoke so regally that he might have been channeling his father's spirit. "You say you were serving your god. Need I remind you that your king counts High Priest of Gyotia among his titles? How do you know that this page is not written in the higher order script, which, as priest of a lesser god, is forbidden to you?"

Rale's eyes widened. "I have no way of knowing that, of course, Your Majesty. I assumed that the code was part of the Tutor's treachery."

Mati held out his hand imperiously, and Rale gave him my heart-verse. My breathing eased as soon as the sheet was in Mati's hand. Mati skimmed the page, and I could see him trying to decide which the councilors would find a worse crime: me carrying a coded page, or me carrying a page written in the higher order symbols. If he told them that it was higher order writing, they would have to accept his word, wouldn't they? Had Rale grown so bold that he would dare to compare it to the writing in the Library of the Gods, and call out his king's lie?

Mati apparently thought so. "This is nonsense," he said. "Not even real writing. You are wasting this council's time."

Rale gave a little bow. "I thought it too unbeautiful to be the language of the gods," he said. "But she has still broken the law by failing to burn it. And dare we overlook the possibility that this is a coded message? After all, her predecessor shared the language of the gods with others, and was caught passing messages to the Resistance. If it is indeed nothing, then why would the Tutor take such steps to conceal it?" The other councilors murmured in agreement.

Mati looked like he wanted to throttle Rale right there in open council. "Perhaps," he said through gritted teeth, "we should ask the Tutor." He turned to me. "Raisa ke Margara," he said, so loudly that his voice rang off the stone wall behind me, making me wince. "What is the meaning of this?" His eyes bored into mine, seeming to plead, *Whatever lie you tell, make it a good one.*

"It was . . . a training exercise for Jera, Your Majesty," I said, the huge room swallowing my trembling voice. "To help her learn to use the quills. I was . . . afraid I would forget the idea if I did not save the page."

Mati turned to Rale, a little too quickly. "Do you still see sinister purpose here?"

Rale eyed me greedily. "Exactly the kind of excuse we might expect from one passing information to our enemies."

Mati looked around quickly. "Nevertheless, treason against the crown requires that the crown see evidence of treason. I see none." He crossed the room in three strides and dropped my heart-verse into the firepit.

Aqil threw his mother to the ground, while Lanea retrieved the tablet. When she presented it to Gyotia, he saw that a large piece of stone was missing from the center.

Gyotia turned on Sotia. "What have you done with it?" he demanded.

Sotia refused to say a word.

THIRTY-ONE

MY HORRIFIED GASP echoed around the chamber. I felt them all watching me, but I couldn't school my expression. I closed my eyes and hid behind my hair.

"No evidence, sire?" said Rale; I knew he was indicating my reaction, but I couldn't look at him, couldn't look at Mati, couldn't look at the smoke rising from the firepit.

Obal Tishe's gentle, reasonable voice came from my left. "We must remember that this Tutor was chosen by the gods through the oracle."

Rale snorted. "As was the last one."

"Indeed," said Tishe mildly, his gaze on Rale, "the choices of the gods can sometimes be baffling." He let his words hang in the air for a few seconds before continuing. "Nevertheless, this council cannot contradict the will of the gods without significant evidence. If she had passed messages to our enemies, surely we would have seen the results of such treachery. Has there been an increase in Resistance activity?"

Mati, who had been looking thoughtfully at me, roused himself and gestured to someone behind me. "Dimmin, report."

Captain Dimmin stepped past me, bowing to Mati. "Disruptions in the city have been minimal since the coronation, Your Majesty. Other than the escape of the traitor Patic Kone and his slave, we have seen no sign of the Resistance at all. As I reported previously, our attempt to bait them with the weapons shipment at the pass failed."

I tensed as Mati's brow crinkled. I didn't have to wonder whether he remembered telling me about his guard captain's plan to entrap the Resistance; I could see that he had already made that particular connection.

Mati's eyes fell on someone to my left, and I turned to see a dark-haired scribe crouched beside Minister Jin, murmuring in the old man's ear.

"What is it?" said Mati sharply.

"Terin has relevant information, Your Majesty," said Minister Jin.

"Speak," Mati barked at the scribe, who stood and straightened his tunic. A wave of dizziness passed over me as I realized why his face was familiar—I had seen it, close up, from my hiding place in the corner of the records room, and my heart had constricted with fear then too.

Terin bowed his head. "Your Majesty, councilors, some time ago I discovered rodent damage in our storage area, and the record of Eral Kone's holdings was among the most damaged. The entire slave listing was gone. At the time, we assumed that it was the work of mice, but with his son's escape, I now fear that someone tampered with our records."

Mati's eyes slowly moved to my face, and I saw him replaying our conversation after I'd been caught in the basement corridor, and my warnings about Patic after the banquet. Any minute now he would realize, if he hadn't already, that I'd avoided explaining exactly how I knew that Patic's slave was with the Resistance, that the only way I could have known was if I'd had more contact with them than I had let on.

Mati turned abruptly to Rale. "When did you find the paper on her?"

Rale seemed to be suppressing a grin. "Just before she was brought here, Your Majesty."

Mati nodded stonily. My stomach dropped, and I understood with miserable clarity what he must be thinking—I had told him ages ago that I'd burned all the pages, so what else had I lied about?

I stared at Mati, willing him to look at me. If only he would look at me, I might be able to tell him, somehow, that it wasn't what it seemed.

Mati spoke to the guards, his gaze arrowing past me. "Take the Tutor to her room while the council discusses this matter."

"Post a guard outside her door," added Rale. Mati slowly nodded his agreement.

Still he would not look at me.

The guards pulled me away amid murmurs from the councilors. I couldn't bear it, the way Mati's eyes had gone cold and his face had become an indifferent mask. "Mati," I called, unable to hold the cry back any longer.

The anguished sound caused him to meet my eyes for a split second, but then he turned away, and I was hauled through the doors and along the corridor.

I didn't even realize I was crying until the guards shoved me into the sitting room and I collapsed on the flowered rug.

"Raisa! What happened?" Laiyonea helped me into a chair. I was vaguely aware of Jera sitting across the room.

He wouldn't even look at me. Why wouldn't he look at me?

"Raisa?" said Laiyonea, alarm in her tone. "Jera said the guards came for you . . . but if you're here . . ."

"They did," I choked out. "I was taken before the Scholars Council."

Laiyonea sucked in a breath. "Someone found out about you and Mati?"

I shook my head, closing my eyes against the image of my heart-verse vanishing into smoke. Despair threatened to over-whelm me. "No, I—I'd kept a page of writing. Rale had me searched and . . . they found it."

Laiyonea's face was stormy now, so I looked away from her and saw Jera. The little girl wore the same arrested look she had in the weaver's stall as she'd tried to follow the adult conversation that would send her to the Selection.

A bright green ribbon gleamed in her hair. That had been a gift from Penta Rale. He'd visited her in the gardens, had doted on her just like the others. But Laiyonea had warned me that Rale hated Tutors. Why hadn't I put the pieces together?

I beckoned to Jera. She came to me solemnly. Whatever happened to me, I wanted her to know it wasn't her fault, but how to say so without making her realize what her questions to Rale had done? So I just held her for a long moment, then said, "Jera, go to your room. Laiyonea and I need to talk."

She nodded and left. I waited for the click of the second door before I spoke again.

"There's more," I said, staring at the floor. Haltingly I told her of how I had helped the Resistance, and how Mati had behaved when he'd realized my lies. Tears came again as I recounted it. "Please, Laiyonea, go to him. Tell him he has to let me explain. He wouldn't even look at me. He thinks I betrayed him."

"Didn't you?" said Laiyonea coldly. Her nostrils flared. "Romantic foolishness I knew you were capable of, but this!" She shook her head. "I *defended* you after Mati was seen leaving your window. Tyno would have sent you away. I told him it was too late to train another girl. I told him you were nothing like . . . and Mati, he lied for you too. Gave quite a performance to convince his father that you wanted nothing to do with him." Her lip curled. "A shame that you turned out not to be worth the effort."

Her words were like a blow to the stomach. "I was only trying to help those children—"

Laiyonea gripped my arm, baring her teeth. "If I had known, I would have turned you in myself."

I leaned away, horrified. I had seen Laiyonea displeased, angry, disapproving . . . but this was something else entirely. Palpable hatred rolled off her.

Laiyonea opened her mouth to say more, but a sharp knock

at the door cut her off. Captain Dimmin stepped into the room. "Come with me, Tutor," he said, no hint of emotion in his voice. I stood and smoothed my rumpled dress. Laiyonea crossed her arms and turned away.

So I gritted my teeth and followed the guard captain. He didn't grip my arm like the others had; oddly, that made him more, not less, intimidating. Two more guards fell into step behind us as we descended the stairs.

They took me through the entrance hall, their footsteps ringing in the silence. The council chamber doors stood open, and the room was empty. I didn't have time to wonder about this, because Captain Dimmin opened the outer doors and gestured me through.

I stepped out, and would have backed up if he hadn't been directly behind me. Assembled silently in the courtyard below were half the council—I saw most of the high priests, and Soraya Gamo standing by her father—as well as rows of guards and a smattering of Qilarite servants. A knot of Arnath children stood behind Emilana Kret.

Mati wasn't there.

The guard captain pushed me forward and I stumbled down the steps. Penta Rale stepped out from the line of high priests, his watery eyes bright. My stomach lurched.

"As Aqil's representative," he boomed, "and on behalf of the Scholars Council, I hereby strip this slave of her title. Where once stood a Tutor, see now only a slave."

I had expected this, of course. Once Rale's words would have made me cower in terror, but now all I felt was numb disbelief.

Losing my post was the least of my concerns.

Rale couldn't conceal his delight as he went on. "As this slave has disobeyed her master, we offer a fitting punishment. Such disobedience must be met with swift and effective discipline. . ."

He went on for some time in this vein, clearly enjoying the sound of his own voice, but I tuned him out and looked around again. Where was Mati? I recognized a young guard in the second row, the one who had found me in the scribe rooms. He was watching Rale, his brow furrowed.

Which made me realize I ought to be paying attention. ". . . as a demonstration to all her kind," Rale was finishing as I turned my attention back to him. My heart stuttered to a stop, then pounded in my chest.

Was this to be my execution? But even that thought couldn't block out the insistent refrain: Where was Mati?

The world seemed to slow, the voices around me to distort. Rale spoke to Captain Dimmin, who took my arm—his grip iron, inescapable, but somehow still not ungentle—and led me to a stone pillar at the side of the steps. I turned to find that the other two guards had followed as well. At a word from their captain, the other two took my hands and dragged me forward so that I was hugging the pillar. I struggled, too late, as they tied my wrists together.

But I still didn't realize what was happening—not until I twisted my head around and saw the guard captain calmly raising a whip.

Gyotia, furious at Sotia's silent insolence, pulled a branding rod out of the air and handed it to Aqil. Its end smoked with unseen fire. "Mark this traitor, and we shall have done with her."

Aqil pressed the rod to his mother's cheek without hesitation. She stiffened, silent tears pouring down her face.

The high cry of an asoti echoed in the valley below.

THIRTY-TWO

I HAD ONE moment of agonizing dread, and then there was just agony. The first lash sliced through my thin dress like a knife through pudding, leaving a slash of fire across my back. I gasped and choked back a cry, forming a deluded resolution not to scream.

That resolution held until perhaps the fourth lash—or was it the fifth? I lost count as I clutched the cold stone and my world narrowed to the endless cycle of a whoosh, then pain, a whoosh, then more pain.

I am certain I screamed and begged for mercy. My vision darkened and I sagged against the pillar, the only thing anchoring me to reality as pain exploded around me, unending and inescapable. I wished for death—anything to stop the relentless rending of my body.

In the distance, between the whistles that brought more

agony, and more, I now heard a voice, angry and loud. Then more voices, and then—it seemed years later, but it couldn't have been—I was being dragged and jostled. I screamed as something pressed my shredded back, and finally I fell into darkness.

Once or twice the darkness lifted and I was aware of something soft under me, a distant scent of willow bark, someone holding water to my lips. I drank, but the effort sent pain like shards of glass scraping down my body, and I groped for unconsciousness. In the darkness I tumbled through hazy images—fire flaring in the dark Library, stones on the shore, a timid girl raising a blank tablet with a gouged center. A dark-haired woman, her heart-shaped face sad, her whispered words incomprehensible but her eyes begging me to understand.

Gradually I came to awareness, but the woman's face, so familiar, lingered in my mind. It was a kind face—was it my mother? I took a deep breath, trying to think, and coughed hard, the movement sending excruciating spasms through my body. I groaned, and became aware that my face was mashed into a soft pillow, a puddle of drool chilling my cheek. A sudden pressure caused one of the raw, throbbing places on my back to blossom with pain. I whimpered, wincing away.

I turned to see who my tormenter was. My heart rose and then immediately fell when I realized that the face was not the one I'd been hoping for, and I closed my eyes again in despair.

"She's awake, sire," said a quiet voice.

Footsteps approached the bed. "Wait outside," said another voice, one that sent a flock of emotions skittering through me. Mati.

"But I need to apply—"

"I'll do it," said Mati.

A door opened and closed, and someone settled into a chair nearby. Something cool touched my back, so gently that I only winced the tiniest bit at the contact on my tattered skin.

I forced my eyes open and focused on Mati. His hair was messy, his face haggard.

Mati met my eyes. "How do you feel?"

"Like . . ." I lifted my head and pushed the sodden pillow away, and wished I hadn't moved. I gritted my teeth through bolts of pain, pressing my face into the bed.

A cool hand touched my forehead. "The fever's gone," said Mati. "You've been delirious for two days."

I took this in. "I don't understand . . . why I wasn't executed."

Mati stayed silent for so long that I had to open my eyes to see his face. He was still looking at me neutrally, but I saw something break in his eyes. "Rale had no proof of anything."

He was still trying to believe in me, even now. It was almost too much to bear. "But I did help the Resistance," I croaked. "You know I did."

Mati only slumped back in the chair, looking exhausted. I pressed my forehead into the bed. Only when I felt the cold, damp sheet below my face did I realize that I was crying.

Mati didn't say anything, only took up a tub of ointment and began to apply it gently to my wounds. For some time the only sound was my pathetic shuddering sobs.

"How long?" Mati finally said, when I had subsided into

sniffles. I looked up at him, but his attention was on his hands at my back. "The whole time we—does that mean you were—" His fingers pressed too hard into a gash near my spine, and I cried out.

Mati pulled back and put down the pot of ointment as if it had burned him, then wiped his hands on a rag.

"No," I said, once my breathing had calmed. "I told you the truth before, just not . . . all of it. I turned them down at the pantomime, but they didn't leave me alone after. They sent me that quill, and then they cornered me at the Festival of Qora earlier this year. They said they needed my help to save Arnath children. I . . . couldn't say no."

Mati sat back and folded his arms. "You're not sorry." The words were an accusation.

"I'm Arnath, Mati. I *was* one of those children." I met his eyes. "But I am sorry that I lied to you. And about . . . your father . . ." The image of King Tyno, lying in the carriage with a hole in his chest, flashed through my mind, and I stifled another sob.

Mati's face went stony. Fear and guilt and pain swirled through me so violently that I thought I might vomit, but I owed him the truth. I started to explain about destroying Ris ko Karmik's record to clear the way for his mission.

But my words trailed off as I saw it: the exact moment when his ability to believe the best about me ran out. How hard had he worked, while I'd been unconscious, to convince himself that the things he knew didn't add up to what he thought they did? It took me back to the council chamber, when he'd turned so cold and wouldn't look at me, only this was a thousand times worse, because now he looked right at me and knew exactly how I had betrayed him.

Abruptly he went to the door. "I'll send the doctor in."

I pushed myself up onto my elbows. "Mati, wait, I—"

"Be quiet, Raisa," he said, his back to me. I couldn't see his face, only his hand gripping the doorknob. "I can't stand another word from you right now. How can I know which ones are true?"

He pulled the door open and went out. I sank down onto the bed, my eyes and nose streaming. When the door opened again, I lifted my head hopefully, but it was only the doctor, returning to finish applying the ointment. I flinched and cried so much that he insisted I drink some foul-smelling black medication to make me sleep. I gulped it, and welcomed the sensation of my eyelids drooping and conscious thought leaving me.

The gods locked Sotia behind walls of stone, even as the ships carried Iano and his followers into their banishment. The other gods drifted away from the mountaintop, until only Lanea and Suna were left gazing at the roiling sea in the distance.

"Wisdom is gone," murmured Lanea.

"Wisdom is but imprisoned," said Suna dreamily. "And every prison must have a key."

Lanea looked at her quickly. Had Suna guessed how much Lanea had known of her husband's plans, and what she had done in the guise of serving him? She clutched the object in her pocket. "That matters little," she whispered, "if no one is brave enough to turn it."

THIRTY-THREE

EACH TIME I woke, I looked for Mati, but he was never there. Sometimes the doctor or one of his assistants was nearby, torturing my back with their rags or ointments. I was afraid to ask how much time had passed or whether Mati had come again, and I gladly took their horrible-tasting medicine and fell back to sleep.

And then one evening I woke with my head clear enough to think, clear enough to remember exactly the way Mati's shoulders had hunched when he had walked out, exactly how I had lied to him at every turn and earned that reaction. My neck ached from the way I'd been positioned on my stomach, so I rolled up onto my side. I caught sight of the gilt-edged side table, and realized for the first time that I was in the king's suite, in the very four-posted bed that I'd glimpsed so long ago when Mati first showed me the secret passage to the Library of the Gods.

The door opened, and I turned to ask the doctor for more medicine, to drown this newest wave of pain in forgetfulness— but it was Mati who had stopped just inside the room. He was properly groomed and dressed now, as though he had just returned from a council meeting.

"You came back," I said softly. "I wasn't sure you would. You were so angry. . . ."

His cheek twitched, and I rethought my use of the past tense. He closed the door, slowly, deliberately, and stayed facing it, as if he couldn't bear to look at me.

I spoke quickly; he might not give me another chance. "I never meant to hurt you. I didn't know what the Resistance was really doing. They told me—they always told me—that it was to help Arnath children."

There was a long silence, and then finally he approached the bed. A chair waited there, but he did not sit, only rested one hand on the back of it and looked at me. "Jera?" he said evenly. "Was that why you selected her even though—"

I flinched. "Yes, I agreed to take her and keep her safe, and I haven't had contact with them since. But she doesn't know any-thing. She's just a little girl." I gasped, suddenly fearful. "Where is she?"

"Laiyonea's got her. She's taking over Jera's training."

Because I was no longer a Tutor. My chest tightened, and I groaned and rolled onto my stomach. "Laiyonea hates me. She said she would have turned me in herself if she'd known."

"She probably would have," he said matter-of-factly. "She despises the Resistance, because of Tyasha. Laiyonea has many opinions about both of our acts of stupidity, but she's keeping her mouth shut and focusing on the current problems instead."

"Current . . . problems?" I asked.

He didn't answer, and I turned to find him measuring me with his eyes, assessing whether he could trust me all over again. I deserved that, but it still hurt.

"Please tell me what's going on," I pleaded.

"Rale," he said at last. "He and the other priests have been stirring up anti-Arnath sentiments ever since my father's death. All except Tishe." He gave a bitter laugh. "I'm surprised, actually, that Rale didn't accuse the Resistance of assassinating my father. He probably thought one of his own conspirators was behind it, and didn't want to raise suspicions. But now . . . the story of my torrid affair with an Arnath Tutor is on the lips of every Scholar and peasant from the city to the western sea, as proof that I am unfit to rule, just as my father always said."

I looked up at him, but he was focused on the door, as if contemplating walking out again. "They know about us?"

"Rale already suspected," Mati answered flatly. "That's why he arranged for the . . . spectacle in the courtyard so quickly, and didn't stop Kirol from coming to get me. Rale *wanted* me to stop it, to make a scene and reveal how I felt about you."

Felt. Mati was using the past tense.

But . . . if he had intervened . . .

"You made them stop," I said weakly.

"Yes. The sentence was one hundred lashes. When I arrived, Rale was counting the fifty-sixth."

One hundred lashes—that was a moderate punishment for slaves in the city. Fifty was light, meted out for minor offenses. Yet here I was, days later, still barely able to move. How many slaves had endured this agony again and again? How many times had Jonis and Jera been whipped? I shuddered.

"I should have seen it coming," Mati went on, his voice unsteady. "The council agreed to a lesser punishment, as long as I made some concessions on . . ." He paused, as if reminding himself that he couldn't trust me with more than the barest details. ". . . on some other issues. The fact that it was a whipping was a message to me, because I'd been trying to outlaw it. Laiyonea told me it was stupid to try to push it through now, but I didn't think . . ." He sighed. "I had no intention of letting them do it. Rale must have guessed that, because as soon as I went to deal with . . . something else . . . he went off and—"

"So you stopped them, even though you knew they would use it against you?" Something large and unwieldy seemed to be making its way through my chest.

My words hung there, accompanied only by the rasp of my breath.

"Soraya left two days ago," Mati said at last. "She wanted the betrothal dissolved, but her father refuses to relinquish his claim. He knows I need his money, and I know he's in league with Rale. Rale had hoped my father would name him regent,

I think—Father hinted that he would appoint one, me being so unsatisfactory, but he died before he had a chance. So now, I think . . . Rale is working up a coup."

Even now, Mati was too good to come out and say it, but this was the answer to my question. He had effectively thrown away his crown when he'd stepped between me and Captain Dimmin's whip.

The lump in my throat seemed to be made of stone, and I had to fight to speak. "You should have let them finish, pretended you didn't care—"

"That was never going to happen," he said, his voice steely.

I looked up at him, tears pricking my eyes, but he was already turning away, muttering about calling the doctor in. I couldn't let him leave; there were still more truths I owed him. "Mati, there's . . . something else I need to tell you."

He turned back, his eyes cautious, as if he were bracing himself. He hovered behind the chair, his knuckles white as he gripped the top of it. I wished that he would sit, but I didn't have the right to ask him to.

"The page . . . that the guards found in my shift," I said. "I didn't write that. My father did." I waited, but Mati didn't speak, so I went on. "He gave it to me when I was six. It was a special message, my heart-verse. That was the tradition on the Nath Tarin, at least among the families of . . . the Learned Ones."

He stared at me. "But . . . if you're . . . how did you survive?"

"My mother sent me to her friend when the raiders came. Margara told them that I was her daughter." I took a deep breath. "My real name is Raisa ke Comun." I hadn't said those words out loud in nearly twelve years, and my skin tingled at the sound. "My heart-verse was all I had left of my father. I've been trying for years to decode it. That's what the pages in the Adytum were, me trying to figure out the Arnath writing. And when Jera found one, I panicked. I burned those, but I couldn't bear to burn my heart-verse, so I . . . hid it in my shift."

"What did it say?"

"I don't know," I said, my voice a thin, anguished cry. "I was never able to read it."

"I'm . . . sorry," whispered Mati.

"It's not your fault."

"Why didn't you just hide it in the Library?" he said with an edge of anger. "It would have been safe there."

I gaped at him. Why hadn't I thought of that? Only Mati and I ever went in there—except for the guards and children on cleaning day, and I knew firsthand what happened when one of them disturbed anything.

But I knew the answer at once, and I was ashamed. It hadn't occurred to me to hide my heart-verse in the Library for the same reason it never occurred to half the slaves in the city that they could run from their masters. Were we all like the asotis in the courtyard, bound by imagined bars?

"I didn't . . . think of that," I said weakly. If I'd trusted Mati with this secret sooner, maybe I wouldn't have brought us both to ruin. I turned to look him full in the face. "I know that you're still angry with me. But . . ." I took a deep breath, and my next words took more bravery than any trip into the scribe rooms ever had. "Can you ever forgive me?"

He inclined his head in something that was nearly a nod. But then he cleared his throat and moved toward the door again. "I have to go," he said briskly. "I'll send the doctor in to check on you."

The next few days passed in a haze; they must have put sleep herbs in the broth they fed me. Once I lay half awake listening to Mati, out in the anteroom, talking with a woman whose voice made my stomach clench with guilt, though I couldn't quite place it.

"Is a stricter curfew really necessary?" she said.

"The council felt it a necessary precaution," said Mati's voice woodenly. "After the raid yesterday."

"Those executions were aimed at you. They will press you until you respond."

"How am I to respond?" Mati snapped. "I've already given them enough to damage me."

"You'll be vulnerable as long as they can use her against you," said the other voice. "That's why they didn't execute her, you know. You should send her away, immediately."

"Where shall I send her? She won't be safe anywhere."

The woman sighed. "But keeping her here puts you both in danger."

The silence stretched out, and I fell back to sleep listening for his response.

The next time I woke, morning sun slanted through the windows. I stretched, working my stiff neck back and forth, then luxuriated in a face-splitting yawn.

The sound drew pattering feet from the next room, and then Mati was framed in the doorway, shirtless, a brown tunic in one hand.

"Feeling better?" he said. I searched his face for clues about what he was thinking, but he'd kept his expression and his voice both carefully even.

"Yes," I said. My body was far less achy than it had been, but I frowned at how grimy I was. "How long have I been here?"

"Six days," he replied, his tone still businesslike. "The physician said the wounds would start to scab over and the pain would be less now. Are you hungry?"

I nodded, aware of a ferocious emptiness in my stomach. Then his words hit me. *Six days*. "Where is . . . are you still . . . ?"

He slipped his tunic over his head, and his voice came to me slightly muffled. "Still king, for the moment, though Rale is doing his best to change that. I'll send for some food, and arrange for a bath, in here. It's best if you stay here for now."

He disappeared into the adjoining room and came back with a pair of boots, which he sat to put on.

I had a thousand questions, but as I was trying to figure out how to frame them so that they wouldn't make him angry, there was a sharp knock at the door. I did not miss the way Mati tensed at the sound. I pulled the blanket up to my chin as he opened the door.

Laiyonea stepped into the room. I fought a childish urge to dive under the blanket, but her cold gaze only swept over me and returned to Mati.

"Jin's man intercepted a message from Pira," she said. "Gamo's coachman arrived there last night on foot, reporting an attack on the western road. Armed men in green. He claimed he was the only one to escape."

Mati sat down hard in the chair and rested his forehead on the heel of his hand.

"I don't understand," I said timidly.

"It means," said Laiyonea frostily, "that your *friends* in the Resistance have kidnapped, and possibly killed, Soraya Gamo."

With Sotia gone, the other gods only occasionally read the scrolls of the world in their great library, for the doings of mortals interested them little. However, they assured one another that sometime—when they got around to it—they would read out the scrolls and call each being to account for its deeds and misdeeds.

THIRTY-FOUR

THE REST OF the day was miserable. Once the promised meal and bath were done—the servants were all polite to me, but none would quite meet my eyes—I was alone. Mati had left with Laiyonea to arrange a search party for Soraya.

I hadn't known what to say to Mati. What *can* you say when you've destroyed someone's life, but that someone won't hold you accountable for it?

Laiyonea had turned away as if she couldn't bear the sight of me. Less than a Shining ago, her quiet nod of approval would have been enough to lighten my heart. Now I would never see it again.

I had plenty of time alone with my guilt. I spent the afternoon looking out the window to where the white-capped waves faded into a green roiling line. I traced the symbol on the stone hanging around my neck and wondered bleakly what my father would think of what I'd done. I believed that my parents would have loved Mati, even if he was Qilarite. They would have seen beyond olive skin and black hair to the good man he was. So why couldn't people like Jonis see that?

Ah, but that question was far too easy to answer: because Qilarites rarely saw past pale skin and curly hair. Even if Mati's proposed changes had gotten through the council, would Jonis and the others trust that Mati was trying to do good?

I left the window and cast around for something to do. If only I had some quills to sharpen—but then, Laiyonea probably would think me unfit for that task now. I wasn't a Tutor anymore, after all. Even the white and green gown the servant had handed me after my bath, previously one of my favorites, seemed to fit all wrong, as if it knew I was no longer the same girl who'd worn it before.

Restlessly I wandered into an alcove off the main room and found a desk stocked with writing materials. Carefully, to keep my dress from pulling at my still-tender back, I sat and selected a sheet of paper. I dipped a quill into the ink and held it suspended over the page.

My heart-verse was gone, but surely the symbols were still there in my mind, after years spent staring at them. Weren't they?

The first symbol, at least, I knew. I drew my stone necklace out and copied its symbol onto the paper, my hand shaking. The result would have made Laiyonea order me to write it again fifty times, but I ignored the pang that thought gave me and moved on. The second symbol had a vertical line on the left, didn't it? And then a large curve? But did the curve touch the line, or was there a gap? *Keep going,* I told myself. The next symbol I was fairly sure of: a series of arches stacked atop one another. Then another vertical line, with a curve facing away from it . . . and there had been curving lines over some of the symbols, hadn't there? Experimentally I drew a few, but none of it looked right.

A hollow feeling in my chest, I wiped the quill on the blotter, then closed the bottle and crumpled the paper in my fist. I looked down at my hand, reminded of . . . but the memory fled as quickly as it came.

I noticed a small pile of scrolls at the edge of the desk. The paper was not the thick writing stock of the king, but a thinner, yellowish kind.

I hesitated, but curiosity overwhelmed me. Slowly I unrolled one scroll and laid it flat, dropping weightstones at the corners. The writing was small and even, with a measured swoop that gave the sense of a proud, meticulous writer. I leaned forward and read.

It is not a question of the gain to this or any other empire, but of the acceptable cost of such gain. It is time to examine frankly the relationship of master to slave, slave to master, and to recognize that the subjugation of one does damage to both. The very conception that another is one's property destroys the inherent humanity in the master, as well as the slave. Surely each of us can think of a man (or woman, for the damaging effects are not limited) who, though otherwise compassionate, generous, and honest with his own kind, acts as a merciless tyrant to his slaves. This happens because his heart

>recognizes that the slave breathes, bleeds, eats,
>loves, lives—just as he does. He resorts to cruelty to
>reassure himself that the slave is the other.

"Raisa?" Mati's voice around the corner was sharp, worried.

I started. I'd been so absorbed in the scroll that I hadn't heard the door. Sweeping the weightstones away, I let the scroll reroll itself as I leaped up from the chair, gasping at the lance of pain in my back. "I'm here," I said breathlessly.

Mati came around the corner. I realized, too late, that the scroll was a foot to the left of where it ought to have been, and my crumpled paper still lay in plain sight. I flushed.

The disappointment on Mati's face was an all-too-familiar sight of late. "You don't have to snoop around. If you'd asked I would've let you read anything there."

"I'm sorry," I whispered, feeling ashamed—and stupid—at both prying and trying to hide it. I cleared my throat. "I was . . . trying to rewrite my heart-verse, but . . ." I scooped up my crumpled page and turned to take it to the firepit.

Mati tugged the paper out of my grip, then smoothed it out on the desk and looked over my badly written symbols. "Is it so different from our writing?"

Our writing. He was including me in that. I wasn't sure how that made me feel. "The Arnath symbols stand for sounds, not words. Like this first one—that means *sa*, like in my name." I held out my necklace. "Remember this?"

He looked from the page to the stone. "But it's just a coincidence," he said.

"I suppose," I answered, looking down at the stone.

"Why didn't you tell—" Mati broke off, then shook his head and handed me the paper, like he didn't want to know any more about my petty deceptions.

"Mati . . . I didn't—"

But he only scooped up the scroll and said lightly, "So what were you reading?" He unrolled it, and made a noncommittal sound as he skimmed it.

"What is it?" I asked.

Mati rerolled the scroll and set it on the stack. "That," he said, "was written by a Scholar named Taro Elis fifty years ago, an open letter to the king—my grandfather—and the Scholars Council. He was executed not long after." He paused. "All copies of that letter were supposed to have been burned. I found it in my father's papers after he died. It gave me a bit of hope that he wasn't as bad as I thought."

"Oh." I took a tentative step toward him. "Any . . . news of Soraya?"

He sighed. "Nothing. We've got guards searching the city, and Gamo's got his own men crawling all over the Valley of Qora, but no sign of her or her attackers."

"Gamo has enough men to search the valley?"

Mati smiled humorlessly. "Caught that, did you? Seems Gamo has been amassing quite an army at Pira. That he didn't hesitate to deploy it for the search says that either he'd do anything to find his daughter, or he's so certain that Rale's coup will succeed that it doesn't matter if he reveals it now. Maybe both. All sorts of accusations have been thrown about in council, veiled in polite barbs, of course. It's exhausting."

"But most of them are still loyal, yes?"

Mati laughed softly, then sat down and removed his boots before answering. "That is the question, I'm afraid. I'm only sure of a few. Obal Tishe, Priasi Jin—"

"I always liked him," I said.

Mati nodded. "He's a good man. And influential." He paused, giving me that assessing look again, and then went on. "Some of the others who're wavering would support me, I think, if he comes out and does so. He's hedging in public, to keep Rale off him, but he's privately offered his support. He understands what Rale is, but most of the others don't. They see Emtiria's victory at Asuniaka and the depleted treasury as signs that Qilara is weak, and the success of the Resistance supports that. Rale blaming the Arnathim for everything makes sense to them." He looked down, focusing on removing his stockings. He didn't say—didn't have to—that the crown's inability to control a certain wayward former Tutor fueled the councilors' doubts.

I sat on the bed beside him. What could I say? That I was sorry? It wouldn't make any difference. I had to *do* something to help Mati, only I had no idea what.

"If they found out how I helped the Resistance and how you protected me, it would make things even worse," I said, my voice trembling.

"Yes," he said slowly. "But they won't find out. Rale says he's investigating, but he can't do anything without proof. Besides, it might backfire on him. The bolder he gets, the more disgusted some of them become."

I buried my face in my hands. "I can't stay here, Mati. Every minute I'm here puts you in more danger."

"You won't be safe anywhere else."

"After what I've done, you should be angry enough to . . ." I took a deep breath. "Why are you still protecting me?"

Mati was silent for so long that I was sure he was asking himself the same question. "I keep thinking about what you said, that night after the banquet," he said at last. "About how maybe the Resistance was doing what they thought they had to. And I think—maybe you weren't only talking about them." He looked up at me, and I saw in his eyes all the pain he'd been hiding behind his detached manner for the last few days. "But you never had to lie to me."

I reached out and took his hand. "I know that now," I whispered. "Let's . . . let's make a promise, that from now on, we'll always tell each other the truth, no matter what. I can't bear . . ."

Mati didn't answer for a long moment—he was thinking, no doubt, of all the ways my untruths outweighed his. But then his other hand covered mine. "Agreed," he said hoarsely.

Then, as if making a decision, he pulled me down on the bed next to him, carefully avoiding touching my sore back. He kissed my cheeks, my forehead, my nose, and then sighed and leaned back on the pillow, his eyes drifting shut.

"I will love you," I told him, my throat catching, "until the gods read out the scrolls."

Mati smiled without opening his eyes. "They do their reading at third bell while we're at luncheon, remember?"

It was the joke he'd made when we'd first gone into the Library of the Gods, and I'd worried about being found out. Those fears seemed naive now, after all that had happened.

And I noted that he'd made a joke instead of saying that he loved me too. So even if he was softening, I wasn't completely forgiven.

"Forever, then," I whispered. I stroked his hair, and his breathing grew deep and even. I let my thoughts drift until I fell asleep beside him.

Mati jumped up, waking me before the pounding on the door even registered. In the time it took me to lurch to my feet, gasping at the stiffness in my back, disoriented by the evening shadows in the room, Mati had already gone to the door, cracked it, spoken to someone in a low, urgent voice, and returned. He pulled me over to the mirrored wardrobe door.

"Wait in the Library," he whispered. "Stay out of the passage."

My heart thundered in my ears. "What's happening?"

Mati pushed me into the wardrobe. "Just go!" He shut the door. I groped for the secret passage in the darkness. I felt my way down the dim staircase to the panel and stepped into the Library.

Poking my head back into the passage, I strained to make out the voices upstairs. One was louder, speaking often, and I could hear Mati answering in a softer tone. Then thumping, and booted feet walking around—lots of those.

A door opened—the wardrobe?—and the voices grew louder. Fearfully I swung the panel shut and pressed my ear against it, but heard nothing. I waited for what seemed hours, the only sound the insistent thrumming of my heart.

At last, the panel opened, nearly knocking me over, and Mati entered the Library. He crossed to the firepit and struck the surface, igniting a flame that did little to chase away the evening gloom.

"Rale's making his move," he said, turning to face me. "He brought guards for you—to complete the sentence, he said."

"But really to use me to make you cooperate."

He seemed surprised that I had figured this out. "Yes," he said wearily. "He's claiming that the High Priest of Aqil holds authority over the Tutors."

I grimaced, imagining Laiyonea's face when she heard that. Then it hit me that Laiyonea would probably approve of whatever punishment Rale had in mind for me, and I had to blink back tears.

"I thought his antics were disgusting the council," Mati went on, "but if he's pulling this now, it means he thinks he's got enough power to succeed. I wonder how much Gamo gold has gone to buy the council's support. I can't fight that, and he knows it." He sank down onto a bench. "The next time Rale comes with guards, it'll be for me."

"Mati, no! What about your supporters? Some of the guards are loyal, aren't they? And Tishe, and Jin . . ."

Mati laughed. "Not enough. Don't you see? Rale's been planning this for a long time. I've played right into his plans, because I was stupid and blind. I don't have allies. He does."

My mind whirled. "But can't you get allies? You're the king, Mati!"

Mati shook his head. "I can't hire mercenaries—no money. I'm sure Emtiria would be happy to come in and take over the whole country, but that wouldn't be any better than Rale. And Galasi's treasury is even worse off than ours." He rubbed at his temples. "I don't have anything to offer potential allies except royal ancestry and . . . gratitude."

I played with my necklace, thinking so hard that my brain seemed to hum. "So . . . you need an ally with armed men willing to fight, who might benefit from your gratitude," I said slowly. "Someone . . . someone who has nothing to lose."

Mati laughed grimly. "Exactly."

I blew out a breath. "The Resistance, Mati. If they knew what Rale was doing, they wouldn't want it either."

Mati stood up abruptly. "Are you insane? They killed my father, Raisa! You said yourself that they wanted to kill me!"

I waved this off. "Because they don't *know* you, Mati. They think you're like your father. They don't know what you've tried to do."

Mati crossed his arms over his chest. "Then they'd never believe it, even if a messenger could find them."

"I think . . ." I had to say it, no matter how it might blight the fragile forgiveness I had sensed growing in his heart. "*I* could find them."

Mati stared at me. "You're unbelievable! You know we've been trying to find Soraya. If you knew where they were—"

"I don't know where they are! I just mean . . . I think I could get a message to them, is all." I balled my hands into fists. "As for convincing them, well, that's why you have to send *me* with the message."

He went rigid. "Absolutely not."

"It's the only way—"

"No! I'm not putting you in danger."

"But I already *am* in danger! *In* danger, and a danger to you if Rale finds me. Do you intend to hide me in the Library forever? Do you think Rale would hesitate to break down the doors? You've saved me over and over. Let me help you for once. I can do this. If I just explain to Jonis how things are—"

"Jonis?"

"Yes, he was my contact. He's Jera's brother, and a good man. Since he asked me to keep her safe, the least he can do is listen to what I have to say, right?"

"But if they know about us, won't they think you've betrayed *them*? I don't like this at all."

"They won't hurt me, Mati. I'm Arnath, remember?" I had to believe this was true, if only because I had promised not to lie to Mati again.

"Rale won't stop looking for you," he shot back.

"Which is why you'll lie to him. Tell him . . . tell him that we argued and I escaped." I laughed. "Tell them I turned out to be just as horrid as they all think I am. If you act like you don't care, like it's over between us, they won't bother to come looking for me."

"It won't be that easy."

"Of course not. But it's better than sitting around waiting for Rale to come for us." Hesitantly, I touched his cheek, and was relieved beyond measure when he didn't flinch away. "I know I haven't given you much reason to, but please, can you trust me to do this?"

Mati closed his eyes. The silence stretched out as I waited for his answer. Then he sighed, his defeated expression piercing my heart, and rested his forehead against mine.

"What choice do I have?" he whispered.

The asotis, sensing Sotia's imprisonment, would no longer
drop their quills willingly for any of the gods. Aqil, enraged, built
a cage atop the mountain and gathered all the asotis into it, where
he bound them to his will.

THIRTY-FIVE

SO THAT WAS how I ended up, early next morning, crouched inside a barrel that reeked of pickled fish, rumbling along toward the docks in a cart driven by Kirol, the loyal guard who'd alerted Mati to my whipping. Minister Jin had arranged for this cargo to be delivered to Horel Stit's ship. At my insistence, Mati knew as little as possible about the plan. It was safer for him that way.

I braced myself against the sides of the rocking barrel and thought of Mati's face before I'd crept out of the Library that morning. He clearly didn't want me to go, but he saw the risk to both of us if I stayed. I'd been apprehensive—I still was—but it had been worse there in the Library, saying good-bye to him after a restless few hours of dissonant dreams, waking often with the feeling that there was an important job I ought to be doing. I was glad now to be on my way to doing it.

The cart lurched to a stop. I stood, easing the top off the barrel so I could hear what was happening outside. Eleven other barrels crowded the goatskin-canopied cart, with mine closest to the front so it would be the last out, in case Kirol needed time to relay his message to Jonis.

"You, boy, where is your master's man, the one with curly hair? The cooper has special instructions for this shipment." That was Kirol.

"Jonis?" squawked a boy's voice. "He did a runner a couple days ago. Master was mad, I tell you. . . ." The boy chattered on, but I didn't hear—I had slid back down to the bottom of the barrel as the entire plan fell apart around me. I had counted on Jonis being here.

A few seconds of panic was all I allowed myself before I rose and climbed out of the barrel.

". . . only eleven," said Kirol's voice outside as my feet thumped onto the floor of the cart. "There are twelve barrels in there, see, but one's to go to the blacksmith." He was lying, trying to keep my barrel in the cart so that he could take me back to the palace. Surely Mati had given him orders to bring me back if something went wrong.

Sorry, Kirol. I wasn't going back until I had found a way to help Mati out of this mess. I crept between the barrels, glad for the green tunic and trousers Jin had given me. A dress would have caught on every splinter and loose barrel stave.

"I'll show you which," Kirol was saying, his voice rising. "Think you can lift 'em?"

"I can," said the boy indignantly. "That's why Master moved me up after Jonis took off. I'm strong, see."

"All right," said Kirol with a strained laugh. Boots crunched on stones, coming closer.

I was ready when Kirol unhooked the back panel of the cart. I leaped out, knocking the astonished boy out of my way, and ran.

"Wait!" shouted Kirol. I caught a glimpse of his face as I took off, and felt a stab of guilt that he'd have to report this to Mati, no doubt feeling that he'd failed in his mission. And what would Mati think—that I had run off, betrayed him again? But I couldn't spare another thought on that, because a moment later Kirol was after me, and I couldn't let him catch me.

I darted into an alleyway and weaved along the harbor until I came to a low wall. I scrambled over and found myself in a deserted garden, a fine white-stone house in the distance. Crouching behind a willow, I gasped quietly as the rush of my escape abated and the stiffness and pain in my back returned.

But pain didn't matter. Making contact with the Resistance was what was important; it was the only way I could help Mati fight Rale's coup.

Footsteps passed on the other side of the wall. I waited, tensed to run, but they soon faded into the distance. Was it possible? Had I lost Kirol?

I exhaled and examined my surroundings. The house wall facing me was curiously blank—but of course the windows and open terraces would have been built on the harbor side. Everything seemed so quiet that I allowed myself a few minutes to sit in the shadows and think.

How foolish I'd been to pin all my hopes on Jonis being where I'd thought he would be, and not plan for this contingency! Mati had said that Rale was continuing his investigation—had he found something that incriminated Jonis? Was that why Jonis had finally run?

Where to now? Kiti? No, the only place I knew to find him was the Temple of Aqil. Going there was akin to walking straight into Rale's arms.

But I couldn't stay here. I crept along the wall to the gate and picked a direction at random, trying to look like I knew where I was going. I mashed my shapeless green hat down over my eyes—Jin had given it to me to hide my hair, which was now braided and pinned up out of view, but I was glad that the wide brim kept my face shadowed. Of course, that was the point of the design, to keep the hot Qilara sun off fair Arnath skin while slaves worked outdoors.

It certainly kept the few people I met on the road from looking too closely at me; their eyes slid right over the green tunic like I wasn't there. It had been a long time since I'd experienced that, and it took me back to my days running errands for Emilana Kret.

Maybe that was why my steps automatically turned toward the market. It made sense, I thought, my brain belatedly catching up with my feet. I'd seen Jonis there before. Surely, if I waited and watched, I'd find a way to get a message to him.

Seven Arnath heads stared ghoulishly from the pikes at the entrance, fresh enough that the faces were recognizable. I scanned them with my heart in my throat, but none were Jonis. I scurried away from them as a guard turned to me, and I tried to blend into the marketplace crowd.

I wandered through the haphazard stalls, examining each green-clad figure. How would I know if one was safe to approach?

What if I was recognized?

The crowd bottlenecked around a papermaker's stall. As I paused to let a man pushing a handcart come through, I caught sight of a candlemaker's stall across the way. A dark-haired girl in a lacy green dress stood behind it, talking to a boy in a green tunic. She handed him something, and he slipped away through the crowd. Then she turned and I clearly saw her pale face and dark eyes, and realized that I knew her. She'd been one of the finalists at the Selection with me, I recalled suddenly. She'd glared at me when I was chosen.

And I'd seen her, too, at the Festival of Qora fair at the palace—talking to Jonis.

The crowd moved again, an old woman muttering a curse at me as she stepped around my frozen form. I darted over to the candlemaker's stall, approaching it from the side. A portly Qilarite woman with a wide curving mouth was helping a customer at the far end. The girl, who was dipping a wick into a pot of wax, looked up at my approach; nothing in her manner said that she recognized me at all.

"You were in the Selection three years ago," I said in a low voice. "I know you."

She narrowed her eyes at me, dipping the wick again. "You are mistaken."

I glanced at the Qilarite woman, who was flirting quite obviously with her customer, and stepped closer. "Do you know a man named Jonis?" I hissed. "I need to speak to him."

She looked up quickly at Jonis's name, then turned her attention back to the wick. It went into the wax three times before she spoke again. "I don't know what you're talking about. Unless you mean to purchase candles, you'd best move on before my mistress calls the guards."

She knew Jonis. And I was more certain every minute that she was with the Resistance. In desperation I reached across the stall and grabbed her hand. She made an indignant sound, but I held tight and traced a symbol into her palm, the same that Jonis had traced into mine so long ago in the Temple of Aqil: a circle with lines flying up on either side. "It's urgent," I said through gritted teeth.

"What's this? Is another boy bothering you, Deshti?" said a voice, and the Qilarite woman bustled closer. I jumped away, hiding my face under my hat.

"No, mistress," said Deshti. I didn't hear the rest of her excuse, because I was already pushing through the crowd.

I didn't stop until I reached the fountain. I wished I hadn't come this way, near the foodsellers' stalls; my stomach was reminding me that it was past third bell and I had nothing to eat. I turned away from the mouth-watering aromas of goat meat and bread and walked down another lane, pausing at a weaver's stall—but of course Jonis's mother wasn't standing behind it. Was the sour-faced old Qilarite there responsible for beating Jera?

I continued to the last row of stalls, finding nothing that might lead me to Jonis. Dejected, I turned back, deciding to hide near the Temple of Aqil until I could make contact with Kiti. It was suicidal, but I had to try.

When I passed the candlemaker's stall again, Deshti was waiting on a veiled Qilarite noblewoman. She met my eyes, then

KATHY MACMILLAN

pointedly looked away. I followed the crowd out of the market.

I left the main road at the first alleyway, relaxing a fraction as I left the crowd on the street behind. But the silence was broken by footsteps behind me. As I turned to look back, something covered my head, and I was swept off my feet and thrown over a burly shoulder.

The asotis wept for their own captivity and that of the goddess Sotia, until their tears burned white markings into their gray feathers that remained forever after.

THIRTY-SIX

I SHOUTED AND struggled, but my captor only held me more tightly. A door creaked open and I was dropped onto a hard floor. I cried out as pain seared my back. Then I was flipped over roughly, but only so that my captor could tie my wrists together behind me.

I heard a door open and close, then the floor rumbled beneath me—I was in a cart or carriage. Moving my head back and forth, I tried unsuccessfully to work the rough cloth off my face. The cloth smelled of oats—a feedsack, I realized, as my jostling sent dust up my nose and made me sneeze.

I shouted again, but the only response was the sound of my own breath, loud in my ears. Each time the cart rode over a bump, I rolled painfully onto my pinned arms—but at least that distracted me from the fire in my back, where it felt like several wounds had ripped open.

Had someone recognized me and reported me to the guards? Surely Rale would want to make a spectacle of my capture, but I could think of several reasons why he wouldn't. He'd probably keep me well guarded, ready to torture me to keep Mati in line.

So I would have to find a way to escape; I owed that to Mati. I couldn't let anyone use me to hurt him again.

The cart bumped on for what seemed hours. When it finally rolled to a stop, I heard voices, and a door opening, and then I was heaved over a shoulder again. I didn't bother to struggle—what good would that do now? I would wait and watch.

The man who carried me breathed heavily—were we going uphill? I had no sense of how far the cart had taken me. I might be in the Valley of Qora by now.

At last I was slung to the ground. Footsteps crunched away from me. I sat up and waited, taking in the packed earth beneath my rear and silence all around.

Someone pulled the sack off my head so abruptly that it took my hat with it. I sat blinking in bright afternoon sun. My eyes watered as I tried to make out the figure above me, and I sighed in relief when I saw Jonis's curly hair.

His face was unreadable. "You wanted to speak to me?"

"Yes! I thought those men were . . . but you're not Rale, and I'm here. When that boy said you'd escaped, I thought that was it." I was sitting on a rocky ledge backed by a wall of stone. The clouds seemed close enough to touch. In the mountains then—but I might have been anywhere along the great ridge that divided the coastal plains from the desert.

Jonis's face was like stone too.

"Could you . . . untie me please?" I said, squinting up at him.

"Not," he said, "until you explain to me why I should. Why are you here?"

"Because I needed to talk to you," I said impatiently. "Obviously, it's important."

"So talk." He stepped forward intently. "Is it Jera?"

"No, she's fine. More than fine, actually. She's charmed half the court." I sighed bitterly. "Even made a friend of Penta Rale."

Jonis narrowed his eyes. "There are rumors all over the city. That Rale wanted to have you whipped, and the king stopped him."

"I *was* whipped, and Mati did stop it," I said.

Jonis stepped back. "Then it's true, you and the king . . ."

I nodded.

Jonis was silent for a long moment, clasping his hands in front of him; I had the sense that he was reining in his anger. "Did he find out you'd helped us and toss you out?" He spoke as if he knew all about me, and all about Mati, and didn't think much of either of us.

"No. He found out I'd helped you and he protected me anyway. If you must know."

"So you're here to spy for him? If so, your methods are . . . ineffective."

I lifted my chin. "I've come with a message from the king. Asking for your help."

Jonis's laughter rang from the rocks. I flushed.

"Is this a ruse, to distract me while the guards sneak up and capture me? Because I assure you, Tutor, no one is coming to save you." His gaze traveled to the ledge a few feet away. I realized the purpose of bringing me here; if Jonis decided I was a threat, he could toss me over that cliff easily. No doubt my broken body would lie hidden in the rocks below for years.

I closed my eyes, pushing my fear away, determined to explain so Jonis would see how important this was—to Qilara and to the Resistance. I imagined I was writing, shaping the symbols in my mind before I spoke the words. I told Jonis how Rale had meticulously built up his allies, how he had inflamed anti-Arnath sentiment despite everything Mati had tried to do, and how he was angling for the crown.

"Even if I were inclined to help, which I'm not," said Jonis, "what makes you think I could?"

"Because you're armed, you're covert, and no one—especially Rale—will expect it. He thinks he's beaten down the Arnathim, but he's just riling them up more. Even those who haven't joined the Resistance will be sympathetic to it now, and would support Mati if you did. And . . ." I trailed off, not wanting to state the last reason out loud.

"And the fact that a Tutor is involved will sway more to either cause," Jonis finished for me, his mouth twisting into something that was not quite a smile. "True." He paused. "I'll consider it."

"Will you also consider untying me?" I asked.

He laughed and produced a knife from his pocket, then bent down and cut my bonds. I rubbed my wrists, working the feeling back into them, and stretched my stiff shoulders, wincing as my tunic pulled against opened wounds.

Jonis's sharp eyes did not miss this. "Come on," he said. "Are you hungry?"

I nodded eagerly, and Jonis led me down a narrow path so steep that I had to cling to the plants on either side to keep from sliding down. Once Jonis even grabbed the back of my tunic to keep me upright.

I didn't realize until we emerged between two boulders that we were in a bare, rocky valley, the tops of smooth stone monuments visible over the next rise.

My mouth dropped open. "We're in the Valley of Tombs?" That carriage must have driven a meandering course to confuse me, only to deposit me in the mountains just above the City of Kings.

Jonis grinned. "Welcome to the new headquarters of the Resistance."

Though he wrote and wrote in the language of the gods, Aqil was never able to manifest the symbols into action as his mother had. He crumpled his paper in his fist in frustration, and it burst into flame. Aqil watched, mesmerized.

"This is my power," he said. "To burn away all that is impure. Behold the fire of sacred knowledge."

With delight in his heart, he hurled his fireballs at the scrolls in the library of the world, for what did Sotia's wisdom matter against the power of the gods?

THIRTY-SEVEN

JONIS LED ME into a stand of scrubby trees and pushed branches aside to reveal a narrow tunnel entrance. We crawled through, the tunnel gradually widening around us until we could stand, packed earth giving way to smooth stone. The Resistance, it transpired, had made their new home not in just any tomb in the valley—but in the long, low, massive Royal Tomb building. I realized this when I saw the inscription over the first door we passed—the serpentine symbol of King Makal—and I stopped in the torchlit hallway, gaping at Jonis.

"What?" he said defensively. "This was the biggest one."

I shook my head at his gall, then realized that this was exactly why Mati needed him.

Corridors of stone stretched on under the mountain, punctuated by rooms of varying sizes. Stone doors blocked many of these, with inscriptions carved above—occupied tombs. But there were other rooms too, doorless, where the offerings buried with the monarchs lay. I didn't ask whether the Resistance had looted those. I didn't want to know.

Jonis took a torch from a sconce and led me along a sloping hallway, pointing out the occupied tombs as we passed. He read the inscriptions nonchalantly, but I bet he had spent hours working them out.

"It was Kiti's idea to move here, after our place by the quarries was discovered," said Jonis. "He used this as a hideout once, and since they only have guards posted at the entrance to the valley, it's easy enough to get in. That rear tunnel was made by the workers when they were building. The Qilarites have forgotten it, if they ever knew about it."

I nodded, squinting up at the inscription over the door we'd just passed—which Jonis had not stopped to read like the others. The symbol combined lion and crown, with *great man* behind. King Tyno. I stopped in my tracks. Jonis slowly turned to face me.

"I know that you were responsible for King Tyno's death," I said.

There was no guilt, no anger, no pride in Jonis's answering nod, only cold acknowledgment. "And you," he said, "told the king about Patic and Ris."

"Yes. Would you have assassinated Mati too?"

Jonis shrugged. "Maybe, if we'd had the opportunity. As you've destroyed the cover of our best man inside the palace, it's a moot point. You might reflect on how that affects the chances of us helping you now." He turned and continued down the corridor, laughing darkly. "Though it seems the High Priest of Aqil may be doing our job for us."

My face grew hot with anger. "If Rale succeeds there'll be ten executions a day."

Jonis just shrugged and kept walking.

I pattered after him. "What about Soraya Gamo? Did you kill her?"

He spun sharply. I glimpsed his anger before he smoothed it away. "We are not barbarians," he said evenly. "Soraya Gamo is quite safe."

He jerked his head toward a doorway, then led me into a vast room full of people practicing with swords. The room was so wide that it was hard to believe we were still underground. Torches set into the walls at intervals lit up the enormous space, and I knew immediately what it was. In ancient days, when a monarch died, all his slaves were sealed into the underground tomb with him, in a space like this. The practice had mercifully fallen out of fashion two hundred years before. A memory of sitting in the Library, reading out old kings' letters about it with Mati, stabbed my consciousness. There were no bones or other signs of dead Arnathim here, though—had they cleared those away?

Jonis must have seen the revulsion on my face, because he said, "You know what this space is for?" He grinned. "Remember, Arnath slaves built the whole tomb. Why do you think they made the tunnel and the back door? Any Arnathim who were put in here were on their way to Emtiria before the king's body was cold." He indicated a burly, balding man who was correcting a boy's sword grip near the far wall. "That's Tomis," he said. "He and Cauti—the skinny one in the corner—are training the rest of us. They both ran from their masters about ten years ago and trained in the Emtirian army."

"Why did they come back?" I asked, and regretted the words when Jonis shot me a disgusted look.

"We've managed to stockpile quite a few weapons," he went on, not bothering to answer me. "We're lucky to have Tomis and Cauti to teach us how to use them."

I wanted to make a snide remark about how he'd used me to get those weapons, but decided it would be wiser to hold my tongue. Jonis went on about training regimens and numbers. I didn't follow most of it, but my heart sank as I realized that the Resistance already had major plans of their own.

"You're not even considering helping Mati," I said, cutting him off in the middle of listing types of pikes.

"There are many factors to consider."

The evenness of his tone made me want to scream. How much time did Mati have before Rale's men came for him? "What about the others?" I said coldly. "Don't you think they have the right to decide for themselves if it's a good idea?"

Jonis shrugged. "All right, present it to them." He clapped his hands and called loudly, "Everyone! Gather around."

The closest people heard and lowered their swords, moving toward us curiously. Seeing them, others followed suit. Whispers ran around the room as they recognized me, but no one seemed surprised—news of my coming must have preceded me to the tombs.

Soon I had an audience of fifty or so, but I had no idea what to say. I looked at Jonis.

"Go to it," he said. The surface of his voice was polite, but I heard the smirk underneath.

The faces turned to me wore expressions ranging from curious to hostile. "Things in the palace are not as they seem," I began. I cleared my throat and tried to speak up. "Penta Rale is trying to steal the crown. The king needs your help."

Tomis, the ex-soldier, shrugged. "What's that to us?"

"The king is a good man," I said. I told them how Mati had helped the palace children, how he'd tried to outlaw whipping, how he'd saved me. "Mati wants to help the Arn—to help *us*. But the Scholars Council is against him. He needs allies. He needs *you*. That's why I've come, to ask for your help."

I looked around hopefully, but all I saw was skepticism and, in some cases, open-mouthed disbelief. I pressed on. "Some on the council still support Mati. Priasi Jin, the Trade Minister, and Obal Tishe, the High Priest of Lanea." I thought Tishe's name might impress them—after all, he'd intervened during the fighting at the temple last year.

The room went completely silent for a beat, and then whispers and murmurs started up. I frowned, not understanding.

Jonis spoke up to my left. "She doesn't know," he said. He looked at me. "The Temple of Lanea burned to the ground this morning. Eight Arnathim were inside, along with Obal Tishe."

My stomach tightened. "Rale did this. Don't you see? Rale

is trying to destroy anyone with the power to help Mati, anyone who might be sympathetic to your cause. He's feeding off fear of us to increase his own power!" My voice sounded hysterical to my own ears. Rale was openly killing people now. How long before he went after Mati? How many more people would die before this was over?

"*Us?*" said a voice to my left. "Suddenly you're one of us, are you?" I located the source: Deshti, hovering behind Jonis, glaring at me. Clearly she had voiced what everyone else was thinking.

"I've *helped* you," I said angrily. "I don't think I—"

"When it was convenient for you," said Deshti. She sounded like Jonis, right down to the deliberate, mocking tone.

"Deshti," began Jonis, but I cut him off.

"*Convenient?* I could have been executed for tampering with those records. And I lied to the council about the oracle, to keep Jera safe, like you asked me to. The only reason I got away with any of it was because Mati trusted me, even when I was lying to him. There was nothing *convenient* about it. I helped you because it was the right thing to do." I pulled in a furious breath. "And now, helping Mati fight Rale is the right thing."

Deshti rolled her eyes. "Do you even know anything? Rale was the one who set Tyasha up. She was too stupid to see it, and look what happened when the Resistance trusted her."

A few people gasped at Tyasha's name, but a curly-haired woman in the front row said, "We don't know that for sure, Deshti."

Deshti ignored her, glaring at me. "It's sweet, really. You're just like the very first Tutor, a king's concubine." She smiled nastily. "How nice that you're carrying on such ancient traditions, falling in love with your master."

I flushed. "Mati's not my—" I began angrily, but then I realized that she was right. It was so far removed from how I thought of Mati as to be almost inconceivable, but that was how everyone else saw it. Including the crowd of people eyeing me with disgust.

My stomach knotted. How could I overcome years of slavery and oppression? How could Mati? I shook my head to clear it, and latched desperately onto the rest of Deshti's outburst. "That story about King Balon's . . . concubine . . . that's not why the Tutors are Arnath," I said. "Maybe that's what they say, but that's not it. It's symbolic—another way to keep us down. They use the Tutors to pass on the thing they've taken from us, to remind us how much they control us." I was speaking at random, but as the words came out of my mouth, I felt their truth. We Tutors, ironically, were the ultimate symbol of Arnath subjugation.

The others had grown quiet, but Deshti snorted. "Easy for you to say, living so easy in the palace, learning to write . . ."

I faced her incredulously. "It's not a gift—to learn how to write, and then not be allowed to. Not for any real purpose, anyway. Not like my—" I bit off the rest of the sentence.

Deshti's voice was shrill. "Oh, please. You come here, pretending to be one of us, pretending to know what it's like—"

"I do know, though," I said quietly. I couldn't keep my secret any longer; the Qilarites had plenty of reasons to want to kill me now aside from my birth, and telling these people who I really was might be the key to earning their trust. I had to say this right. "I admit, I wanted to learn to write, more than anything, when

I became Tutor. So I would know the language of my father, the language . . . of the Learned Ones of the Nath Tarin." A wave of grief for my lost heart-verse hit me.

But I couldn't think about that now. I cleared my throat. "My true name is Raisa ke Comun. My parents sent me to their friend when the raiders came, because they knew what would happen to them, what would happen to me, if anyone knew who I really was. I came from the Nath Tarin. I was ripped away from my home, and I've had to lie about who I am since I was six years old. So don't tell me that I don't understand how things are."

Deshti still looked dubious, but the old man beside her nodded sympathetically. The curly-haired woman in the front row reached out a hand as if to touch my arm, then dropped it to her side. Jonis just watched me thoughtfully.

"Please," I said fervently, meeting the eyes of anyone who didn't look away. "Mati is trying to be a good king. He needs your support. If you do this, he'll . . . he'll free all the Arnathim." Mati hadn't said so, of course, but I spoke with certainty. He would if he could.

This earned me many skeptical looks. Even the sympathetic man in the front raised his eyebrows in disbelief. Deshti opened her mouth as if to say something, then glanced at Jonis and stayed quiet.

I couldn't let myself waver. I lifted my chin and forced myself to speak loudly and clearly. "He will," I told them, holding each person with my gaze before moving on to the next. "If you fight this enemy with him, King Mati will give you your freedom."

Lanea watched Belic and his people, but, fearing Gyotia's wrath in the wake of Sotia's imprisonment, she dared not approach them. One day she returned to the great house on the mountaintop to find Lila just leaving Gyotia's bed. Lila's proud face was bruised, for Gyotia was not gentle with either of his wives. Lanea went to her storeroom, her hand pausing briefly over the poisonous lantana, but she selected instead a jar of willow bark salve. She returned and handed the jar to Lila. Lila's haughty expression did not abate, but she took the jar with a nod of thanks and left the house.

THIRTY-EIGHT

"WHY DO WE need anyone to *give* us our freedom?" said Tomis loudly. "I say we take it, just like they took it from us. We don't need a king. If there's a coup, we take advantage of it and attack. Get 'em all out of there, I say." The others nodded and murmured agreement. Tomis turned on his heel. "Come on, you lot. Seems we'll need to be ready earlier than we thought."

Abruptly I was alone as the others returned to their practice. Jonis said something softly to Deshti. She shot me a hate-filled glare over his shoulder. Jonis touched her arm and moved away from her, and I saw the flash of wistful longing in her face before she turned away. Clearly Deshti did *not* hate Jonis.

"Come on," Jonis said to me. He led me through to the next chamber, where six people sat on the stone floor, a meal spread on a cloth before them. Jonis gestured to a corner, and I sat dazedly.

I'd thought, for a moment, that some of them understood. My head felt heavy.

Jonis's voice seemed far away as he sat next to me. "Kitchen's down there. It's the only room with enough ventilation—if you call a giant piece of stone ripped out of the ceiling 'ventilation.' Only place we can build a fire without smoking everyone out. I don't know what we'll do during Qorana—the rain'll come right in."

"Who knows what'll happen by then?" I said softly.

Jonis grunted. Everyone had gone quiet, watching us. A girl brought us bread and cheese and roasted meat.

The others drifted away as soon as they finished eating. At first I thought this meant they all felt uncomfortable around me. But the more I saw Jonis with the other members of the Resistance, the more I realized that he wasn't just *a* leader; he was *the* leader. He was often called away while we ate to deal with some situation or another. The fourth time this happened, I was alone when he returned.

Jonis sat down. "It's a shame about Tishe," he said, no trace of irony in his tone.

"Rale only went after Tishe to hurt Mati."

"True," said Jonis. "The king's allies *are* in considerable danger these days."

"That's not what I meant!"

"But it's so," he responded. "Who knows what they would

have done to you if you hadn't escaped?"

"That's *not* why I came."

Jonis crossed his arms. "Why are you so eager to support him?"

"I love him."

He rolled his eyes. "Why?"

"Because he's the kindest person I've ever known—he's saved me more times than I can count. Because he's doing his best to be a good king. He does want to free the Arnathim. He *will*."

"You believe that?"

"I do. He's . . . he's never let me down, even when I've given him reason to." I blinked back tears. Talking about Mati was making me miss him fiercely. "Why else do you think I came? Everyone here hates me. Especially Deshti."

Jonis sighed. "Don't mind her. She's still mad that she wasn't selected as Tutor. She was supposed to be our operative in the palace. She was ready for it even at thirteen."

I nodded. That didn't completely explain her attitude, but it made sense. "Why didn't you tell me about Rale setting up Tyasha?"

Jonis made a face. "That's Deshti's theory. I don't believe it. Tyasha was smart, and Rale seems too petty to plan something that big."

I laughed. "*Seems.* He hates the Tutors. I didn't see the danger either." I played with the hem of my tunic. "There's something else I need to tell you. Rale used Jera to get information about me, to bring Mati down. Mati will protect Jera as best he can, Laiyonea too." She *would* protect Jera, wouldn't she? Even if she was furious at me, I had to trust that she would take care of the little girl. I looked up at Jonis. "But if Rale succeeds, I don't know what will happen to your sister."

Jonis blanched before his blank expression fell into place. "I'll consider your request," he said.

For the first time, I actually believed he might. I cleared my throat. "You . . . command the Resistance?" I asked tentatively.

He nodded.

"Aren't you, well, young to be in charge?"

"Amazing how quickly one moves up the ranks when your sweetheart keeps executing our leaders."

I winced, recalling the fresh heads on pikes at the marketplace. "That wasn't Mati. That was the Scholars Council."

"So the king is completely powerless."

"No," I said, "not completely, but Rale's gaining support, and Mati can't—"

"Can't stop senseless deaths?"

I sighed. I'd thought I was making progress, but now I was saying everything wrong. "Mati hates violence, and didn't see what Rale was doing until it was too late. My stupidity got in the way too. Mati won't do anything to hurt me, and Rale knows it. That's why I had to leave. It was my idea to ask for your help. Mati didn't believe you would agree, but I told him . . . that you're a good man too, that you'd understand. I just hope I was right." I peeked at his face. His expression was impenetrable.

I shook my head. "Well, please decide soon, so I can go back and tell him what's happening."

"Oh, you're not going back," said Jonis.

I whipped my head up so quickly that my neck hurt. "I'm a prisoner here?"

"No," Jonis said, "but I'm responsible for the safety of a large number of people, and I need to determine how best to protect them. Letting you leave is not in anyone's best interest, including your own." Something in the way he spoke reminded me strongly of Mati, but it must have been a trick of the echoes off the stone walls.

I snorted. "Is that what you told Soraya Gamo?"

"No, actually, it was difficult to say anything to her—she never stopped spewing insults."

I grinned, for some reason enjoying the image of Soraya screaming at Jonis. Then I remembered what Jonis was capable of. So he hadn't killed Soraya—that didn't mean he wouldn't. "Why did you kidnap her?" I asked.

He cocked his head. "Leverage. To make the king and the Scholars Council take us seriously."

I shook my head. "Haven't you been listening? It's not Mati you have to worry about, it's Rale, and Gamo. . . ." I trailed off.

Jonis smiled unpleasantly. "Exactly. And now you're here, so we're covered however this turns out."

My stomach turned. "You'd use me against Mati too? I thought you were better than that." I stood. "I want to see her."

"Soraya Gamo?"

"Yes."

Jonis didn't move. "Why do you care about a Qilarite princess who'd spit on you as soon as look at you?"

"It's my fault she left the palace in the first place."

Jonis stared at me, then got languidly to his feet. He told me to wait, and came back a few minutes later with a thin slab of stone. Hunks of meat, cheese, and bread lay on the makeshift tray, along with a goblet.

"You can deliver dinner to her, since you're so sympathetic," he said with a smirk.

"Fine," I replied airily.

He took a torch from a sconce and led me down a set of narrow steps, and then along a deserted hall that ended in more steps. Down those steps and around a corner, and I saw a torch in the distance. Under it two men sat by what looked like an occupied tomb—a stone slab blocked the door, but no inscription above told of an occupant.

One of the men looked up as we approached. "Quiet all afternoon," he said.

Jonis turned to me. "Well, go ahead."

My blood ran cold. Not that Soraya and I had ever been friendly, but I could imagine what it must be like for her, shut up in a dark tomb.

I stepped forward with the tray. The two men stood. One took an astonished look at my face, and then at Jonis, who nodded wryly. They worked together to push the stone slab aside. Jonis handed me a torch, saying, "Don't get too near her with the flame, or you'll regret it."

I balanced the tray on one hand and stepped into the dark room. Soraya lay huddled on the cold floor, her eyes glittering in the torchlight. A sharp tang in the air attested to the presence of a chamber pot nearby.

"I have food," I said softly.

She sat up. I recognized the spangled blue scarf she'd been wearing at the council meeting, in tatters over her hair.

"You!" she spat. "I might have known that you were behind this. Humiliating me wasn't enough? You had to dispose of me too?"

"No!" I said. "That's not—"

"When my father finds me—and he will, have no doubt—I will see *you* flayed alive. Your punishment will make that whipping seem like nothing."

My hands shook. Quickly I set the tray on the ground and backed away.

Soraya let out a contemptuous sigh. "I can't reach it there, slave." She lifted her hands to reveal manacles around her wrists, with chains leading to a ring set into the wall at waist height.

I eased forward and nudged the tray toward her with my foot. Soraya watched me beadily, and I realized that, though her behavior hadn't earned her any friends, it also kept her captors from touching her. Surely that was her greatest fear, born of hundreds of thoughtlessly pronounced opinions in Scholar parlors: that the barbaric Arnathim would beat her if given the chance . . . or worse.

I understood in that moment that Soraya Gamo was not stupid, but still I underestimated her.

"He never loved you," she said, when I was close enough that her voice would not carry to the corridor. "Maybe he found you amusing to play with, but don't think he's ever forgotten what you are. Once I'm his wife and take my rightful place on the council, you will be nothing to him."

I stepped back, heat rising in my face. I knew she was shooting wildly, saying anything to wound because of her own fear, but that didn't mean her arrows fell short of the target.

"You won't be harmed, as long as you don't harm anyone else," I said, trying to force the emotion out of my voice, the way I'd heard Jonis do.

Soraya lunged forward and launched the goblet at me. I stood sputtering, covered in wine, laughter echoing in the corridor behind me. Soraya's lips spread into a satisfied smile. She'd go thirsty now, but she seemed to think it was worth it.

I backed out of the room, not daring to take my eyes off her until I was outside and one of the men took the torch.

Jonis was still laughing as he slipped off his tunic and handed it to me, revealing a pale, lean torso. "Here, dry off. Now you see why we keep her chained. I should have warned you, but you were determined to be sympathetic."

I mopped at my face and sodden clothes, then shook my hair out of its braid to dry. Wordlessly I handed Jonis his tunic and he draped it over one arm and led me back up the corridor.

The only sound was our footsteps until we got to the second staircase. "Why do you want to help them?" Jonis finally said. "So they can treat you like that?"

I sighed. "Not all Qilarites are like that. And even those who are—well, did you ever consider that slavery is just as damaging to them as it is to us? 'The master is cruel to reassure himself that the slave is the other.' Or something like that. I may be quoting it wrong."

Jonis looked at me as if I'd spoken a foreign language. "Do you know why I was sold to Horel Stit when I was fourteen?"

I thought back to what I'd read. "Part of his wife's dowry, right?" I flushed, realizing too late that his question had been rhetorical.

He looked at me quickly, but didn't ask how I knew this. "My benevolent master, Kladel Ky, had sold my father to the mines the year before," he said, his voice dripping with sarcasm. I cringed; being sold to the mines was as good as a death sentence. It was just slower and more painful than execution. "My father wasn't gone half a Shining before Ky started raping my mother. She nearly died in childbirth a year later, when Jera was born."

Jonis continued down the corridor, and I hurried to catch up. "I was . . . not good at controlling my anger then." He jerked a thumb over his shoulder at the crisscrossing scars on his back, denser than his sister's, denser, I knew, than mine would be. "So Ky sold me to someone even worse than himself, someone he thought could control me." He shuddered. "I've been facing Qilarite cruelty all my life, as have most of the people here. Whatever happens, don't expect me not to hate them."

He marched away, leaving me standing in darkness.

That night, Lanea prepared for Gyotia a feast—meat dripping from the bone, steaming rice, and sweet concoctions to lighten his dark mood.

"Where were you today?" he said as she served him.

"I . . . merely wished to see that Belic's people were using your gift as you intended, mighty husband," Lanea replied.

"And?" he said, ripping a chunk of meat from the bone with his teeth.

"There has been no change," Lanea whispered. "Nor, I think, will there ever be."

THIRTY-NINE

I HOVERED IN the makeshift dining room for the rest of the evening, forcing myself to talk about Mati's cause to anyone who came in. Jonis stayed away, but it didn't matter; every one of them left eagerly as soon as they had finished eating.

Eventually I was alone in the room. I stretched my legs out in front of me and leaned against the wall. This was impossible. I couldn't even make these people trust me, so how could I convince them to trust Mati? How had Tyasha ke Demit gotten them to accept her?

She taught them the language of the gods.

I bit my lip, remembering how I had vowed to do just that,

right before I'd gotten caught in the scribe rooms. How quickly I had forgotten it, when life had swept me back into Mati's arms.

It had been days since I'd really written anything. My stomach did an odd flip at the thought of teaching others what had so long been held inside the Adytum. A discarded wooden spoon lay in one corner of the room; thoughtfully I picked it up and ran my fingers over its rounded handle. It would work.

Standing on tiptoe, I lifted a torch from its bracket, then moved to an empty corner of the room. I held the spoon handle in the flames until the end was charred with soot. Then I knelt and started writing the first tenset of the lower order symbols on the stone floor. I had to return the spoon handle to the flames often to get more soot, and the spoon's shape made it an awkward quill, but the result was legible, and large enough to attract attention.

I'd planned to write the second tenset as well, but now that my mind was turned to writing, I'd started thinking about my heart-verse. I moved to a new patch of floor, burned the spoon again, and wrote *sa* with bold, black strokes. Then I faltered; this was where I'd gotten hung up before, on the symbol with the vertical line and the curve. Did the curve touch the end of the line, or was there a gap? Both ways matched symbols in the lower order script. So I wrote them one above the other, and moved on to the next, the arches that I was almost sure went with the sound *ano*. I kept writing, stacking multiple symbols where I wasn't sure which was right.

Soon I had over a dozen symbols. I pointed with the now-shortened spoon handle to each one, saying aloud those I had deciphered so far. "*Sa* something *ano heli* something *yoti ev* something *qilan goday* something something—"

"*Sa noano heli gri, yotieven qilan godesha,*" said a voice behind me. *Light of wisdom, bold, brave, bright, bless us all and what we write.*

I whipped around and stared at the speaker, a middle-aged woman with curly blond hair, the one who had looked like she'd wanted to comfort me after learning about my father. She stood by the door, smiling at me. "Is that what you were trying to say?"

"What was that?" I asked, my mouth dry. Her words had tugged at something in my mind.

She shrugged. "Just something my mother used to say, when the master couldn't hear, of course. I'm Anet, by the way."

"I'm Raisa," I said absently.

"I know," she said, laughing. She had a bold laugh that echoed off the walls, more joyful than I had ever expected to hear from any Arnath in Qilara.

I swallowed hard. Anet had recognized the sounds from my heart-verse, even with the gaps. It couldn't be a coincidence. Her mother's words and my heart-verse were the same thing.

I looked at her keenly. "Say it again. More slowly. Please."

Anet grinned, but repeated the lines, and even held the torch for me when I fell to my knees and frantically pointed to each symbol, trying to burn the sound for it into my memory.

"Keep going," I ordered breathlessly.

Despite my rude tone, she laughed again. "That was it. It was just something she used to say."

My heart crashed with disappointment—my heart-verse had three more lines. But some of the symbols repeated, so maybe the new sounds would help me after all . . .

I charred the end of the spoon again and sketched another

symbol on the stone floor. Anet watched me for a few minutes, then put the torch back in its holder and sat down beside me.

"What is this, anyway?" she asked.

"It's . . . writing. Arnath writing." Briefly I told her about my heart-verse and thanked her for her help. I might be stuck again, but now I knew far more of what my heart-verse said than ever before. I ran my fingers under the symbols, wondering what message my father had been trying to give me. *Light of wisdom, bold, brave, bright—*

"It's different from the Qilarite writing," said Anet, indicating the tenset I'd written in the far corner.

"Yes, Arnath writing is based on the sounds of the words, and Qilarite symbols each stand for an idea. The symbols themselves are very similar, but—" I looked at her in surprise. "You can read."

She smiled. "A bit. My son convinced me to go with him to Tyasha ke Demit's secret meetings a few times. He learned far more than I ever did, though."

I straightened. "Well, I can teach you. Your son too, anyone who wants—"

She looked away. "My son is dead. He attended *all* of Tyasha's secret classes. Including the one guards raided."

I fidgeted with the spoon. "I'm sorry."

"Don't be. He would be glad that you want to teach us. It's as much a means of fighting against them as lifting a sword."

I hadn't thought of it that way. I wasn't sure I fully agreed, or how I felt about the fact that, to the Resistance, Mati was one of "them." I hesitated, then asked, "What was she like—Tyasha, I mean?"

Anet cocked her head. "She was . . . a wildfire. She was as worked up about the Resistance as any of the leaders. It was all they could do to convince her to go back to the palace every time she sneaked out. She was in love with the idea of being a rebel—and, in the end, a martyr."

I'd only seen Tyasha a few times in the palace, but I pictured her now with dark eyes bright in her smooth brown face, straight black hair flying as she stood before a roomful of Resistance members, inspiring them with her fiery words—the complete opposite of the impression I must have made in the training room earlier. What had it been like for Tyasha, to know so clearly where her loyalties lay?

"A wildfire," I muttered. "Whereas I'm more of a candle."

Anet patted my knee. "Ah, but candles burn more steadily."

I looked into her kind, motherly face. "Do you think the others will come, if I offer to teach them?"

"They'll come."

I smiled. "Do you know where Jonis is? I should tell him. . . ."

She jerked her head toward the door. "I'll take you."

She led me down two flights of steps and along a narrow passageway. When we emerged, I had a sense that we were near the front of the tombs.

"They're in there," Anet said loudly, indicating a doorway ahead. I didn't realize that her volume was a warning until Jonis poked his head out into the corridor. He turned and spoke to someone behind him, and then Kiti stepped into view.

All my nervous thoughts about what I'd been planning to tell Jonis fled. "Kiti!" I cried, so relieved to see his familiar face that I only just stopped myself from hugging him.

Anet said something in a low voice to Jonis, and he nodded.

"Have a seat," said Jonis, gesturing me and Kiti into the room, which was barely ten feet across. There were no torches here, but a firepit crackled in the corner, shedding plenty of light. Several wooden shipping crates lay scattered around the room, a map open on one of them. Jonis quickly rolled this up as I sat on one of the crates, but not before I saw that it was a map of the city.

"I'll give you two a few minutes," said Jonis, and as he stepped back into the corridor to join Anet, I realized that Kiti was still hovering by the door, studying his hands.

I'd thought that Kiti, of all people, would be willing to hear me out. "You know why I'm here?" I began.

"Jonis told me," he said softly.

"Then you probably also know about the whipping, and what Mati did."

Kiti looked straight at me. "I know what *you* did. I can't believe you and the king—" He broke off, but there was no mistaking the disappointment in his tone.

If Jonis had said it, I would have bristled and shot back, but the sadness in Kiti's voice left me momentarily speechless. I understood at last how deep a betrayal it felt to Kiti and the others, me falling in love with Mati. As Tutor, I was supposed to be the most Arnath of the Arnathim, and I had failed them miserably.

I heaved a sigh of frustration. "If you knew Mati, you'd understand."

Kiti shook his head. "I thought you were with us, and all the time—"

"I was! I *am* with you. I did everything you asked."

"Ris and Patic?" he said quietly.

I bit my lip. There was nothing I could say. Warning Mati was a choice I would make again in a heartbeat, but saying so wouldn't do any good. I had a sinking feeling that Kiti thought less of me with every word.

"Please come sit," I said.

Reluctantly he sat on one of the crates. As he did, his tunic sleeve fell away, revealing an ugly burn that ran from his wrist up his arm.

I grabbed his hand. "What happened?"

"When Rale found out you'd escaped from the palace, I . . . didn't get out of his way quickly enough."

My mouth fell open. I stared at the burn, hating Rale even more. Kiti gently disentangled his hand from mine and pulled his sleeve back down.

"I'm sorry," I said. Why was it that no matter what I did, someone got hurt? "But you of all people understand what Rale is. If he and Gamo are allowed to take over the throne—"

Kiti tipped his head back, as if seeking answers in the shadows above. "I'm the one who brought you into the Resistance. How is Jonis supposed to believe anything I say now? I convinced him to trust you." He met my eyes. "And I was wrong."

His words cut me deep, but at the same time I felt a flicker of annoyance. "You weren't wrong," I said icily. "But you didn't have to lie to me."

Kiti dropped his eyes, and I knew that my intuition was right; Jonis might not have minded manipulating me, but Kiti did. "That was Jonis's idea—"

"You're the one who knew me. You gave him the idea. So don't tell me that you *trusted* me."

"It was . . . for the greater good."

I seized on that. "So sometimes you have to do things you'd rather not do, for the greater good. Like join forces with someone whose goals are similar, even if you don't like that person?"

Kiti shook his head. "I can't help you, Raisa."

"But—"

Kiti stood up. "Let me rephrase that. I *won't* help you, Raisa." He squeezed my hand, as if to ease the sting of his words, and then he left the room.

Jonis appeared before I had even processed Kiti's refusal. He'd probably overheard every word of our conversation. But he only told me to follow him.

When I reached the corridor, Anet was gone. I wondered what she had told him, and whether Jonis had sent her to spy on me.

"Care for some dinner?" he said jauntily.

"So you're my host now, not my jailer?"

"I could be fierce, if you prefer. I just didn't think it was necessary."

"I'm not hungry," I said with disdain, just as my stomach gave a ferocious growl.

Jonis laughed. "Fierce doesn't suit you," he informed me.

"I know," I said miserably. How had I ever thought I could succeed at this?

"Have something to eat, and then you can join in the training," said Jonis.

I stopped, offended at his stupid joke, but then I saw that he was serious.

"Why would you want me to—" I began, but he kept walking and cut me off.

"I'd rather have you seen as fighting for our side. It's good for morale."

"I won't stop talking to people about Mati," I called after him.

"Fine. Talking hasn't done you much good so far." He turned back to face me, his features shadowed. "Maybe seeing you with a sword in your hand will make an impression."

"You're helping me?" I asked suspiciously.

He just shrugged. I thought hard for a moment, and then my stomach sank. "You know it won't work," I said. "No matter what I say, none of them will believe me, so you don't care how many of them I talk to."

"Oh, maybe it will, I don't know," he said. "But these people are here because they've put their faith in the Resistance. There's very little any Qilarite could do to make us trust him, after what we've seen." He paused. "And whether you want to believe it or not, you belong here. Part of you knows it. That's why you helped us in the first place."

I do belong here, I thought. *Because this is the only place where I can help both Mati and the Arnathim.* "Fine," I said. "I'll join in the training."

He nodded and started walking again, but I didn't follow.

"You're just as bad as they are, you know," I called after him. "Rale and Gamo and all the rest."

He wheeled around. This time he did not bother to hide his anger.

"You are," I pressed on. "They judge us by our skin color, by our birth, but you're doing the same thing to Mati. You're not giving him a chance at all."

He crossed his arms. "He had his chance—"

"When?" I said, taking a step toward him. "When you killed his father and thrust him into the midst of a council full of conspirators? He's tried to make things better. Why can't you believe that? You trusted his cousin."

"Patic proved himself trustworthy," said Jonis with a frown.

"And so has Mati!" I cried. "The only reason I'm still alive is because he risked his crown to save me. Doesn't *that* tell you something about him?"

Jonis's frown deepened. I wasn't positive, but I thought he might be softening. "Tyasha saw what he could be," I pressed on. "She told him once that he wasn't like other Qilarites, that he was different. Braver."

"Tyasha was a good judge of character," said Jonis reluctantly.

"Yes." I took four steps more, until I was standing right in front of him. "You said the people here put their faith in the Resistance. Well, so am I. So is Mati. If . . . you help him, I'll teach you to write. All of you. Whoever wants to learn. It'll help you spy on them and it's . . ." I thought of what Anet had said earlier. "It's fighting back as much as picking up a sword is."

Jonis didn't look surprised; Anet must have already told him. But he smiled. "Now you're giving me something to consider," he said.

Though Lanea would not risk her husband's wrath by visiting the mortals again, she continued to help them in small, secret ways. She caused silphium to grow in abundance in the valley below, so that when Gyotia turned his attention to a mortal woman, she could use the herb to protect her womb from his seed. No mortal woman could bear the pain of birthing Gyotia's child. Gyotia thought nothing of this, seeing the plant as a lowly weed. The mortal women praised Lanea, but quietly, for she was a goddess of shadows and secret gifts.

FORTY

"JONIS WANTS YOU."

The words, accompanied by a jostling of my shoulder, tore me out of uneasy dreams. The stone around my neck dug into my breastbone; I slept on my stomach now, to spare my still-tender back, and no matter how I positioned the stone upon going to bed, I always seemed to wake up with it under me again.

I rolled onto my side and squinted at the man standing over me with a torch. It was Adin, one of the men who'd witnessed my drenching by Soraya Gamo. He'd enjoyed telling the tale to anyone who would listen, but his face now was serious.

I heaved myself up off the pile of blankets and followed Adin down the corridor, rebraiding my hair as I went, my mind still on the fading, urgent images of my dreams. I'd been in the Library again, looking for something—why did my dreams always take me back there?

Because Mati was there, of course. What must he have thought when Kirol returned to the palace without me? Did he think I'd truly left him this time? Would his trust in me extend this far?

It wasn't difficult to guess where the sense of urgency in my dreams had come from. Jonis still hadn't told me *how* the Resistance would help Mati, even though I had been conducting writing lessons for three days now. So many people had shown up for the first lesson that we'd had to take over part of the training room, and by day two, the crowd had swelled so much that Tomis and Cauti had to halt sword-training entirely during the lesson. They looked just as doubtful about the whole business as many of the others, but they joined the class. As I kept reminding them, it was just as brave for an Arnath in Qilara to pick up a quill as it was to pick up a sword.

Jonis had insisted on practicality in these lessons, so I'd begun with the lower order symbols they would most likely see when spying on Scholar documents. It felt wrong to disregard the tenset sequence, but then, so much about teaching the language of the gods to others felt wrong. I reminded myself that I was helping Mati as much as I was helping the Resistance. I often reminded my students of this as well; they didn't think much of my sample sentences like *The king is kind and generous* and *We must help the king fight his enemies,* but if they wanted to learn to write, they had to copy my examples.

And when I hadn't been teaching, I'd been talking to anyone who would listen about Mati's cause. It was easy to tell, now, who the newcomers were—they were the ones who didn't leave the instant I walked into a room.

I'd assumed that Jonis wanted to yell at me about my teaching methods, but as Adin led me down corridors and across empty rooms, taking me deeper underground, my trepidation grew. Flickering light spilled out of a door ahead, and as we drew closer I heard a man's voice speaking. Adin motioned me through and I stepped inside.

Ten people sat around a huge firepit. Half of the faces were familiar. Jonis, closest to the door. Beside him, his mother, Dara, her light eyes serious. Across the firepit, Tomis and Cauti. And beside them, still talking between bites of the bread and cheese he held in either hand, Ris ko Karmik.

"—so when I got to the mountain camp . . ." He trailed off as he saw me. "What's she doing here?"

Jonis folded his arms. "She brought a message."

"She double-crossed us, and you let her walk right in?"

"You might notice," replied Jonis flatly, "that she hasn't been able to walk right out."

Ris pointed at me with the hand clutching the cheese, his eyes deadly. "It's because of her that Patic Kone is dead."

I gasped. "He's dead?"

"Yes," said Jonis. "Ris and Patic had been hiding at the harbor. They found something important and decided to make contact again. A shipmaster's slave alerted the guards as they left the docks, and Patic took an arrow in the back."

"Another Arnath turned them in?" I asked, looking at Jonis to avoid Ris's murderous gaze.

Ris answered anyway. "The guards can execute anyone they think is helping us on the spot now. Between that and the reward out for the Gamo girl, it makes for a nice cooperative herd of slaves."

I felt sick. If Mati had been unable to stop such a decree, that meant he was losing support faster than ever.

Jonis pointed to the empty place next to him. "Sit down, Raisa. Go on, Ris."

I sat. Ris took an insolent bite of bread. "Not while that's here," he said, spraying crumbs into the firepit.

"Go on, Ris," said Jonis in exactly the same tone he'd used before. "Tell them what you found on the ship."

Ris swallowed his bread, then turned pointedly away from me and addressed the others. "We'd been hopping between different cargo holds, but Patic thought we ought to stow away on a ship bound for Galasi. Soldiers came every day, if not the city guards, those others in blue—"

"Gamo's men," supplied Jonis.

Ris nodded. "One night they searched every ship. It was Patic's idea to go over the side and duck underwater till they passed. I thought we were done for, but it worked." I felt a pang at the way he spoke of Patic—like a friend. Did Mati know about Patic's death? If I walked into the market again, would I see Patic's head on a pike?

I shuddered. Jonis looked at me curiously. I forced myself to pay attention to what Ris was saying. "—sneaked into the scribe's cabin to make sure of the route. We found out it was going, wouldn't you know, to the Nath Tarin."

A tremor went around the circle. I sat up straighter as Ris continued.

"I saw a fancy paper with a wax seal, and I showed it to Patic. He took one look at it and turned as pale as me. I couldn't read it fast like him, but when he showed me the symbols I understood. That's when we lit out of there and tried to find you." He paused. "You know what happened next."

"What was the paper?" asked Jonis's mother softly.

Ris chewed for a long time before answering. "Orders sending slave raiders to the Nath Tarin, signed by the king himself."

The room was suddenly cold, despite the fire. I couldn't move.

Ris shook his head. "Saw it with my own eyes. Dated ten days ago. Raiders set to go out at the Shining."

I had trouble getting enough air to speak, and by that time others had started talking. My voice was a tiny pebble to their stones. "That's impossible," I whispered, then forced more air into my lungs and said it again. "That's impossible."

I'd spoken too loudly, and my words echoed as the others shut up in surprise. The flames blurred as I leaped up and ran into the dark corridor. I ignored the shouts behind me as I stumbled down steps and turned a corner. I made for another torch in the distance, not caring where I was going, just trying to get away from where I'd been.

More darkness beckoned beyond the torch. I went forward without thinking—thinking was dangerous, and painful. At the edge of the light I descended a shallow staircase and turned another corner. Five steps along, I stopped, throwing up my hands against the blank wall that cut off the corridor.

I fell into a heap, hugging myself as I realized I was shaking.

Ten days ago. Mati had signed that order ten days ago, while I was in the palace, my back in ribbons from a Qilarite whip. Was the ink even dry when he had come to me, full of indignation at my secrets? When I had burned with guilt for lying to him? When we had pledged to be honest with each other?

Neither the boy I had loved nor the man I'd fallen in love with again would ever do such a thing. Not willingly.

My head snapped up with such force that it struck stone. *Not willingly.* How did Ris know that those orders were really signed by Mati? And even if they were . . .

It would be easy, here in this place, surrounded by people who hated him, with Soraya's poisonous words echoing in my mind, to believe that Mati would betray the Arnathim, would betray *me*. But I knew him better than that. How many times did Mati have to prove himself to me?

This changes nothing, I told myself. I had to trust that Mati was struggling along, doing what he could, just like I was.

I'd wavered, though. How could I have wavered? What was wrong with me, that I still didn't trust Mati, after all he'd done for me?

My guilty heart pounded as I realized I had to get back, to convince Jonis that the situation wasn't what it appeared. I leaped up, trying to remember which way I had come. I sped down a corridor, then felt my way along another, cursing when I reached a dead end. I stepped backward and almost collided with someone coming around the corner with a torch.

I squinted, but all I could make out was a silhouette.

"You have come far," said a woman's soft voice. She bent closer, and the figure resolved into a familiar heart-shaped face framed by dark hair. I must have met her in one of the halls upstairs, but I couldn't recall her name.

"I didn't pay attention to where I was going," I jabbered in relief. "I was upset. Did Jonis send you?"

She smiled. "These tunnels are deep, and old. So much to see." She lifted the torch and gestured behind me. It wasn't a wall, as I'd assumed, but a door, like those to the tombs above. Only it bore no inscription or marking of any kind.

"I don't see anything," I said.

She touched the door lightly. "You're not looking yet."

I stared at her. That was when I noticed her dress—not lacy like Deshti's, but still of finer fabric than I had seen since I'd arrived, its green so pale that it appeared white in the dim light.

"Who are—" I started to ask, but she looked over her shoulder, as if someone had called her from the corridor. When she turned back, I saw a flash of fear in her eyes before she leaned forward.

"Take this," she said, handing me the torch. "See for yourself." She gestured toward the door and backed up a few steps.

Curiously I pushed at the door; despite its weight it swung open easily. I turned back to ask if this was a shortcut to the upper levels, but the woman had already disappeared back up the corridor.

I shrugged and poked my head through the door, holding the

torch aloft. Its light glinted over bones. At first I took them to be littering the floor, but once I had gotten over the initial shock, I saw that the bones were spaced evenly. Someone had laid out the bodies in this room carefully, respectfully.

This was how the people of the Nath Tarin laid out their dead, in the caves under the mountains.

Of course—Arnath slaves had built the entire tomb. Those who had labored in these tunnels had probably come from the islands, and had laid out these bodies, long ago. Some were turning to dust. The air in the room was heavy and stale, as though no one had breathed it for hundreds of years.

I began to withdraw the torch, to close the door and leave the dead to their realms, when the firelight flickered across the far wall and I saw a familiar shape scratched onto it. But it couldn't be what I thought it was, I told myself. I should leave now—I had to get back and explain to Jonis that Mati must have been forced to sign that order.

Nevertheless I stepped across the room, carefully avoiding bones. On the far side of the room, next to a low door, I held the torch close to the scratching on the wall. My heart thundered in my ears at the sight: three wavy lines, joined by a straight one. The first symbol from my heart-verse, the symbol I had seen nowhere else since coming to Qilara, save on the stone I wore around my neck.

Sa. Light of wisdom.

Belic, the mortal chieftain, stood often before the tablet given to him by the gods, pondering this gift for which he had sent his own brother into exile. But never did he speak of his regrets to anyone, not even when he was an old man with a great city full of temples and slaves to tend them.

FORTY-ONE

I MOVED THE torch along the wall, looking for more markings, but found none. So I ducked through the open doorway to explore the tiny room beyond.

Symbols covered the wall to my left, the top of which was barely a foot above my head. Some were scratched faintly, while others had been carved with a sharp instrument; they seemed to be the work of several different hands. I touched the grooved symbols in wonder. Surely I was looking at a record left by the very Arnathim who had labored on this tomb.

This was Arnath writing; it had to be. Every symbol had a sound, and the symbols were placed together to mimic the sounds of the words as one spoke them. I closed my eyes, picturing my heart-verse, remembering the lines I had worked out already, and when I looked at the wall again, some symbols seemed to leap out at me. I whispered the sounds for the ones I knew, skipping the ones I didn't, and sense began to emerge from the bits

I understood. As a record, it was haphazard, seeming to contain whatever each carver had felt like recording—births and deaths and arrivals in Qilara, descriptions of raids on the islands, and, near the bottom, a summary of the building of the secret tunnel. And through it all, the sense that these people had no intention of giving up their writing, no matter what their Qilarite masters did.

And yet, they had—or their descendants had. Years of oppression and the extermination of the Learned Ones had stolen this ability from them, until the only Arnathim in the city who could write were Qilarite tools like me.

I traced a line about halfway up the wall. It seemed to be a listing of names, some I could make out: *Vas. Lyga. Iltara.* I'd become so used to the Qilarite way of referring to the islands as a collective, the Nath Tarin, that I'd almost forgotten that each tiny island had its own name. *Iltara.* That had been my home.

With a gasp I realized that every single symbol from my heart-verse appeared on the wall before me, repeating often. I sank to the floor, writing in the dust with my finger, memory stirring with certainty now that I had models to copy. At least I knew now that I was writing the symbols correctly, even if I still didn't understand what they all meant.

When I had finished, I sat back on my heels. "*Sa noano heli gri, yotieven qilan godesha,*" I whispered, pointing to the first line.

The rhythms of that line had sounded familiar when Anet had said it, but now, in this dark, close space, surrounded by the writing of my people, it seemed to whisper all around me. *Light of wisdom, bold, brave, bright, bless us all and what we write.*

Some of the symbols in the next line were the same, though

in a different order, and I remembered sounds for a few of the others too. "Something *kareve qilrai esha qil go* something *qilan* something *kar* . . ." With a feeling like an explosion in my chest, I heard children's voices in my mind, years ago, reciting a prayer to the goddess Sotia:

Light of wisdom, bold, brave, bright, bless us all and what we write.

Hand of wisdom, lead us true, lend your might to all we do.

There were still two more lines, lines I couldn't remember how to write, but maybe I could remember enough sounds to work them out. Hope rose and spread through my chest and throat, and I labored over the symbols, whispering their names, searching the writing on the walls for clues. When they appeared under a connecting arch with another symbol I knew, I could work out the words from context, and then extrapolate the new sounds to my heart-verse.

And then—it seemed like seconds later, but it must have been hours that I worked—I read aloud, in a shaky voice:

Light of wisdom, bold, brave, bright, bless us all and what we write.

Hand of wisdom, lead us true, lend your might to all we do.

Heart of wisdom, guide each deed, forgive our folly, see our need.

When light and hand and heart be one, then may wisdom's work be done.

I let out a sound that was half laugh, half sob. I'd done it. After twelve years, I could finally read my heart-verse. Tears of triumph stung my hungry eyes, which couldn't stop running over the symbols as I chanted the sounds under my breath.

The children's voices of my memory seemed to grow stronger, chanting along with me, and all at once, in the middle of a line, I stopped.

It wasn't a message at all. It wasn't anything—just a child's prayer, a writing exercise like the ones I'd been preparing for Jera. I counted the symbols, and sure enough, twenty individual symbols appeared in the verse. I would have bet they represented the first two tensets of the Arnath writing, the ones my father would have started teaching me if the raiders hadn't set my house on fire and my life on a different course.

I sagged against the wall, my chest hollow. All the risks I'd taken to protect my heart-verse, all the people I'd betrayed to keep it safe. And it was *nothing*.

This was all writing was, in the end: markings in the dust. It didn't *do* anything, couldn't change anything. They kept it secret, made it seem powerful—and that had made me want it more. But it was nothing.

Angrily I lifted a hand, but stopped it a few inches above the stone floor. Even now, I had worked too hard on this verse to wipe it out—that would be too much like burning it in a firepit.

I rubbed my eyes and blinked away dust and tears. I looked up at the markings on the other side of the tiny chamber, expecting more of the same haphazard writings, but this wall was quite different. The writing was neat and beautiful, as if the carver had approached the wall as a giant scroll. It was punctuated by pictures—ocean waves, ships, men, and some circular objects I couldn't identify. It had to be the work of a master, like my father—a Learned One.

I jumped up, sidestepping my heart-verse on the floor, and stood on tiptoe, holding up the torch so I could see the writing at the top of the wall. The regularity with which my heart-verse symbols appeared seemed to taunt me with the reminder that they were the most common, the ones that would be taught first.

Using the symbols I knew, I picked out *Gyotia* in the first line, and *Lila* and *Aqil* not far from it. I guessed that the names of the other gods appeared there too, though I didn't know how to read them yet. I followed the lines of script down to the pictures of ocean waves and ships. It had to be the story of the banishment of Iano and his people, of Sotia's imprisonment for daring to think she could use the language of the gods as she liked. The same story my parents had told me in the firelight of our cottage, about how our ancestors had brought Sotia's gift with them to the islands, had protected it despite the incursions of the sons of Belic.

Then my eyes roved down the wall to the two circles. Up close, I could see tiny symbols spiraling around their surfaces. My heart leaped as I recognized the tablet, just as I'd seen in its case in the Library. But why were there two?

The second circle was blank at the center, like the one in the Library, but the first was not. I leaned closer and saw the tiny symbol etched carefully in the center of the others: *Sa*.

Again. Light of wisdom.

I turned to the writing underneath the circles. Two symbols grouped together stood out to me: *Sa* and a symbol that looked like a square with pinched corners. Those symbols repeated again and again in the next few lines, with others in between. My stomach fluttered. I knew now that I could work this out, and my chest burned—suddenly it seemed very important that I do so.

Sa I knew. But what about that second symbol? It meant an open scroll in the higher order Qilarite script, but what else could it represent? I thought of all the words used to describe such scrolls: *kresmin*, for a royal decree (with the royal determinative above it, in Qilarite writing) . . . *joklim* for a secret message (when combined with the symbol *spy*) . . . *tia* when one wanted to disparage the quality of another's writing . . .

Tia. As in *tialik*, that horrible word that Qilarites applied to the Arnathim, meaning *a thing to be burned like unwanted scrolls*.

As in the name of the goddess Sotia.

I looked at the symbols again, a thrill of understanding flooding my chest. The first stood for *Sa*, I knew, but I felt sure now that it also stood for the sound *So*. Meaning the cluster I saw again and again was the name of the goddess Sotia.

I touched the first carving of the tablet, where the symbol *Sa* stood out at the center. That symbol didn't exist in Qilarite writing; that place on the tablet in the Library of the Gods was empty, gouged out, taken in revenge, the stories said, by Sotia before the gods had bound her for eternity.

So how had these ancient carvers known to put it there?

Because, of course, Sotia had given the tablet to Iano before the gods took it back and sent Iano's people—my people—into exile. Before the center piece had been removed. At least, that was what the story said.

I groped for the stone around my neck and examined the

lines upon it. I saw now that the symbol had been carved so deeply and carefully that it might have been done by the gods themselves, that only such carving would have withstood the currents of the ocean where it had lain for—how long?—before Mati had found it.

In that moment, I knew, with utmost certainty, where the stone belonged. It was ridiculous, impossible, and yet I didn't doubt it. This was the missing piece of the tablet.

I stumbled back through the room of bones and pushed open the door. After passing a torch in its sconce, I chose a direction at random, aiming only for higher ground.

I clattered up a staircase and around a corner, and heard a shout in the distance.

"Jonis! I found her!"

Footsteps pounded down the hall toward me, then Tomis gripped my arm.

Jonis met us halfway up the hall, followed by another man bearing a torch. I thought I saw relief pass over Jonis's face before he glared at me.

"Thought you'd run off," Jonis said.

"No, I was in the lower tunnels. The woman you sent after me showed me something amazing. Did you know that there's a room—"

Jonis held up his hand. "What are you talking about? We've been searching for you for hours." He jerked his head at the other two men. "Bring her up."

His manner deflated me. I recalled all at once how, and why, I had run out in the first place. "Jonis, I know what it looks like, but Mati didn't send those raiders. I know it!"

Jonis waved me off. "Don't waste your breath. Whether or not the king can be trusted is irrelevant. *We* are going to take the palace, and you're going to help us."

Incensed at Lanea's sad compliance, Gyotia sought the fierce
arms of Lila more and more often. And each time he lay with her,
the power of their coupling brought war upon the land.

FORTY-TWO

THIS TIME I was careful to stand back when I visited Soraya
Gamo.

"Jonis is letting you go," I told her.

She snorted. "You speak as if I can tell them apart."

"Jonis," I said slowly, "is the leader. The one who could have
killed you but didn't."

"And why would he let me go?"

"Because I asked him to. Killing a prisoner is what Qilarites
would do. We are better than that."

Her head jerked up at the word "we." She studied me,
and I knew what she was seeing: a pale face framed by wavy
auburn hair, worn loose around my shoulders for the first time
in ages.

I cleared my throat. "There's one condition. You will deliver
this to the king." I flipped a scroll across the room; it landed a
foot away from her.

Slowly she reached out and lifted it by the edges. "Is this a
trick?" she spat.

"Read it yourself." I stepped closer, holding up the torch so she could see.

With a wary glance at me, she unrolled the scroll. I worked to keep my face blank as she read the letter I had composed in the lower order symbols that morning.

Mati—

I know about the raiders. I wondered, at first,
how you could break your promise to me. Then
I realized: I know who you are, no matter how I
have deluded myself in the past. My feelings now
are like a stone hung around my neck, one I will
never remove.

So go marry Soraya Gamo and be the king. And
I, too, will be who I am. I will join my people. Our
paths will not cross again until the gods read the
scrolls.

Good-bye.
Raisa

Jonis believed the letter would convince the Scholars Council that I'd abandoned Mati. But would Mati see the hidden message? I could only hope that he'd be more willing to believe in me than I had been to believe in him.

Soraya finished reading, but I could tell from the set of her jaw that she still wasn't convinced.

"Were you there when they decided to send the raiders?" I asked, working to keep my voice from shaking.

She nodded smugly. I looked away, longing to ask what had made Mati agree. But if Soraya realized that I still loved Mati, it could blow the whole plan apart.

I was saved when Soraya spoke. "Why would this . . . Jonti . . ."

"Jonis."

She waved this off, her chains clanking. "Why would he let me go, because you asked?"

I shrugged. "Being Tutor means something to the Arnathim."

"You're not a Tutor anymore. And I don't want your pity."

"You don't have it." I gestured to Adin and Tomis, hovering in the doorway. "Take her out."

Soraya cringed, but they only unlocked the manacles and heaved her up by the arms. I backed into the corridor and set the torch in a sconce as they led her out.

"How's your mission of mercy going?" said a wry voice behind me. "She bitten you yet?"

I turned to find Jonis lounging against the wall, arms crossed. Soraya craned her neck to look at me, but I ignored her.

"No biting. She can be civilized. You might try it sometime," I said.

Jonis laughed as if I'd said something dear and clever, and then stepped close and swept me into a kiss. I stiffened, but his hands gripped my waist, his mouth hard on mine.

I registered the sounds of Soraya and the guards clattering

up the stairway, and I shoved Jonis with all my might. He broke away, laughing.

"Was that really necessary?" I hissed, wiping my mouth.

He smirked. "Her story'll be more convincing with visual details."

I stomped away down the corridor; Mati didn't need any more reasons to doubt me. Jonis caught up with me and grabbed my sleeve. "You shouldn't wander in those lower tunnels. Some are caved in."

I hesitated. I had crept down there the day before, looking for the hidden room full of writing I'd seen two days ago, but I hadn't been able to find it. I'd tried to tell Jonis about the ancient carvings I had found there, but he'd been too full of plans to listen.

I changed the subject. "Do you really think this will work?"

He grinned. "As it depends on Qilarites believing that we're lazy, stupid, and disorganized, it ought to go just fine."

He was right. I crouched beside him on the slope above the Valley of Tombs two days later, watching the king's guards and the Gamo army attack the token force we'd left in the Royal Tomb building.

"Soraya thought that *we* thought she didn't know where she was being held?" I asked. "How did you know that would happen?"

Jonis was tracking the battle below so anxiously that I was surprised when he actually answered me. "She'd have to see us as equals to believe we could use strategy. She's incapable of that. Most Qilarites are."

"Mati's not."

"Doesn't matter. If he wants to fight for our side when we get there, maybe we won't kill him."

I cringed at his matter-of-fact tone.

"It was a good plan, Jonis," said Deshti on his other side, smiling up at him. She wore a ruffled green dress today, and had come up from the city as soon as the guards had started marching toward the Valley of Tombs. I had learned that her mistress, the portly Qilarite I'd seen in the market, doted on her like a loving aunt, even passing on her own gowns for Deshti to alter and dye. Deshti could come and go as she liked, and, because her mistress's shop supplied the candles that burned all night outside the tombs, she always had a plausible reason to visit the Valley of Tombs. She made sure to get back to the shop before curfew—but only because her mistress worried about her.

Below, the guards drove the last of the ragtag Resistance fighters into the Royal Tomb. Soldiers shoved the giant doors closed and piled wood in front. A tall figure in a white robe walked down from the back of the group, and the guards gave way. Penta Rale's high forehead shone as he set fire to the wood. The soldiers laughed, enjoying, no doubt, the image of the Resistance fighters trapped inside, helpless against the stone door swelling shut with the heat.

"I saw Talin wounded, but Adin was helping him. Ranal too, but he might have been faking it." Jonis's voice was low, his eyes trained on the escape tunnel in the copse below.

A few minutes later, we saw them emerging from the tunnel, then moving silently into the trees and up the mountain. Jonis counted under his breath as the men exited, and when they stopped coming, he continued to watch expectantly. At last a big man—I recognized Adin's thick beard—exited the tunnel and reached back to help another man crawl out. Adin looked up at the ridge and shook his head. Jonis swore.

"Talin didn't make it?" asked Deshti shrilly.

Jonis didn't answer; his teeth seemed to be clenched too tightly together for speech. This strategy had been his, and he'd wanted to be down there, but the others had insisted he sit it out.

I touched his shoulder timidly. "Thank the gods it was only one."

"The gods have nothing to do with it," he snapped. He dropped to the ground and scuttled back over the ridge to the other side.

Deshti was at his side by the time I heaved myself to my feet and followed them down the rocky path.

"It *is* a good plan, Jonis," she said. "There's something else I came to tell you. They're talking about it all over the city. It was the big news until the guards started marching."

Jonis sighed. "What news?"

Deshti looked at me triumphantly. "That the royal wedding will be happening at First Shining, just like it was originally planned."

After his mother was imprisoned, Aqil made his home in the great library, ordering it to his liking. It pleased him to take charge of the scrolls of the world and burn those he found unworthy. The other gods avoided the library altogether; this suited Aqil, for he guarded jealously the sacred knowledge that Gyotia had given him.

FORTY-THREE

CROUCHED INSIDE A giant urn was hardly the way I thought I would return to the palace. I hugged my knees, hips curved at an awkward angle to accommodate the wool-swathed daggers beside me. I ached to move, but doing so might upset the balance of the urn and cause the two Arnathim carrying it—Adin and Tomis—to drop me.

The urn was plain enough not to be recognized as a funeral offering for a long-ago king. I heard Ranal, in the haughty tones of a Qilarite servant showing off to his master's slaves, producing papers for whichever scribe had been assigned the task of documenting the wedding offerings. Apparently Ranal's black hair and olive skin fooled the guards and the scribe, because the urn was soon swaying along again.

The Resistance had been moving into place over the last four days. Scholars from all over Qilara had been sending slaves to assist with the wedding, some on loan, others gifts for the royal couple. The slaves were being housed in the palace outbuildings, and many of our people had been able to slip in among them, their presence explained away by the accompanying papers from their masters—all forged by me. Jonis hoped that, once inside, they could quietly recruit the other slaves. More of our people waited in the crowds outside the palace gates, ready to strike when Anet, stationed in the tower, tolled the bell three times at his signal.

Things had gone well so far—but why shouldn't they? The council believed that the remnants of the Resistance were trapped, starving in the airless underground tombs. Rale had even held a special service to praise Aqil for his assistance in crushing the blasphemous Resistance. Kiti had slipped away to tell us about it one night. He'd said, with an apologetic glance at me, that the entire council had attended, along with the king and the queen-to-be, and that all seemed in high spirits, looking forward to the wedding.

I wondered, not for the first time, what Mati was thinking. Did he believe I had abandoned him?

I knew that the only reason I hadn't been left behind today was that Jonis planned to use me to ensure Mati's cooperation. But I had no intention of being Jonis's pawn. Once in the palace, I'd be on familiar ground. I'd spent three sleepless nights wondering what to do with that advantage. I'd be useless in a battle, and which side would I fight for, anyway?

So I would find Mati and we'd get away. Keeping him safe was my first priority, and I didn't trust either side to do that.

The urn tipped and swayed, and at last was set down. I knew

where we were from the glimpses of friezes I could see by the ceiling—in the council chamber, though today it would act as a giant altar where wedding guests could make their offerings to the various gods in honor of the royal couple.

The wedding would begin in the garden at fourth bell, and it had to be nearly third bell now. I was supposed to wait for Jonis to come for me; surely Adin or Tomis was lurking outside, ready to grab me if I tried to escape before that. Though I had taught them the language of the gods and provided forgeries for them, they still didn't trust me.

Luckily I had other ways to get where I needed to go.

As soon as all was silent, I pressed against the sides of the urn and stood. The lip of the urn was above my head, but I mashed the bundle of daggers down and stood on it, pulling myself up to peer over the lip.

A veiled Scholar noblewoman knelt on the prayer rug, her forehead pressed to the floor. I crouched and waited, hardly breathing, until I heard footsteps leaving the room. When I looked again, the room was deserted, but the number of jewels, chests, urns, and other offerings attested to the presence of many wedding guests. Most of the urns had been sent by the Resistance, and held daggers and swords. Jonis had told me to take my pick of weapon, but as my skill with a sword was questionable at best, I'd selected only a short knife.

I rocked the urn so that it leaned against the nearest wall, then scrambled out and steadied it before it shattered on the tiles. I didn't bother to look at the open doors as I darted across the room. If someone spotted me, I'd know it soon enough.

Ducking into the corner, I ran my fingers along the decorative molding. Mati had told me about this passage, but I'd never used it before, and my nerves frayed as my fingers searched for the hidden latch. If a Scholar happened to come in and look to the right, I was doomed.

I wiped my sweaty palms on my trousers, then forced myself to pass my fingers slowly over every inch of the molding. And—Jonis would have laughed—my mind automatically slipped to prayer. *Gyotia, greatest of the gods, lend me your might. Aqil, patron of Scholars, grant me your wit. Suna, goddess of memory, guide me. Qora, god of the fields, fill me with your strength. Lanea, goddess of the home—*

Something moved under my fingers, and the wall before me swung silently forward, revealing a patch of shadow beyond. Gratefully I tumbled inside and clicked the door shut behind me.

I groped along the dark passage, heart pounding, nearly tripping when I came to shallow stairs. I lost all sense of direction—was I under the entrance hall or near the kitchens? The passage opened at last onto another. I chose a direction at random and came to a familiar door behind a tapestry: the exit near the dungeons. Which meant that if I followed this passage up to the other end, it would lead me to the Library.

I ran back up the passage, and I could have sworn that the stone around my neck grew warm as I swung the panel open.

The Library looked the same—except that I'd rarely been there on sunny days, so the shafts of sunlight striping the rugs seemed out of place.

Mati sat on the bench. My breath whooshed out of me at the

sight of him, beautiful in a white and gold tunic, a thin golden circlet gleaming in his dark hair, a sword at his hip. He looked up at
the sound of the door, and was across the room, his arms around
me, before I could speak.

"You came," he murmured into my neck. I heard the relief in
his voice and vowed never to give him reason to doubt me again.
"Thank the gods you're safe."

I didn't get to respond because his lips were on mine. The
warm stone pressed against my chest. I broke away from his kiss
and adjusted it.

I heard a low humming. I looked around, but saw nothing
unusual—just the desk and the wooden tablet case at the center of
the room. My eyes lingered on the case, until Mati's voice jolted
me back.

"You did it! You got them to agree."

"I didn't," I confessed sadly. "Mati, they didn't come to help
you."

"I don't understand. Your letter said—"

"I know. I was afraid you'd think . . . but you understood the
message."

"Not at first. I got the part about the stone, but Rale, of all
people, made me see the rest. He got quite a laugh out of you
forgetting the 'out' in 'until the gods read out the scrolls.' But I
knew you wouldn't be that careless, and then I remembered how
we used to joke about the gods doing their reading at third bell.
So I've been coming here at this time every day. Gods, if I'd had
to go through with this wedding—" He smoothed my hair away
from my face. "Raisa, what's happening?"

My throat felt tight, and the humming in my ears was growing louder. I spoke over it. "The Resistance plans to take the palace. Jonis will give the signal in the middle of the wedding. Mati, I thought they might agree to help, but then the news came about . . . the raiders."

Mati gripped my hand, watching my face as he spoke. "Don't you know, Raisa, that there was only one way the Scholars Council could have made me agree to that? Rale saw it, and you're much smarter than he ever was."

I thought hard, and, with a shudder, I did see it. "That was the compromise? So they wouldn't execute me?"

Mati nodded. "Those raiders never went to the Nath Tarin, though. I gave them maps that would lead them straight to the wastelands of Illana."

I buried my face in his shoulder in relief. I'd been right to trust him. Despite my failures, my heart sang. "We've got to get out of here," I said into his tunic. It was what I had come to do—get Mati and get as far away as possible—so why did I suddenly yearn to stay in the Library? The pull of this place was as strong as it had been in my dreams at the tombs, and my ears buzzed dizzily with it.

Mati didn't answer right away. I lifted my head and looked at him. "I don't think Rale ever intended to let me live long after the wedding," he said. "Once Soraya is queen, they don't need me."

"Jonis would rather use you as a bargaining chip than kill you . . . I hope . . . but Mati, I don't see what we can do." I squeezed his hand. "I won't lose you again."

Mati took a shaky breath. "Run or die. Are those the only choices?"

My stomach hurt with how much I'd let him down. The buzzing in my ears was nearly deafening. "We've got to go, Mati," I practically shouted.

He nodded and pulled me toward the passage. I had to work to hear him over the noise in my ears, and every step felt strained, as if something held me back.

"There's a ladder up to the observation tower. We can climb down over the Adytum from there," said Mati. "We'll swim around to the docks, find something bound for Galasi. We've got to leave the city before Gamo's reinforcements from Emtiria arrive. Tell me you can swim, Raisa."

But I had frozen, staring at him. One word had broken through the din in my mind. "Reinforcements?"

He turned to face me. "Yes, Gamo's made a deal with Emtiria. He thinks I don't know, but the emperor sent an emissary to me— thought he might squeeze money out of both sides. Only I don't have any." He sighed. "Gamo's got ten thousand soldiers coming through the pass this afternoon. He's probably timing their arrival with my assassination."

My head pounded. "Jonis doesn't know about the Emtirians . . . even if the Resistance wins the palace, they'll be slaughtered when the reinforcements come. We have to tell him!"

"But you just said—"

I let go of his hand to grab the stone around my neck; it was now blazing white-hot. "I know what I said!" I snapped. "But we can't just leave them to die! We have to warn them!" Despite my words, I turned back to the tablet case. The humming was inside my whole body now, inescapable, undeniable.

"Where's the key for the case?" I shouted.

"Up in my room, under—Raisa, what are you doing?"

Propelled by a force I couldn't explain, I leaped forward and ripped the tapestry off the case, then shoved my knife into the lock and rocked it back and forth. The lock popped open; I threw it aside and opened the case.

I was vaguely aware of Mati's voice behind me, but the rushing in my ears drowned him out. It roared like waves, like wind. I stared at the tablet, and my head dipped as the stone around my neck grew heavier.

I ripped the stone from its thong and laid it into the gouge at the center of the tablet.

The roaring stopped. The Library of the Gods was perfectly silent.

The edges fitted perfectly, though the broken stone had worn smooth over time. I saw now how the lost symbol sat in the center of the tablet, all the other symbols both pointing to and radiating from it.

The tablet beneath my fingers grew hot, nearly burning. I cried out as the symbols shone with a pure white light, some glowing even brighter, searing themselves into my vision.

Then the world went dark. Like the first time I had touched the tablet, my lungs compressed, unable to pull in enough air. Was I remembering the Stander again? Then why did I feel powerful, and brimming with rage?

A point of light in the distance. I squinted as it spread in lines over the stone walls of my prison. Leaping forward, I crashed through stone, and the world exploded into light around me.

Then I was standing on the shore, perfectly balanced as the earth bucked and heaved around me. I lifted my hands and wrote a symbol in the air with my finger, and the ocean rose in a giant wave. I laughed as it crashed down around me. My mouth opened, and a strange, powerful voice came out. "I shall erase this place of hate, and with it those who imprisoned me."

I came to myself lying on my throbbing back in the Library of the Gods, a dull roaring in my ears, the bitter aftertaste of rage in my confused mind. I rolled onto my side and gulped for air. Wood and stone and charred paper littered the floor. Birds fluttered across my vision.

I sat up and rubbed my eyes. No, not birds—scrolls, blasted from their slots and sailing about the room.

Mati lay a few feet away, covered in debris. I crawled toward him, but he was lost to my sight as golden light filled the library. It came from the place where the tablet case had been, a wide beam that lanced up at the ceiling and sent its light over the shadowed statues of the gods.

As I watched, the light moved across the wall, over the letters that remained in their slots. All at once the letters ignited, sending embers and ash through the air. Mati and I huddled together, and he beat at the sparks that landed on the sleeve of his tunic.

Then the beam of light moved on, and shone right at the face of Gyotia, set into the wall. With a deafening crack, the statue split down the middle. The earth shook as the light sped out through the great crack in the wall. Mati and I threw ourselves flat as furniture toppled around us.

A splintered piece of wood slid across the floor in front of me—a remnant of the tablet case.

"It's stopped," said Mati. I pulled myself to my feet beside him and looked around. Brilliant sunlight flooded in through the ruined wall. The statue of Suna lay on the floor amid bits of paper and wood. The firepit, choked with blown scrolls, had gone out.

Every fragment of stone from the tablet, however, had disappeared.

In the distance, a bell began to toll without stopping.

"What did you do?" Mati asked, his voice shaking.

I swallowed hard. "I think . . . the stone was a kind of key. The tablet was a prison, and the stone unlocked it." I started to explain about the room in the tombs, but Mati cut me off.

"And who was inside?"

I could see in his eyes that he already knew the answer, but it was illogical, impossible, and he needed me to say it out loud. "Sotia."

As if in response, the earth rumbled, and the statue of Qora toppled from its base, narrowly missing us. "We have to get out of here," I said, grabbing Mati's hand.

We raced for the doors, which were hanging off their hinges. Mati started to heave one aside. The statue of Suna, lying prone a few feet away, rolled into a pillar and shattered. I skidded on the fragments and fell, but Mati pulled me to my feet and dragged the door open.

We spilled out into a crowd of people running from the direction of the front doors of the palace, pushing, shoving, and screaming their way toward the stairs. I caught sight of Soraya

Gamo in a purple dress, the white flowers in her hair askew, dragging her sister Alshara, and old Priasi Jin clutching the rapidly reddening sleeve of his tunic.

Pursuing the crowd were Resistance fighters with swords—familiar faces among them. Adin. Tomis. Ranal. Kiti.

We pressed back against the ruined Library doors to avoid being trampled, Mati angling his body in front of me as he drew his sword.

The hall cleared. "Are you all right?" Mati asked me.

But my eyes were locked on the front doors of the palace, where Jonis, sword held high, had just caught sight of me.

Finally free from her prison, Sotia turned her thoughts to revenge. First she found Suna and Qora in Qora's garden, where she wiped them from the world as easily as crossing out a line of script.

Next she dealt with Lila. The goddess of war thought to fight her, but wisdom always defeats might, and Sotia's quill moved far faster than Lila's arrows. Sotia pried Lila's bow from her stiff fingers and crushed it to dust beneath her feet.

No pity tinged Sotia's vengeance, for the others had felt none for her.

FORTY-FOUR

JONIS SHOUTED AND ran at me, but Mati's sword blocked his. Mati glared at Jonis, and Jonis glared at me.

"Traitor," Jonis snarled.

I had been called a traitor so often that the word no longer hurt. But all at once I realized how things must look to him—Sotia's release had touched off the battle prematurely, and he thought I had informed the other side.

"Jonis, no, it's not—"

"Don't bother to lie." He sidestepped Mati's blade and swung, but again Mati blocked him. Mati was tense, his eyes following Jonis's every move. My stomach dropped. Mati had years of training—he could dispose of Jonis easily if it came to that.

"Jonis, the goddess. Sotia was . . . in the tablet. . . ." The story tumbled out of me incoherently. "You felt the quakes—the city isn't safe!"

Jonis's face registered confusion. I seized on that. "Gamo has reinforcements coming from Emtiria. Mati told me and we were on our way to warn you when—"

Jonis shook his head and lunged. Mati whirled and forced him farther away from me. "More lies," Jonis shouted at me over Mati's shoulder.

"She's telling you the truth," said Mati.

Jonis snarled and sprang at him.

"Jonis, you have to—" The floor lurched beneath me and I staggered to my knees, my words lost.

Jonis and Mati both went down too, but Jonis swung for Mati's shoulder before he'd even righted himself. Mati blocked him from the floor, then jumped to his feet in one swift motion, already ducking Jonis's next thrust. Even with the golden circlet askew and dust covering his fine clothes, he looked every inch a king. He fought with calculated efficiency, never wasting a stroke, not pressing Jonis back but not allowing him to gain any ground either.

Jonis, on the other hand, made up for what he lacked in skill with sheer ferocity. He swung savagely at every opening, his eyes burning with hatred.

I heaved myself up, leaning on the wall. Mati warned me with a glance not to interfere, but I had to do *something*. I thought about throwing myself between them, but, as Jonis would undoubtedly kill me right now, that wouldn't do any good.

I couldn't let them hurt each other, though. So I cast around for something I could use, and my eyes lit on the shattered stone of Suna's statue, which had rolled out into the corridor. I seized the goddess's head and maneuvered behind Jonis. But he sensed me just as I was bringing it down on his shoulder, and he whirled around. The stone glanced off his arm, but disrupted his aim enough that the thrust meant for my heart only sliced my left thigh.

I yelped and clutched my leg as I crumpled to the floor. I didn't see what Mati did, but a moment later, Jonis was on his back, Mati's sword at his throat and Mati's foot pinning his sword hand.

"Drop it," Mati growled.

Jonis's fingers curled more tightly around the sword, and he called Mati something that would have gotten him immediately executed on a normal day.

"Mati is not your enemy!" I shouted. "If he was, you'd be dead by now. Rale is the real enemy, and this is exactly what he wants—us fighting each other so we won't fight him!"

Mati's eyes went to the blood spreading across my trousers, and he looked like he wasn't quite sure he agreed about not being Jonis's enemy.

"It's shallow," I lied. "It just stings a little."

"I thought we'd agreed," Mati said evenly, "that we weren't going to lie to each other anymore." Before I could respond, he brushed his sword lightly across Jonis's throat, just enough to get his attention. "She doesn't want me to kill you," he told Jonis flatly. "And you won't even listen to her. Maybe I'm not a great leader, but one thing I know is that leaders get all the facts before they make a decision. And *you're* missing some."

I pressed my hands against the gash on my thigh and looked at Jonis. Uncertainty had crept into his expression, and I knew why—he couldn't believe that any Qilarite would have him at his mercy like this without immediately killing him. Still he didn't let go of his sword. "I'm supposed to believe some nonsense about a goddess?" he said.

"Sotia," I said. "She was imprisoned in the tablet and we freed her."

Mati looked just as skeptical as Jonis, but he obviously didn't want to contradict me. "You were there!" I told him. "You saw it!"

Mati shook his head. "I don't know what I saw. But I know the city's not safe. The earthquakes—"

"The quakes will set off a tidal wave," I said with certainty. The vision I'd had sharpened in my mind. Somehow, when the tablet had exploded, I'd seen through Sotia's eyes, seen her controlling the sea with her symbols. My chest constricted with remembered rage.

Mati didn't question how I knew this. "Then we need to raise the floodwalls, get everyone to higher ground," he said. He looked at Jonis. "Do you care about your people's lives, or just about winning?"

The earth shuddered, and Mati swung his sword away from Jonis's throat. It might have appeared that he was thrown off balance, but his foot stayed firm on Jonis's wrist, and I knew that he was trying to avoid hurting Jonis, even by accident.

Jonis seemed to realize this too. He pursed his lips, then said, "Where's the floodwall?"

"We'll take care of that," said Mati. "You work on getting your people to the temple hill—that's the closest high ground. They won't listen to us. And once you get there you can start figuring out what to do about the Emtirians." Jonis nodded and moved to sit up. But Mati pointed his sword at Jonis's chest. "If you hurt her again, I *will* kill you."

Mati's eyes were hard, and Jonis's were equally hard as he stared right back at him. But the two of them seemed to come to some silent agreement. Mati lifted his foot and Jonis stood, shifting his sword to his left hand and flexing his right wrist. Mati watched him warily, but Jonis only made for the doors.

As soon as Jonis was gone, Mati crouched beside me. "Can you walk?"

"I think so." Leaning on him, I got to my feet and took a few steps. My legs trembled, and I thought it was from the injury, but then I realized that it was the earth, reminding me that I had no time to dwell on pain. So I grabbed Mati's hand and ran across the entrance hall, ignoring the ache in my thigh.

The front courtyard was in chaos, a mass of humanity roiling in blinding sunlight. It took me a moment to distinguish individual shapes, green-clad Arnathim, and here and there darkskinned Resistance fighters dressed as Qilarite servants, battling with guards and Scholars.

A distant rumbling sounded. Gray clouds blocked the sun, extinguishing the light. "This way!" Mati shouted, pulling me down the steps and to the left. "The controls are in the guard tower. If we get the palace floodwall all the way up, that will trigger the harbor wall going up too. We'll have to—"

Someone slammed into his right side. He went down, but caught himself on one knee and shoved me behind a pillar as he turned to face his attacker, who wore the uniform of a King's Guard.

I clung to the pillar—the same I had been tied to when I'd been whipped—and watched as Mati forced the man away from me. This was no half-trained Resistance fighter, but a skilled soldier attacking his king. Mati fought just as confidently as he had inside, but I saw sweat on his brow and his chest heaving as he and the man moved in and out of the other battles raging in the courtyard.

Nearby, I heard familiar voices, but I couldn't turn away from the battle. "Where're the others?" Jonis was shouting.

"Still outside the gates," Deshti replied. "Why'd you give the signal so early?"

"*I* didn't," shouted Jonis. "This area's going to flood. We have to get everyone to the temple hill."

Deshti grunted, and swords clanged. "Guess you haven't seen Rale and his fire-shooter then," she said.

"What?" Jonis and I said together, and I pushed myself up on tiptoe to see over the fighters.

And there was Rale, by the outer gates. His high forehead shone with sweat as he did something to the long metal tube in his hands—the same he had used for his fire effects at the pantomime. Flames poured out of the end and caught the back of a curly-haired woman in green—Anet. She rolled on the ground, screaming, to put out the flames. Before she could rise, a guard put a sword through her throat. I gasped, my fingers digging into the stone pillar, as Rale gleefully shot flames into the crowd without seeming to care if he hit friend or foe. The fighters pressed away from him, back toward the palace.

My eyes raked the crowd, but I'd lost sight of Mati in the battle. My throat constricted. But then I saw a flash of white by the orchard—Mati, huddled behind a tree with Laiyonea and Jera. Their white and green dresses were streaked with dirt, and Jera clung to Laiyonea's singed skirt, hiding her face. Mati's white tunic was spattered with blood and ripped at the shoulder, but he seemed unhurt as he spoke urgently to Laiyonea.

I ran around the edge of the courtyard, dodging swords and skirting fighters from both sides. I slammed into Mati and wrapped my arms around him.

He held me close and spoke into my hair. "I have to get up to the tower. Go with Laiyonea and Jera to the temple hill. I'll come find you there."

"I'm coming with you."

"I need you to keep them safe," he said. But his eyes said, *I need* you *to be safe.*

"How are we supposed to get out?" I argued. "Did you see what Rale has? And we're not even armed!"

"Yes, we are," said Laiyonea. She darted out from behind the tree and returned with two bloody swords. She handed me one of them and held Jera to her side, eyeing me coldly. I knew what she was thinking—I was being a distraction again, one Mati couldn't afford.

So I pulled Mati to me and kissed him, hard, and then said, "Go. We'll be waiting at the temple hill."

I turned away before I could change my mind, and started toward the gates. I didn't see Rale anywhere, just isolated fires burning wherever there was something to fuel them. The stench told me that a great deal of that fuel was human. On the far side of the courtyard, the garden was alight.

I turned to tell Laiyonea that the gates might be clear if Rale was in the garden, but the ground shifted and screams filled the air as the heaving earth threw the fighters off balance. With a great crack, a slab of the palace roof slid into the courtyard, crushing people under its weight.

Some of the fighters tried to run then, but found themselves trapped by debris and fire. A mass of people pressed up the steps and into the front doors of the palace.

"No!" I screamed. "Not inside! What are you doing?" But they couldn't hear me, of course.

Suddenly Laiyonea shoved me to the ground, so hard that my knees cracked against stone and my wounded thigh burned. I rolled onto my back and swung the sword up wildly—why had she given it to me if she'd planned to attack me?

But Laiyonea wasn't looking at me—her sword went unhesitatingly through the neck of the tall figure in green who had come after me. The man dropped to the ground, and the lifeless face of Ris ko Karmik stared at me, eyes accusatory even in death.

"Well, your new friends seem nice," Laiyonea said as she pulled me to my feet. I gaped at her. How did she know how to use a sword like that?

There was no time to ask. I clutched her arm, and she clutched Jera, as thunder rent the air and the front doors of the palace caved in, showering us with rock and dust.

I squinted through the haze. Most of the Scholars had fled into the palace in the wake of the roof's collapse, and the destroyed doors cut them off. Three pillars had fallen in the tremors; the remaining four wavered as though they might go at any moment. A few fights still raged around the courtyard, but mostly people were getting to their feet, looking dazed, or lying on the ground, never to get up again.

I saw Jonis helping another man up. Just as I registered the blood on his tunic, someone ran past me.

"Jonis!" It was Jera, launching herself at her brother.

"Jera, no!" Jonis cried, holding one hand out to stop her while trying to support the man beside him.

I wondered, for a second, why he was warning her away. Then I saw Penta Rale nearby, his face split in a horrible grin, a stream of fire shooting from the tube in his hands toward the little girl. It happened so quickly that all I could do was gasp and shut my eyes.

I heard a cry of agony, but not from Jera. My eyes flew open and saw Mati lying on the ground in front of her, his tunic afire. The odor of burning flesh filled the air.

Penta Rale stood above Mati. He lifted the tube again, his hands working at the end, and aimed it right at Mati's chest.

Laiyonea and I moved at the same time.

She swung the bloody sword down on Rale's shoulder, but he'd already ducked away. I threw myself to the ground beside Mati as Rale's next blast of fire shot past me.

"Don't touch him, traitor," said Laiyonea, placing herself in front of us.

I beat at the flames engulfing the right arm of Mati's tunic as Laiyonea pushed Rale back with her sword and her words. "You sent Tyasha to her death," she said. "You used her in your plan to take the throne."

"For Tyasha ke Demit!" cried another voice. Others echoed his words, and I sensed, rather than saw, them step up beside her with their swords. I couldn't look away from Mati.

"No," said Laiyonea in a clear, ringing voice. "Her name was Tyasha ke Laiyonea."

Firepits illuminated the library as Sotia entered. Aqil did not even look up from his work at her approach; this insolence fanned the flames of her fury.

She laid a hand on his head, the touch not gentle despite its lack of force. "My son," she said softly.

He did look up then. If any regret had tinged his expression, she might have wavered. But his eyes held only contempt and audacious righteousness, so Sotia traced upon his brow the symbols she had created just for his torment, sending him to the miserable death he had earned.

The firepits went out, and Sotia laughed in the darkness.

FORTY-FIVE

I LOOKED UP, astonished, but Laiyonea was already forcing Rale backward. Soon they were halfway across the courtyard.

I needed something to put out the flames. I spotted a discarded cloak nearby and leaped over Mati to grab it. When I pulled it, however, I found that it was attached to the body of Aliana Gamo. Her throat had been cut.

I gagged, looking away from her open, lifeless eyes as I unfastened the cloak and yanked it off her. Then I ran back to Mati and beat at the flames, inhuman sounds of grief coming out of me.

When the fire was out, I crouched next to Mati's unmoving

form. His right arm and side were a sickening black mass, but his chest moved with breath. "Mati," I said, touching his face.

He didn't answer.

The earth shook again, and I heard a shout. I looked up in time to see Laiyonea maneuver Rale right under one of the swaying pillars. His teeth were bared; though five others harried him with their swords, his target was clearly Laiyonea. She said something that made him lunge toward her. I saw her satisfied smile, and then the pillar broke free from its foundation, crushing them both as it crashed to the earth.

I stared in horror at the place where Laiyonea had stood, but only broken rock and dust remained.

"Raisa?" The whisper shouldn't have carried over the clamor of death and destruction around me. I whipped my head down toward Mati. His eyes seemed to search the sky above before focusing on my face.

"You're hurt." My chest hitched with what I had just seen, but now wasn't the time. "I'll find the doctor, you'll be fine—"

His mouth moved, but his voice was so low that I had to put my ear right by his mouth to hear him. "The floodwall," he said. "You have to. The path through the orchard will take you to the tower."

"I can't leave you!"

"You have to," he repeated. His gaze, glassy with pain, held mine. "I'm trusting you to do this."

He must have known how those words would hit me, after all I'd done. I nodded, my throat too tight to speak, and kissed his lips before I pushed myself unsteadily to my feet.

Jonis was nearby, holding his sister, her face buried in his bloody tunic. She was shaking—she'd seen what Laiyonea had done too. I looked around, realizing that with Laiyonea's destruction of Rale, the fighting had stopped. I grabbed Jonis's sleeve and pointed at Mati. "Help him!" I shouted.

Jonis, still in battle mode, swung up his sword, but I ignored it. "I'm going to raise the floodwall. You have to help him." I shook him a little. "Promise me!"

Jonis just nodded, and I let go. With one last look at Mati, I ran for the orchard.

The path was close. Mati must have been on it when he'd seen Rale target Jera. I sped along it and came to the spiraling stairs that led to the tower perched a hundred feet above on the mountainside. I raced up, even though my injured leg was unsteady and the narrow twisting steps had no railing.

It's just like balancing on the Library platforms on cleaning day, I told myself. *At least there aren't any nervous guards shaking this one.*

As if in answer to my thought, the stone beneath me wavered. Another earthquake.

I grabbed the stone column that formed the center of the staircase and squeezed my eyes shut, waiting for the tremor to pass. When I finally opened them again, there was less dust in the air than I'd expected; the quake had probably stopped some time ago. What I had been feeling was my own trembling.

I forced myself to keep moving. Mati trusted me to do this, and I wouldn't let him down. Not this time. I gasped my way up the last few turns and flew onto the ledge.

A guard stood inside the tower with his back to me, hauling

at a wooden lever. His neck muscles strained as, with a grunt, he pushed it halfway up its track and into a slot. Through the open front of the tower, I saw the floodwall scrape partway up.

And beyond the wall, I now saw the sea—a deep green, roiling mass. A white-capped wave formed out of the choppy waters and smacked up against the partially raised floodwall, like an invader testing the defenses.

The wall held, but I knew what the guard didn't: that water would rise.

I stepped into the tower, and the guard whipped around, his sword at my throat so fast that I didn't even see him draw it. I raised my hands to show that I was unarmed.

His eyes narrowed. He recognized me. Of course he did, I thought with a sick swoop of my stomach. I recognized him, too. He was the one who'd removed my dress when I was strip-searched in the garden.

"It's the traitor," he spat. "Come to destroy the floodwalls, have you? Or just lower them and let your tialik friends attack by sea?"

"There's a tidal wave coming," I said. "You need to raise the floodwall to the highest—"

Without warning he swung the sword, and I skittered backward through the door, throwing myself to the right to clutch the mountain wall. The rocks rang where his sword struck them instead of me. The earth trembled, and I clung to the mountain, ducking my head to avoid the rocks falling from above.

"There's more water coming. Please, raise the wall," I said in my most reasonable tone. "Or just climb down now. Go to the temple hill, and let me get the floodwall up."

He didn't even seem to hear me. "On your knees, slave," he snarled, slashing at my cheek when I didn't immediately comply. I cried out, clutching my face, and he pressed the flat of his sword against the top of my head, forcing me downward. I sank onto the narrow ledge. "It would be easier to kill you now," he said thoughtfully. "But Rale will give me a bigger reward if he gets to do it himself."

"Rale's dead," I spat.

I felt, rather than saw, his shrug—his sword was still pressing my head toward the ground. "Gamo, then. There are plenty of powerful people who want to see you die, slowly, and will pay me well for delivering you to them."

Terror and fury slammed together into a hard knot in my chest. "There won't be anyone left if that floodwall doesn't go up!" I forced out.

Before he could respond, the ledge below me undulated. The pressure on the back of my head lifted, and the guard scrabbled at the sheer wall, trying to keep his balance. Staying low, I lunged at him and wrenched the sword out of his hand, then, without thinking, without planning to, shoved him over the edge.

He was gone so quickly that I stared at my hands, wondering how they had done it. Then there was a scream and a thud from far below, and I started to shake.

I rubbed my eyes, remembering the frightening, overpowering rage I had felt from Sotia in that vision. I recognized it—I'd felt it when I had pushed the guard. And it terrified me.

Was this who I truly was?

Taking a deep breath, I dropped the sword and forced myself to walk into the tower room, to do what I had come to do.

The water was rising at an alarming rate now, pooling a few feet below the wall, occasionally sending a white-plumed sally over it.

The lever waited in the corner. I sank to my knees, pushing up on it with both hands, pressing my legs into the stone floor, not even caring when the tower shook and swayed around me. I pushed until I met resistance, then shoved the handle sideways into the slot that would lock the wall into place.

I pulled myself up onto shaking legs and peered out at the floodwall. It towered above me now, and relief and pride mingled in my chest. I'd done it. I hadn't let Mati down.

And then white foam dribbled over the wall and down the nearest side. I didn't understand at first—the water surely hadn't risen so high, had it?

It wasn't until I looked past the wall, and saw the wave in the distance, high and white-capped and larger than I could have imagined, that I understood: getting the floodwalls up didn't matter—not when a goddess was determined to destroy the city.

Sotia faced the great stone house of the king of the gods, fear tempering her fury now. But she would not allow Gyotia to exist any longer, even if she destroyed herself in the process. She drew five shimmering symbols in the air, and the roof collapsed inward.

Wreckage flew aside as she strode into the great hall. She found Gyotia, face down, interrupted at his meal. He did not move, yet none of his divine blood stained the table—there was no sign that the falling ceiling had harmed him at all.

FORTY-SIX

WHEN THE NEXT quake came, I let it push me to my knees, not even trying to keep my balance. My thigh burned and my muscles ached and my arms and face stung and my eyes were wet and nothing mattered, because whatever we did, any of us, it would never be enough. I would never see Mati or Jonis or Jera again. Mati would die thinking I had failed him. The city would drown beneath the sea-without-memory, and none of us would have a chance to make up for our mistakes. We would all die together, Arnath and Qilarite and master and slave.

I'm sorry, Mati, I thought dimly, my hand reaching automatically for the stone around my neck. But it wasn't there, of course, and my heart swelled with anger.

"I freed you!" I shouted at the oncoming wave. I dragged

myself to my feet and screamed at the water that crashed over the floodwall. My voice was lost in the clamor of the ocean.

Dimly my father's voice came back to me. *"One does not entreat the gods through shouted prayers or offerings, but through their greatest gift to us, writing."*

But what words could I give to Sotia, I, who had barely begun to decipher the writing of the Nath Tarin? Surely Qilarite writing would only infuriate her more. And all I knew of Arnath writing was my heart-verse, a simple child's prayer.

But it would have to be enough. I tore my eyes away from the next wave as it crashed over the wall. I heard a smashing noise, and guessed that the bathhouse was gone.

Ink. I needed ink. But there was nothing in the tower, not even dirt on the floor to write in with a stone or stick.

I swayed on the spot, not sure if the earth was shaking again, or if it was just me. I did have ink, and it was exactly the kind Sotia would understand best: the blood of her people.

The cut on my cheek still bled freely, so I dragged my finger across it and swept a patch of stone floor clear of debris with my other hand. Then, my finger oddly steady, I began to write.

I had no idea whether the order of the strokes mattered, as it did in Qilarite writing, but where symbols were similar to the ones I had learned in the Adytum, I followed their order.

Light of wisdom, bold, brave, bright, bless us all and what we write.

I went back to the inkwell of my cheek again and again, and when the blood there dried, I gritted my teeth and ripped my trousers away from the wound in my thigh so that it bled anew.

Hand of wisdom, lead us true, lend your might to all we do.

I wrote faster than Laiyonea would have said was proper, but every symbol was infused with my own longing, my plea to Sotia to end this suffering, to forgive, to spare the people of the city.

Heart of wisdom, guide each deed, forgive our folly, see our need.

When light and hand and heart be one, then may wisdom's work be done.

Dazedly I touched the first symbol of the final line. *Saolbe*—light and hand and heart joined, knowledge and action and feeling all pointing in the same direction. For the first time I truly understood what that meant. But would it be enough?

I leaned back, every part of me hurting. A wave smacked over the wall—was I imagining that it was less fierce than the previous ones, that the water level seemed to have gone down? But no—the beach below was now a lake that rose to the second floor of the palace. The Adytum and the orchard were underwater.

And in the distance, something white was speeding toward the city. I forced myself to my feet to see, but the sun broke free of the clouds, and reflected dazzlingly off the water. I threw my hands up to cover my eyes, and so was off balance when the next quake came, a swift juddering that seemed to shake the mountain itself.

I tumbled backward, too weak to grip the ledge as I swept past it. As I fell toward the dark water pooling below, I remembered, absurdly, that I had never answered Mati's question.

No, I couldn't swim.

Just before the water closed over my head, I saw something white flashing in the brilliant sunlight above.

An asoti, wheeling against the bright blue sky.

Sotia stared at Gyotia's lifeless form, uncomprehending. Then she heard a moan, and saw Lanea on the floor, broken and bleeding.

Sotia's shuttered heart at last felt the horror of the death she had brought upon the gods. She knelt and brushed a lock of dark hair away from Lanea's heart-shaped face.

"You are free," whispered Lanea. "I knew that this one would use the stone well."

"The stone . . . ," Sotia repeated, and she recalled that it had been Lanea who had handed the tablet back to her husband with the piece missing. "You stole the piece of the tablet. It was you all along."

Lanea shuddered in pain. "A key is nothing without the courage to use it," she said. "I was too afraid of him. Your people freed you, not I. But I kept him from stopping you. Do you remember the lantana?"

Sotia looked at Gyotia, and saw now the deep brown stains of lantana poisoning upon his lips.

"I would have done it ages ago," rasped Lanea. "But the others would have destroyed me. I could not leave you without allies."

Sotia gathered the broken goddess to her. "I will heal you. The language of the gods can write you well."

Lanea smiled fondly. "Not if it has already been written otherwise. I earned this, beloved, for my actions and my inactions." She closed her eyes. "You shall rule now, alone of the gods. None shall hide your wisdom in a tomb again. So it shall be until the goddess reads out the scrolls."

Lanea's spirit left then, passing from the realms of mortals

*and gods. Desperately Sotia sent her symbols flying after it, but it
sailed blithely on.*

And Sotia wept.

FORTY-SEVEN

AWARENESS CAME SLOWLY. I was comfortable
and warm, and opening my eyes might ruin that. So I let my ears
wake first.

I heard voices speaking softly, at least one that I recognized.
The creak of wooden floorboards. The low coo of an asoti. Soft
breathing close by.

At last I let my eyelids flutter open. I lay on a bed, covered
by a soft linen blanket, in a large, open room. Tasteful murals of
trees covered the walls. At the foot of the bed stood an empty
firepit.

Mati sat by my bedside. He squeezed my hand as I looked up
into his relieved face. "Finally," he said.

Bandages covered the right side of his neck, and his right arm
and hand were wrapped in dark fabric. Abruptly I remembered
his mutilated body in the courtyard. "Oh, Mati, your arm—"

I ran my finger lightly down his arm, but he caught my hand
and kissed it. "You saved me this time, and everyone else too."

I frowned, remembering the dark water closing over my head.

Like the last time I'd woken with Mati's concerned face beside me, I didn't understand how I was still alive.

A loud coo from the windowsill interrupted my thoughts. Mati turned and flapped his good arm at the asoti perched there. "Shoo!" The bird examined me with one beady eye, then took off when Mati stood. I watched it fly away, an odd sensation in the pit of my stomach.

"I haven't seen a single other bird since the flooding, but that creature won't stop begging for scraps," Mati said, shaking his head. Then he crossed to the door and called, "Jonis! She's awake."

I wasn't sure which shocked me more, the casual way Mati called for Jonis, or the fact that Jonis responded to the summons. He looked different as he stepped into the room; it took me a moment to realize that this was not only because of the gash over his left eyebrow, but also because he wore a brown tunic. I'd only ever seen him in green.

Jonis and Mati came to stand on either side of the bed. "It's about time you woke up," Jonis said. His tone was mocking, but I sensed relief underneath.

"How long . . . have I been asleep?" I croaked, looking between them.

Mati poured me a goblet of water from the pitcher on the bedside table. I took it gratefully and drank, using the time to study the two of them. They seemed on friendly terms now, but I hadn't missed the way they stood on opposite sides of the bed, or the wariness with which they looked at each other.

"Four days," said Jonis.

I felt so disconnected that I wouldn't have been surprised if he'd said four years. "Where did . . . how did . . ."

Mati sank down into the chair again and took my hand. "They found you on the Adytum roof. You must have swum there after you got the floodwall up."

I shook my head, and was surprised that the motion did not hurt. I felt fragile, as if any swift movement should pain me. "I can't swim," I murmured, looking past him, at the windowsill where the asoti had perched. There had been an asoti in the sky, too, right before I had gone under. . . .

"Well, you must have—"

"The floodwall didn't even work," I said over him, as memory rushed back like white water pouring over the wall.

"It worked," said Jonis, and it took me a moment to recognize his tone as one of respect. "We saw them go up, from the temple hill."

"No," I insisted. "The waves were too high, it didn't make a difference. But I wrote my heart-verse, and then . . ." I lifted my fingers to my cheek, where I had taken the blood to write my message to the goddess. They met a crusty scab that hurt when I touched it. My thigh, too, felt tender under the bandages someone had wrapped around it.

I looked up in time to see Mati and Jonis sharing a concerned look. I cast around for a matter-of-fact question that would show that I wasn't crazy. "Where are we?" I asked.

"The priest's residence at the Temple of Aqil," said Jonis. "It's the only part of the temple that survived the earthquake—"

I couldn't help myself. "You mean Sotia," I said softly.

Jonis raised a doubtful eyebrow, but Mati stroked my hand

and said smoothly, "It's the highest ground in the city, so it was spared the worst of the flooding. And fortunately this is where Rale stockpiled all the food for his priests too, so we've been able to feed people."

"This is headquarters until we can make repairs to the palace," said Jonis.

"Which would have been completely destroyed, along with everyone in it, if not for you," said Mati, his eyes shining at me in a way that made me blush.

Jonis looked back and forth between the two of us and abruptly excused himself to have food sent up. As soon as the door shut behind him, Mati leaned forward and kissed me.

Even as I kissed him back, I felt myself retreating into silence, into fear of what he would think of my secrets. So as soon as the kiss broke off, I clutched his hand and made myself tell him everything—the hidden room in the tombs, the terrible disappointment of my heart-verse, my conviction that writing to the goddess had saved the city, not the floodwalls.

"Do Jonis and the others even believe, do you think?" I asked. "About the goddess?" I wanted to ask if *he* believed, but I was afraid of his answer.

"I told them all about the tablet, but it's hard to know what anyone believes now. One thing's certain—they're all in awe of you. The heroine who raised the floodwalls. And once the whole story gets out . . ." He looked at me. "But you need to rest. I don't have to tell you all this now."

I clutched his hand. "I want to know."

Mati sighed. "Gamo was killed in the battle. His reinforcements never came—the quakes set off an avalanche that destroyed the pass. Rale's dead too."

"Laiyonea did that," I said softly. "Did you . . . did you know that Tyasha was Laiyonea's daughter?"

"Yes," he said soberly. "Tyasha told me, when I went to see her before she was executed. She'd only found out herself a little while before that, because Laiyonea tried to help her escape."

"*Laiyonea?*" I gasped.

Mati nodded. "Laiyonea told her she'd had an affair with a Scholar from the south. My father helped her hide her pregnancy— he sent her to one of the healing houses in the valley. When Tyasha was born, she was supposed to be left on the mountain to die, but Laiyonea begged a sl—an Arnath woman to take her. She arranged for Tyasha to be selected as Tutor when she was old enough, and my father never knew who she really was."

"Do you believe that, about the Scholar?" I asked quietly. "Laiyonea and your father were so close. . . ."

The pain in his eyes told me that the idea of Tyasha being his half sister was not a new one to him. "I don't think that my father would have—" He broke off, and I couldn't tell how he'd been planning to end that sentence. His father wouldn't have had an affair with an Arnath? Or wouldn't have ordered the baby's death? I opened my mouth to ask, but Mati went on, his voice shaking slightly. "That's how I made Laiyonea keep quiet about us. I threatened to tell my father about Tyasha."

I shook my head. I was only beginning to understand how many layers there were to Laiyonea now, after her death.

"She loved you," said Mati quietly. "She was proud of you. But you helping the Resistance was hard for her to stomach. She was afraid she'd lose you too."

I blinked back tears, remembering how she had saved me from Ris ko Karmik's wrath without hesitation. At least Laiyonea had not left this world despising me.

I took a deep breath. "So you and Jonis aren't trying to kill each other anymore, I see."

Mati answered my unspoken question. "It seemed prudent to work together. It's a chance to rebuild a new way. If things are really going to change, the Arnathim need to be a part of that."

"But what about the Scholars Council?"

"Most of them are either dead or have fled the city," said Mati flatly. He smiled. "So we'll need a new council. But it's only going to be four—two Qilarites, two Arnathim. With you and Jonis, we're covered for the Arnathim. But finding another Qilarite has been tricky. If only Jin had survived—"

My brain caught up with his words. "Me? Why me?"

"People already think you're a . . . priestess of Sotia, because of the tablet."

"But I'm not—"

"You said yourself that you communicated with her," said Mati. "If not you, then who?" He looked uneasily over his shoulder at the empty windowsill.

"There was an asoti at the tower, too," I said reluctantly. "Right before I went under the water, I saw it, and then—"

"And then you were on the Adytum roof," said Mati softly. "They'll see that as her choosing you." He leaned forward. "But if it's not what you want, we can keep this quiet. I don't want you to be forced into anything." *Not again*, his tone implied. A year ago, I might have thought this was just Mati being unusually sensitive, for a Qilarite, to the fact that I'd had so few choices in my life, but now I understood—he knew the crushing weight of the expectations of others, and would protect me from it if he could. His thoughts seemed to be traveling in the same direction as mine, because he added, "Now that everyone knows who your father was, they seem to think it's only natural you be on the council."

I frowned, a memory tickling my mind. "A council of four, including the High Priestess of Sotia . . . like the Learned Ones on the islands."

Mati nodded. "That's where Jonis got the idea."

I furrowed my brow. "But the Learned Ones were all equals on the council. They didn't have a king. You don't think Jonis is trying to—"

"Raisa," said Mati gently. "I'm not going to be king anymore. I don't want to be."

I stared at him. After all I had done to prevent Rale's coup, now he was losing his throne anyway. "Oh, Mati . . ."

"It's better this way, don't you see? It's a chance to really change things." He gave me a sly look. "Unless you'd rather I go tend goats . . ."

I smacked his good arm lightly, and he laughed and kissed me again. There was a soft knock at the door, and we broke apart breathlessly as Jonis's mother, Dara, appeared with a tray of bread, olive paste, and broth.

Mati went to talk with Jonis while I ate and took a bath. When I had dried off, Dara handed me a bundle of rose-colored fabric. I didn't realize until I shook it out that it was a dress. I slipped it on, then combed my hair and sank back down on the bed. I felt much better now that I had eaten and bathed, but there was still a haze of unreality hanging over my mind.

Jonis appeared at the door. "Are you strong enough for visitors?"

I shrugged. "I suppose."

"Good," he said, as he turned away and started down the hall. "Some of the petitioners have been waiting for days, and we need the space."

Sotia entered the great library, the symbols of the mortal girl's prayer still dancing before her eyes. Light of wisdom, bold, brave, bright . . .

It was time to read out the scrolls, to call all to account at last. She summoned a scroll to her and opened it, ready to read out its contents, but found that it was her own.

When light and hand and heart be one . . .

Sotia bowed her head, for, goddess though she was, she could not bring herself to judge anyone.

FORTY-EIGHT

"PETITIONERS?" I REPEATED, but Jonis was already gone.

I hobbled after him down a narrow hallway and a curving staircase and out into a tree-lined courtyard. The ruined temple loomed in the distance, its platform a misshapen heap.

But that wasn't what made me stop short. The courtyard was packed with people, and more were entering from the two paths leading from the main road.

Suddenly Mati was beside me, taking my hand. "Jonis, what are you doing? She's not ready for this!"

"She'll be fine," said Jonis shortly. "We need to get them out of here before the food runs out."

"Did you at least explain to her?" hissed Mati.

Jonis stopped and looked at Mati. "I thought you did."

"I did, some of it, but I wasn't planning to dump all this on her yet!"

Jonis looked quickly at me, then at the crowd. "Bit late to turn back now."

Mati grimaced. "Yes, but talk to me next time. Isn't that the point of a council?"

Jonis smiled, but there was an edge to it. "Still getting used to that idea. Come on."

I started. "Where?"

Jonis grabbed my hand and led me through the crowd. I clung tightly to Mati with my other hand. People melted back when they saw them—all except one. A tiny figure sprang forward and attached itself to my middle.

"Jera!" I bent down and hugged her.

"You're well now?" she whispered.

"Yes, I . . . think so."

"You can talk to Raisa later, Jera," said Jonis, gently prying her off me. "Go see Mother."

Jonis took me to a chair under a canopy. I sank down onto it gratefully.

That's when I realized that everyone was facing me. I looked up at Jonis and Mati, but they were both watching the crowd. Jonis gestured to someone across the courtyard.

Kiti, grinning widely, led a young couple forward. They approached my chair slowly, almost reverently. The young man was fair, with reddish-brown hair, and the young woman had olive skin and black hair that curled around her shoulders. A tiny fist waved from the bundle in her arms.

The people here wore brown, white, blue, red—any color except green. I fingered my soft rose-colored skirts. No one, it seemed, would wear green again.

To my utter shock, the young woman knelt and held the baby out to me. The young man knelt beside her.

"We ask your blessing on our daughter," she whispered, her eyes downcast. "She was born the night after you saved us all."

I stared at them, unable to speak. "I . . . I . . . bless her?" I choked out at last.

They took it as a statement, not a question. "Oh, thank you!" said the young woman. She dipped her head. "We have named her Raisa, in your honor."

I leaned back against the cushions, bemused. "Thank you," I managed to say. I reached out and touched the baby's cheek. Her eyelashes were dark against pale skin, and she sucked on her tiny fist. "She's beautiful," I said.

"She'll grow up free," said the young man in a gruff voice. He looked quickly at Mati, then away.

Jonis gestured them back, and an old man with a bandaged leg limped up. He tried to kneel on the stones, but I protested. Jonis produced a chair for him.

The man sat down and slowly removed the dressing on his leg, revealing a greenish, smelly wound. "One of them guards did this," he announced. "They might have to take it off if it doesn't heal right."

I gaped at him. "I'm not a physician," I said at last. A rustling went around the courtyard, and Mati squeezed my shoulder—whether in warning or support, I couldn't tell. I looked around at the eager faces, and realized—they had nothing to believe in now, and for some reason they'd chosen to believe in me. This was exactly what Mati had warned me about.

But, somehow, though their expectations terrified me, they didn't constrain me. I wasn't a slave any longer. I could get up and walk away in my rose-colored dress, if I wanted to.

I didn't want to. I wanted to help them. I didn't have the power to heal wounds, but I might be able to ease their minds. To share what I knew. That was a power too.

I leaned forward and flattened a patch of dirt at the edge of the stones, then used my finger to trace a circle with a line through it, and a line with a curve like a tail in the middle. "This is Arnath writing," I told the old man. "It means *tabay*—whole. You write it." He only gaped at me, so I took his finger and traced it in the dirt next to my writing. "You must practice these symbols—" *Fifty times to make it stick* floated through my head, and I bit back a tearful laugh. "Make them a prayer to Sotia, and the goddess will read them."

All around the courtyard, people stared at me, stunned, as if they were waiting for guards to come, for lightning to strike, for the punishment that would surely come from such open use of the language of the gods.

But the sun only continued to shine on the silent crowd, and the old man wrapped up his bandage and moved soberly away.

I leaned back against the cushions, exhausted beyond explanation, as if writing that word had drawn more out of me than mere symbols.

"She's too tired for this, Jonis," whispered Mati above me, taking my hand. "Tell them to come back tomorrow."

Jonis bent down and spoke to me, but his eyes were on Mati. "Think you can handle one more? You'll probably be glad to get it over with."

I closed my eyes wearily. "I don't understand you."

"You'll see," he muttered darkly.

"I'm sorry about this," whispered Mati, gently disentangling his hand from mine.

I opened my eyes. Soraya Gamo stood before me. She wore a simple gown of yellow, her shining black hair uncovered, but her bearing was just as imperious as ever. A few feet away from her stood Mati, looking at me apologetically. The courtyard was silent. Somewhere a child babbled and was quickly hushed.

"I want my betrothal dissolved," Soraya announced.

"Soraya," said Mati reproachfully.

She shot him a begrudging look, then sighed. "I suppose I should thank you," she said. "For saving our lives." Her voice wavered, and I cringed, remembering Aliana's lifeless face, and the shouts of the guard I had pushed over the ledge.

"If you want your betrothal dissolved, why are you coming to me?" I said testily. "You need a high priest."

Soraya laughed bitterly. "There *aren't* any priests anymore. They're all dead. Looks like you're the priestess now, whether you like it or not." She looked down at me, a hint of uncertainty in her eyes. "So will you dissolve the betrothal or not? I don't think I need to explain why," she added acidly.

"Let it be dissolved, then," I said. I contemplated Soraya,

standing so haughtily in the midst of the motley crowd of Qilarites and Arnathim. She had kept that unbowed pride even while chained in the tombs. Whatever else could be said about Soraya, she was not weak.

Almost as if I'd been thrown into another vision, I saw the world as it must look to Soraya Gamo: the daughter of a Scholar, educated and petted beyond any other woman in the city, but all her education and intelligence mattering not nearly as much as the quality of husband she could catch. She'd been told she would be queen, would have a seat on the Scholars Council—and then she'd been publicly humiliated time and again because Mati loved me. I realized, thinking back over her words in the tomb, that it wasn't even really Mati that she wanted, but the things that being his wife would have given her—power, and respect. A measure of control over her life.

Mati was right—we had a chance to change things for the better. And the Arnathim weren't the only ones who needed it.

"Soraya," I said impulsively, "will you take the fourth seat on the council?"

Murmurs started up around the courtyard, and Mati and Jonis both made sounds of shock. I ignored them and kept my gaze trained on Soraya. She studied me for a moment, then lifted her chin and turned away. "Fine," she said, but I could see the pleased look she was trying to suppress, and knew that my intuition about her had been right.

Jonis and Mati hustled me out of the courtyard then, no doubt to question my sanity, but I just smiled, tired and satisfied.

Sotia made her home in the great library, and watched the
mortals as they rebuilt their city and penned tales of the disaster.
Her wrath was great, as was her forgiveness. She would not allow
such injustice to fester in the land again.
    And so she would watch.

FORTY-NINE

THREE DAYS LATER, Mati, Jonis, Soraya, and I went
to the palace to survey the repair work. Adin was overseeing the
Arnath workers, Kirol the Qilarites, but it was an uneasy truce.
They worked in separate areas of the palace and rarely interacted.
We wanted them to see the four of us getting along.

And for the most part, we did. Soraya was still jumpy around
me, and especially Jonis, but I had come to respect how much
she knew about finances—clearly she'd been paying attention to
her father's mining operations. Jonis and Mati, though still a bit
guarded, managed to speak to each other civilly, and even to joke
on occasion.

I commented on this to Jonis as we lagged behind the others
in the main hall of the palace.

"He threw himself in front of Jera," Jonis said, as if that
explained everything. And I supposed it did.

We stepped through the doors to the Library. The debris had

been removed, along with the statues and ruined furniture. Two barrels by the far wall held salvaged scrolls. The place where Gyotia's statue had been was only a lopsided hole in the wall.

"Well, that'll make a nice window," said Jonis wryly.

"A training room here, do you think?" said Mati.

Jonis lifted his eyebrows. "Why not a library?"

"No," Mati and I said together. We looked at each other.

"No library," I said.

Jonis looked around speculatively. "I know why you're saying that, but what if we made it a different kind of library, one where *anyone* can come and learn?"

I pondered this. "Sotia would like that," I said softly.

"Who's going to teach them?" said Soraya.

"Raisa and Mati," said Jonis, as though this should have been obvious. Mati and I looked at each other. Just that morning he had begun practicing writing with his left hand, as his burned right one might never be dexterous enough to hold a quill again.

"You too, if you want," Jonis said to Soraya, challenge in his eyes.

Soraya's perfect composure slipped. Quite apart from what he'd said, it was the first time Jonis had addressed her directly. She stared at him for a long moment. "Well, it sounds expensive," she said, then looked around critically. "Especially with this architecture. If slave labor is no longer an option—"

"It isn't," Jonis snapped.

Soraya rolled her eyes. I sighed, stepping between them. This would take time.

"The friezes would have to go anyway," I said quietly. "That's the only way I'd agree." That was the least I could do for all the children who'd ever had to balance on a platform.

"That would bring costs down," conceded Soraya, "but if this is open to anyone, there should be an admission price."

"People will pay whatever they can—crops or livestock if necessary," said Mati. He looked at Jonis. "It's the *idea* that's important—that anyone is welcome."

Jonis nodded. He seemed surprised that Mati had understood this so easily.

We continued our tour of the palace. The scribe rooms were in the worst shape, with mountains of soggy paper everywhere, but the second floor was virtually untouched, and the first floor, apart from the Library and the main entrance, had suffered only minor damage.

Then Jonis went with Adin to discuss fortification of the walls, and Soraya went with Kirol to examine the remains of the bathhouse. Mati and I made our way out to the Adytum.

The gate, untouched, was closed, and Mati pushed it open slowly. Part of the canopy had fallen in—no doubt from the blast in the Library. Beneath it the damp writing chest poked out, one corner mangled. The asoti cage stood bare and empty, and there were no signs of dead birds. Had the asotis flown free of their imagined bars when the goddess had burst out of the tablet? I liked to think so.

I'd only seen a few asotis since the one on the temple windowsill, and they were always in the distance, watching. As if Sotia herself was watching to see how we would handle this new cooperation, to see if we were worthy of this chance.

Mati and I walked over to the wall, where the firepit had fallen from its base. The sea was calm today, fading into the greenish sky in the distance.

I sighed. "This isn't going to be easy."

"No," said Mati, taking my hand. "It'll take a long time." He didn't sound discouraged though.

I leaned against him. "Wouldn't it be easier to just be king and order people to get along?"

He laughed. "It didn't work that way, even when I was king," he said. "Besides, it didn't mean anything without the ability to make real changes. Or"—he took a deep breath—"without you as queen." He gripped my upper arms and turned me to face him. "I guess this is as fitting a place to ask you as any. Raisa, will you marry me?"

I stared at him, and he looked nervously back. "I know there aren't any high priests anymore," he said. "Well, except you, so I don't know how we'll work that out, but—"

His next words were cut off, because I pounced on him and kissed him.

We broke apart and I pressed my forehead against his. "As far as I am concerned, we're already married," I whispered. "Can I declare it, just like that?"

Mati laughed giddily. "You probably can. Say it out loud, and it will be so because the High Priestess Raisa says it is." He bowed.

I swatted his hand, reddening. "Stop that," I said. "I feel ridiculous, being on this council. I don't know a thing about ruling anyone. All I know how to do is write."

Mati smiled. "Luckily, you write extraordinarily well. And I saw you with Jera. You'll be a wonderful teacher."

Teacher. For three days something had been fluttering around in my chest—now that I wasn't a slave, wasn't a Tutor, I didn't know what I was. *Councilor* and *priestess*, the labels tied to me by others, were uncomfortable too. Mati's easy words brought the fluttering thing to rest. Yes. I was a teacher.

I gripped Mati's hand. "I want to teach them everything. Arnath writing and higher order and lower order . . . none of it should be hidden. Only . . . it won't be just ours anymore."

"I know," said Mati, his smile growing wider, reminding me that every time I'd held my secrets and my words close, it had only ended in pain. He was right—it was time to open up. He'd taught me that too.

Unable to speak, I hugged him fiercely.

"What should we call this new library, anyway?" Mati said into my hair. "The Library of the Goddess?"

"No," I said decisively. "The Library of the People." I felt Sotia smiling down on my words, and I trembled with excitement. "We should gather as many scrolls as we can. Even . . . from the islands, if we can get them honestly. The best from everywhere."

Mati smiled. "Then you'll have to put your own scrolls in there."

"I burned them, remember?"

"So write more." He led me to a table, then went to the cabinet and pried it open. He returned with paper, several battered quills, and ink, and set them before me. The scent of ink took me back so powerfully to my early days in the Adytum that my head swam.

"Tell the story," said Mati. "Your story."

"It's not that interesting," I said doubtfully, but Mati only pulled a fresh piece of paper from the stack and laid it in front of me, then handed me a quill.

"Now," he said, imitating Laiyonea, "lines in the correct order, please. No sloppiness."

I shook my head. "If I'm going to do this, I'm going to do it my way," I said. I closed my eyes, opening myself to the memories of my father's language, remembering my heart-verse and the symbols that had blazed with white fire on the tablet. And I found it within me—the language of my people.

I opened my eyes and began to write.

I never knew Tyasha ke Demit, but her execution started everything. . . .

$\mathcal{A}$CKNOWLEDGMENTS

This book has been a long time in the making, and there are so many people to thank that I will inevitably leave someone out. Still, I have to try.

Mountains of thanks go to my agent, Steven Malk, who kept believing even when I was a tortoise; to Lindsay Davis, who got this whole journey started; to Alexandra Cooper and Alyssa Miele and the whole team at HarperTeen for making Raisa's story something beautiful and tangible and out in the world; to my chief beta reader, Manuela Bernardi, whose insights never fail to astonish me; to my very first reader, Erin Harrison, who's been reading this story for over ten years now; to Elaine Benson, Kate Bradley-Ferrall, Kelley Finck, Helen Harrison, Megan Morrison, L. V. Pires, Laura Shovan, Diana Stevens, Patrick Stewart, Kali Wallace, Olivia Yancey, and probably about a million other people I am forgetting who have read various versions of this story and given feedback on it over the years; to Claire Jerram, Waldorf School of Baltimore class teacher, for lending lines from the beautiful ninth birthday verse she wrote for my son to Raisa's heart-verse; to Laiyonea Branch for letting me borrow her name; to Kristin Brown, photographer extraordinaire, and Megan Morrison,

Maureen Knight, Jennie Levine, and Lisa Campos, for always keeping the creative flames lit; to my fellow authors in the Sweet Sixteens for being amazing and supportive and awesome; to my parents, Dorothy and Frank Kelly, for their unyielding support; to all the librarians who have inspired me and believed in the right to access for everyone; and last but definitely not least, to Jimmy and JX, for always being there.